Audrey

'Angel of Death'

A teen paranormal romance novel
by
Christopher Westley

CMWAUTHOR@gmail.com
Burnt Ridge Publishing

Manufactured in the United States of America

10 9 8 7 6 5 4 3 2 1

Audrey©

'Angel of Death'
A teen paranormal romance novel
by
CHRISTOPHER WESTLEY

Cover art by Marika Kraukle 2016
Latvia EU

MARIKA RAVEN
DIGITAL ARTIST

First edition hardback April 2017
Printed in the United States of America
ISBN10:069284291-8
ISBN13:978-0-69284291-1

For all the wallflowers…you know who you are.
Summon the guts to find your Audrey or Chloe, move away from the wall…and dance like nobody is watching.

In memory of Scott G

for

Kat and Callie

Now a thing was secretly brought to me,
and mine ear received a little thereof.
In thoughts from the visions of the night,
when deep sleep falleth on men,
fear came upon me, and trembling,
which made all my bones to shake.
Then a spirit passed before my face;
the hair of my flesh stood up.
It stood still, but I could not discern the form thereof:
an image was before mine eyes, there was silence,
and I heard a voice saying...Job 4:12-17

She will come for them—one by one, and she will know what evil lurks in their hearts.

PART I

THE RETURN

1

POLAND 1722

ANIELA MOVES AROUND the ballroom, gliding in the arms of her love, her elegant ivory gown plunging deep in the neck. Although she is not royalty, she holds an air over the sophisticated crowd, enamoring them with her youthful beauty and prose. Her shoulder-length auburn hair curls on the ends, and her bangs fall over her eyes, a constant nuisance, which requires the flick of her hand to clear her vision. Dozens of guests are at the winter ball that is hosted by a wealthy land baron and his wife, their home an opulent mansion in the center of a small town in western Poland. Across the room, a new mirror has been installed. It is an item only the wealthy can afford, displayed in a prominent place in their home for all to see. Aniela, barely in her twenties, holds her husband tight.

"Look, she casts no reflection," a lady sitting next to the mirror gasps, catching the attention of the room.

"A witch," a gentleman shouts as he jumps out of his seat, pointing a finger at Aniela.

"Be gone witch, leave us," another man yells.

A hush falls across the room as Aniela and her husband stand alone in the middle of the deserted dance floor, his reflection cast in the mirror—her reflection absent. The flash of a muzzle and smell of gunpowder fills the room. Aniela's dress grows red as she slumps into the arms of her husband.

“Stay back,” Andrus Andrysiak yells at the crowd. He pushes through the onlookers near the door as he carries Aniela out to their carriage.

“Pavlo, take us home, quickly,” Andrus yells to his coach driver.

The coach rumbles across the cobblestone streets, sliding around corners in the rain. Andrus holds his wife in his arms as blood streams down her side into his lap. The driver pushes the team of horses hard to outrun their pursuers. Slapping the reins harder, the driver spurs the team to go faster, the carriage nearly tipping as it bounces up and over an arched bridge on its way toward the castle. The four horses gallop in unison, enraged by the driver’s constant whipping. A mat of sweat is lathered around their harnesses as they pull with all their strength. The coach rolls over the hills through the dark countryside, the narrow roadway closing in. The driver can see the castle ahead of them, its entrance guarded by two gargoyle statues above the gate. The coach rumbles past them, sliding to a stop in front of the castle, and the young lady stumbles out of the back, blood dripping off her hand. Her husband throws her arm around his neck as he carries her inside.

“I’m sorry, I didn't know they were waiting for us,” her husband says, as he cradles her in his arms. Her auburn hair lies in tangles, the color draining out of her face. Andrus rips her dress open, exposing the wound. He steps away, returning with a hot iron from the fireplace and pressing it against the open wound, cauterizing it. Aniela screams from the pain as her vision narrows and she passes out. Within minutes, the hoard of villagers have made it through the front gate and are pounding on the door.

“Andrysiak, come out. You have been found in violation of harboring a sorcerer. The demon must perish! Release her to us and you may be spared.”

Andrus shakes his fist at the door. “You shall not enter this residence; there is no pursuance that allows it.”

Motioning for the caretaker to help him, the two men carry Aniela through the castle and into the gardens as the young woman regains consciousness, her legs barely able to support her. “Pavlo, take her and go. I will stay behind. They will not harm me; I’ve done nothing wrong.”

"Yes my lord," their servant replies.

The front door strains as the villagers pound on it with a large log, the hinges yielding with each blow. Over and over, they throw the log into the door with all their might. The door busts off the hinges, crashing onto the floor inside.

A townsman steps through the door, his torch sending fiery shards up into the rafters.

"Be warned, those that enter this domicile shall forever be cursed and his families family after that for a hundred years." Andrus's words do nothing to stop their assault into the castle, their torches flooding the castle walls with dancing light. Fiery shards of ash climb into the rafters.

"Where is she, Andrus? Where is the sorcerer? She has violated the laws of the church and she must pay for her sins." The villager stands in front of him, wielding a sword. The other villagers quickly surround Andrus.

"You have no jurisdiction here. We've done nothing wrong. Leave here and never return."

"Take him outside," the lead villager barks as his comrades grab Andrus.

Andrus is pulled outside the castle into the courtyard and shoved onto the ground, his face cut open as it is thrust into a rock. Blood pours down his cheek.

The villagers tie rope to his wrists and legs and toss the ends up to four horsemen. The horses neigh as they are jabbed in their flanks by the riders, spurring them to pull on Andrus's limbs. The horses inch slowly backward, tightening the ropes and swinging Andrus off his feet into the air as he is splayed out.

"Andrus, do you have any last words?" a villager asks him. He doesn't reply.

The villager motions to the riders and the horses back up step by step, their hooves slipping in the muddy courtyard, stretching Andrus to the breaking point as he is pulled apart.

"Find her. She has to be close."

They search the grounds behind the castle, holding their torches high overhead, looking into the darkness for their prey. The horses' hooves click on the stone walkways as the statues in the garden cast haunting shadows into the night. They circle the horses back and forth, weaving up and down through the shrub rows.

In the darkness of night, the caretaker watches as the torch lights dance in the distance. The lights move to his left and appear to go away. A minute later they come straight toward them.

"Come, my lady. They are getting close; we must keep going." The caretaker pleads with his employer to keep going. Her strength is leaving her, the wound oozing.

"Leave me.... Save yourself," she gasps.

The caretaker leaves her in the garden alone, returning a few minutes later, the clop of hoof steps filling Aniela's ears. He pushes her onto the saddle then climbs on behind her, taking the reigns in his hands. He spurs the horse and they gallop away from their pursuers.

There she is! After her!" a townsman yells, pointing into the darkness.

The chase leaves the castle grounds into the countryside. An hour later, their horse played out, the caretaker dismounts and leads the horse by hand. Aniela is slumped over in the saddle. The caretaker pulls on the reigns to coax the horse further. Aniela hears a loud thump as a spear pierces the caretaker's back. The caretaker falls over dead. Aniela slides off the horse and lands on the ground.

Fear strikes Aniela as the soldier towers over her, stopping her crawl to freedom.

"Aniela Andrysiak, in the name of the father, I accuse you of sorcery. Do you have anything to say to these charges?"

Her lips quiver as she tries to speak, the words coming out in a whisper.

"The destroyer shall come for thee, his action swift, and in your final hour you will know you have sinned."

Drawing his sword, the townsman plunges it into her chest, leaving her for dead. The blood drips off the blade, his clothing stained. The torch light fades into the night, Aniela muttering incoherently, her lips covered in blood, her left arm reaching skyward.

"All shall feel my wrath; I am the one who brings the end, the one who watches while you sleep."

Her dying breath vanishes above her in the cool night, the bright moon above the last thing she sees.

AUDREY RETURNS

Two hundred sixty years later...

Carl leaned over the edge of the train trestle looking at the water twenty feet below. The river was the likely hangout for him and his friend Pete this summer. A small crowd of teens had gathered at the local swimming hole as well, due to the intense heat, unseasonal for western Washington. The mercury had hit the 100 mark for nearly a week and the teens were seeking relief the best way they could.

"Do it, do it!" the crowd of teens chanted.

Carl glanced at the water again, then leapt into the sky, leaving the trestle behind. His feet slapped the water hard, plunging him to the muddy river bottom. Carl pushed off the bottom with force, pulling his way to the surface. His face broke free of the water's grasp and he sucked in the hot air. Above him, another teen had stepped up, ready to jump, her skinny frame a sliver amongst the huge trestle.

"I'm not a chicken," Carl said as he swam over to his friend Pete. Carl was barely fourteen and trying to keep up with his friend, who was one year older.

"Whatever, douche," Pete replied.

"Jump," one of the teens yelled at the girl above them.

Carl turned to see her body splash into the water. He waited for her to surface. A minute passed and she was still under water.

"Do something," a girl on the riverbank yelled.

Carl was the closest, still knee deep in the pool. He sprang into action, swimming as fast as he could directly above where she splashed. Carl tucked his knees to his chest then kicked downward, the water growing icy cold and black as he reached the muddy bottom. He groped around in the dark, then felt the squishy stomach of the girl. Clasping his arms around her waist, Carl pushed off the bottom and shot toward the surface, his face breaking the water as his lungs filled with air.

"Pete!" he yelled.

Pete had already reached him before he could yell again, the two of them swimming the lifeless body to shore. Carl knelt above her in the mud.

"She's not breathing," he said as he leaned over her.

"Do that mouth-to-mouth thing!" a girl behind him yelled.

Carl placed his mouth over her ashen lips, blowing gently, her chest rising and falling with each breath.

"More!" the girl yelled again.

Carl looked across her chest at the yellow bathing suit covering her stomach as it rose up with the next breath. She sputtered and a stream of river water shot into his face. A fit of coughs followed as she cleared her lungs. Carl cradled her head in his lap, and it was then that he saw how beautiful she was as the color returned to her face.

"She's alive!" the girl in the crowd yelled. A few of the other's clapped.

"Damn Carl…" was all Pete could get out.

She stared directly into Carl's eyes.

"What's your name?" Carl asked.

"What year is it?" she asked.

"Man she must have lost her memory or something?" Pete replied.

Carl brushed her wet hair out of her eyes, the auburn locks highlighted by the summer sun.

"1982," Carl replied. Her eyes grew larger.

"I think her name is Audrey; she just moved here," the girl in the crowd said.

"Aniela," she whispered to Carl, his nose just inches away from her face.

He could feel her hot breath brush his nose and was intoxicated with her.

"I'm Carl, are you okay—Audrey?" he asked, not aware she had said another name.

"What happened? Where am I?" she asked.

"You drowned. But you are okay now," Carl replied, "…and you are at the Skook, I mean the Skookumchuck River—that's where you are."

"Oh okay."

Carl helped her to her feet and that is when he noticed everyone around him was wide eyed—shell-shocked.

"Do you need someone to walk you home?" he asked.

"I'll do it," the girl in the crowd piped up.

"Is that okay Audrey?" Carl asked.

"Sure," she replied.

Carl watched the other teen girl help Audrey up the bank as they disappeared into the wood line.

"Do you think she will be okay?" Carl asked his friend Pete.

"Yeah man, she's good."

Carl had been best friends with Pete since third grade. Although Pete was a year older than Carl, they hung out together all the way through middle school. They were inseparable and did everything together, including bike riding and throwing scavenged beer bottles onto the railroad bridge over the river. Late nights found them playing hide and go seek with the neighborhood kids, then passing out in lawn chairs on Pete's front porch covered with blankets. When he ran with Pete, Carl never knew what they would do next. Their adventures during summer were epic. Pete was always the daredevil, constantly plotting ways to one-up Carl. Earlier that summer, he had talked Carl into floating down the narrow Skookumchuck River to shoot the rapids where it spilled into the Chehalis River. It was a harrowing trip down the chute, the rapids close to a class-four kayak run, because Pete had them floating it just after the late spring rains.

The water raged that day, Carl hanging on for dear life as they shot down the narrow river, trying to keep the inner tube centered, their faces just above the surface as they lay belly down on the tube. Their arms flailed wildly as the current pushed them toward the bank, where tree limbs dipped into the water. It was a surefire way of gaining a few scars if they were pulled underneath the overhanging brush. If they didn't paddle hard, the limbs would scratch their half-naked bodies or drag them under the water to a submerged branch that would pin them until the last bits of air left their lungs. Their lifeless bodies would be stuck until the winter floods broke them free.

"Paddle, paddle," Pete yelled at Carl, their arms moving frantically as they pulled the tube through the current. Water splashed up into their eyes; their vision blurred. Carl saw the worst spot up ahead as they slid around the next corner. A large tree had fallen across the river and it was the only way to go: underneath it and with only a fraction of an inch to spare if they were lucky. The tube shot into the trough of water that seemed to suck them toward the narrow slot under the tree. Carl twisted his head sideways as the tree loomed above.

"Damn it Pete, if we live through this, I'm going to kill you." Carl could see Pete was having the time of his life, laughing while he screamed. Pete showed no concern on his face as the tree passed over them, bodies pressed flat on the tube. The inner tube bounced across the last two rapids and out into the deeper water at the confluence of the Chehalis River, where the current slowed.

Carl walked up the boat launch and shook the water out of his ears, his old tennis shoes sloshing with each step, as the river drained out of them. He yelped once, pulling his shoe off to toss out a small rock, sliding it back on. Pete rolled the tube up the steep ramp, thrusting it forward and down the road into Borst Park. Dirt stuck to the black tube as he pushed it along, making it look like a donut in the display case at Fuller's market downtown. Right then and there, Carl vowed to never do anything that crazy again.

A week later, Carl was still pushing Pete for information about Audrey.

"Well? I went on your crazy adventure. Tell me, what's she like?"

"She's a nice girl Carl, besides, she's too young for you." Carl could tell his friend was getting tired of all the questions, but he persisted.

"How old is she?"

"Thirteen." Pete didn't know her actual age, but figured it was close enough based on how tall she was in relation to his little sister.

"Really? She looks older than that."

"Hmm, maybe fourteen next year?" Pete tried to play it off. Audrey was just a friend he met a few weeks earlier and nothing more. They were from the same neighborhood essentially, except for the fact that they were not in the same economic situation. Pete's parents had money.

"Hey, no biggie. I'm only fourteen; we are practically the same age." Carl tried to get his friend to see his point, but Pete was not having any of it as he walked away from him.

"Technically you are closer to fifteen than fourteen."

"You're a great friend; thanks for smashing a guy's dreams."

"No problem, douche bag, that's why I'm here."

"You're the douche bag, Peter Chambers." Carl called him by his full name when he wanted to get under his skin, and it usually worked.

"Screw you, and the horse you rode in on," Pete jabbed, adding, "Let's go shoot the rapids again."

"No way Pete. We barely lived through it the last time." Carl wasn't kidding; it had nearly killed them. One false move on their trip down the swollen river would have capsized the inner tube and thrown them into the 48-degree water, possibly smashing one or both of their heads into the rocky bottom.

"You wimp. It's not that bad now. I checked it yesterday; the water is a lot lower."

"It may be lower, but I'm not going under the tree again."

Pete had failed to mention it on their first trip down.

"Whatever. I'll find someone else," Pete said, but Carl knew from experience Pete was bluffing. He wouldn't go with anyone else.

They bantered for hours as they rode around town. Pete started singing, Carl following close behind, nearly rear ending him, their bike tires overlapping. "Eeeny meeny, mynee moe, catcha whiffer whaffer by the toe," Carl added the second verse: "If he hollers let him go." It went on like this for a few minutes, Carl picking back up with the first verse. "I woke up Monday morning and I looked up on the wall, the bedbugs and the skeetlows were playing a game of ball." Pete finished it off: "Score was nineteen twenty and the skeetklows were ahead, the bedbugs hit a home run and knocked me out'a bed." They finished the song in unison: "Eeny meeny, miney moe, catch a whiffer whaffer by the toe...."

Pete had asked Carl what a skeetlow was the first time he heard the rhyme. To Carl, it was obvious, but Pete had no clue that it was Carl's reference to a mosquito.

Carl remembered the first time he had sung it after coming back from summer camp, but he had been taught a more colorful version, complete with the *N* word. His mother did not respond well when she heard him singing it in the house one day, making him chomp down on the bar of soap that his dad used to wash his grimy hands at the end of each work day. One taste of the soapy lye was enough for Carl. Whiffer whaffer was how it would be sung by him from then on. The same questions and songs were revisited all summer. Pete never gave up pushing him to go down the rapids again either. Carl had hundreds of questions about Audrey. What was she like? Did she have any brothers or sisters? What was her phone number? Pete never budged an inch, blowing off Carl's inquiries day after day.

The warm summer breeze was replaced by the falling of leaves signaling its end. The small town at the foothills of the Cascade Mountains bustled with energy; log trucks blowing past them as they hung out in town. The town itself was not much, its ebb and flow of population never exceeding fifteen thousand, the small four-block radius of downtown a cornucopia of nineteen forties stone and brick buildings. No, Centralia would never be destined for greatness; what it lacked in sophistication and refinement, it gained in popularity with the college crowd during weekends home from school, the nine taverns within that small downtown radius a pub crawler paradise. It was a one-horse town, if they ever had one horse. Besides the overabundance of taverns, there were three banks, an old theater that was barely functioning, a music store, six antique stores, and an outdoor pool that was crowded all summer long, rain or shine. It rained a lot in the Pacific Northwest. The industry had changed little in over a century. Three sawmills toiled away day and night, and four dairy farmers kept the residents supplied with whole milk. Other than that, the town was a virtual dead zone for real career opportunities, besides the junior college, one of the few ways to escape. The nineteen eighties was the decade the city truly fell into ruin, its final death blow coming after the closing of the sawmill across town.

Fall came with the start of the city league soccer season upon them; Carl's hounding was relentless. He knew Pete's sister had befriended her, so he must have known something.

"Do you think she would go for a guy like me?" Carl was still in the stages of finding himself, his self-confidence not as strong as it should have been for his age.

"Carl, man, give it up already. She's a churchy girl. You know, the bible thumper kind that goes to church three times a week and twice on Sunday. Besides, she just moved here; she doesn't really know anyone."

"Where is she from?" Carl prodded.

"Don't know, I never asked her. I'll tell you what, if you shoot the rapids one more time, I'll ask her for you."

"Really?" Carl couldn't believe what he was hearing. It was the one thing that would get him back on the tube.

"Yes, really. Just go down the rapids and it is as good as done."

"Okay, I'll go."

Carl put the trip off for over a week, preferring to spend his afternoons at the outdoor pool. That was the summer Pete would get them kicked out. The outdoor pool was not much, the concrete in-ground structure having weathered nearly forty years of winter weather in the Pacific Northwest, leaving the concrete pad next to the pool cracked. The texture of the cement around the pool was similar to a cheese grater, with the exposed aggregate snagging the unwary. None of this would dismay the kids from seeking relief in the cool water, regardless of its shortcomings. Pete had a plan to prank the lifeguard, and Carl followed his lead. Carl would remember that event for the rest of his life.

Pete climbed up the back of the lifeguard chair, slowly untying the lifeguard's bikini top, the young lady unaware he was behind her. Carl put the rest of Pete's plan into action, as he climbed up the fifteen-foot-tall high dive. Carl stood at the end of the high dive, waved at Pete, then jumped sideways, propelling his body as close to the lifeguard as he could. Pete hung onto one end of the lifeguard's bikini top as the wall of water engulfed her, making her stand and blow the whistle at Carl. It took another five seconds for her to realize the crowded pool had gone silent as she froze in place, Pete still hanging onto the bikini, her breasts standing at attention like two radar beacons. For some kids, it would be their first exhibition of the upper female body. Others would hardly notice as they splashed around in the shallow end. They never returned to the pool that summer, unofficially banned by the young lady lifeguard.

The act had pushed them back to the river, and that was all Pete needed to seal the deal and get Carl onto the inner tube. Riding their bikes across town with the inner tube straddling Pete and his bike, Carl started in on another camp song. "A yellow bird, with a yellow bill, was sitting on, my windowsill. I lured him in, with a piece of bread." Carl finished it up, "—and then I smashed his—efffn head!" It was the raw and gritty version Carl's camp counselor had taught him when nobody else was around, the counselor learning it from one of his friends that had just returned from Army boot camp in Fort Benning, Georgia. Carl could not come to say the *F* word, after chewing on the bar of soap for the second time that summer.

Later that afternoon, they shot the rapids again, the flow of water a mere trickle due to drought. Pete never ran back into Audrey; his promise to Carl to find out about her went unfulfilled.

Carl couldn't get her out of his mind, no matter what he did to occupy his time. She stuck with him like a bad pair of underwear, creeping up when you least expected, her fiery auburn hair emblazoned into his subconscious. He was delirious and obsessed with the young girl and couldn't wait to get that first kiss, as his heart ached with longing.

She, on the other hand, had kept tabs on Carl, running into him at the Fox Theater downtown. Carl was unaware she had followed him that first Thursday evening when they met again.

"Hey Carl, how are you?" she said, while seated on an old couch in the middle of the mezzanine on the second floor, where she waited for the movie to start.

Carl could not believe his luck.

"I—I'm fine." His throat burned as his tongue twisted into knots.

"Do you wanna sit down?" She patted her hand on the couch seat next to her. Carl nodded. His face turned deep red.

Audrey grabbed his hand, lacing their fingers together. Sweat pooled in Carl's armpits as he studied her green eyes—eyes that pierced his soul.

Audrey leaned in close to his face; their noses touched as she kissed him lightly. Carl kept his eyes closed. It was short, warm, and wet. His stomach stirred within, and then she was up, running off to her movie, and Carl sat there glued to the seat. He wanted to move but couldn't. He was past infatuation. Carl's body felt as light as air. His heart pounded. Thump, thump—p—ker thump. His chest pulsated up and down as he regained his breath.

Carl pushed the door open and looked inside theater number two, his eyes peering into the darkness searching for Audrey. He walked up the aisle looking left and right.

"Audrey—Audrey," he whispered. "Audrey are you in here?" he whispered again, eliciting a stern glare from an elderly gentleman as he walked by him. He reached the back of the theater and scanned for the redhead but she was gone.

Carl took in every Thursday night movie for the next year, and he never ran into her again, although she was always present on his mind.

2

CARL KNEW THAT HIGH SCHOOL would either be a cruel joke, dismally boring, or the time of his life. Carl had already figured out his role in school. He didn't define himself as a preppy, nor was he a redneck farm kid, and he certainly was not a jock. He was just there, not really interested or worried about being associated with one clique or the other—not really caring if he belonged or didn't belong. Popularity was not his thing. It was a benefit that he had complete invisibility. On most days, he would skip a class, going unnoticed, to return the following day as though he were never absent. Even the instructors did not pay much attention to Carl, a fact he exploited to its fullest extent—something any guy would have done if given half a chance.

Carl ambled down the hallway, head down, shuffling his feet as he turned the corner, when—bam: there she was, standing directly in front of him, between her two friends. His heart pounded hard in his chest. He stood there speechless, his brown hair mottled, spiky, sweat pooling on his brow. His feet were glued to the floor. Carl's voice turned to gravel as he tried to squeak out a hello. He was a lanky 5'10" tall, 145-pound mess of a boy trying to act like a man.

Her hair was longer now, but the same shade of auburn. A hint of summer still lingered in her locks, as it shimmered and swayed with every movement. Her chest had grown while she was away, a voluptuous young woman emerging. She carried her slim 5'6" figure with confidence.

"Hi Audrey."

He did it; he mustered the courage and spoke. Her head turned and he waited, hanging on for a reply, anything—a subtle look was all he wanted. One glance—just one glance was all he needed. The hallway closed in around him, everything and everyone moving in slow motion. Carl saw nothing except her, the flow of students around him a blur. His stomach flip-flopped.

"Hello Carl," she said, smiling, her friends giggling.

Audrey swung her head back around, hair circling her face, arm and arm with her friends. Her green eyes pierced his soul—all innocent, yet taunting, something girls her age seemed to be so good at—a teenage girl's rite of passage to torture high school boys. Carl noticed the girl on Audrey's arm was none other than Pete's younger sister Chloe. He had known Chloe most of his life and he considered her to be a sister to him, he knew her so well.

He wondered if he had made a good impression. Was she interested in him or just being polite? Where was Pete when he needed him?

Audrey turned to leave, and he watched her walk away. His moment was vanishing.

Carl ran after Audrey and grabbed her shoulder, catching her by surprise. As she spun around, he felt her breast brush his hand. His face glowed beet red as his heart pulsed wildly out of his chest. Audrey stared at him, her green eyes focused on his.

"You—you going to the dance Friday night?" Carl asked, trying to suppress a stutter as he bit his lip.

Her reply was delayed as her other friend, Lauren, stepped between them. Oh how he loathed her friend already. She was deliberately blocking Audrey as he tried to step to the side to talk to her. Pete's sister was still hanging onto Audrey's arm, her bubbly nature infectious, blond hair covering her eyes as she giggled. She was a full six inches shorter, petite and cute, with a perky little nose and two dimples at the corners of her mouth. Her eyebrows were plucked neatly into points at the sides of her face, dark, smokey eye shadow framing her lids, mascara thick on her bushy lashes.

"She might be. What is it with you Carl? Can't wait to ask her to dance?" Lauren spat.

"Well, I just thought I would see if Audrey was going, that's all."

"You will have to see when you get there," Lauren growled.

His fists tightened as his face grew a deeper shade of red. He looked around Lauren and smiled at Audrey; his heart skipped a beat as he locked eyes with her.

Lauren was the antithesis of her friend Audrey. She was brash, obnoxiously loud, and knew how to get under your skin with a single phrase or word. She was pretty as well. Not drop dead gorgeous like her friend, but good looking enough and confident enough to know it. Lauren owned the ninth, tenth, and eleventh grade, her red hair and fiery attitude a precursor to her future. Anybody who was somebody wanted to be in or around the group these girls were in. They were a class of distinction all in themselves, standing completely on their own. Why shouldn't they? Lauren being the daughter of a wealthy lumber tycoon and Chloe's father the local bank manager gave them status.

Audrey was the exception. She was the leader of the group, unknowingly at first, and definitely not by family wealth or distinction in the small town. No, her calling card was her extreme beauty—what the French call *je ne sais quoi*, it literally means; "I do not know what," and in her case it was exactly the quality you could not describe.

"Bye Audrey," was all Carl could muster to say to her as he stood there, mouth open, gathering flies.

"Bye Carl, see you at the dance!" Audrey's eyelids fluttered rapidly. Carl brushed his hands through his dark hair as his lean frame wobbled from excitement. His pounding heart slowed its pace to a steady cadence. Palms sweaty, he raised a hand to wave goodbye and opened his mouth—no words.

Carl listened to the girls as they skipped away, arm in arm, singing, "*Children behave, that's what they say when we're together,*" their voices waning as they disappeared around the corner. The clanging of the second bell sent Carl on his way, with the girl's words bouncing around his head. He finished the next line of the song as he walked to algebra class: "*—and watch how you play.*" He had listened to that song many times on the radio but could not finger who the artist was. He could picture the singer, another fiery redhead with a natural beauty and gravelly voice in the right places when she sang. It was the teen girls' anthem of the time.

Mr. Thomas's algebra class was one of those courses you took because you had to, not because you wanted to. Carl slipped through the back door, late and unnoticed, taking his seat behind Pete Chambers. Pete had become the larger than life football star at school. He was one of those gentle giants that everyone loved; he had stretched out into a 6'6" 235 pound formidable force.

Carl punched Pete in the small of his back. Their friendship had yet to carry into high school.

"Hey douche," he whispered.

Pete turned his head, slightly mouthing a phrase only Carl picked up on, the rest of the classmates around him either half asleep or glued on the teacher, not noticing the transaction taking place.

"Got my stuff?" Pete whispered. Carl nodded.

Mr. Thomas stood with his back to the students the entire class. His teaching style had not changed for nearly thirty years: effective, to the point, and boring. Mr. Thomas didn't care; he simply threw the information out and watched to see if it would stick. His method at the chalkboard was just as unnerving, pulling the chalk down the board as he wrote, making the chalk squeak, sending a screech into the students' ears, making them cringe. There was only one thing worse than his writing style, in Carl's mind, and that was when Mr. Thomas would get ticked off at the class, usually once a quarter, and drag his fingernails down the chalkboard. His teacher was a genius, scoring in the top four percent of smartest professors in Washington State during a teacher's conference, but where he excelled in brains, he lacked in common sense and compassion.

It was Carl's third attempt at passing the class; too many days skipping sent him behind every semester, the building blocks not coming to him in order, an instant failing grade by the middle of the semester. Carl would not succeed as a mathematician, but, in other areas, he had good skills at turning fives and tens into hundreds. In his mind, he didn't understand how adding a's and b's mattered.

Carl's thoughts burned inside him, thinking about Audrey. After years of infatuation, the fire was fanned again. His heart did flip flops dreaming of Friday night's dance. Would she dance with him? That would be the question. Friday could not come soon enough. Carl was not a good dancer, but she had his whole attention and he was willing to lay it all on the line just for a chance to be near her again. Hour after hour, class after class, he stared aimlessly at the chalkboards, not copying nor comprehending a single word said by his teachers.

Carl strolled down the hall, shuffling, head hung low, pushing his way through the crowd of students on his way to his next class. He lifted his head in time to see her. His face lit up as he watched Audrey approach from the opposite end of the hallway.

He smiled, his mouth opened. "Hi," was all he could get out as she passed by, smiling back at him, her shoulder-length auburn hair swaying from side to side. Lauren glared.

Carl watched her walk away. She turned her head and mouthed. "Hi Carl," waving her left hand, curling her fingers back and forth. He smiled back. At least she was responding to him, he reasoned. He knew that he was underweight for a guy in his class and that he did not have the muscles he should have at his size.

Carl sat alone, staring at her from across the lunch room, watching her interact with her friends. Even from this distance, nearly forty feet away, he could see her green eyes, her curly hair enticing him. She glanced his way a couple times in twenty-five minutes, smiling at him.

"Dude, who you staring at?" Pete blocked Carl's view.

"Nobody, what's up?" Carl asked.

Pete looked over his shoulder, then around the cafeteria for the teacher, who was monitoring the lunch hall. No teacher had bothered to show up that day, or had left early to smoke.

"Can you hook me up tonight?"

Carl stared around Pete at Audrey.

"What? It's Wednesday night? Who drinks on a Wednesday?" Carl asked, glancing at Pete as he said it. He turned his gaze back at Audrey and Pete caught on.

"You like her, don't you man? She is hot, but there is something I don't quite like about her." Pete turned back to face Carl. "Well? Can you get me a six pack or not?"

It wasn't a question of if he could get it, it was how much it would cost him on short notice, and Carl did not like working on short notice.

"Yeah, but it is going to cost you."

"Okay, whatever, just bring it by tonight, I'll settle up then," Pete replied, standing up, his huge frame towering above Carl.

"Sure man. Now beat it, I don't like meeting at school like this," Carl grumbled, trying to keep his voice low. Pete glared back at him.

Pete left the table and Carl had unfettered access of Audrey again. He stared so long, he had not realized the lunch hour was nearly over. Carl was infatuated, so much so that when the lunch bell rang, he could not stand up for another five minutes. It was another fact of teenage boyhood: rock hard erections when you least expected it and at the most inopportune time. There was not much he could do about that but sit and wait, arriving at his next class late and gaining another afternoon in detention. What was Carl to say for being late? "Uhh, excuse me Mrs. Clark, I could not make it to class on time because I had a delicate problem with my manhood that precluded my punctuality."

Every lunch period, he kept his gaze upon her, summoning the courage to approach. His opportunity came when Lauren was sick on Thursday. Audrey and Chloe were seated alone, nibbling away at their sandwiches. He walked across the crowded room, making his way around the tables, her back to him. The lunchroom was abuzz with chatter.

Carl tapped her on the shoulder. "Hey Audrey." Chloe looked up and smiled as Audrey turned to face him.

"I thought you would never come over," she replied, turning back to face Chloe.

"Took you long enough Carl," Chloe jabbed.

"Can I sit with you guys?" Sweat pooled under his pits as his face reddened.

“Of course you can,” Chloe chirped, pushing the chair out with her foot.

Carl pulled himself up to the table between them. He had made it this far and had not thought of anything else to say.

It was awkward silence for another minute until Chloe spoke up. “You still going to the dance tomorrow night?” Her word’s slurred through the squishy sandwich.

“Yep—you going Chloe?” His nerves lessened in her presence, although Audrey still made him edgy.

“Sure, right Aud?” she replied, and Audrey nodded, not speaking until she cleared her mouth of food.

“We will be there—” the bell rang, ending lunch period, cutting her off.

“Can I walk you to class?” he stammered.

Chloe jumped up and grabbed Carl’s arm. “Heck yeah," she said, then giggled. Chloe nuzzled her face into his shoulder. "You smell delicious Carl," she said as she giggled again.

"Thanks Chloe," he replied.

"Is it that French dude's stuff?" she asked.

"Yeah, something like that."

Carl wondered if Chloe was messing with him or if she could tell that he had a deep crush on Audrey. The three of them strolled out of the lunchroom, Chloe hanging on tight as Carl walked them to their next class. He had no words, but Chloe yammered away.

“You going to join us for lunch now?”

“Sure, if Audrey doesn’t mind?” he said, waiting for her rejection.

“It’s okay with me,” Audrey replied.

Carl stood outside their class as Chloe slipped inside. He caught Audrey by the arm, stopping her.

“I still think about our kiss. You remember when we kissed in the theater?”

She batted her eyelashes twice. “Yes, how could I forget. You were so innocent, so cute,” she replied, adding. “I have to go. See you tomorrow at lunch.”

"For sure, see you tomorrow." His shirt heaved up and down, his heart pounding again. She had remembered him. Elation was building inside.

The 1980s were the big hair days. Most girls would spend their first hour and a half after waking up spraying on two cans of hairspray into the bushy hairdo just to repeat the process two hours after they got to school. Not Audrey though, she was one of a kind: natural; it would take Carl the rest of the year to find out and the rest of his life trying to figure out what happened. Carl's obsession with her was bordering on madness as his mind thought of what it would feel like to move his hands down her curvy hips.

Carl ran through the crowded halls making his way to the lunchroom. Rounding the corner past the offices, he caught sight of Lauren, taking a seat next to Audrey at their table. Carl moved in slowly and Lauren's eyes squinted as she glared at him, even though he was still twenty feet away. He glared back, then slid into the chair next to Audrey.

"And who said you could sit with us?" Lauren spat.

"I did—" Audrey said, staring down Lauren. Lauren lowered her head and dove back into her lunch.

"Hey Carl, remember when you used to stay over and you and Pete would have a farting contest?" Chloe giggled as she said it.

He blushed. "Yeah, those were fun times."

Audrey smiled.

"How is Pete? We don't hang out anymore, not now that he is the big star athlete."

"He's good, just full of himself, and Mom says he is nearly a man so I have to give him his space."

Carl chuckled.

"What's so funny?" Chloe chimed in, snorting.

"Nothing. Well, I was just thinking about the time we made root beer floats at your house and Pete made you laugh and you snorted root beer out of your nose, all over the counter."

"Did you really do that?" Audrey asked. She had not laughed when she said it.

"Yep, just get me giggling and it is all over. Cookies, root beer float, or whatever is in my mouth is coming up like a missile."

Carl stuck two French fries up each side of his nose and Chloe started sputtering again, with two snort snorts coming out like shotgun bursts.

"Damn it Carl, don't do that; you know I can't handle it," she said, sputtering some of her sandwich across the table.

"Gross," Lauren growled.

Audrey played it all off as she finished her lunch, turning to speak to Carl.

"Can you dance?" she asked him.

"Well, not really. Never been much for going to the dances."

His pits felt slimy again. He was trying to maintain his cool, but sitting this close to her made his stomach flop over. Carl was about to leave the table when the lunch bell rang, sending them back to class. He walked hand in hand with Audrey, their fingers interlaced, Chloe hanging onto his other arm. Lauren would have disapproved verbally, but she was in gym class and it was the other direction, giving him the opportunity to spend time with Audrey. Audrey's hand slipped away from his, their eyes stealing that last glance as she disappeared inside history class behind Chloe. Carl shuffled down the hall, beaming.

Three classes rolled by, as the clock on the wall in Carl's sixth period class crept around to a quarter after two. Carl had fifteen minutes to sit suffering, waiting, and thinking about Audrey. Time seemed to stand still. He was not sure how long he watched the dial go round and round. It almost seemed as though it was going backwards for a few minutes as the teacher rambled on and on about the Vietnam War. Mr. Jones was vibrant about his war stories, having been a veteran serving over there years before Carl was born. All Carl heard was "blah, blah, Vietnam, blah, blah blah." Not that he wasn't patriotic; it was just a means to an end. Besides, how many students in that class really cared about anything more than going to the football game that night followed by the dance and after party and the prospect of getting laid? The bell rang, stirring Carl out of his deep trance, sending him scrambling to the door into the hallway and out to his car. He wondered why he did not ditch class. The crisp fall weather chilled his arms as he slipped into the black leather biker's jacket to ward off the cold. In front of the school, he could see his grey 1972 Chevy Nova. The paint job peeling, half the work done towards restoring it, Carl had primed a few of the panels, waiting to spray a fresh coat of paint. The driver's side door was dented in the center.

Carl slipped behind the wheel and started the 327 cubic inch engine, the pipes rumbling underneath as he rolled through the parking lot. He frantically searched for Audrey the whole way, made harder by the hundreds of students walking home along the road. Carl scanned girl after girl, finally spotting her next to the front gate. Carl reached over to roll down the window, stopping to talk to her. Audrey was alone; at last the evil redhead Lauren was nowhere to be seen.

"Audrey. Do you need a ride home?" he asked, his voice shaking. He hoped she wouldn't shoot him down.

"Sure, I would love a ride home."

Carl hi-fived himself in his head; it was the first real girl he had asked to ride with him, except for Mona, and she was his cousin, so that did not count. Although Audrey had walked hand in hand to class with him, he still wasn't confident enough to consider them boyfriend and girlfriend yet.

"Jump in."

His stomach churned, flippity flop, flippity flop as she slid into the seat beside him.

"Thanks Carl."

Her words drifted across the interior of the car as they drove down the street into town. Her aroma filled the car, intoxicating him. His hand wanted to reach out and touch her hair, a move that would be out of line. He glanced over at her every two seconds while trying to keep the car between the white lines. Every time he looked at her, he could not believe she was actually sitting next to him.

Silence filled the car as he pushed himself to speak. Audrey stared back at him.

"That is nice smelling perfume you have on, what's it called?" It was an innocent question and the only thing he could think of saying.

Audrey crossed one leg underneath the other, sitting sidesaddle on the bench seat next to Carl. She continually brushed the auburn hair out of her eyes. The quick twist of her head made her hair swish from left to right, and it was done just for effect. She had ignored his question or at least that was what Carl thought.

"Carl, can I ask you something?" Her smile infected him, soothing his heart.

"Sure Audrey, anything. What is it?"

"Would you pick me up and take me to the game and dance tonight?"

Would he? Of course! It was the only thing he had thought about for the entire week—actually the only thing he thought about for the last two years: getting close to her, especially after she kissed him.

"Yes, definitely," he said automatically. She could have asked him to rob a bank and he would have done it.

"It is not really a date though. I mean, I can't call it a date, and you have to meet my mother. Is that okay?"

"I get it, no problem."

"Awesome, you can pick me up at seven."

"Okay, seven," he replied.

The drive across town took Carl ten minutes longer than usual, driving out of the way to add as many minutes as he could before dropping her off. Maneuvering the car through the narrow downtown streets, Carl slowed as he approached each intersection, waiting to see if the light was going to change from green to red, allowing him another two minutes time with her. Two lights disappeared behind him and his plan was failing, the traffic lights stuck on green that day. He watched the traffic light three blocks away, the green light looming, not changing. Carl resumed the speed limit of 25 miles per hour, gliding toward the intersection fast as the light changed to yellow, catching him off guard. Carl slammed on the brakes, bringing the car to a stop at the red light, giving him an extra minute with her.

Audrey broke the silence. "I live out at the old Andrysiak ranch."

"Yeah, I know," he croaked, his voice shaky. His sweaty palms gripped the steering wheel tighter

"Really, how do you know where I live?"

"I know that you live out there, not the address, or what they call that place."

"You didn't answer my question, Carl." Her statement made him nervous; what if she decided to back out on the dance? Carl was at a crossroad. Should he tell the truth and risk her possibly never talking to him again, or embellish it to make him look smarter than he was?

The traffic light turned green and a horn blared behind him. The Chevy rolled forward, resuming their trek across town.

"After we met at the river. You know, the day you went underwater and I pulled you out, I have thought about you every day since then—even followed you home once."

Dang, had he said too much? Stop talking. Just give her the basics. That's all he had to do. It sounded creepy to him as he played his own words back in his head. Followed her home? Who does that?

"You followed me? Really? Why didn't you just come up and talk to me?"

"I—I, don't know. Too nervous I guess." Carl played it cool, and maybe it was enough to just act like himself. His mother had always told him to just be himself and people would accept him.

"Nah, you're cute. Only a little creepy, the following part, but you were just a boy then. I was wondering if it was going to take you all week to ask me out?"

Her lips curled at the corners, while something wicked gleamed in her eyes. She was toying with him like a cat batting a mouse around before the fatal deathblow, Carl surmised. Audrey was wise beyond her years, and Carl was just beginning to understand that.

"I'm kind of shy I guess." This was the truth with Carl; he had never approached a girl before this week. For some reason, he was drawn to her, other than the first kiss and their meeting at the river. But to him there was more to it than just good looks. She had an aura about her that he had keyed into years ago. Carl had been in tune to her spiritual side just as much as her physical side, whether he realized it or not. They were drawn together by a force outside their control. Fate had intervened on that riverbank years earlier.

The Chevy bounced, making the springs squeak as it rolled around the corner, past the Logan district and out into the valley as Carl soaked in the last few minutes with Audrey. The defroster in the car never worked that well, the front window still half fogged up as he stared ahead. The road out to the valley took them through a thick forest of Douglas fir trees, most of them towering far above, casting long shadows on the road. It was a narrow two-lane country road, similar to other country roads: long, winding, and full of blind curves and steep hills. Leaves were scattered about the crumbling asphalt, blanketing the road in many spots, disguising a pothole or two, the car lurching up and down as it pounded through them, the tires splashing the water up out of the hole and across the road.

"It's there, in front of us, the old house in the distance," she said, pointing over the dash.

The ranch home, which sat at the end of a long gravel driveway, was now in its final stages of decline. It was the former glorious residence of a prominent Slavic family that farmed the valley for more than 120 years. Surrounded by 440 acres of pristine farmland, the fields lay fallow now, the fence along the long gravel driveway falling over, the wood fence posts rotten. Across the driveway, the huge wood barn stood in stark contrast to the landscape, still full of hay from years past.

Farm equipment sat inside the abandoned single story machine shop just past the house across from the barn. The home sat at the base of a tall hill. An apple orchard unkempt from years of neglect stood between the home and the hill. A forest of towering fir trees stretched up the hill away from the home.

Carl parked the Nova in front of the house, noticing the grass had gone to seed. The house was unpainted; its cedar siding missing in a few spots. The shingles were weathered grey. It was a regal home in its heyday, with the wrap-around covered porch and ornate cedar railings. The wide porch was perfect for entertaining guests on a hot summer afternoon. Now it was barely recognizable as the mansion it used to be.

Carl didn't care, nor did he notice anything amiss with the large two-story residence. You could have hit him with a two by four across the face and he would have thanked you for doing it, that is how enamored he was with her. She, however, was still very reserved, and guarded.

“Thanks Carl. Seven o’clock. No, wait. Make it six thirty and you can meet my mother.”

“Sure, six thirty. See you then.”

“See you Carl. Don’t be late. My mom hates that in a person—and wear something nice.” Carl’s hands trembled at the thought of meeting her mother.

“Okay I will, bye.”

Her hips swayed as she walked in front of the car, mesmerizing Carl. He watched her closely, studying every move, every mannerism. It was odd what he saw, but Carl had a déjà vu’ moment when she looked back at him when her face was framed just right in the afternoon light—a face that did not look like the gorgeous porcelain complected beauty sitting next to him just seconds earlier.

Carl blinked his eyes as she disappeared up the hill into the house. Was there something there? Carl chalked it up to jitters and infatuation. He knew he thought about her too much, too often, too immoral. Carl put her out of his mind momentarily as he drove back into town to his cousin’s house. His stereo scratched as the radio station faded in and out. Carl pushed on the cassette tape that was hanging half out, the stereo sucking it in, the rock & roll coming out of the speakers at a point in the song where he had left it this morning before turning the car off at school. “*Oh—I’m a getting it—*” He sang along with the catchy tune all the way into town. “Bump pa, bump pa,” he hummed.

Rolling up in front of the two-story garage, he honked twice, and the garage door jerked upward. Frankie’s mom’s place was a hodgepodge collection of old cars sitting in the alley, broken lawnmowers that were rebuilt into go carts, and an antique Coke machine sitting on the back porch. Carl loved every detail of that house, including the 1970s orange shag carpet in the living room. It was a home full of oddities right down to the cat clock on the kitchen wall that ran backwards.

“Hey there asshole, what’s going on?” Carl’s cousin always gave him a hard time, although they were closer than most first cousins, their love of muscle cars and whiskey unparalleled by their love of the female body. Carl studied the half naked bodies on the tool calendars that plied the garage walls.

"Not much, just thought I heard a tick in the engine; can you check it out?"

"No problem."

Carl's cousin Frankie was the only one he would trust to look at his car. Frankie had been working on cars since he was old enough to walk, toiling away in the garage for weeks on end trying to build the hottest and fastest race engine around. After many years of working on cars, he eventually got the nickname Greasy Frank. Most people in school just called him Greezy; Carl always called him by his childhood name, Frankie. Frankie had taken every shop class he could since seventh grade. It was evident early on that his life would be spent under the hood of a car. There was nobody in town that was a better wrench than Frankie, and Carl knew it, relying on him whenever his car was on the fritz or just to keep it in top shape so it would perform better. Carl had deep respect for him.

"So Frankie, what does it look like?"

"Nothing out of order. Start her up," Frankie replied, jutting his head out from underneath the hood.

Carl started the car, the low ticking coming out of the engine catching Frankie's ear.

"Got it, turn her off," he yelled from underneath the hood, poking his face around to look at Carl.

"What is it?" Carl asked.

"Just a valve knocking, I'll pop the cover off and tighten her up." The grease on Frankie's arms disappeared under his shirtsleeves as he cranked on the ratchet, removing the valve cover.

"So man, saw you with the prude today after school. How was the ride to her house?" Frankie never looked up as he said it, twisting the ratchet like a mad man as he worked.

"Don't say that man, she's not a prude—she's, she's amazing. I think about her all the time."

"She's a prude and a virgin, at least that's what I heard, but if you like her it's fine with me."

"I don't care; she's nice to me," Carl said as he shifted his feet. "We're going to the dance together too," he replied.

"Man, you're shitting me, don't do that, it will ruin your high school career." Carl could tell Frankie was just kidding him. It was how it was with them, jabbing each other in the ribs as much as possible. First cousins were like that—nothing was off limits. No matter what, they had each other's backs. Many times they had gotten angry at each other and said something they regretted days later, but the apologies never came, they just moved on. They had a tight bond.

"I don't have a career Frankie; I'm nearly invisible at school." This was very true; Carl was unknown to most of his classmates.

"Dude you're hopeless, after this week you got half the underclass girls wishing they were with you. Now that you asked her out, word is already going around the town; I got two calls already asking about you. There is something about that girl; she has got all the other girls in a tizzy. Just the mention of her name can incite a riot among the girls in eleventh and twelfth, the younger girls worship her; you can see it."

"I'm not worried about other girls. They're just jealous of Audrey, that's all."

"Alright man, done under here. You owe me a fifth," Frankie said as he closed the hood. "Probably right—girls do get jealous often."

"You know I always pay up. I'll bring it by for you later," Carl replied.

"Right on Carl, one of these days you will hook me up with your connection."

"Not likely, but thanks for the help man." Carl would never give up his booze connection—not unless he was under duress.

"Just be careful Carl. That girl is different. There is something about someone that beautiful; it's as though she sold her soul to the devil to get looks like that. It is not natural."

"You worry too much man."

The 327 engine purred as Carl backed out of Frankie's driveway. Turning north on Pearl Street, the Skookumchuck River was just a trickle underneath the bridge as the car rumbled overhead. Carl lived on the top of Davis Hill, one of the more prominent neighborhoods in Centralia, even though his parents were classified as a lower-class family, having bought an older home on the hill before the money families arrived. The home sat on the south side of the hill. It was a two-story 1600 square foot Cape Cod home that was out of place in the neighborhood. Cedar shingled siding sat worn and unfinished from forty years of neglect. It was home to Carl his entire life up to this point: the only place he knew. His father was a state highway worker and drove a sanding truck during the winter at night. He was rarely home, leaving Carl and his mother to fend for themselves. His mother was a homebody, and he knew she would be sitting up when he got home.

"Hello the house." Carl always announced himself that way when he walked through the back door, having read about it in a book about John Wayne. Every day after returning home from the movie studio, John would announce to the occupants: "Hello the house," or at least that is what Carl had remembered from the book, and he liked it.

"Carl, how was your day honey?" Mrs. Newkirk's voice bellowed from the other side of the home. She was an avid horror book reader, rarely getting dressed, preferring to lounge in her robe all day. The ashtray overflowed with smoldering butts, sending wisps of smoke to the ceiling above. Her tiny frame and weathered face hid her compassion for her son. She had read every horror novel to date and was deep into one of the most recent 700 page super novels, as she would call them. Carl did not read them, preferring to have good dreams versus the night terrors he often heard coming from his mother's room when she was having a bad nightmare shortly after reading a scary chapter.

"Good Mom, guess what?" He wanted to just blurt out what had happened that day, but decided he would try to engage her in the conversation. Abigail was a good mother to Carl, not that he would complain, although she did have her vices: cigarettes, alcohol, and an incessant need to read scary fiction.

"What dear?" she asked, to his surprise.

"I met a girl the other day, and I'm taking her to the dance tonight."

They had always had an open relationship, talking about anything. It was the one thing Carl loved about his mother; although she had demons to deal with, habits he was not proud of, Carl appreciated her interest in his life.

"That's nice dear," she said, glancing up from her novel, dismissing him for another chapter in her book as she flipped the page. She adjusted the bifocals perched on her nose.

"She is wonderful mother. You need to meet her. You will see how amazing she is." Carl stood there fidgeting as his nerves built up thinking about meeting Audrey again.

"That's nice honey. Bring her by sometime."

Carl's eyes locked onto the glass of whiskey sitting next to the ashtray; a single ice cube floated alone in the middle of the tan mixture. He knew her favorite whiskey glass rarely went dry this time of day. Rubbing his hands together briskly, subconsciously, Carl considered not asking his next question.

"How bout tonight? Please do not drink too much; I want to bring her by around seven thirty."

"Okay dear," she said as she glanced his way, flipping the page. Carl wondered whether she had heard a word he said or was merely repeating her usual pleasantries while her mind sailed through the fiction world. Carl knew she was deep into a weekend bender already, and it would only get worse by Sunday. Leaving his mother to her novel, Carl retreated to his room to get ready for the dance. The steam from the hot shower in the upstairs bathroom spilled out from under the door, fogging up the mirror. His voice floated out of the shower, singing off key: "*I'm a soul man, bamp, bamp, bah, bamp bah bah.*" Carl wiped the fog off the mirror with a dry towel. His ruddy complexion glared back at him; the mirror directly behind him reflecting back a foggy image of the back of his head. It was a weird arrangement for any home, opposing mirrors, a decorating style his mother decided just had to be. Carl stared at himself as he wiped down the opposite mirror, shifting his eyes sideways to look at the mirror over the sink. That's when he saw her—or at least he thought he saw Audrey. Was she really there, in the mirror? Carl looked again, shifting his eyes slightly to the right, but he saw nothing but the back of his head. He wondered if his obsession with her was playing tricks on his mind. Yes, that must be what it was, he reasoned, just tricks of the mind. Or it was an anomaly of the two mirrors sitting across from one another, showing the back of his head in one and his face in the other, producing an endless reflection if you looked at it from the right angle. If you looked deep enough into the mirror above the sink, it appeared as though you saw multiple mirrors behind you, a phenomenon made into reality by the early manufacturing process of the antique mirror. This mirror was not extremely old, installed in the home when it was built in the nineteen forties, when the mirror industry abandoned the silvering process, using mercury instead; the liquid mercury provided a nearly identical reflection to the silvering process of years past. All Carl knew was that he liked the mirrors in the bathroom. It was easy to comb his hair, adding hair gel to get the brown locks lying in the perfect direction. The eighties saw many hairstyles for high school boys, and Carl was not exempt from spending countless hours each week perfecting his style.

Lying back on his bed, Carl drifted off to sleep; his last thoughts of Audrey's face filling his mind, her tight lips curving upwards at the corners. He dreamt about her auburn hair lying on her bare shoulders those many years before when he held her lifeless body in his arms on the riverbank.

Carl blinked, but his eyes were fuzzy as he strained to make out the clock. It read a quarter past six. "Dammit, I'm going to be late." Scrambling to get dressed, he slid into his jeans and short sleeve button-down shirt, jamming his feet into his dress shoes, the brown slip-on loafers engulfing his feet. They were a poor choice for someone trying to move fast, the soles slipping on the stairs as he descended. It happened on the third step, his feet sliding out from under him, sending him flying down the stairs on his butt. The commotion of his fall did nothing to upset his mother's stupor, as she went about her routine in the kitchen, whipping up a batch of tomato soup.

"Carl, you need to eat something before you leave," she yelled as he flew through the kitchen.

Carl ran past her and out the door, hobbling on a sprained ankle. "No time Mom, I'm late. I'll bring Audrey by later if we get the chance."

"Carl, Carl!" she yelled as the Chevy's tires barked on the asphalt driveway. Carl knew he could make the trip to Audrey's house in fifteen minutes if he pushed it. He swerved in and out of traffic, passing multiple cars in the twenty-five mile per hour zone, exceeding the speed limit by thirty miles per hour. Flying across the river bridge, the lights and siren signaled him that he would be late as he pulled the car over on the south side of the bridge. Officer Spence exited the patrol car, and his image grew larger in the side-view mirror. The glare of the lights on top of the patrol car caused Carl's eyes to squint as they flashed through his windows. Carl waited until Officer Spence got up to the car before rolling down the window.

"Where you going in such a hurry, Carl Newkirk?"

The officer knew him by name, having pulled him over multiple times, and for the same reason. Carl loved to drive fast. The thrill of driving fast was like a drug pulsing through his veins, making him delirious. There was only one other thing that did that to him, and she was waiting on him.

"I'm late picking up my girl."

"Is that so? Maybe you should leave a little earlier so you don't have to speed." Officer Spence glared at Carl as he leaned through the window. "I'm going to let you go this time, but next time you won't be so lucky. Now get out of here and don't let me catch you drinking and driving." The officer flicked Carl's nose with his bony finger.

"Yes, officer."

Driving at the speed limit deepened Carl's pain; his foot was anxious to go fast, throbbing from the trip down the stairs. Holding back, he drove up the long gravel driveway slowly. The only light was from the yellow glow of the single lamp spilling through the window into the front yard. At 6:45 p.m. in the fall, the Pacific Northwest was completely covered in darkness. Carl approached the house with trepidation. A raven sitting on the power pole squawked twice. Carl looked back over his shoulder. Raven's were considered good luck, according to Carl's research a year earlier for class. This raven did not give him a warm fuzzy feeling as it squawked over and over, the familiar qwark qwark, making him jump. The door shuddered as Carl knocked on it with his fist.

"You're late, come in," Audrey said as she swung the door open.

"I'm sorry Audrey. I fell asleep, lost track of time, then I got pulled over by the cops."

"It sounds like a great story, but I'm not buying it, do you think I am stupid?" Her face told it all; she would not let him slip by without calling him out.

"No, not at all Audrey. I mean, well, you, you are Audrey, how would I ever think you were stupid." Carl stumbled through the conversation.

Stepping inside the small parlor just off the living room, Carl strained to see around the bleak interior of the home, the damp chill of evening soaking into his body. The home felt cold and clammy, not just from the cool evening but from something else. "Did you hear that raven outside?" he asked.

Audrey ignored his question.

"I'll be right back, I still need to get ready, then you can take me to the game." Audrey left Carl standing in the parlor alone, her voice trailing off as she disappeared into the back of the large home. Sitting on the worn-out leather couch, the home was quaint and sparse, and the furnishings looked like nothing he had ever seen. The chair across from him was a high wingback that was ornately carved with figures from the afterlife. The small cherubs with demon faces stared back at him. They were overlaid with gold paint. At least, that is what Carl thought they were painted with. As far as he knew, Audrey and her mother were not well off, but the antique furnishings intrigued him enough to elicit a question or two.

"Okay I'm ready." Her voice was soft and sweet again. Carl breathed in the perfume he smelled earlier when he dropped her off from school. Her hair glowed brighter than normal.

"Can I use your bathroom?" Carl bit his lip, his voice low and uncertain.

"Sure, it is just down the hall, second door on the right." Audrey pushed her arm out, pointing her index finger.

"Thanks, I'll be out in a minute."

His shoes echoed on the bare wood floors as he shuffled out of sight. The partially open door to the bathroom guided him to the string hanging down from the single light bulb in the ceiling. He pulled the string and the light flickered, then came on, the interior of the small bathroom glowing from the yellow light. Carl washed his hands and then it hit him. There was no mirror in this bathroom. He couldn't wrap his brain around a bathroom being built without a mirror.

"Carl, are you ready?" Her firm voice echoed through the living room and into the bathroom.

"Be right there."

"Is something wrong?" Audrey asked, Carl unaware she was behind him.

"You startled me." Carl's heart pounded when he turned around and met her fierce gaze piercing his eyes.

"You will have to meet my mother another day; she had to go out tonight."

"Okay."

Carl dried his hands on the towel as he studied the antique sink and marble base that held it up. It was a fine installation in an old house. Another oddity, but he decided not to ask any questions about the furnishings in the home.

Audrey's arm slipped inside Carl's, up against his chest, sending his stomach into an assault of euphoria. He wasn't prepared for her directness as they strolled out to the car together, his heart thumping wildly again. Carl swung the door open for her, a gentleman's move, then closed it. Carl glanced at Audrey inside through the curved windshield as he moved around the front of the car to the driver's side. He got a haunting image of her through the windshield from the glare of the security light hanging off the barn. It sent a chill up his spine, reminding him of when he thought he saw her in his bathroom. No, it was just nerves, that is all it is, he convinced himself. Carl opened his door and Audrey was there, staring up at him. She had moved over on the bench seat. "Is it ok if I sit here next to you?" The familiar qwark, qwark, qwark of the raven's call faded away as he slid into the driver's seat next to her.

"Sure, if you want to." The engine sputtered to life with a rumble and they were on their way to town. Carl searched the road ahead, waiting to see whether the local cop was still there. The corner of Pearl Street, where he was pulled over, was empty, Officer Spence nowhere to be seen. Carl mustered the courage to speak. "Where's your mom? Is she working?"

"Yes, something like that; she will be out all night, probably all weekend."

"Oh, okay," he replied.

"That means I don't really have a curfew. Do you have a curfew Carl?" Her tongue rolled across her lips and she popped them once sharply.

"Yeah, 11:30, but it won't be a problem if I stay out late; Mom will be asleep by 9:30."

"Cool."

Her words slid across his brain, encompassing his mind, the siren call of a teen girl, enticing a young man into her world. Carl steered the car through town, past the drive-in theater, not realizing Audrey's hand was on his thigh, her soft touch sneaking up on him, making his leg twitch. Looking down, he realized why his leg trembled; the emotions boiled up inside him. *Okay,* he said to himself, *be calm, she is a nice girl, just play it cool.* He worked to keep his cool. It didn't help that Audrey's blouse plunged deep in the neckline, showing just enough cleavage to spawn a boy's imagination.

"Do you love me, Carl?" Her whisper floated through the car.

"What did you say?"

"Nothing, I didn't say anything."

He was sure he had heard her say something. Did he imagine it? Or did she say it out loud? Carl could not come up with an answer. They drove the rest of the way in silence, her hand not moving an inch in either direction. They walked hand in hand outside the stadium, then met up with Audrey's friends at the entrance.

"Come on Audrey, why did you bring him?"

Lauren's words cut like a dagger, the red-headed heathen attacking all out. He loathed her even more than before. Carl's hand throbbed in pain as Audrey's grip tightened on it.

"Lauren, he's with me—end of story. If you don't like it then you can go sit by yourself."

Lauren and Chloe just stood there in disbelief.

"No, I don't have a problem, do you Chloe?" Lauren said, backpedalling.

Chloe was not big on words, rarely speaking at times like these, a true follower—an introverted lonely girl who somehow ended up as Lauren's friend and was now enjoying a new level of heightened popularity. At other times you couldn't shut her up. She was like a chainsaw buzzing away at a log, words coming out, two thousand per minute.

"Nope, he's fine with me, and he can drive," Chloe chirped.

It was the one thing Carl had going for himself, the fact that he could drive and that one other thing that he already forgot about, the one thing he promised his cousin he would get this evening. "I have to go to the men's room."

"Sure Carl, don't be long, I'm missing you already." Audrey squeezed Carl's hand again, her smile deepened across her lips.

Carl found the pay phone behind the stadium, depositing twenty-five cents. "It's me man; I need a case, and a fifth." He paused, waiting for his supplier to finish talking. "Yeah, bring it over to the block building next to the stadium. I left the cash in the trunk. I know, I know, just do it man, I owe you."

Carl navigated through the crowd of students and parents, noticing Audrey sitting between Chloe and Lauren, jogging up the concrete steps, joining them in the stands.

"Move over Lauren." The red head complied with the order without recourse, letting Carl sit next to Audrey, and an uncomfortable feeling came over him. Lauren's discord for him was evident. Her eyes burned holes in him as he glanced at her, the red hair flailing around as she cheered for her boyfriend on the field.

"Go Alan; kill those bastards."

"Lauren, be quiet, you will get us thrown out."

Chloe chastised her friend as she searched the stands for her parents. They were prominent citizens in town and booster club members who attended every game; no matter what sport, they were there and for good reason. Their son Pete, Chloe's brother, was bigger than anyone in his class, the obvious choice for football, recruited to the varsity squad in the ninth grade, playing in every game all the way into his senior year. Pete was a gentle giant; he always took care of his little sister, knowing her every move, and acquaintance—except for this new girl who seemed to come from nowhere, having only seen her a few times in the last two years. It was a fact that made Pete uncomfortable, even though he had run into Audrey a few times after the river incident.

On the field Pete would glance into the stands at Chloe and Audrey, then it struck him who was sitting next to Audrey: his supplier and childhood friend Carl—the guy that everyone wanted to know on a high school campus, but only a few had the direct knowledge of who it was, the supplier of all things illicit. He was the guy who could get you booze, fake I.D.s, condoms, and anything else you were either too embarrassed or too young to buy. It was a secret that Carl had worked extremely hard to protect for three years. The game ended with the tigers winning twenty-one to nothing, a blowout game.

"Yeah Alan, I love you—You rock baby."

Alan waved from the field as the team headed into the locker room.

"Carl, take us into town to the burger bar before the dance, I'm hungry." Lauren's words dug into him again.

"Don't you need to wait for Alan?" he asked.

"Nope, he won't be out for another hour; we'll meet at the dance, the coach will bad mouth them for the next forty-five minutes before letting them go."

Audrey gripped Carl's hand tightly as they walked out of the stadium to the car. Carl opened the door and waited for Audrey to slide in, Lauren sitting on the other side, Chloe riding in back. "Your car is kind of a junker, Carl." More assault from the brash redhead.

"She's a work in progress," he replied. Carl had worked on the car more than a dozen late nights recently just to get it to look this good.

"I like your car." Chloe's kind voice wrapped around Carl. "Thanks Chloe Bear."

Chloe smiled back at him. Audrey squeezed his hand again, making him blush.

This evening, the town had come alive, with hundreds of cars taking to the main street, cruising, the rage of the Pacific Northwest on a Friday night. Teens lined the streets block after block. Some hung out of their car windows as they cruised by their friends, the muscle car of the era a status symbol. Carl turned down F Street as he drove them away from the burger bar and cruise scene.

"Where you going, dip-shit?" Lauren spat.

"I've got to stop by my cousin's house before the dance. I told him I would drop something off."

"It's okay Carl, we have all night, do what you have to do, then we can get a burger," Audrey purred. Lauren rolled her eyes.

"Who's your cousin?" Chloe's softness soothed Carl.

"*Greezy* is your cousin?" Lauren spat again, as they pulled into Frankie's driveway. Carl didn't mind telling them about Frankie, and he was not ashamed to tell them either. This was the first time he had brought them there and he didn't want to reveal where he kept his stash.

"You guys don't even look alike. He's a redhead like me and yours is dark brown," Lauren growled.

"We have the same last name Lauren, maybe that would mean we are related." Carl's loathing of Lauren was growing bigger by the minute. The side window shuddered as Frankie pounded on it. "Hey Lauren."

"Hey Greezy, what's going on." Lauren's voice trailed off.

"Not much, just tuning up the Chevelle, going to take her out tonight if it doesn't rain."

"That rust bucket? It couldn't get out of its own way if it had to."

"Ha ha Lauren." Frankie leaned into the back seat. "Hey Chloe Bear, how are you?"

"Good Frankie, you coming to the dance tonight?" Chloe hugged him, squeezing his neck hard.

"Maybe, will have to see."

Frankie leaned against the edge of the door, looking at Audrey and his cousin. Nodding his head up and down once, he motioned for Carl to get out of the car. They met at the trunk, where Carl pushed the hidden latch he had installed just under the bumper, popping the trunk open. Greasy had helped him hook it up a few months prior.

"Who is the case of beer for man?"

"You know I don't talk about those things, Frankie."

"Come on man, let me in on it, it has to be for a party tonight right?"

"It's Pete's."

"Chloe's brother?"

"One and the same."

"Man, watch out for them, they are cool, but their parents are hard asses, if they find out you are the guy who supplied their son and daughter with alcohol there will be hell to pay."

"Point taken."

Audrey stretched her body out of the driver side window. "Hey, getting hungry in here, Harold's is waiting."

"Be right there, almost finished."

"Man she is a looker, I will give you that cousin. Think that red-headed bitch Lauren is good in the sack?" Frankie never minced words no matter the company.

"I don't know Frankie, ask her if you want to know."

"That's okay, thanks anyway. Come by sometime next week, we'll work on this bottle."

"Sure thing man, gotta go, the ladies are waiting on me."

"Dude you are PW'd."

Carl flipped off Frankie as he slammed the trunk lid, the word PW'd echoing in his head. Who came up with that saying anyway? Pussy whipped?

"See you Lauren, maybe I will come to the dance, just to give you a hard time slim," Frankie said sharply.

"Bye Greezy." She spoke softer, the fire leaving her voice as she flipped her hair back with her hand, flirting.

"Frankie and Lauren sitting in a tree—*K I S S I N G*—" Chloe buzzed.

"Shut up Chloe, not funny," Lauren spat, adding. "Okay Carl, you both have the same last name, but that doesn't mean you are related, lots of people have the same last name, like Jones and Smith you know, normal people."

"Sure Lauren, a relative in a small town would be way too convenient. You are right, Newkirk is a familiar name, and many have it." He wondered what she meant by normal people.

"I'm just busting on you Carl, lighten up."

"First comes the baby—" Chloe rambled on.

"That's enough Chloe, I don't like him that way," Lauren growled.

"Sure you don't," Chloe chirped. The chainsaw was gearing up.

Audrey's hand curled around Carl's as he backed the Nova out of Greezy's driveway, a spot of rain signaling that cruising would end soon; everyone who was anyone would retreat to the high school. The two girls sat in the back of the car, pushing each other back and forth.

If cruising was the event of the decade in a small town, the local burger joint was the other gathering spot for teen America. Centralia had both, a good cruise scene and a better burger joint. It was the type of burger stand left over from the nineteen fifties, the small square building with no inside seating opting for drive up service only. This was the quintessential burger, the best Carl had ever eaten: tomatoes the size of hockey pucks, onions that made you cry, and a side of fries with the skin still left on. They were the best fries you could find south of Seattle, smothered in ketchup or fry sauce, sliding down to your stomach where they would churn for hours. If you weren't a local, you would never find this burger joint, its location tucked away on the East side of town on South Gold Street. Harold's burger bar was the only place Carl would frequent, even though there was a rival burger joint on the opposite side of town closer to his home. These two competitors had been plying their trade for nearly three decades but were now battling corporate burger America. A thought that Carl had not fathomed—eating a corporate burger. Blasphemy!

3

HIGH SCHOOL DANCES AFTER A big game were the second right of passage for all teens beside cruising, and especially so in this small town where there were few options for entertainment. If you were anyone on a Friday night, and not cruising, you were either at the dance, making out with your girlfriend in the back of the theater downtown, or hopelessly alone at home. Until tonight, Carl was the latter, hopelessly alone, cruising the streets with an empty car, waiting to sneak in the back door of the theatre when his cousin Mona was working; he was hitting all gamuts of the geek scale, a perfect score. Tonight would be different, his first time to join in, fraternizing with the in crowd, a crowd that he did not associate with except for a select few that he had business dealings with. He knew Pete would be there, but Pete could be counted on to keep a tight lip, at least so far. This time he would be on the arm of the most beautiful girl in school.

"Hey Carl." Pete's athletic frame towered over him. "You ladies go on inside; I got to talk to Carl a minute, you know, guy stuff." The weight of Pete's body felt like a ton of bricks as he placed his arm on Carl's shoulder. They strolled away from the building into the parking lot.

"Pete, this is not how it works; we never meet in person, and we never do the deal in person." He wondered how they went astray so quickly, the duo that did everything together—blood brothers: sleepovers, tubing down dangerous rapids, sneaking out of the house at midnight to go egging. Marauders of the night. That was one of Carl's best adventures with his friend Pete, the pair of them cashing in nearly forty pounds of aluminum cans to earn the seventy-nine cents to buy a dozen eggs to throw at the sheriff's house just down the block from Carl's home. In retrospect, Carl wondered if that was why he had multiple run-ins with the law. Carl missed the chummy old Pete and their friendship, even if it was skewed.

"That's not why I wanted to talk to you, and I always stick to my end of the deal. You got my stuff though, right?" The growl rolled out of Pete.

"Yes it's in the trunk; we just can't do it now."

"Cool, you're the man. Drop it off at Alan's house later. His parents are out of town, nobody will know," Pete said enthusiastically.

"Alright you whiffer whaffer." The statement did not seem to phase Pete, and Carl knew he would have to shoot at him straight. "What did you want to talk about?" Carl queried.

"It's my sister man. Ever since she has been hanging around Audrey, something is different; I am not sure what it is. Just keep an eye on her, okay?" Pete's sternness had moved on to concern.

"Man, anything for you. Your sister is cool, we grew up together; you know I will watch out for her."

"Right on man, let's get jiggy with the ladies. Try to keep your hands off Audrey tonight." Pete poked at Carl, ribbing him a bit, a side of Pete Carl had not seen for a long time. It was a moment they shared that told him, "Hey you're cool man, and we are still childhood buddies." It had to be unspoken now, the code of a cooler upperclassman.

"I mean it man. Keep an eye on my little sister; she means the world to me."

"She's my number one priority. I'll keep her safe; you can count on me." Carl was ready to protect the one girl he really adored, although he was not physically attracted to her. To him, she was his little sister too. Everyone loved Chloe, and how could you not. She was a pint-sized fireball rolled into a teenage female package of bubbly awesomeness. Chloe was the friend that would lift your spirits no matter how down you were. She had witty antics and the best smile. If you added that in with one of her signature Chloe-style bear hugs, the kind of hugs that gave her the nickname Chloe Bear, your depression melted away.

The unlikely pair entered the brick building, where the principal checked them in as Carl stared up at him, sweating. That was the thing with Carl; he would get nervous if the wind blew in the wrong direction.

“Let’s see what you have in your coats gentlemen.”

The principal was a gruff man, nearly sixty years old, and had been in the school district for nearly forty years; Carl wondered if it was obvious that he was nervous.

“Mr. Hollings, why would you think we have something to hide?” Pete held up his hands, gesturing in innocence. Carl shifted his feet nervously.

“Boys like you always have something to hide. Mr. Chambers, don’t make me call your parents. Get inside and have a good time.”

“Right O, Mr. H.”

“Get in there young man. Not sure we have met before, but you’re clear, nothing under your coat worth bothering.”

“I’m Carl Newkirk sir.”

“Are you new to the school Mr. Newkirk?” It was a regular statement Carl was used to hearing.

“No sir, I have been here all my life, since I was born,” Carl replied, noticing the principal had already turned to search the next group of students.

Inside the darkened lunchroom, light from the disco ball bounced around the room, reflecting the multicolored lamp shining on it. Audrey spotted Carl just as the DJ spun up a slow tune, dragging him into the crowded dance floor. She pulled him tight into her body, wrapping her arms around his neck. Her head pressed up against his chest, and she closed her eyes, drifting around in circles, not thinking. Carl’s hands were another matter: should he leave them where they were at the sides of her stomach or move them around back? He couldn’t make up his mind. Opting for halfway, Carl slid his hands around her back, leaving them unclasped. She pressed her body up against his tighter and Carl shivered. Why was she so cold? Carl slid his hands underneath the back of her shirt against her bare skin. Was he imagining it? Or was she really as cold as ice? Minutes later, the song ended, followed up by a fast-pace jive that livened up the nearly two hundred students on the dance floor, Audrey still hanging on tight to Carl.

"I think it is time to dance a bit faster Audrey." He did not mind that she still wanted to dance slow, but he felt a bit awkward standing there not moving while the rest of school was dancing fast.

"Sure Carl, whatever, I like the slow dance best of all. Why don't you dance with Chloe, I'll be right back."

Audrey wandered off the dance floor, disappearing into the crowd, replaced by Chloe.

"What's up with her?"

"I don't know Chloe Bear, she said to dance with you, so let's dance."

"Right on Carl. Show me what you got."

Chloe was a real pro at dancing, spinning around in the mid eighties style with a mix of disco thrown in. Her many years of ballet and sport dancing competitions paid off because she danced better than everyone.

Pete joined the pair with his girl of the night, dancing just off Carl's right side. "Thanks buddy."

"My pleasure Pete; besides, it was Audrey's idea."

A scowl rolled across Pete's face. The music subsided into another slow dance, Chloe opting to dance, at her brothers prodding, with one of the senior football players. Carl stepped into the interior courtyard just outside the dance and Audrey was there sitting alone. The courtyard was usually used by teachers that would hang out and grab a smoke while the students were taking a test or during lunch hour. Sitting on the concrete bench next to her, the small pool of water behind them reflected the moon above. That was the first time he saw it; the first time he thought he saw her as a spirit. He wasn't prepared to believe it. Sure, there he was, at his first dance, having the time of his life and sitting next to him was the girl of his dreams. Carl looked at the reflection in the water, then back at Audrey, then back at the water—his face reflected perfectly, hers just a ghostly apparition. Audrey took his hand in hers, distracting him momentarily.

“Carl, there is something you need to know about me.” Her voice cracked.

“What is it Audrey? ”

“I’m not sure you can handle it.” Her voice wavered. “Not now anyway, not here.”

“No, go on, you can tell me anything, really—no judgment.”

Her reflection in the pool faded in and out. Carl searched her eyes, gathering as much as he could, searching for a clue to who or what she was.

She had heard the same phrase spoken in a dozen other languages before, and the outcome had been all the same: her new acquaintances running off scared. But these times and this generation of kids were different. America was different. She was not living in the dark ages anymore, nor were the citizens afraid of their own shadows and things they did not understand. This—was the MTV generation.

“You wouldn’t understand. Nobody ever does, not now, not then, but if you would keep an open mind, I would let you know everything about me and who I am and where I came from.”

She wasn’t sure he was ready to accept her. Maybe this time would be different; something about Carl told her that he was the one man that would understand her. The one she could tell her secret to. The one that would keep her secret. They say there is only one way to keep a secret, and that is if the other person is dead. Audrey knew this; it had been engrained in her long ago. Long before her time in Centralia.

“Carl, I’m not who you think I am.”

“You kids get back to the dance,” the principal barked.

The words shocked the pair, sending them running back into the dance, the moment delayed for another time. Audrey held onto Carl’s hand, her grip just as icy. They joined their friends on the dance floor, just in time, landing right in the middle of their classmates as another slow song spun up. Carl’s friend bumped into his back, a girl on each of his arms as he walked through the crowded dance floor.

“Hey Moose, nice one, she’s a looker.” Carl nodded at Clint Mirvens, happy to see him walking, and with two younger classmates.

Clint brushed up against Audrey's back as he lumbered by, and Carl caught the strange look coming across her face.

"Clint's got a health condition. It's his heart."

She didn't reply.

The conversation was soon lost as they danced on, Audrey swaying to the beat, hanging onto Carl's neck as she stared into his eyes. It was so loud that talking was impossible. The pair spun across the dance floor, Carl watching his reflection in the mirrored ball overhead as he passed by, and only his reflection. He knew she was dancing with him, her icy grip encompassing his neck. He strained his neck to catch a glimpse of her in the mirror. She pressed her mouth up against his right ear and whispered.

"I'm an angel."

"Hey butt head, I'm cutting in," Lauren yelled, prying Audrey's arms off Carl's neck, placing them around her own, the two girls laughing as they danced together for a few minutes. Carl stood off to the side, unaware of what she had just said.

"Going to borrow your girlfriend Carl, girl stuff," Lauren yelled over the music.

Audrey, Lauren, and Chloe pushed their way through the crowd as they ran to the bathroom.

Lauren stood at the mirror and brushed her hair, as Chloe added another layer of mascara.

"How do you do it Aud?"

"Do what Lauren?" She was good at playing with them, keeping them guessing but close enough to be good friends and far enough to conceal her secret.

"You look fabulous all the time, never a hair out of place." Lauren glanced at Audrey

"Yeah Audrey, let us in on your secret, inquiring Chloe Bear minds want to know." Chloe talked about herself in the third person a lot, and tonight she was just as silly.

Standing off to the side of the mirror, Audrey watched the girls work their hair and makeup over, as she waited to go back out to the dance floor.

The girls turned to face Audrey, pressing her for more details. "Come on *biatch*, tell me how you do it!" Lauren's voice pitched up an octave.

"Yeah, Chloe Bear needs to know babe, please, please, please, tell me!"

"Nothing but a bit of hairspray and makeup applied sparingly I guess." It wasn't the answer they were looking for, neither satisfying them nor disappointing them.

"Call of nature." Lauren laughed as she disappeared into the far stall.

"Can you help Chloe Bear with her hair?" Chloe was still dependent on friends, her confidence, although outwardly high, inside she was just as shy as the next girl. She relied on what her big brother told her to get by those first few difficult teen years. "Fake it till you make it," he explained to her. Most if not all of the outgoing students and athletes did it, and Pete was right. You were either faking it, running with a group that was helping you fake it, or you were that one guy or gal—that one person that no matter who they were around or where they were, they were cool and they knew it. Nobody, no teacher and no classmate, could shake that from them. They had confidence exuding out of their every orifice. Clint was that guy and Audrey was that girl. There were a few others as well. Carl was not one of them; until now, he had not known what it was like to have that much confidence or be around a girl that was on top of things.

"Sure, turn sideways. What do you want? single pony? Or a bun?"

"A couple braids would be cool."

Audrey stepped in front of the mirror, Chloe staring at the far end of the wall as she twisted her friends hair, weaving the sandy blond locks back and forth into a neat pony tail, every hair perfectly in place. Chloe turned around to look at Audrey then glanced at the mirror. Only seeing her reflection staring back at her, she spun to face Audrey, who had stepped away from the mirror. The shock in her eyes told Audrey she saw something that she should not have seen. Chloe glanced at the mirror then back at Audrey again, brushing it off. Chloe was tired, so she didn't believe what she had witnessed.

"We're going back out to the dance, slim," Chloe yelled at Lauren, using her nickname.

“Okay be right out,” Lauren croaked back.

Chloe could hear the iconic rock tune as soon as she stepped out of the bathroom. The thump thump thump of the bass drum and guitar riff told her that her song was on. It was the song she was meant for—her anthem. She knew her classmates expected to see her in the middle of the dance floor, one arm raised, yelling out the lyrics, and the song was ten seconds into the first chorus. She pulled on Audrey’s arm. “Come on, it’s playing.” Audrey listened to the words for the first time. “—Here she comes now sayin' Mony Mony.”

Audrey and Chloe ran together, hand in hand, right through the crowd of students and into the dance floor, where they found Carl. Chloe started jumping up and down, chanting verse for verse. “Shoot 'em down turn around come on Mony.”

The crowded dance floor pulsated, waiting for their time to yell out a few words of improv. They were teenage rebel words added to a song that was already racy and had made the list for banning by the feds, spurned on by a middle-aged politicians wife. Chloe yelled it the loudest, to the cheers of the crowd. “—HEY HEY GET FUCKED, get laid get screwed!” The music rambled on—students yelling along—“Don’t stop Chloe, come on Chloe.” They were replacing the song title name with an elated Chloe, who was popping her head up and down, swinging her blond hair in circles, pumping her fists in fury!

Some of the students would tell the principal afterwards during a makeshift interrogation that she only said F’d and not the cuss word. Pete’s teammates boosted Chloe up on their shoulders at the end of the song, and the student’s chanted her name ‘Chloe, Chloo-ee!’

“What took you so long?” Carl asked Audrey as the noise of the music died down.

“Just taking a break in the bathroom, tidying up Chloe’s hair.”

“Yeah, I see, you did a great job,” he said, pointing to Chloe’s messed-up hair.

Audrey smiled.

Carl was not sure if it was an excuse or if she was really doing Chloe’s hair in the bathroom; either way, he didn’t care as long as she danced with him the rest of the night, and she did. She embraced him during the last dance and Carl could feel her heartbeat, the strong thumping jarring his chest as it reverberated through his whole body. Her energy flowed through Carl as they pressed together, and Carl could feel her warmth for the first time. She—was alive.

"I'm tired Carl. Can you take me home?"

"Did I do something wrong?" Tonight had been the time of his life. He had already planned on cruising that night with her, and if all went well, maybe going up to Seminary Hill, near the armory, where everyone would go on a rainy night to make out.

"No Carl, you were wonderful, but I need to go home now."

"Okay," he replied as his head slumped. "You need a ride Chloe Bear?"

"Sure, can you drop me off after Audrey?"

"No problem Chloe. You gals wait here, I'll pull the car up."

Carl left them just inside the double glass doors, the cold fall rain chilling him even under the heavy black leather biker's jacket. The Chevy sat alone at the end of the parking lot, two rows past the other cars. Carl was a nervous nelly, not wanting to park next to anyone that might ding his car with their doors. Carl honked, sending the girls running through the rain. Audrey slid across the bench seat, snuggling up to him for body warmth, while Chloe slammed the door next to her, making the car shudder.

"Easy on the door, Chloe."

"Sorry Carl. It's so heavy and it sticks; I can hardly pull it closed."

"I know, I have to get that fixed."

Carl drove into town and spotted the remnants of the cruisers sitting inside their cars at the Jackpot gas station and food mart on the last corner before downtown.

"HEY CARL!" They couldn't hear Frankie yell across the parking lot at them.

"Isn't that your cousin over there?" Chloe's finger darted out the window at Frank's green Chevelle.

"Yep, that's him. Mind if I pull in a minute Audrey?" Carl looked into her eyes, judging whether he should ask.

"No not at all, I just want to get home in the next fifteen minutes."

He did not want to make her wait, but his cousin had always had his back, and he felt obligated to stop.

"What's up Frankie?" Carl yelled over the top of the car, standing between the door and the roof.

"We're going out to the corner, going to try out the new engine. Meet us out there man, gonna be awesome. I think I can get it under twelve seconds in the quarter." Frankie leaned back against the fender crossing his legs as he rubbed his knuckles on his leather jacket, a pack of Camel cigarettes jutting out of the left pocket.

"That's sweet, what time?"

"Whenever you're ready man, I need someone to time me."

"Let me drop the girls off, then I will be right out."

"Right o' Carl. Why don't you bring them along?"

"Audrey wants to go home and I think it will be past Chloe's curfew."

"No worries man, meet us out there in a half hour."

"Alright Frankie, but no funny stuff this time."

Usually, when Carl would join his cousin, the seemingly benign event would lead to something more devious. It happened that way a few years back, before they could drive. Frankie had invited Carl over to help him work on his go-cart. It was supposed to be a quick project and test run down the alley behind his house. Years later, Carl would explain it as the Indy 500 of Centralia. Carl had no sooner finished bolting the rear wheels on the cart when Frankie asked him if he wanted to ride with him down the alley and back. It was a judgment call that would nearly cost him his life. Frankie shoved the gas pedal to the floor, spewing gravel up behind them as they shot down the alley. He came up with the brilliant idea of continuing onto the city street right into downtown, where they immediately passed by the police station acquiring the attention of Officer Spence. The next fifteen minutes would go down in history, as Frankie cranked the engine wide open, hitting speeds above fifty-five miles per hour. Carl sat there hanging onto the side of the cart, no helmet, and screaming at the top of his lungs to take him back before they ended up in juvenile detention. That day would go down in Carl's memory as one of his more exciting and harrowing events. The police never caught up to them, and Frankie left the cart in the garage for six months before he took it out again.

"Sure man, on the level; everything will be okay, trust me," Frankie replied with a smirk. The fact that he would be breaking laws speeding down a country road did not occur to Frankie as illegal. Carl knew something in Frankie's radar was broken.

Carl drove past Logan district, the dark winding road and spindly tree branches above sending his stomach into knots as the hair on the back of his neck stood up. He didn't like traveling down this road at night, especially alone. At least Audrey and Chloe were with him; it was still creepy. Cresting the top of the hill for the turnoff to Teitzel Road, a narrow two-lane country road that led down the hill to Audrey's driveway, Carl's eyes strained, looking for the fog line marking the right hand side of the roadway. He knew if he took that corner too fast, it would be all over and they would end up in the ditch, plowing the car into one of the many large cedar trees down the embankment. Carl slowed the car as they drove down the hill, the asphalt pitch black. He turned sharp at the corner, taking the car away from the main road and into Audrey's driveway. Carl stopped the car in front of her house, opened his door, and reached for her arm.

"It's fine, I can walk myself up. Besides, it's raining and Chloe is waiting."

Her light peck on the cheek sent an icy chill up his spine as he watched her walk away.

"What's your number, I'll call you tomorrow," he yelled to her as she jogged up the path through the rain.

"We don't have a phone, Carl, just stop by," she yelled back.

Her statement struck him odd. *Who doesn't have a phone these days?* he thought to himself. "Okay, will do. Goodnight Audrey." She had already gone out of earshot, the foggy drizzle of rain muffling his voice.

Carl watched through the windshield as Audrey disappeared into the house, Chloe sitting across from him breaking the silence.

"What do you think about Audrey?" Chloe asked.

“I think she is amazing Chloe Bear, why?"

“Oh nothing, just wondering.”

“You’ve known her longer than I have; she just asked me to the dance this week, you have been around her for years.”

“I haven’t really known her that long. I mean, I remember seeing her around, but just started hanging out with her.”

“I know. She’s mysterious. Ever since the riverbank, I’ve thought about her every day.”

“Really?” Chloe asked. “Every day?”

“Nearly. It’s like I have some kind of connection to her, I just can’t put a finger on it. Something is strange about her. I feel like I’ve known her forever.”

“Deja vu—,” Chloe whispered. “She has something about her that is haunting.” Chloe’s voice trailed off and they sat in silence for a few minutes as he drove away.

Carl’s mind raced as they crested the hill to Chloe’s home; his thoughts of Audrey spun in his head. He had seen some weird things, but her good nature and attitude to him clouded his judgment.

“Night Carl. Thanks for the ride.” Carl felt the warmth of Chloe’s high-pitched voice hit him in the sweet spot; his heart was happy.

“Night Chloe Bear. Love ya.”

“Ditto!” Chloe yelled back.

Carl drove out to the strip, where Frankie was waiting to make a run. He noticed Clint’s car sitting just on the other side of Frankie’s as he cruised by. Setting his car up at the opposite end of the road, Carl left the headlights on, pointed at the finish line. The roar of the engine filled the night air as Frankie’s car shot toward him. Halfway down the strip, he nearly lost control on the slick road. The rush of wind blew Carl’s coat up away from his chest as Frankie rolled by him.

“Not good man: fourteen nine,” Carl mumbled.

Frankie leaned out the window as he drove up next to Carl, shaking his head. “Too wet. Catch up with you at school.”

“See you later Frankie.”

The wipers skipped back and forth on the windshield and Carl felt alone once again as he drove home. Walking inside his parent’s living room, his mother sat passed out in her chair, one hand hanging onto a paperback, the other hand holding a burning cigarette, a long ash ready to drop onto the floor. He sighed as he removed the cigarette, snuffing it out in the ashtray next to her.

Carl climbed the stairs up to his bedroom, falling asleep seconds after hitting the sheets. His dreams of Audrey and their week together filled his head. It nagged him all night; her features blazed across his subconscious, leaving a permanent imprint in his mind. All of a sudden Carl realized that he never saw Lauren again that night after the girls' trip to the bathroom.

4

CARL LOVED HIS NOVA MORE than anything in the world, at least until Audrey came along. His friend Clint Mirvens was exactly the same way, driving a 1973 blue Nova that had been completely restored. Clint and Carl went way back, years before, when Clint began suffering from a heart defect. They first met when Carl joined his father cutting firewood. Clint had also rode along with his father that afternoon but stayed in the cab of their old Chevy pickup to keep out of the rain. Carl would not know it that day, but they would become friends a few years later, sometime around eleven years old, when Clint would ride his dirt bike up to the little league field where Carl was playing ball. From that day on, Clint and Carl had a mutual friendship and respect, getting together often when Clint wasn't sick. Clint always called Carl by the nickname he had given him a few years earlier. It was also the name of the baseball team Carl was on at the time they first met: Moose.

Carl ran into Clint frequently, the two of them parking their cars at the end of the cruising strip near the Jackpot food mart. Today was no different, as Carl rounded the corner of Harrison Avenue near Main Street. He spotted the blue Nova backed into the parking spot in front of the convenience store. Carl rolled his window down as he pulled alongside his friend's car, not surprised to see a young blond girl sitting in the passenger seat. That was the thing with Clint; he always had the coolest girls with him and usually they were from the city four miles south. Something about those Chehalis girls got to Clint, or rather, Clint was unique enough to garner their attention. Two more blond gals poked their heads around the back seat of Clint's car to get a look at Carl.

"Hey man," Clint yelled across the seat of his car. "What's on the agenda?"

Carl shook his head back and forth, then shrugged his shoulders. He wondered how Clint did it. But there was no doubt about it: even though he was gimpy, Clint was a charmer; sweet to the ladies and that's what they sought out when they had run the gamut of the football squad in their hometown. Clint was ready, willing, and able to pick up the slack when they came calling. Today, three of them had.

"Come over to the house. MTV is playing a marathon of Headbanger's Ball," Clint piped up. The young blond smiled at Carl, then Clint coughed in a fit of spasm as he sucked the cold air in.

"I'll be over in a while. Gotta see a girl first. What time you gonna be home?" Carl looked at his watch; it was nearly three thirty.

"Leaving now man, see you when you get there." The little blond girl rolled the window up as Clint drove off. Carl pulled the car back onto the street, driving it out of town toward Audrey's house to see if she was around. The long driveway up to the old farmhouse was as deserted and foreboding as the last time he had been out there. Carl rapped his knuckles on the door, then glanced left and right, moving to the edge of the porch as he looked around. He was aware that he was being watched but unable to locate by who or what. The home echoed a hollow sound inside as he knocked on the door again. He was not sure how long he stood there, but if it was more than three minutes, it was enough time to make the hair on the back of his neck stand up. A raven flew past the porch, startling him. Carl stepped backward, and the porch boards squeaked. The combination of freaky bird and squeaky porch sent him back to his car. Carl watched the home grow smaller in the rearview mirror as he drove down the dirt driveway on his way to Clint's.

Carl shut off the car and looked through the garage door window to see if Clint's car was inside. The 1973 Nova lived indoors all its life. Today was no different; the car was put away, out of the harsh Pacific Northwest weather. Mrs. Mirvens greeted Carl at the front door. A heavy metal song floated out of Clint's room, infiltrating the rest of the house.

"Go on in Carl, Clint is waiting for you," she said, her sweet voice and caring demeanor the same for every one of Clint's friends.

"Thanks Mrs. M."

Carl liked Clint's parent's. They were real cool, even though they were in their late sixties, and maybe that is why they didn't seem to mind the endless stream of teenagers traipsing through their home at all hours of the day and night, nor the loud music. Or they were senile, either way, Carl would have traded his parents in on them in a heartbeat. Nothing surprised Carl about Clint, but today, he was taken off guard when he swung Clint's bedroom door open, shutting it behind him just as fast. Sitting in bed, on both sides of him, the three gals were cozied up to Clint, watching head bangers ball on a floor console television. It was 27", the largest TV available. Clint's parent's gave it to him for Christmas the previous year.

"Grab a seat buddy, some good bands coming up soon," Clint said, as he lowered the volume on the television with the remote. Movie posters of monsters, slasher flicks, and heavy metal bands plied the walls. On one side of the room, past his king-size bed, a nine-foot-long leather couch spread out next to the wall. A motorhead, heavy metal poster was tacked up above it. At the end of the couch next to his bed, a full size refrigerator sat stocked with soda, fruit juice, and medicine that was the reality of Clint's condition as well as an occasional six pack of beer that Clint was warned by his physician not to partake of heavily. Vintage floor lamps that stretched upward stood towering above Carl by at least a foot, their brass stems tarnished, disappearing into an inverted cone that threw red light across the ceiling. Clint replaced the regular sixty-watt incandescent bulbs for twenty watt red bulbs. Mood lighting he called it. On top of the television, fish swam in a Disney-themed forty-gallon square saltwater aquarium, complete with a replica pirate ship straight out of the Caribbean. A chest full of fake gold coins sat at the bottom, opening and closing in the current as tropical fish swam by, wary of the eel that lived under a rock structure behind the ship. Somewhere while traveling the states with his family, Clint's father had come across a street sign with his name on it. Clint Street lived above the fish tank, jutting out from the wall.

"Beer?" Clint asked, nudging the blond on his left side. She opened the fridge and grabbed a beer, tossing it over to Carl before he could reply. "Thanks brother, not really thirsty," Carl replied.

"Hey Moose, we ain't gonna live forever," he laughed.

Having lived five years longer than the life expectancy doctor's had predicted, Carl knew Clint wasn't kidding. "Besides, when am I going to get a chance to drink with my buddy?"

Carl obliged him as always, popping the top open, sucking down the frothy suds as the liquid tried to exit the sides of his mouth as it shot out of the can at lightening speed. The girl on the right side of Clint rubbed his chest up and down, and Carl was sure the comforting touch of a pretty girl was keeping him alive. The commercial on the TV ended, and Clint turned the volume up as the next song played. It was a song and band Carl had never heard of before, the band members wearing yellow and black spandex, their bushy hair and glamorous makeup akin to a Vegas strip show; that was the mode of most rock and heavy metal bands, each one more gaudy than the last. He immediately forgot their name when the next song came on.

"The girl you were with the other night, very good looking Moose." Carl had resigned himself to being called Moose for the rest of the days while Clint was alive. He also knew that Clint would always have two to three gals at his side until the end. "She's kind of mysterious though—better keep an eye on that one," Clint added.

"Nah man, she's a nice girl—kinda churchy," Carl replied.

Carl sucked his beer down, barely catching the next one, as the blond gal on the left had anticipated him finishing off the first one and rocketed another one across the room at him. Carl nearly missed the catch as it sailed overhead toward the wall. He raised an eyebrow at her, recognizing her but not remembering her name. She smiled back, then popped the top of her can open and slowly sipped on the beer before passing it across the bed to the other girls, each one of them taking a sip as they passed it back and forth. Soon, a mound of beer cans had piled up on the nightstand next to the bed, the four of them, sans Clint, were getting rather warm and toasty, their vision narrowing. One of the girls on Clint's right side had joined Carl on the couch, and Carl was sure that Clint had whispered into her ear a few minutes before she had abandoned the bed. Her touch felt good as she nuzzled up next to him, pulling her feet up onto the couch, bringing her knees up to her chest as she latched onto Carl's right arm.

"I have a girlfriend," Carl said to her. The green-eyed blond with dark winged eye shadow smiled back.

"I know, but I don't care if you don't. Were just cuddling, that is all," she purred.

Carl hesitated, choking on his guilt but spurred forward by his blurred mind. The quest for good versus evil was at hand; Carl was caught in unfamiliar territory. In front of him, his life played out like one of those Saturday morning cartoons, the kind where a devil stood on one shoulder of the cartoon character and an angel on the other. The devil telling him; *Go on, nobody will know. Besides, you are just cuddling with her*. The other shoulder, the angel, telling him, *Don't do it Carl. Audrey will find out and then you will be in trouble. It is not worth it*. The devil piped up again, fueled by the alcohol. *You only live once Carl, enjoy yourself, for Clint's sake anyway. He isn't going to live forever.*

Carl shook his head, staring into the eyes of the girl still clinging to his shoulder. She seemed content to sit there hanging onto him, watching television, and cuddling. If that was all that she was interested in, Carl saw no problem with it. They were just cuddling, no problem he decided—no problem at all. No harm no foul, nobody would find out and Clint had always had his back. Her sweet perfume wafted into his nose. She giggled as she stroked his hair. His neck tingled, Carl unaware that it wasn't the alcohol tickling him but the lips of the blond girl as she explored him. Carl enjoyed this, stretching his legs out farther away from the couch as he kicked off his shoes. He glanced over at Clint and could see he was equally involved with the girl on his other side.

Her lips slid across his neck methodically as he closed his eyes tighter, blocking out her face. But Audrey's face filled his mind. His lips tingled as hers locked onto his. The kiss lingered. Carl's heart pounded faster, eyes squeezed tighter. Audrey filled his head as he realized that he may have gone too far. It hit him in the stomach and he felt nauseated. He sat up and pushed the little blond girl off him.

"I've gotta go, Clint, thanks for the beer. Forgot I have to work tonight." Clint hardly heard what Carl said as his face leaned out away from the girl on his left.

"Okay Moose, catch you later."

The blond that had cuddled up to Carl rejoined Clint and the other two girls. Clint bumped the volume up three notches as Carl left the room. Iron Maiden had arrived—guitars were screaming as the band danced through the TV. Clint had waited a week to see them.

5

CARL HAD LEFT CLINT'S HOUSE, reeling from the effect of the alcohol and his new acquaintance. He tossed and turned all night until he fell asleep at four a.m. A knock on his bedroom door startled him as his eyes adjusted to the dim light coming through the windows. Carl stared at the alarm clock, the red numbers coming into focus. It was only 5:45, and then it dawned on him that it was evening already. He was supposed to meet up with Audrey for a date in an hour. "Carl, are you okay?" His mother's voice was raspy, cigarette scarred.

"Yeah Mom, I'm getting up."

He scrambled out of bed, aware he would be running short of time. The steam from the shower filled the bathroom, fogging the mirror. Carl stood under the hot water humming a rock tune, washing away the hangover—washing off the blond girl. Her perfume still lingered on his body.

The mirror was cool to the touch as he rubbed an open spot in the fog with his fist. Dark circles hung underneath his eyes. He was up, but was walking dead. His head pounded through the dull ache. Dressing in blue jeans and a t-shirt, semi casual, Carl ran out of the house and jumped into the Nova, thinking about Audrey.

A second date was something Carl would have never thought in a million years would happen. Nor would it happen immediately after the first date. His teenage years up to now had been a virtual desert in the dating world. He was on his way to her house. Carl could not think about anything other than her. He longed to be with her: her auburn hair, the sweet-smelling fragrance of her perfume, her laugh, and most of all her kind demeanor pushed him into a bliss he had never felt before. He knew he would fall in love at some point in his life, but this was bordering on pure obsession—an unhealthy obsession. The house looked less ominous as Audrey bounded off the front porch, jogging up to the car. He was afraid he still had the smell of the blond girl on him even though he showered. Was there anything lingering? Would Audrey notice? He sniffed his shirt.

Audrey slid up next to him and kissed him lightly on the cheek, making Carl blush, her hand grabbing his right hand. "Can you take me up to the point?" It was magic to his ears, the one place he had not driven to with a girl, let alone a girlfriend. "Sure." It was a one word answer that rolled off his tongue naturally. The Chevy bounced along the streets as he maneuvered it up the winding curves to the end of the road overlooking town. Days in Western Washington during winter were made for times like this, the constant rain, perfect cover for teenage activities in obscure places. Fog was rolling into town, and darkness was overtaking the grey sky.

"Carl."

"Yeah?"

"I want to tell you something," she said.

It was Carl's make or break moment and his mind weighed the options. Should he make the first move, kissing her, or was she breaking up with him? Throwing caution to the wind, Carl slid his hand over her shoulder, pulling Audrey's face to his. Their noses touched. He kissed her. It was long, wet, and vibrant. His eyes were closed the entire time. Had he kept them open, maybe he would have seen her eyes, maybe he would have seen the flash of brilliance that had crossed her eyes as they turned deep red then faded black again. For Carl, it was perfect.

"What do you want to tell me?" he asked, coming up for air.

She never answered him, pushing her lips up against his again, the kiss making him forget. Carl never brought up the previous afternoon's event at Clint's house, although he suspected that Audrey was wise to it, but they were not going steady at the time and nothing had really happened.

"Let's go to the pool hall. I have not been there in years."

Her statement seemed odd, but at the time Carl would have done anything for her. He mulled it over in his head. Why would a nice girl like her want to hang out in the seedy pool hall.

"Sure, I like pool. Are you any good?" he asked.

"I can shoot."

"Audrey Anderson, you are on, be warned though, I don't take it easy on the ladies."

"I wouldn't expect you to Carl."

Rainy afternoons sent the town kids to the billiard hall, and this Saturday afternoon it was packed. There were twenty-four tables, stacked into a small space with dozens of kids betting their allowances or last week's paychecks.

"I'll rack em' Audrey, grab a stick."

"I shoot first," she laughed.

She never let him shoot. From the break to the eight ball dropping in the corner pocket, Carl just stood there, his mouth gaping. It was another clue that this fifteen-year-old, was older than she seemed. An old soul, he chalked it up to that. He was beginning to think she was more like thirty than fifteen, at least a young looking seventeen.

"That's game. Sorry Carl. I told you I had skills."

"Re-match. You rack, I will break this time."

Carl got to break, then it was another run. Audrey slid around the table like a pro. Billiard balls flew around the table in curves and complex angles that Carl had never seen before. Her movements were effortless, her skill top notch. He watched her slim body lean over the table again and again, mesmerized, infatuated, excited.

"I win." She was happy, her smile growing bigger after each game.

"Hey man, your girlfriend is good, and hot too. Mind if I play a round with her." Carl recognized the voice. He had never played the town pool shark, but he knew him. At least by face and voice, preferring to only call him by his first name.

"Sean, that's Audrey's decision, you will have to ask her."

Sean was a lean, scruffy man, his pock-marked face fending off the roughest gals. He was a thug, and Carl had kept his distance until now. Sean had taken advantage of everyone he could, bilking them out of every red cent and dollar, a true predator when it came to gambling or playing pool. Sean was scum, plain and simple. If there were something unlawful happening at this end of town, he was into it. The neighborhood around the pool hall was sketchy in Carl's view.

"I'll play him," Audrey chirped. She spun the stick between the palms of her hand, then let it go. It stood straight up, spinning like a child's top, it's inertia keeping it aloft.

A sharp smile spread across Sean's lips. The shark got excited and cocky when he saw new competition. Months had passed waiting for a worthy adversary, and now he had his chance to showcase his skills. It was a moment he wouldn't let pass him by. He stood looking at Audrey and Carl like a lamb being brought to the slaughter house. It was an easy kill. Sean leaned back against the table, grinning.

Audrey took the first break, sinking a ball, then ran the table, finishing the game without giving him a chance to shoot. Sean took the next break, shooting twice before scratching the cue ball. She ran the table on that game too, his demeanor souring as the games played out. Hour upon hour, Sean threw down more money. Ten dollars per game first, then twenty per game. Eventually, she wiped him out as she emptied his wallet.

"It's not natural shooting like that. I don't know how you do it, but someone who shoots like that is either possessed, or they sold their soul to the devil." His anger boiled over, as his fist's balled up waiting for an answer. He loomed over top of her, a full head taller, his nasty breath billowing across her face.

Audrey stared straight into his eyes, not backing down an inch. "Practice. That is all, practice, and time, maybe you should spend more time practicing and less time mouthing off."

Her reply pissed him off. The pool stick silenced the pool hall as it shattered against the table. "This is not over," he spat. His words echoing in her head did little to unnerve her. Carl's hand's trembled.

"Let's go Audrey; I think you've done enough damage."

The two players stood there, just two feet separating them, neither one backing down. Sweat poured off Sean's head, streaming down the sides of his face. Audrey stared down Sean, never taking her eyes off him as Carl drug her out of the pool hall.

Carl saw a side to his girlfriend he had never seen before. She was still pleasant, but the sweet demeanor seemed stowed away temporarily. Audrey was on guard. He was pretty sure she could have kicked Sean's ass if she wanted.

"Carl, was that wrong? To take his money like that?"

It was a weird statement, another oddity coming out of an even stranger girl. It was almost as if she did not fully understand what it meant to dethrone the top pool shark on his home turf.

"No, not at all. He will get over it. Besides, I'm the luckiest guy around; who else has a girlfriend that can kick ass at pool."

"Nobody does Carl. There is nobody like me around. You can rest assured, I am a one of a kind girl; guys have looked for centuries. Ladies have looked for centuries for a man like you."

Carl danced around in the street clapping his hands. He had just watched his girl play like a professional. She had won more money in four hours than he could make in a week washing dishes at the restaurant where he would toil away for gas money. He caught the last statement too, that she really wanted to be with him. Their early afternoon escapade left Carl famished, and there was only one place on his mind to go.

"How would you like to take me out for a burger with your prize winnings?"

"You can have it all; I don't need it," she said, pressing the wad of bills into his hands.

"I can't take it; you won it fair and square. Just buy me a burger, that's all. You keep the rest."

Audrey bought the burgers and filled his tank, and they stopped by Frankie's house on their way home before dropping her off. The weekly shipment was waiting in Frankie's garage. Frankie never saw it delivered, the delivery man sneaking into the shop in the wee hours of the morning.

"I'll just be a minute."

"Sure Carl, take your time."

Her sweetness had returned; the glow of her skin appeared luminescent as she smiled at him, batting her eyes. Carl loaded up three cases of beer in the trunk and was set for the weekend delivery. The jocks would be set for their next beer bash.

Driving down the long dirt driveway, Carl's stomach churned and his pits felt slimy as they approached the house.

"Come inside," she said.

He thought she would have had enough of him. He was elated that she wanted him to stay. Their footsteps echoed into the bedroom.

She had no false pretenses as she lay on her back on the bed, motioning with her finger for him to join her. Carl moved forward, willing his legs that felt like they were in concrete onward. His knee pushed into the soft mattress, smashing it down as he straddled her. Audrey caressed his face with her hands. Her hands slipped inside his shirt, as she stripped it off. Carl's lips meshed with hers. His heart thumping away, hands groped across bare skin. Carl sucked on her neck.

"That tickles," she giggled.

Carl moved across her neck to her lips, kissing her softly. Audrey breathed in deeply, then sighed as she whispered in his ear, then she bit his lobe. "I'm here, but not here. Do you understand?"

Females were still a huge mystery to Carl. He barely knew how all this started in the first place, let alone what she meant now.

"I've been here before, long before, years ago," she said.

"I know. I've been in love with you since I pulled you out of the river."

"I have been around much longer than that, Carl—for generations."

"You grew up here, so did I. I just don't remember you in school." The intimate moment clouded his mind.

"I've been gone a while, but now I am back," she purred.

“I’m glad you’re back.”

Carl seemed to understand nothing. Not really much of a deep thinker, he brushed it off as girl talk. To him, she was perfect.

They lay in bed together, caressing each other for a couple of hours longer, Carl wishing he could stay all night.

“I’ve got to go to work. Can I pick you up for school on Monday?”

“Sure.”

Carl left her in the bedroom, the glow on her face bright as it was hours earlier, her porcelain complexion perfect in every way, her eyes luminescent pools, piercing deep into his soul, capturing his heart. Warmth took over the home, and a small fire was burning in the fireplace as he walked through the living room on his way out, another oddity that he brushed off, unaware of how it got started—or had he not noticed it before?

6

AUDREY BRUSHED HER HAIR WITH long sweeps, removing the tangles. The mirror in front of her was blank. She could hear the voices of the girls before they pushed their way into the tiny bathroom just outside the chemistry lab. Three of them walked past her, not noticing her lack of reflection in the mirror. Audrey stood there wide eyed, afraid to move, waiting for the girls to notice her. Snickering laughs floated out of the last stall, along with the pungent smell of marijuana, and it was all too clear to Audrey. This was the bathroom the bad girls used. It would be the one she would use as well, because it was obscure, private.

Audrey ran down the hallway and burst through the classroom door seconds after the bell rang, taking her seat behind Chloe. The teacher gave her the evil eye as she continued the lesson, keying in on Audrey, who was now whispering into Chloe's ear.

"Ms. Anderson, can you tell us what is so important it can't wait until after class?" Mrs. Carver said gruffly. Audrey sat there quietly, thinking of a reply that would be suitable.

"Well, the class is waiting," Mrs. Carver pressed.

What came next could only be described as a battle of wits between two superior intellects. Audrey unleashed a torrent of perfect German verbiage, most of it in a dialect Mrs. Carver had never heard before and was having a hard time deciphering. For two minutes Audrey spoke, her voice growing louder and faster as the foreign syllables slid off her tongue perfectly. Mrs. Carver sat there dumbfounded. It was the first time in nearly forty years teaching German that she had run into a student who had a grasp of the language beyond the university level. Audrey spoke as though she were a German citizen standing at the gates of hell, three centuries earlier. The more she spoke, the more the arteries on the side of her face pulsated. At the two-minute mark, Chloe spoke up, breaking her concentration.

"Uhh, Audrey, you okay?" she asked, staring right into her friend's eyes as she broke through the fog.

"I'm good Chloe," Audrey replied, snapping out of the trance. "You may continue the lesson Mrs. Carver. I'm sorry I disrupted the class. I was just telling Chloe about my boyfriend Carl and how we nearly went all the—"

"That is enough, Ms. Anderson. Class, open your books to page 245." Mrs. Carver stared at her often during the rest of the class, not hearing much of the conversation between the students as they took turns practicing. The bell rang forty-eight minutes later.

Chloe chased Audrey out of class and into the hall, laughing loudly and snorting as she hung onto Audrey's right arm.

"That—that was epic, really Audrey. You kicked her in the ass so hard, she won't be able to sit down for a week."

"That wasn't my intention Chloe, but she pushed too hard; she should have let it go."

"Come on. It is killing me, did you do it or not?" Chloe asked as they walked arm in arm down the hall. They could hear the buzz of voices from the other students echoing out of the cafeteria into the main hall as they passed by the principal's office. Audrey looked in past the secretary at Mr. Hollings, he sitting at his desk with his head in his hands. Chloe pulled on her friend's arm harder as Audrey paused in front of the doorway, dragging her into the lunchroom.

"Aud, let's go, I'm hungry—tell me—"

"No, Chloe we didn't do it. But we did have a good time."

"That's okay. You have all the time in the world; it is not like Carl will find someone else."

Audrey didn't know Chloe was privy to Carl's interlude with one of Clint's groupies. It was just gossip, told as it always was, passed along from one person to the next, the story getting more embellished each time. Small towns and small schools operated that way, gossip spreading just as a wildfire shoots through the forest after a careless citizen sets it ablaze with a discarded cigarette butt.

Chloe and Audrey pushed through the crowd and into the lunch room, joining the friends at their table. Audrey scanned the room for Carl and wondered if he was in the lunch line or just late from leaving his class. He never missed a day sitting by Audrey. The group consisted of Chloe, Audrey, Pete, and a few guys on the football squad. Lauren was there one day, gone the next, as her mood swung violently. Frankie would stop by now and then, but preferred to hang with the rednecks and farm-boy crowd, or as he would put it, "The real people."

Later on, Audrey and the rest of them would come to realize Frankie was right, the real people were the farm kids and rednecks.

"Has anyone seen Carl?" Audrey asked. Chloe glanced around, then shook her head no.

"Pete, have you seen Carl today?" Chloe asked, after slugging him in the shoulder, nearly spilling his tray full of food.

"Damn it Chloe, you were almost wearing this pile of slop. You know I need the sustenance for football practice." Pete had started using big words since he joined advanced-placement English, although he rarely knew what he was talking about; in this instance, he was correct. He spaced out a few more seconds before answering her.

"You were mulling over the word sustenance, weren't you?" Audrey poked.

"More or less, and no, I haven't seen him today, probably playing hooky," Pete replied as he stuffed half the burrito down his throat, finishing it one bite later.

"Pete, Mom told you to chew your food; you're going to choke."

He opened his mouth and stuck a tongue full of burrito out at her, a piece of it falling off and back onto his tray, splashing down in the applesauce. It sprayed Chloe and Audrey in the face.

"That's gross you idiot," Chloe yelled as she grabbed his sleeve to wipe the applesauce off her face. Audrey took it in stride, only taking two small, dime-sized splatters on her cheek. Pete immediately picked up the chunk of beans covered in applesauce, cramming it back into his mouth as he craned his head skyward. The whole table cringed with the combined gasps and yells of "yuck, gross man." "That is twisted dude," came from the other end of the table from one of the football players.

"I guess he is not going to show," Audrey said as she slumped down in her seat.

Clint crossed the lunchroom, his slow gait and right legged limp taking him a few extra minutes to navigate through the tables of students as his groupies high-fived him. His hair was past shoulder length, and the head-banger crowd were following his lead on maintaining their rocker looks. He was legendary with those kids.

"Hey Peter; what's up my brother from another mother?" Clint said as he shuffled closer.

Pete high-fived Clint, causing him to stumble.

"Easy on the goods my big friend," Clint replied.

"I'm sorry bud, how's things? You feeling okay?" Pete asked.

"Good man, thanks for asking."

Audrey looked into Clint's eyes, reading his thoughts, and that is when it hit her. They stared at each other for a few seconds, exchanging enough in those brief moments to come to an understanding, and she knew he was in worse health than he put on.

"Gotta go my friend, I see some ladies over there that need my assistance." Clint patted Pete on the back as he walked away, keeping his eyes locked on Audrey.

"What's wrong with him?" Audrey asked.

"He has a bad ticker," Pete chimed in.

"That's rude," Chloe said. "He was born with a heart defect and was not supposed to live this long, but he is still here. Been in the hospital a dozen times and nearly died twice. But he keeps on going, you know—energizer bunny type of stuff."

"Oh. It hasn't stopped him from making friends," Audrey said as she pointed at Clint, who had joined two younger girls, sitting between them.

Audrey left the table and walked up behind Clint, grabbing him on the shoulder, sending him a direct message through a vision of his death.

"We need to talk." Audrey's eyes looked deep into Clint's, stirring his soul.

"You can wait can't you? I'm not ready yet."

"That is not why I am here," Audrey replied. "You know something and you're going to spill it."

"Step into my office," he said as he got up and walked out of the cafeteria, while Audrey walked next to him less than an arms length away. Clint pushed the door of the men's locker room open, stepping inside, and Audrey followed him.

"What was Carl up to at your house the other day?" She pushed her face up to his, just inches from his nose. Her hot breath sent the pulse of death across his face. She did it on purpose.

"It was nothing Audrey. He had a few beers with me and a few friends," Clint gasped, coughing loudly.

"What friends?" She pressed her arm up against his chest as she leaned her weight into him.

"A few girls from Chehalis. Nothing happened, really."

Audrey studied his eyes and could tell he was covering up for Carl.

"If nothing happened, why are you lying to me?"

Clint shifted his feet nervously.

"Carl had a few beers, then one of my friends sat next to him, next thing I know, he was out of there—I think she may have kissed him. I don't really know. I didn't see it happen. I was preoccupied."

Audrey took her hand off his chest, letting him catch his breath. "Okay, but next time Clint, next time. You know what I am talking about, don't you? You know who I am." It wasn't his time, but she wanted it clear that Carl was her boyfriend and was off limits.

"I know what you are; it is not my first visit with your kind."

They had an agreement that was unspoken, a reckoning that was coming, and she made him aware he was on borrowed time. Audrey left him in the bathroom, rejoining her friends in the lunch room just before the bell rang. She had considered what Clint told her as she sat next to Chloe, finishing her tuna sandwich. Her mind worked overtime thinking about the Chehalis girl's advances toward Carl. She couldn't decide what made her more furious: Carl getting kissed by another girl or the fact that he had not told her. She was determined to find out soon.

7

CARL PUSHED THE WASH BRUSH down the side of the Nova, pulling the soapy suds along the body panels. His car was rarely dirty; he washed it weekly because it was his baby. Dipping the brush back into the bucket of soapy water, Carl pulled it out, pushing it down the rear quarter panel, nearly hitting Audrey in the chest. The soapy water splashed onto her crossed arms, but she did not flinch. Carl could sense Audrey was mad at him.

"Hey Aud, how'd you get here?" he said as he pushed the brush down the fender panel again, wiping away a dirty spot. He averted his eyes from her in an attempt to sway the conversation his way.

"Carl, I'm going to ask you one time and one time only. How you answer will set the stage on how our relationship will continue." Her hands were on her hips. "Did you kiss another girl?"

He didn't like it when she spoke in such a spirited tone using perfect vernacular.

"I—I—yeah this is not going to sound good…" he paused, catching his breath. He knew he was on the precipice, sinking into the abyss and it was his reckoning. Carl pulled his right hand through his hair while leaning on the brush handle, its end sticking out of the soap bucket.

"Go ahead, I'm waiting," she said, standing her ground, her eyes narrowing as she glared at him, her right toe tapping furiously. The tapping echoed in his head like a metronome, clicking back and forth, rhythmically. Grinding on him. *Click, clack, click, clack.* His head buzzed.

"The other night at Clint's house—I kissed a girl—well, she kissed me first though."

Click, clack, click, clack, she tapped.

Her face reddened and her arms went from crossed to balled up fists hanging down by her legs. Sweat rolled down Carl's face, the tension between the two boiling. He didn't know what to do or say. He knew he had screwed up, plain and simple, and it was too late to fix it.

"We're done Carl. I don't want to see you anymore," she said, turning around so quick a gust of wind blew past Carl's face. Carl released the soapy brush handle, grabbing her arm.

"Don't touch me," she said, her voice low, the tone menacing. Audrey shook his hand off her arm and kept walking down the driveway. She disappeared around the corner, leaving Carl standing next to his car. Carl slipped down the side of the car, landing on the ground, his butt making solid contact. Any other day and it would have hurt; today he was numb and didn't feel the pain. He sat there for a few minutes gathering his thoughts.

Carl slid behind the wheel and cranked the engine over and over, but it would not fire. This had happened to him before, after washing the engine down with degreaser. He had got the distributor cap wet, soaking the points inside. He opened the hood and pulled the cap off to dry the points, then replaced it. Behind the steering wheel again, Carl prayed for a moment then tried his luck. The engine coughed and sputtered as he turned the key. It infuriated him that it wouldn't start as he banged his head against the steering wheel.

He twisted the key again and the engine rumbled to life. Carl slammed the shift lever into drive, and the back tires squealed as they spun on the wet pavement, the rear end sliding sideways down the driveway. At the bottom of the hill, Carl glanced left and right, not slowing down as he shot out onto the two lane road toward Audrey's house. She had been gone for twenty minutes and he was sure he could catch up to her and apologize. The car flew down the road, the speedometer passing seventy in the thirty mile per hour zone. Two miles ahead, the crossroad for Pearl Street was flooded with traffic. Carl slammed on the brakes as he closed the distance to the intersection, the car not slowing. The brake pads were not gaining any purchase as they slid around on the wet brake discs and brake drums on the rear wheels. Carl stared at the intersection, waiting for the crash. Fifty yards from the intersection, the brakes grabbed hold and slowed the car down to fifty, then forty. He cranked the steering wheel hard left as the car slid through the intersection, missing a large sedan by inches. Carl stomped the accelerator to the floor, the tires squealing as they caught traction, propelling the car North on Pearl Street. Ahead, the side of the road was empty.

She couldn't have walked this far this soon, he reasoned. At best she should have been just up the road. *She must have walked toward town,* he thought. He mashed the brakes and the car slid to a stop. Carl spun it around as he stomped on the accelerator. Black smoke erupted from the tires, leaving two strips in the asphalt as the car catapulted toward the river bridge a mile ahead. The Nova flew across the bridge as Carl searched the side of the road, but she was gone. He drove the entire road to Audrey's house at breakneck speed, and the car's engine overheated as he pulled up in front of the old farm house. Steam poured out of the radiator overflow. Carl pounded on the front door frantically.

"Audrey, Audrey," he yelled. "Audrey, are you in there?" He couldn't see any movement inside as he peered through the window. He hung his head down as he stepped off the porch. His feet shuffled across the pavement as he walked back to the car with legs of rubber.

The drive into town was empty, his heart breaking as he realized he would not be able to hold her anymore. Darkness was falling fast, the blackness of the road sucking in the headlights as a few street lamps flickered above while he drove to Clint's house.

Carl looked into the garage through the hazy glass. Clint's car was inside. He knew Clint could boost his spirits or at least help him finish the six-pack he had taken out of the trunk. Clint's older sister answered the door; she must've been back from college for the weekend. She eyed the beer and then held out her hand. Carl placed a ten in her palm as he walked back to Clint's room.

"Hey man, you awake?" he called out as he opened the door. Clint was lying in bed, watching MTV.

"Moose, good to see you man. I see you brought my favorite beverage." Carl pulled a beer out of the carton, handing one to Clint. He collapsed into the couch, grabbed a beer, and popped it open, spraying foam across the room. He guzzled the first one down and was well into the second, finishing it off quick.

"Easy does it Moose, what's the hurry?"

Carl looked at Clint with pain in his heart as a tear rolled down one cheek.

"Is it over?" Clint asked.

Carl struggled to get the words out. "I lost her man, I lost her," he said between guzzles of beer.

"That sucks man, don't worry about it. Maybe it's for the best." Clint grabbed the phone off the nightstand. His fingers flew around the dial as he scrolled through the numbers. His speech was inaudible. Carl didn't hear a word he said, still numb from Audrey breaking up with him. Twenty minutes and two more beers later, the little blond girl and her friends knocked on the window. Carl slid it open and helped them climb inside, two of them joining Clint as they snuggled up to him in bed. The little blond girl, Callie, as Carl would find out a few hours later, grabbed a seat next to him on the couch.

"I'm sorry Carl, I didn't mean for you to get into hot water with your girlfriend." She rubbed his shoulder, placing her head on it as she pulled her feet up underneath her. The night slipped away in a beer induced haze.

He wasn't sure how he got home that night, and his hangover reconfirmed his resistance to drinking in excess previously. The phone rang over and over, Carl stumbling downstairs, his mother not around. Fumbling with the handset, Carl placed it up to his ear gently, his voice raspy, head pounding.

"Hello?"

"Hi Carl, I hope you don't mind me calling you so soon."

"Who is this?" he asked.

"Callie. Callie Elliot, Clint's friend," she replied.

Carl sobered a bit, swallowing the lump in his throat.

"Oh hey Callie, how are you?" It was a fast turnaround for him, and he knew Clint was behind it.

"I'm great Carl. Can you come over and pick me up?" Her request shocked him.

"I guess so, where do you live?"

"Right behind Safeway in Chehalis, on the next street up. I'll wait outside for you," she said, her voice higher pitched and softer than Audrey's.

"Be right over," Carl replied, hanging up the phone as he rubbed his throbbing head.

8

CARL COULDN'T BELIEVE HE WAS driving over to Callie's house a day after Audrey broke up with him. He was upset about Audrey, but Clint was his friend and was responsible for hooking him up with Callie. A twinge of appreciation and duty pushed him to hang out with her, and she was good looking.

Callie sat outside her parents 1940s craftsman style home, on the front steps. She ran up to the car and jumped in as soon as Carl pulled up. It was the second girl that had ridden with him. A smile pursed Carl's lips again. Here was another beautiful girl that wanted to spend time with him. When he kissed her the other night, he had felt guilty even though he didn't consider Audrey and him together. He put Audrey out of his mind as Callie smiled at him. He breathed in the fruity essence of her perfume.

"What's that perfume called?" he asked her.

"Poison," she replied.

"I feel ill already," he laughed as it intoxicated him. She giggled.

"Where we headed?" she asked, brushing the blond locks away from her eyes "—and please, call me Cal."

He hadn't considered where or even what they were doing; his head still ached from the hangover.

"How 'bout a burger from Harold's?" he asked, waiting for her answer.

"Harold's is good, but if you don't mind, could we go to the Dairy Bar? It's just down the road."

"Sure whatever you want—*Cal*."

Carl didn't know much about the burger bar in Chehalis but figured it couldn't be too bad. Traffic in the small town of seven thousand crawled around the streets of the downtown shopping area at a dismal twenty miles per hour, a speed Carl was unaccustomed to driving. He turned onto Main Street and the Nova's muffler snorted as the car strained to keep under twenty miles per hour. Carl could not stand the narrow streets and multiple crosswalks in Chehalis. He wondered who came up with such a travesty? The low speed limit, crosswalks with flower planters jutting out from the side of the streets and, to make matters worse, Dairy Bar was just beyond the railroad tracks, where the cars would pile up waiting for nearly a half hour at times just to drive another three hundred yards. Today, the train sat there for only a few minutes before slowly pushing north. It was ample time for them to get acquainted, and Callie was chatty.

"Do you mind if I change the station?"

"No not at all," he replied.

"What music do you like?" she asked as she twisted the dial off the rock station in Seattle to the local pop station in town.

"Hmm, just about anything I guess, but metal is my favorite," he said, assuming she was a metal head as well. "What are you into?"

She paused as she thought about it, taken away by a catchy pop song on the radio. "Bon Jovi, Poison, those groups. Yeah, Jon Bon Jovi, I like him the best! He rocks and he is hot too!"

Carl wasn't really into the big hair bands but did enjoy some of the songs Callie was into. She cranked up the volume, and the sixteen-inch woofer in the trunk rocked the car up and down as it thumped to the beat. Audrey flowed back into his subconscious. He realized he was thinking of her and pushed her out of his mind and back to Callie.

The last rail car scooted across in front of them, and the crossing arms lifted, the Nova sliding underneath just as the arm cleared the roof. The Dairy Bar sat alone in a parking lot just beyond the Darigold Cheese processing plant. The car coasted to a stop in front of the burger bar, and Carl rolled down his window to order. The man stash on the older gal leaning across the drive through window reminded Carl of a side show performer in the circus. He guessed her to be a few pounds past the 250 mark, as she filled the window.

"What can I get you kids?" she asked, leaning further out of the sliding window. "Hey there Callie Mae, is that you?"

"Yes Mrs. Blackburn, how are you?" Callie answered.

"I'm good honey, you know, I've told you a hunerd times to call me Mrs. B."

"Yes, Mrs. B."

"When you gonna come work with me honey?" Mrs. B asked.

"I'm only fifteen ma'am. I can't legally work yet,"

"That's not true honey, you can work a few hours a week as long as you are off early; besides, we're only open till 9 p.m. You want a job, you come see me. Now what would you kids like?"

Carl studied the menu painted on the side of the building the whole time the conversation went on around him, hardly hearing a word, until Callie said, "I'm only fifteen." A year ago, it would not have mattered, but now he was approaching eighteen, and someone that young could get him in trouble. His cousin's words echoed in his mind. "Fifteen will get you twenty!"

"Thanks Mrs B. I turn sixteen next month and dad said I could get a job after my birthday."

"Good, good honey. What will it be young man?" Mrs. B asked.

"I'll take the double double, and an order of fries," Carl replied, relieved that she would be sixteen—not jailbait.

Carl listened to Callie as she ordered a kids burger, a small fry. and a large chocolate malt. Carl watched her devour the burger and fries before quickly sucking down the malt. The straw pulsed in and out, collapsing as she sucked the chocolate creamy concoction through her small pouty lips. Halfway through the malt, she placed her hand on her forehead.

"Brain freeze, brain freeze, rub it Carl—damn," she replied, while sliding over next to him. Carl rubbed her forehead softly.

"Ahh that's better. Thanks."

Carl was a lot wiser with women now, or at least he thought so, but she had taken him by surprise, although he came to the realization minutes later that it was just a ploy to sit near him.

9

SCHOOL WASN'T THE SAME FOR Carl, as he skipped more days than he attended, although he was in school in the town just to the south nearly every other day during lunch. Callie was more than happy that he visited her, the excitement on her face and giddy laughter she got when the office delivered a dozen red roses that day to her home room threw her over the top. Carl received a warm hug and kiss when he met her for lunch; the other girls at her table were jealous.

"Thank you, thank you, thank you Carl, this is the sweetest thing anyone has given me," Callie said as she wrapped her arms around his neck, kissing him again on the lips. His cheeks turned rosy as he blushed. A girl next to Callie spoke up as her jealousy throttled, unable to resist.

"Damn Cal, how do you rate?" the brunette growled.

"Shut up Kitty Kat, I deserve them—cuz' I'm beautiful—right Carl?"

He wasn't going to disagree with her and had learned that not too long ago—never disagree with a woman or fight with them. The outcome of an argument always goes to the superior mind, and Carl knew that wasn't him.

"For sure Cal." He kissed her on the side of the cheek, to the cat-calls, whistles, and claps at their table and the one behind. The brunette stood up from the table and walked around behind Callie and Carl.

"I'm Kathy; you can call me Kat." She jutted her hand near his, and he clasped it. "If you get tired with Cal, I'll be waiting for ya."

Carl's face grew a darker shade of red.

"I'll take that under advisement Kat," he replied.

"He's off limits bitches—he's all mine," Callie said as she wrapped her arms around his neck. Carl blushed again as his stomach did a flip flop.

Audrey was stewing more and more as she looked for Carl. She was still pissed at him, but the absence was making her heart ache. Their lunch table was not the same without Carl, even though Pete was up to his regular antics of sticking his tongue out with half-digested food on it to the chagrin of the girls. The "Yuck"s, "Ahh, that's disgusting" and heads turning around to avert their eyes gave him enough satisfaction to do it over and over throughout the week.

"Has anyone seen Carl lately?" Audrey asked the group around her, the multiple nos coming in unison. Clint walked by a few minutes later and Audrey followed him to his table, catching him before he sat down.

"What do you want this time?" Clint grumbled.

"It's not about that. Do you know where Carl is?" she replied softly.

"Maybe. What's it worth to you?" he said, posing a question she hadn't thought of having to answer. Audrey pondered what he was really asking her.

"Okay, you've earned two more years," she answered.

He thought about it a few seconds, rubbing his scruffy goatee.

"He's with Callie, the blond that you asked about the other day, probably having lunch with her as we speak."

"Thanks. I'll be seeing you—soon," she replied, her voice trailing off.

Audrey had given him a stay of execution—something she had never done before. Time was on her side, not his.

"It's a date!" Clint replied as she walked away from him.

She turned, stared directly into his eyes, and whispered under her breath, "Yes it is. Two years Clint, no more."

He nodded.

Carl made it back to school a few minutes after the second lunch bell rang, slipping into the back of class unnoticed. Audrey shared the same class with him. She glared at him from three rows over trying to catch his attention. He could see her but was playing the, *I'm not interested in you card,* now that they were not a couple. This infuriated her more. The longer she stared at him, the more he acted like she was not there.

"Dude, she's pissed at you. If I didn't know it, I would say she is 'bout to blow a gasket," Pete whispered over his shoulder at him.

"What did I do? She broke up with me." Carl whispered back.

"Don't kill the messenger, just telling you that she is gunning for you, you know, probably stalking you when you are sleeping, maybe tearing up a stuffed animal you gave her and dousing it in ketchup before throwing it on your front porch. You know, 'bat-shit crazy' stalker chick," Pete replied. "Remember when that psycho stalked me for two months after we broke up last year?"

"No, I don't remember? Do they really act like that?" Carl asked.

"Yes, you idiot! Girls go ape-shit crazy when you mess with them. Hormones my brother, hormones got 'em all screwed up in the head and the heart."

He had never realized the differences between a girl and a guy before, other than the physical stuff. Carl thought a girl was just a version of a guy with a part missing in one spot and two parts added up top.

"What should I do?" Carl whispered. "Help me out man, we go way back."

Pete paused before answering him.

"What's in it for me?" Pete asked.

"Booze, I'll get you some more booze, on the house," Carl answered. "And I'll throw in a bag of weed."

Carl knew that Pete did not smoke pot, but he needed his help.

"Deal. Don't worry, I'll keep her at bay for you," Pete replied.

Audrey stared at Carl the entire class, moving rapidly through the students as the bell rang.

"Hey Audrey, what's shakin'?" Pete asked while Carl slipped out the back door of the classroom, disappearing into the hallway among the hundreds of students.

"I don't have time for this, Pete. Get out of my way." She pressed her hand into his chest and was surprised to see that she couldn't move him. She pushed harder and Pete stepped back, letting her pass by. Audrey moved through the crowded hallway but lost sight of Carl. She bumped into multiple people as she searched. She knew what his next class was and made a b-line for it, as she navigated quickly through the students. Audrey was near a dead run as she ran around the next corner and into Clint.

"You said two years," Clint replied, as he was nearly knocked off his feet, Audrey grabbing him by the arm.

"Yeah, sorry Clint, I didn't mean to run into you—yet," she said as she loosened her grip on his arm, letting him go. Their minds meshed with the bodily contact—a bad vision for Clint.

"Sure thing Audrey, sure thing," he replied, his breathing labored.

Audrey continued through the crowded hallway to Carl's next class. She searched the rows of desks as she peered through the narrow window of the classroom door, the last one on the right, Carl's spot, was empty.

Carl had walked right by the class and into woodshop across the hall, having switched classes that morning with the registration office. He was failing typing anyway, and a withdrawal would boost his grade-point average if he could get an *A* in woodshop. That was not a far stretch even for a slacker like Carl; the instructor was a goofy old guy that everyone loved. Nobody failed woodshop—nobody.

Audrey crossed the hallway, opening the woodshop door, the machinery drowning out the students' voices inside. Carl was nowhere to be seen, having ducked out the back door on his way around to his car. She knew he had just been through there; it was the obvious exit point. She could sense him.

10

CALLIE STOOD OUTSIDE THE CHEHALIS high school, next to a statue of a Greek goddess as the Nova rounded the corner, pulling alongside the curb. She slid up next to Carl, taking the spot that was recently reserved for Audrey. Carl felt like it was the natural course of events, another nice girl next to him. He gave her a light peck on the cheek, making her smile before driving downtown. She pulled his right arm off the steering wheel and held his hand in her lap. Carl knew that skipping school was new for her. She was a straight A student, and he could tell she was excited to be with him. He even noticed that her friends were happy they were together. She had already latched onto him as his girlfriend, but Carl did not see it that way, at least not yet; they had just met, and now she was holding his hand in hers as her petite warm body pressed up against his side. She leaned in, curling her feet up across the seat next to her.

Callie Mae Elliot was the younger daughter to a professional couple in Chehalis. She was an unpretentious girl; although she had come on strong initially, her tendency was toward bashfulness. She did hold a status among her friends as the nonchalant leader and good friend, they called them BFFs in Chehalis: best friends forever. Carl listened as she chatted non-stop, one story going into the next as the car swung past the old theater downtown on their way to the mall. She didn't leave anything out during the twelve-minute drive. Her parents, the older sister, which Carl immediately forgot her name, their cat Willow, a full-size twenty-two pound Maine coon and what her favorite color. He forgot that too.

Carl steered the Nova around the Lewis County Mall parking lot through the back alleyway parking across from the nondescript rear entrance to the arcade.

"Aladdin's Castle! How'd you know that I love this place," she squealed.

Video games were an addiction for Carl; just about every spare quarter he had available went into the upright machines at Aladdin's arcade or in the machines at the Seven Eleven convenience store.

"Just a hunch," he replied.

Carl had been skipping school and visiting Aladdin's for nearly two years now, even when he had to ride his bicycle across town for three miles to get there. Now he had wheels, and a quick trip during lunch was more feasible.

"I heard the principal stops by here often?" she asked.

She was right. The principals from both high schools frequented the arcade, sending students back to school and a stay in detention. But Carl had already made the appropriate adjustments to his game play, sticking to the machines at the middle of the crowded arcade, giving him full view of the front and rear entrance.

"Don't worry, they will never find us if they come in," he told her, their eyes adjusting to the darkened interior, pinball machines clanging away as players racked up points. The video games flashed vibrant colors across the ceiling and onto the walls.

"I didn't bring any money," Callie said, batting her eyes at him.

"It's on me," he laughed, pulling out a wad of twenties, shoving one of them into the coin changer, the quarters clanking into the tray below. Callie grabbed a handful, then skipped off to the machine closest to her. Carl stood alongside, watching her maneuver a frog across a city street, cars running over her character time and again. It was a girly game to him. Although he had played it a few times, he was more interested in one of the newest machines that was near the front of the arcade. Game

Over flashed on the screen in bright red, signaling the end of her play. Carl grabbed her hand and led her up to the front of the arcade, sitting down in the seat of a race-car game. He plopped in four quarters, a fortune in his mind for a video game, but this game, Pole Position, got his heart rate going.

"Come on, take a seat," he said to Callie, sliding back as far away from the steering wheel as he could. Callie planted herself between his legs as she grabbed the wheel, her feet barely reaching the pedals. The countdown timer scrolled backwards; 10, 9, 8, 7, she giggled, 4, 3, 2, 1, her foot shoved the throttle to the floor sending the car up the race course and around the corners. *She is good,* Carl thought to himself. The car slid back and forth around the corners, Callie hanging onto the steering wheel as Carl rubbed her shoulders. She passed car after car until she was in first place. She had two corners to go and was going to win the race and go into overtime, allowing her to race longer, when Carl kissed her softly on the back of her neck, moving around to the side. At first, she held it together, making it around a corner successfully, straightening out before shooting up to the next corner. Halfway through the corner, Carl nibbled on her ear, making her lose control as she giggled. The car crashed off the course and she giggled again.

"That's no fair, I was going to win," she said, as she pushed the throttle back to the floor, the car rolling through the finish line in fourth place, ending the game.

"Sorry, you smelled so good. Wanna go again?" he asked.

"No, you drive this time. I'm going to sit in back." She slipped her body around Carl, squishing between him and the back of the seat. Carl deposited four more quarters, and the countdown timer started. He was a real pro, as the car slid around the corners effortlessly gaining first place in less than a minute. Callie wrapped her legs around his chest, snuggling up against his back as she gave him a light kiss on the neck. He ignored her advances, obsessed with winning the game while her hand caressed the side of his face. The car slid around the last corner and through the finish line, signaling extra play, Carl pushing it harder and faster through the course.

"There is nothing you can do to distract me," Carl laughed.

"Really? Nothing—" she laughed as she stuck a moist finger into his ear.

"Damn it Cal," he fumed.

"Wet Willie," she laughed.

His anger quickly left him and he laughed with her, returning the favor as they struggled inside the confines of the race car, Carl finally getting the upper hand and a repeat Wet Willie in her ear.

"Oh gross Carl, that was a lot of slobber." She rubbed her ear on his shoulder, trying to dry it off.

In the front entrance to the arcade, a tall older gentleman in a business suit stepped inside. Carl glanced his direction, straining to see who it was. Callie looked around him.

"It's Mr. Blake, my principal," she said, as she scrambled out of the race car, running to the back door. Carl was close behind. He was not sure if they were spotted as they disappeared through the crowd and outside.

The Nova's tires squealed on the bare asphalt, catapulting the car away from the back door. Mr. Blake shot out of it and Carl could see him staring at him in the rearview mirror. He wasn't sure if Mr. Blake knew who he was or if he was able to get his license plate.

Carl sped up Gold Street, past the giant statue of a crow made out of fiberglass and plaster that sat out in front of the old Yard Birds shopping mall, the store where you could get it all. The smell of peppermint filled their nostrils, Carl braking hard as they entered downtown Chehalis just past Callison's mint factory. Carl breathed in deeply; he had fond memories traveling to Chehalis with his father in their 1967 Ford pickup, just to smell the sweet mint that wafted out of the factory from the vats of mint oil destined for candy shops around the country.

He dropped Callie off at her school, then bid her farewell, for a few hours at least—their plan to attend the dance later that evening already solidified. Carl liked the silky smooth touch of her lips as she kissed him goodbye, and it was also the first time he really noticed how petite her body was, her 5’4” one hundred six pound body underneath her long blond hair making her appear taller.

11

CALLIE AND KAT JUMPED DOWN the front steps as Carl drove up. The drizzle of rain, falling slowly, signaled another dreary evening. At least they would be inside, their destination the dance at Carl's high school. Chehalis students were allowed to attend as long as they had a student identification card from their school, even though most of the Chehalis kids stayed away due to the rivalry between the opposing schools in support of their football team. Each side felt as though they had a better team.

"Carl, you met Kat the other day," Callie said as she slid up next to him; Kat slammed the door behind her.

"Hey Kat, how are you?" he asked.

"I'm good. Thanks for taking us to the dance Carl," she said as she brushed the rainwater out of her hair, flicking it on the carpet. The wipers swished back and forth intermittently, streaking lines across the windshield. Carl strained to see the fog line as they drove to the high school in Centralia. The windshield fogged up around the edges as the heater went in an out, the motor rattling in the dash.

A large crowd had already gathered as they parked the car at the far end of the lot.

The line of students in front of the school stretched past the building into the driveway as they waited their turn to enter. Callie stood hand in hand with Carl, his coat draped over her shoulders to fend off the waning rain. Audrey was in front of them, nearly two dozen students separating them as she glanced back over her shoulder. She nudged Chloe with her elbow.

"What?" Chloe asked, rubbing her arm.

Lauren kept her distance as she watched them from across the parking lot.

"He's here," Audrey said to Chloe, nudging her again.

"Forget him Aud; he screwed up, he's not worth worrying about," Chloe replied.

Audrey looked back again as the line moved forward, noticing Callie standing next to Carl, holding his hand.

"—and she's with him," Audrey said as she punched Chloe in the shoulder.

"Ouch, that hurt. Who's with him?" Chloe asked. She stepped out of line to look back just as Callie pressed her lips up to Carl's, giving him a quick kiss. Chloe watched Audrey's eyes narrow with fury. Lauren stood a few people behind Carl. Chloe waved at her, not getting a return gesture.

"The blond, that's who," Audrey said, her voice strong and deep, the hatred coming out for everyone within spitting distance.

"Yeah, I saw her, and she kissed Carl too," Chloe said, her voice trailing off.

Audrey's fists tightened to the point her knuckles cracked. A commotion behind them stirred up the crowd as Clint limped past the line of students, his friends high-fiving him as he walked by. He had a Chehalis girl on his arm.

"Hi Clint," Callie yelled out as he walked past. He threw a hand up, waving, dragging his leg behind him, steadied by the girl he was with.

"Hey Clint," Chloe yelled.

Clint shuffled over to her and gave her a hug.

"Who's your girlfriend?" Chloe asked.

"This is Brandie," Clint replied.

"I'm Chloe," Chloe said as she stuck out her hand.

"Charmed," Brandie replied. Clint pulled her away as he shuffled into the dance, cutting into the front of the line.

"Man—Clint can sure pull in the pretty girls can't he!" Audrey laughed.

"Yeah for sure, she's gorgeous," Chloe chirped. "How does he do it?"

"Smooth talker I imagine," Audrey replied.

Callie, Carl, and Kat joined the large crowd in the middle of the dance floor and were surrounded by his classmates, nobody noticing these two girls from Chehalis had infiltrated their ranks. Kat cut it up as she spun around, shaking her butt up and down and popping to the rhythmic beat, her arms moving in sync with Carl and Callie. Clint slow-danced nearby, with his girl hanging off his neck, making out the entire song. The dance floor pulsated with the music, the crowd gaining and losing numbers similar to the ebb and flow of a tidal pool, until a slow song spun up. Callie and Carl embraced as their arms intertwined. Kat moved off the floor and found her guy, dragging him into the dance floor. The lights flickered greens and yellows, spilling off the disco ball above onto the teens' faces below. Carl swayed back and forth, Callie gripping him tighter as the song played on, the top of her head barely coming up to his nose. He could smell the sweet strawberry-scented shampoo in her hair as he breathed in deeply, closing his eyes to savor the aroma.

Audrey filled his view when he opened his eyes. She was standing five feet away, glaring, burning holes into him, and he could tell what she was thinking before she approached them.

Pain radiated through Callie as Audrey's icy hands pried her away from Carl. Audrey stood nearly four inches taller, as she stared into Callie's eyes, neither one of them speaking. She clamped her hands around Callie's wrists. Carl rambled on, but neither of the girls heard what he was saying.

Audrey searched her memory through the centuries. Her head was spinning with a vision as she passed through the ages where she first ran into Callie as the Kestrel, her rival. Now here she was, standing in front of her, just a foot away. Her eyes cleared as she stared directly into Callie's eyes, looking for a sign that Callie knew who she was. Nothing was there. Callie swallowed hard, shook her hands loose, and ran for the door.

12

CARL CAUGHT UP TO HER as she crossed the street into the parking lot.

"Wait, Callie. Stop," he said as he ran in front of her, Callie pushing around him.

"We aren't together anymore; come back inside," Carl pleaded.

She wouldn't speak, running away from him down the street, leaving Carl standing in the rain alone. There was only one thing on his mind now, and she was still inside the dance. Carl searched the crowded school until he found Audrey, catching her by surprise as he spun her around, grabbing her by both shoulders.

"Why did you do that?" he asked. "Tell me!" he said as he shook her. Audrey pressed her hand into his chest to push him away.

"She's not right for you Carl, trust me," she replied.

Carl dropped his arms to his sides as he left her, retreating to the Nova in the parking lot. He lowered his head and rested it on the steering wheel, the rain on the windshield masking the figure standing just feet away from him. Carl strained his eyes, pushing his face forward as he flipped the wipers on. The swish, swish of the wiper blades cleared the windshield, revealing Audrey. Buckets of rain tumbled out of the sky and she was soaking wet. Carl turned the steering wheel to the right and motored past her slowly, keeping his gaze on her. Her face disappeared into the dark, then was highlighted by his taillights in the rear-view mirror.

Further down the road, Callie walked briskly as Carl pulled the car in front of her. Callie walked past.

"Stop walking, are you insane? It's forty degrees and raining out here," he yelled.

She ignored him, her hair and clothing soaked through. Walking farther away, the headlights cast her shadow down the road in front of her. Carl drove alongside with the passenger window down.

"Cal, get in, you are going to catch a cold." *What is wrong with her?* he thought. What if some pervert decided to pick her up off the side of the road or if she got hit by a car?

"Please —get in Callie. Please."

Callie stopped, grabbed the door handle, and buckled into the seat on the far side of the car, away from Carl. He drove across town, with the heater blasting, neither one of them talking, the fifteen minute ride to drop her off an eternity. It wasn't his fault that Audrey had confronted her. He couldn't blame her for being mad at him, *But that was just crazy,* he thought. He had done nothing wrong and was still feeling guilty about it. She broke the silence as they rounded the corner, passing the Safeway grocery store before turning onto her street.

"I'm not insane Carl; never call me that again," she said, shivering.

"You're right, I shouldn't have said that to you. I'm sorry Cal. Can I call you tomorrow?" He didn't know what else to say or do, her silence and delayed response ripping at his heart.

"Sure, I guess so Carl," she said as she pushed the door open and ran up the stairs onto the porch, slipping inside her house.

13

CALLIE SLIPPED IN AND OUT of a dream as Willow the cat stretched his paws along her side yawning, his whiskers twitching as he purred himself back to sleep.

The dream started the same as it had before. She was inside a large castle centuries earlier working for a wealthy family, as their chamber maid.

Callie went about her duties, but unlike the previous dreams, she was physically present in the room. She touched herself. The flesh was real. Her breath exited into the cool room. It was more than a dream. She could smell the dank castle and feel the cold against her flesh. Audrey stood next to the window just across the room in the morning sunlight as it pierced the darkness, casting her shadow onto the bed. Her auburn hair sparkled in the sunlight.

Callie looked up and recognized Audrey for who she was for the first time. She was the same girl that Carl had dated—the girl that had accosted her at the dance. It was so surreal to her, she did not believe she was really there in the room with her even though her mind told her it was true. Audrey walked across the room, her long burgundy night gown swishing as it trailed behind her.

"Where are we?" Callie asked.

Audrey approached her. Callie could feel her chest tighten against her dress as she breathed harder. Audrey stepped closer, then cupped Callie's face with her hands.

"I know what you are," she said as she squeezed Callie's face hard. Callie winced.

"Stop it, that hurts."

Audrey pulled Callie around in a circle, then shoved her, pinning her up against the stone wall.

"You thought you could come in here to kill me?" Audrey spat.

"Please madam, I don't know what you are saying."

Callie glanced at the mirror behind them, noticing her image was the only reflection.

The icy touch of Audrey's hands around Callie's throat was spine tingling.

"You are the one that has come to finish me," Audrey said, "You are the Kestrel and my enemy; it has always been this way."

Callie looked into Audrey's eyes as they turned deep red, then was swept away from the room in a vision of Audrey's past.

The room faded away for a meadow, and three soldiers were standing around Callie as she gripped a long sword in her left hand. Fog rolled across the ground. Across the meadow, Audrey rode up a small hill on a pale horse. Callie looked over at the soldiers next to her. They all shared one thing in common: they were teen girls.

The pale horse snorted and steam billowed out of its nose as it galloped toward them, Audrey was kicking it madly as she wielded a sword above her head. Callie raised her sword. The horse and rider flew past her, sending a crashing blow into her sword. Sparks flew as she deflected the blow. Audrey dismounted, swinging the sword round and round as she approached the first soldier. The sword spun around lightening fast as it decapitated the first girl. The severed head bounced on the ground, the torso left standing for a few seconds before toppling over. The other soldiers sprung into action in a fight with Audrey, steel clashing against steel. Audrey was gaining the upper hand as she thrust the blade into the chest of one, then the other girl. Callie caught her off guard as her blade sunk up to the hilt into Audrey's chest. Audrey stumbled backward, gripping the blade as she dropped her sword, then fell. Callie stood over her with dagger in hand.

"It's not supposed to go like this," Audrey spat, blood trickling down her cheek.

"Good will always prevail," Callie replied as she pulled the sword out of Audrey's chest.

Inside the chamber, Audrey loosened her grip as Callie's eyes refocused on her.

"You see, I have been here before and I will be here after—it never ends," Audrey said as she threw Callie across the room, her body crashing into the stone wall. Callie tightened her grip on the dagger as Audrey approached.

"If you plan on using that, I recommend you do it while I am asleep," Audrey said as a grin pursed her lips.

Callie knew she had to kill her—but the dream ended abruptly as she shot straight up in bed. Willow lifted his head, then buried his face back in his paws, purring.

A Bible verse came to her and it was clear. *Behold, a pale horse and the riders name is death. Hell followed close behind.* She shivered and could feel the sweat running down her forehead. She was burning up as a fever took hold. The stairs creaked as she walked down to the kitchen. She rummaged the medicine cupboard for the bottle of aspirin. She wasn't worried about waking the house up; her sister was the only one home. Her parents were still gone, traveling around South America; last she heard they were mining opals in the Peruvian Mountains. She shook the thought out of her head, the throbbing bringing her back to what she needed: a max dose of pain killers. She popped three tablets into her mouth, washing them down with tap water; the cool liquid quenched her thirst momentarily. Retreating to her covers, she tossed and turned again, trying to go back to sleep, her hot flash turning into an arctic blizzard as she shivered uncontrollably. Audrey flashed across her mind when she closed her eyes. She understood the dream but was having trouble accepting it. She re-played the dream over and over, pressing the rewind button mentally, until she passed out from exhaustion an hour later.

The red rotary-dial phone jangled over and over downstairs, nearly rattling off the hook. Carl was in a deep sleep, not noticing it until the fifth ring. He always thought they should have installed a phone upstairs, for cases like this when someone called before the waking hours. He scrambled down the stairs in his boxer shorts. Carl slid into the kitchen and yanked the phone off the hook, his eyes still slits as he tried to mash out the sunlight coming through the window nearby.

"Hello," he said. His voice was scratchy, mouth full of cotton.

"Carl, it's Callie, are you awake?"

Carl rubbed his eyes with one hand, the other holding the large handset up to his ear. "Yeah, I am now, what is it?" he said, head groggy. He spun around in circles, stepping over the phone cord as he untangled it.

"Can you come over? I need to talk to you, it's important," she asked, her voice was demure.

"Are you still mad at me?"

"Not as much Carl, just come over—please." Her voice dissipated.

"Okay, I'll be over in a half hour," he replied as he hung up the phone, smelling one armpit. His nose wrinkled; a shower was needed for sure.

Callie was standing on the front porch as the Nova pulled up to the curb. She didn't run out to the car as she had done before. Carl twirled his keys around his thumb as he moved across the street and up the steps. Callie waited for him to reach the top step before throwing her arms around him.

"I'm scared Carl." She hugged him longer than usual, keeping a tight grip around his neck.

"What is it? What's wrong?" His knowledge of a female had increased the last few months, but their mood swings still caught him off guard. *Is it that time of the month?* he thought. *Or is she worried about something else*? He could never figure them out.

"I had a bad dream last night and woke up with a fever." He placed a hand on her forehead and it was cool.

"No fever now; how are you feeling?" he asked.

"Better. I'm glad you came over," she replied.

She led him into the house, where he could hear her sister humming away in the kitchen, the smell of cookies hitting his nostrils. It was the first time he had come inside the 1940s craftsman-style home. Her parents had decorated the place with trinkets and oddities they had picked up on their travels around the world. They were things Carl had never seen before: a mask from Fiji on one wall, beaded artwork from the Jalisco Indians in Mexico hung from another wall, and many more that he couldn't describe if he tried. Willow brushed up against his legs. Carl reached down, stroking him. Purrs.

"I'm lots better now." She sat on the long leather couch across from the fireplace, the flames low as they licked the glass door. She described the dream in detail, everything down to the weather at the time she was with Audrey. Carl sat in disbelief, although some of what she said resonated with him. There were similarities she described that he had noticed as well. An hour, six cookies, and two glasses of milk later, Carl listened intently as he sat next to Callie, with his arm wrapped around her.

"I don't know what she is or why you had a dream about her, but don't worry, this is the twentieth century; there are no spooks or specters anymore." Carl couldn't tell if this was any comfort to her.

"There is more to it than that Carl. Last night at the dance, when she grabbed me, I had a vision. It was the same vision as my dream, except I was awake. Audrey was there, in my dream and vision. I don't know what she is now, but she must have been royalty. Like I told you, the castle, the grounds—she was a princess or something. I'm not sure, but the way she battled, it was unreal and I—" Callie had left off the part about her killing Audrey.

"Or an evil witch…" he surmised. Witches lived in castles, at least in the Hollywood movies.

Her words flowed around his brain, seeking an open port, her sister interrupting them again.

"More cookies Carl?" She pushed the plate in front of his face, his hands moving on their own as he stacked four cookies on his palm.

Carl shoved one in his mouth, whole. “Thanks Leanne.” His mumble came around the cheek full of cookie mash. “These are really good.” Her sister ignored them. A college girl did not pay attention to the ramblings of a younger sister and her boyfriend, no matter what tactic she thought Callie was employing to snare the young man. She knew her sister had a vivid imagination and chalked it up to idle chit-chat from a dreamy eyed-girl she hardly knew anymore. Cookies were her passion when she returned from college on weekends; she was using Carl as her tester.

Carl lifted a hand up, chewed the last bite, and swallowed hard. “Suppose she is what you say, someone that has come back, then what are you to her? She told me last night after you ran out that you weren't right for me.”

Callie's brow furrowed into a wide arc as she considered what he was saying. This had gone way past two girls fighting over a boy. Willow jumped up next to Callie, circled three times, then sat next to her, purring as Callie stroked his back. Carl wondered how Callie had come into the mix with him and Audrey and what her role was. He knew she was an analytical thinker. He could feel it. He also was waiting, to see if she would bring up what he was thinking.

“She cast no reflection in my dream Carl. What does that mean?” His eyes grew wide. She read his mind. He didn't know what to say to her, nor did he want to spend the rest of the day inside when he had plans. He tried to put it out of his mind. But it lingered.

“You just need to get out in the fresh air,” he said, taking her hand in his. His mind raced back to Audrey's bathroom. No mirror. The school. No reflection.

“…and do what?” she asked.

Carl had already made plans with Frankie earlier that week to help him prep his race car at the Seattle International Raceway; now he had a reason to ask her to come along, other than to spend time with her.

“I'm going to Seattle this afternoon. Frankie is racing. You should come.”

She nodded her head up and down, hugging him tight again. "Thanks for listening Carl, I really appreciate it." He was figuring out what worked with women, one piece at a time. Sometimes, it paid to just sit and listen. If it was that simple, why was he having problems with two girls? Another question Carl couldn't answer, as the mystery of Audrey and now Callie raced through his head.

14

FRANKIE PULLED THE FULL FACE helmet over his head as Carl helped him zip up the fire-retardant race suit that was required of all drivers. Seattle International Raceway had a drag strip and a circle track where the professional and amateur driver could push their car or motorcycle to its limits. Originally opened as Pacific Raceway in 1960, the name had been changed to S.I.R. in the late 70s. Frankie had prepped a green 76' Ford Maverick with a Boss 351 cubic inch race motor he acquired from a friend at the track. Tweaking the carburetor and adding nitrous oxide, he was able to push the stock 383 hp engine up to 435 hp, giving him runs down the track in the high 10s. Ten seconds was respectable—not bad for a budget motor running on race fuel. Carl explained all of this to Callie.

"Oh okay Carl, sounds…interesting," she replied after he finished.

Callie leaned against the beat-up rear quarter panel of the car as Carl helped Frankie strap into the five-point racing harness.

"Wish me luck cousin, I'm pulling out all the stops tonight. She's either gonna break the ten mark or—" Frankie didn't finish, throwing a gloved thumb up as Carl helped him snap the race steering wheel back onto the column.

"Give 'em hell Frankie," Carl replied.

The engine chugged over, and a deep throaty roar came out of the exhaust pipe when it fired up, startling Callie. Frankie lit the tires up, spinning them in place, sending smoke into the air to the cheers of the bulging crowd in the stands. Carl and Callie took to the pit area just next to the starting gate and light bars. Frankie pulled the car up to the Christmas tree as Carl explained to Callie why they called the light bars a Christmas tree and how it worked. Frankie was staged up, rolling the car up to the first set of lights to start the Christmas tree running through the sequence of yellow lights on the countdown to his release and green light. Frankie gripped the floor shifter tight, revving the engine up and dumping the clutch milliseconds after the green light registered. Callie put her hands over her ears to cover the shocking sound coming out of the engine. Seconds later it was all over, as the car launched down the strip, Frankie scoring a 10.4 second run—respectable, but nowhere near the high 9s. The car rumbled down the back course and into the pit area, where Callie and Carl were waiting.

"Nice run cousin, it was sweet," Carl said as he helped Frankie get out of the car. An official from the track came up to them and wrote the run time, 10.4 seconds, in white grease pencil in the upper left hand corner of the Maverick's windshield. Callie had never been around the red-neck southern style sport before and was in awe. It wasn't her thing, but she got a rush from it.

They hadn't realized Pete and the rest of the group had been watching from the stands. Pete made it down to the pit first, coming up behind Frankie, slapping him on the back.

"Nice Greezy, good run. The burnout was kickass!" Pete said, laying an arm across Frankie's shoulder. "Thanks buddy!" Frankie replied.

Chloe and Audrey followed close behind Pete. But then a silent standoff began between Callie and Audrey as they stared at each other intently. They had an unspoken dialogue going on until Chloe startled them when she began talking.

"Hey Callie, how are you?" she asked.

"I'm good; it's Chloe right?" She knew who she was and that she ran with Audrey, but that didn't mean that Callie did not like her. She was willing to keep an open mind at least for now.

“Good run Frankie,” Chloe said to him, as she gave him her signature hug.

“Thanks Chloe Bear!” Frankie replied, wrapping an arm around Chloe’s shoulder.

“I’m going to the concession stand, anyone want anything?” Carl laughed nervously while walking away, escaping the drama and tension between the girls.

“Yeah man, get me a Mt. Dew, huge one, thirty-two ouncer cousin, I’m thirsty,” Frankie said. Carl gave him a thumbs up. His mind went over scenario after scenario, each one coming up with the same answer. Audrey and Callie, Callie and Audrey, the two of them like oil and water; they would never mix. He could feel the tension that had built between them when he noticed their eyes locked in battle.

Carl returned with a box full of hot-dogs, three 32 ounce sodas, and a red vine for Chloe.

"Thanks Carl, you are so sweet," Chloe said as she snatched the long red vine from his hand, pulling hard on it with her teeth. She munched on it like a cow chewing stale hay.

“Frankie, want a bite?” she asked, handing him the rope.

“Hell yeah.” Frankie bit a chunk off and chewed on it as he sucked Mt. Dew through the straw, draining half of the cup in one sitting. “Love this stuff, it is like crack man, never can get enough, not that I have ever tried crack, not my thing, but Mt. Dew is to die for!” he replied.

Pete and Carl devoured four of the hot dogs before the rest of the group could stop them; the remaining two were split with the group, Callie eating her portion slowly as she watched Audrey. Their glares swept back and forth, cutting into each other. Callie's knowledge through the dream made her dislike Audrey even more. But there was more to it than that. She could feel that their tension was visceral. Maybe it was her odor, strange and musty, something that her friends had not keyed in on. Callie’s senses were heightened. She was on full alert since their first contact and especially since her dream. She didn't fully believe she was a soldier against evil. Yet.

"I'll be right back Carl," Callie said as she walked away. "Call of nature."

Carl nodded.

Callie moved around the bathroom corner, pushing her way past the crowd of young women standing in line, waiting their turn. Stepping through the line to exit, she stopped dead in her tracks before coming into direct contact with Audrey, the two of them just a foot away from each other. She bit her lip to keep from lashing out at her and moved to the right a step to pass by. Audrey blocked the exit as she moved in front of her.

"It's not over. Not then and not now. I know what you are," Audrey said, pushing her face up close to Callie. Audrey loomed over her. Callie didn't back down this time, nor run.

"At least one of us knows," Callie replied, her fists in tight balls, wringing her fingers back and forth across her knuckles. "We don't have to be enemies; that is your choice, not mine."

"It's not about choices, you will see, you are destined to be what you are." Audrey pushed her aside, leaving her at the entrance to the bathroom, closing the stall door behind her. Callie shoved it open.

"What am I and how are we connected?" Callie glared at her, then pushed her up against the back wall. The two of them alone in the stall, the door swinging shut automatically.

"You don't want to start this here—not the right place, not the right time. Soon enough my old friend. But if you must know—" Audrey paused, pulling Callie's hand off her chest. "—you are the Kestrel, the destructor, and my sworn enemy."

Callie stepped back, pushing up against the door to get out, the door holding fast, only opening inside. The harder she tried to get out, the tighter the door held on it's latch.

"You need to get out, I'm busy."

Callie slipped out of the stall and rejoined the group, where the guys were helping Frankie load the car on the trailer for the ride back home.

"Carl, can we go now?" Callie asked, her hand gripping his, pulling him toward his car.

"See you guys later, were heading back to Centralia," Carl said as he waved good bye.

Audrey was exiting the bathroom and had just turned around the corner to watch Carl and Callie drive away, when Lauren's face blocked her view.

"Not with Carl anymore Audrey?" It was a rhetorical question from Lauren. Audrey could tell she was nervous talking to her, having avoided her recently. She glanced around Lauren before speaking, the Nova disappearing. Audrey was not prepared to deal with Lauren at this point, torn between her love for Carl and her run in with the Kestrel. Audrey was sure that Callie was still unaware who she was, even now with more information. It would be a while before she believed it and a lot longer before she would accept who she was and what she was destined to do. Lauren glared at her, and Audrey knew she should say something, but did not have it in her. She just wanted Lauren to accept her.

"Lauren, it's not what you think," Audrey said slowly, choosing her words careful. "There are a lot of things going on right now and you won't understand."

Lauren pushed past her. She could tell that Lauren was irritated but afraid. She knew that she had to connect with Lauren—calm her down. Open up to her.

"Lauren, wait…" Audrey called out to her as she walked away, and Lauren stopped a dozen feet away, turning around.

"Our time is coming. Stay away from me," Lauren growled as she slipped around the corner into the bathroom.

Audrey let her go. Her heart was conflicted with the loss of Carl's love and companionship, the run in with the Kestrel, and now, Lauren was in direct defiance to Audrey's attempt at saving their friendship.

15

THE NEXT MORNING, CALLIE SEARCHED through the encyclopedias on her parents bookshelf, grabbing the volume labeled J-L. She thumbed through the pages as she sat on the couch in front of the fire. Page after page flipped by. She was looking for the word *Kestrel*. She had no idea what it meant. The term and definition was half-way down the page. Callie read it aloud, but could not make sense of it. She wondered what a hawk would have to do with being an enemy of someone like Audrey. She read further through the definition, finally noticing it had a footnote, the 1 coming at the end of the last sentence. Callie had remembered going over footnotes, endnotes, and definitions with the librarian a few years ago while she was working on a research paper for her advanced-placement English class. Looking down at the bottom of the page, she read the reference for footnote number one:

1:Kalaviṅka, a mythical birdlike creature, half human half bird, the long feathery plumage extending beyond the torso. Believed to be the defender of man during the thirteenth century. Callie slammed the book shut. She opened it back up and read the last sentence again.

Also known as: The Kestrel.

Her mind could not accept what she was reading even though it was racing with possibilities.

The front door rattled, the noise startling her, as Carl's face peered through the window. Callie opened the door slowly.

"Can I come in?" Carl asked, the cold air flowing in around him.

"I guess, might as well," she replied. Carl stepped closer to kiss her, Callie's hand meeting his face inches before they touched.

"That's probably not a good idea Carl, not right now." She wanted to kiss him, but something told her they were finished and she was sure they would never be intimate again. The two of them would not work out no matter what he said or did. It was becoming clear to her that she was different. Maybe there was something to what Audrey said. She had always had vivid dreams, memories of past experiences. Now she was believing them. Now things were starting to clear up. Dreams that were once confusing, cycled through her mind in lightening speed and clarity. Callie was reliving centuries of past lives, battles won and lost. The flood gate in her mind had opened.

"Carl, do you know what Audrey is?" she asked point blank.

"Just a girl I guess," he replied, his body shivering from the cold as he stood next to the fire.

"She's not from this world Carl, I know that now..." she paused, catching her words before they escaped her. "...She's from over there, and I am her enemy. I don't understand it all, but I'm beginning to believe it."

Willow the cat sprinted out of the kitchen and around the couch, flopping down in front of Carl's feet. Carl reached down to stroke his long grey fur and was slapped hard, playfully.

"That's ludicrous Callie, you guys just don't get along; I get it, not everyone likes everyone else," he said. "Would you like to go out tonight?"

"We can't be together Carl. It's over. We can't happen, that much I know...." She knew it was harsh talking to him like that and could tell she was breaking his heart. "...We're done Carl, I'm sorry. Please believe me, I really care for you, so much so that I have to let you go, even if it means that you will return to her."

She watched the tears stream down his face as a lump in his throat moved up and down. Callie showed him to the door, giving him a light peck on the cheek as he slipped outside.

"I'm sorry Carl, this is the way it is. Please don't be angry with me."

Carl trudged down the front steps. He turned as he reached the bottom step and tried to speak, but the words would not come out. He left her standing there in the doorway. She could see it was too difficult for him to accept what she was saying. Callie stood there for another few minutes, watching the Nova slip around the corner, the cool air chilling her as goosebumps raised on her bare arms.

16

THE MONSOON RAINS HAD STARTED and would not let up for another two months. Carl moped around, skipping classes, dodging Audrey as much as possible, and keeping to himself. Callie wouldn't return his calls after she had broken up with him, and he gave up trying after a half dozen missed calls, although he held out hope she would come back to him.

Days turned into weeks as Carl kept up with his side business, supplying the much needed ingredient for a high schooler's party and making a hefty profit that he quickly pumped into his car, the new tires and wheels making the Nova shine brighter. Cruising continued downtown on Friday nights, with Carl and Clint tagging along together, draining their gas tanks nightly. Carl pressed Clint for information about Callie but would get nothing for his troubles, as Clint had told him the night they broke up. "She's just not into you man."

Carl resigned himself to solitude and was nearly over both girls when he ran into Audrey between classes, the two of them startled, neither one speaking, the silence was deafening. Carl stepped to his right just as Audrey stepped to her left. Stepping left, he met her at the same point as she stepped with him on accident. The tension between them was still there—a spark that had never burned out. She opened her mouth, pausing before she spoke.

"Carl," she squeaked. "I wanted to say..." She didn't get through her sentence, cut off by Carl's head shaking back and forth.

"Don't bother, I'm not in the mood to be abused," he replied, walking away from her.

"Wait…it's not like that. Talk to me." She ran after him, grabbing him by the shoulder, stopping him in his tracks.

"What do you want from me?" he asked.

Audrey couldn't get the words out. For once in her life, she was speechless, even though she knew what she wanted to say. She could see the hurt in his eyes and it was too late, the damage had been done, she had waited too long.

"I've got to go to class," Carl said, and then he walked away.

A tear streamed down Audrey's cheek and her heart felt heavy. Audrey knew Carl needed time to come around; time was not on her side now that Callie was becoming aware of what she was. She sat in class after class, numb.

Audrey stood outside the school, leaning up against the brick pillars, just underneath the overhang of the roof. Rain rocketed out of the sky, pelting students as they ran for their cars. A stream of water trickled out of the drainpipe next to her feet. Most students had left the building, and class had been over twenty minutes. She looked for Carl, keeping an eye on his car, where it was sitting alone at the end of the parking lot. Audrey saw him before he noticed her, exiting out of the side door by the gym to avoid her. Carl trudged across the parking lot.

Audrey ran across the parking lot, her feet splashing through the puddles.

"Carl," she yelled. "Can I talk to you?"

He turned to face her. Audrey stood there, hair soaked, waiting for him to say something, anything. Her heart ached. She wanted to tell him she was sorry. She wanted to tell him she loved him, but now she was speechless. His face was broken. She could see the damage she had done by not coming to him sooner.

"I'm sorry Audrey, I don't want to see—" She barely let the words come out of his mouth as she pushed him up against the car, kissing him passionately on the lips. She could see he was confused but pulled out all the stops, kissing him madly.

He pulled his face away from hers. “Wait—I—”

She pulled his face back to hers and kissed him again.

He pushed her back. “But I thought you—”

“I don’t care—let’s not talk about it anymore,” she said, interrupting him again as she locked lips with him. She gripped the sides of his face with her hands, kissing him over and over.

The two stood in the rain for another minute, staring into each other's eyes before slipping inside the car, where they kissed for another forty-five minutes, fogging the windows.

17

MONTHS PASSED; CARL AND AUDREY spending as much time as they could together. Tuesdays nights in Centralia had a unique twist: the town, small for its stature, was able to keep a three-screen theatre in commission, even with the advent of the video rental stores. The theatre was a patriarch of the early twentieth century. The huge four-story building stood above all the others downtown for nearly sixty years. Originally a one-screen venue, it had been converted into three screens: one on the main floor and the balcony split into two smaller theaters. It was an odd arrangement for a movie house, but what it lacked in stylistic remodel, it gained in elegance from yesteryear, with the old building having secret passageways, catwalks above the main auditorium and dressing rooms below the stage. Some say it was haunted.

Carl had slipped in the back door multiple times; tonight was no different, except for the fact that Audrey was with him holding his hand. The look of surprise on his cousin's face as she opened the door to the alley spoke volumes. She knew who Audrey was in school and had spent an entire dance watching her, wishing to be involved with the in crowd. Now her chance had presented itself.

"Hey Audrey, Carl."

"Audrey, this is my cousin, Mona."

"I know who she is," Audrey replied. The two girls studied each other.

"What movie are you going to watch?" Mona asked.

Carl had not thought about it yet, his mind was back on Audrey full time. His thoughts scrambled.

"I would like to stay down here in the main auditorium Carl, the movie doesn't matter." Carl knew what she had in mind and he did not protest.

Mona left them in the main theatre. Carl and Audrey sat in the back row just below the projection booth. The movie was a precursor to the events that would follow later that night. The whole reason for coming to the theater on a Tuesday, and multiple Tuesday nights after that, would play out like a nineteen fifties TV drama.

They never saw the credits roll across the screen in front of them, nor could Carl recall a single scene. It was a passion filled two hours of kissing each other in the dark, the five other patrons hardly noticing the young couple in back. Carl's hands moved from her thigh to her side, her body lean, the ribs running across his fingers as he kissed her. He nibbled on her neck.

"That tickles; you didn't shave today," she giggled.

She brushed her hand against his cheek in the dark, their faces in shadow. Carl wasn't the full beard in two day type of guy, nor was he a full beard in two months, his face barely a stubble of hairs here and there, periodically placed. He could feel her hand on his thigh, rubbing him, and his breathing quickened. Audrey ran her hands through his hair, messing it up as the movie clicked off. The house lights came up and they were alone in the theatre.

"Audrey, you are the best thing that has ever happened to me."

She smiled as her face lit up, showing her porcelain complexion and rosy cheeks.

"I know."

Carl did not care that she was sassy; he enjoyed her comments and companionship even when she was taunting him. In his mind she was really good for him and he was happy that they were back together. Grabbing her waist, they strolled out of the theater into the lobby, where they waited for Mona. Mona said goodbye to the last patrons leaving the building, who were carrying a leftover half-filled bucket of popcorn.

Mona locked the front doors and shut off the marquee, dimming the lights to the concessions, while waiting for half of the high school to show up. The after party, which started a few minutes later, was an epic event. Dozens of teens arrived at the back door, waiting for her to let them in, alcohol in hand.

Carl and Audrey waited on the second-floor mezzanine as they cuddled on the vintage couch, the noise of the crowd growing louder as they climbed the stairs towards them. The mezzanine was an anterior room, just between the balcony where they had divided it into two screens, blocking off the view to the main screen below. It was near the bathrooms, the ladies' slightly larger than the men's, complete with a sitting couch and huge mirror on the wall. Decades earlier, the mezzanine was also the smoking lounge, when that was permitted in a theatre. After a few movie houses burned down, due to the film stock being highly flammable, smoking in the theater was banned. Wall sconces hung down halfway to the floor, their art deco style a throwback to 1931. The carpet was ornamental, with flower designs in deep burgundies, greens, yellows, and blues, from the same era. The flooring had seen its best years a decade earlier, its seams jutting up, a precarious spot to catch an unwary high heel.

Chloe flung herself on top of her friend, smothering her, the effect of one beer she had just guzzled making her lush and flirty. Chloe was still the no-holds-barred teen when it came to the Tuesday night get-together, her tight jeans and skimpy shirt showing off her perky b-cup breasts.

"Dial it down a bit Chloe Bear. I think Carl is getting jealous," Pete said. Audrey laughed at his comment.

"Yeah Chloe, take it down a notch," Audrey chimed in.

"Come on you guys, party time. We're gonna raise the roof!" Chloe hollered.

Her brother was always the voice of reason: overprotective, but fun as well. Pete was the instigator in getting a party going at the theater, pushing Mona to let them stay after hours. Sure, she was the assistant manager, but letting twenty to thirty teenagers inside a place of business for the sole purpose of drinking could have sent her to jail or at least got her fired. They were brash and young, throwing caution to the wind. But if things did get out of hand, Mona would just call on Pete, and his six foot plus size to take care of business. It rarely happened; usually everyone would heed a warning from Pete, but on occasion, he had thrown out an unruly teen braggart that let his mouth run off before his brain had engaged. Tonight, the group was all friends; with a few outsiders joining, as a friend of a friend.

"Let's play hide and go seek," a girl in the back yelled, her intentions to get a certain guy into a dark place obvious to those that knew her. It was a game only kids played, but the alcohol gave it a new twist for these high schoolers. They were caught between trying to act like young adults and wanting to hang onto their youth at least one day a week. Winters in western Washington were harsh: an indoor place to party and play, now that was a rare treat, something they capitalized on.

"Who's going to be It?" the girl said.

"Not me, I'm not walking around in here alone," one of the boys replied.

"I nominate Chloe." Pete's words were prophetic, the group cheering her name over and over. Chloe was actually excited to be It. She had no problem waiting while everyone hid, but wanted at least a co-person to be It with her.

"I choose Audrey as my second It."

The whole game was childish; really, who would even think of playing hide and go seek after hours in a huge theatre.

"Better watch out for Sofia," Pete said.

"Who's Sofia?" Audrey asked.

"She's a ghost—well, a little girl ghost that some have seen here," Chloe added. "But I'm not scared, as long as you are with me Aud."

"I'll be *IT* with you; this will be fun. It has been centuries since I've played this." Nobody caught the meaning in her words, not even Carl. She, on the other hand, truly wanted to play. Centuries ago, playing hide and go seek after dark would have been viewed as suspicious activity. People were afraid of the dark and still are, a fact that these teens played off, as long as they had a friend that was close by.

The teens fanned out, scrambling down the stairs, into the balcony and out into the theatres, choosing hiding places they thought would keep them safe. Their version of hide and go seek had a twist. The It would seek out their friends; anyone could reposition themselves around the theater and back to home base near the bathrooms on floor two. The catch: if half the group made it to home base, the game was over and the It person would have to be It again. Audrey waited in the girl's bathroom, steering clear of the huge mirror, while Chloe sat on the long couch. Audrey could see the hazy look of intoxication coming over her friend.

Chloe was in love with Audrey—not a physical love, but she loved her looks, the way she walked, and how she held herself. She was infatuated. She could tell Audrey was unique; although most people thought Chloe was an airhead, she just played dumb so they would like her and it worked, her antics and spastic attitude making all but the most stoic teen laugh.

"No more beer Chloe," Audrey said as she pried the half empty can out of Chloe's hand.

"Yes Mom," she slurred.

"Seriously Chloe, you're drunk—and we have to go find everyone."

"Okay mother!" Chloe chirped, her lips tightening up into a devious grin. Audrey squinted her eyes at her then smiled.

"One two three, ready or not here we come," Audrey and Chloe yelled out in unison as they left the bathroom. They moved across the mezzanine as they searched.

It was the announcement that would send the last few teens into hiding. The pair crept down the stairs hand in hand to look around the long bannister at the opposite stairs that led back up the other side of the mezzanine. On the bottom step, Chloe spotted her brother running in front of her, towards the other staircase. She chased after him. Audrey's movement seemed effortless; in less than a fraction of a second, she was standing at the top of the other staircase in front Pete.

"Gotcha Pete, you are out." She tagged him, sending him to the sidelines.

"Damn Audrey you move fast."

"Faster than you know Pete," she replied. "I move like a phantom!"

Hour after hour, the group played on through the night, the alcohol disappearing before one a.m. Most of the teens slowly sobered up. They were sweaty and getting tired from the multiple trips up and down the long staircases.

"All right people, I have to go home and sleep, got a test tomorrow."

Mona's words echoed through the group—the spoiler.

"Come on Mona, one more game."

"Yeah, one more game."

She relented but was thrown in as the It girl; her chance to get close to Audrey was at hand.

"I choose Audrey."

Audrey was not surprised, nor did she mind, it was the most fun she had had in a long time. Mona never drank a drop of any alcoholic beverage that evening, and Audrey could see that Mona was thinking more about her than the game.

"Bye Audrey, missing you already," Carl crooned, kissing Audrey goodbye.

"Goodbye my love," she answered.

"Go Carl, jeesh already, making me sick with all this mushy stuff," Mona grumbled.

Chloe stepped in front of Mona, stretched up on her tippy toes, and kissed her friend on the lips.

"Chloe, you are drunk!" Mona laughed. "Get outa here."

"I may be think you drunk I am, but I still love you," Chloe chirped, throwing her arms around Mona's neck.

"Go, you have to hide."

"Yes Chloe, time to go," Audrey buzzed as she pulled Chloe's arms off of Mona.

"Okaaay, If fuh.....must," Chloe slurred as she stumbled away.

Audrey and Mona stepped into the bathroom, giggling at their friend's drunkenness.

"Audrey."

"Yes Mona."

"Do you think we could be friends? I mean, not just friends—good friends like you and Chloe."

Audrey could hear the nervous twitch in Mona's voice. She knew if she said no it would crush her, and besides, it was Carl's cousin. She also liked her, even though they had not spent much time together. She could tell Mona was an outsider, and a loner, but very smart and mature for her age.

"I know it is weird that I am Carl's cousin, but I won't get in your way," Mona said, her face quizzical.

"No, it would not be weird, I would love to be your friend Mona," Audrey replied.

"Cool, thank you." A smile parted Mona's lips.

18

THE GIRLS WAITED IN THE bathroom for five more minutes before stepping out into the mezzanine.

"One two three, ready or not here we come," the girls yelled.

Audrey and Mona walked hand in hand past the concession stand, the large mirror behind the counter reflecting a contorted image back at Mona. Audrey squeezed her new friend's hand. Mona looked into her eyes, then back at the mirror. Audrey knew she had seen the lack of reflection.

"What is it Mona?"

"Nothing," Mona replied. Audrey pulled her past the mirror as they skipped through the lobby, both of them watching Officer Spence drive past the front of the theater.

"Crap," Mona gasped.

"Think he saw us?"

"I'm sure he at least saw me, not sure about you?" Mona's voice trailed off as they scrambled up the stairs and out of view of the officer's spotlight as it swept through the downstairs lobby. They waited, holding their breath just around the corner of the bannister. The light disappeared as Officer Spence drove off, the red glow of the tail lights fading in the distance.

"That was close. I don't think he saw anything," Mona said, breaking the silence. Audrey gripped Mona's hand tight as she looked directly into Mona's eyes.

"I don't think he saw me, but maybe you," Audrey replied.

"True, you were a few feet in front of me. We have to get everyone out of the theater in case he comes back."

"Yeah, party is over," Audrey finished.

The mass exodus out the back of the theater into the alley happened minutes after the officer drove by. The party had ended abruptly after Mona yelled that the cops had looked inside.

Carl drove Audrey home, neither one talking. The house was completely dark as they approached, the car headlights illuminating the front porch.

"Pick you up in a few hours?"

"I'll be waiting for you," she said, the tension in Audrey's voice palpable.

Audrey's reply was uncaring, making Carl question what was going on between them. Carl could sense her demeanor was off kilter, something he had keyed in on was amiss with her. He didn't want to think too hard about it. He wanted to maintain his ignorance despite what Callie had said to him. It would be a discussion he would put off for another day; sleep needed to come as soon as he could get home.

Carl glanced at the home in the rearview mirror, waiting for the inside lights to come on as he drove down the long dirt driveway. He squinted as he looked behind him. A lump twisted knots in his stomach. He couldn't understand why she hadn't turned on the lights. His imagination was rampant, wondering where her mother was. How did she live out here without anyone knowing her all those years before? They were questions that he had no immediate answer. The long driveway out of the ranch curved to the right, next to the large hill above, the trees hanging out over his car as he drove onto the country road. The Nova pulled into his parent's driveway fifteen minutes later. A chill crept up Carl's spine, sending goosebumps over his skin as he stepped out of the car. The vision of the ranch house in the dark sparked his imagination with images of vampires, beasts, or any other number of creatures he had seen on the big screen at the theater. It haunted his dreams all night.

19

LAUREN THUMBED THROUGH THE CARD CATALOG system in the city library. The Timberland Regional Library was located in the center of Centralia, in George Washington Park. The grounds around the building were full of tall fir trees, flowering cherry trees, and an arboretum of roses. On the south end stood a large octagon gazebo made of concrete and stone, where many politicians, local and national, had stumped, plying their campaign promises or lies to the local citizens.

The two-story brick-and-mortar library was filled with nearly every volume a high schooler would need to research anything from a to z, except what Lauren was looking for. Lauren searched for hours through the card catalog. It held all the books on 3"x5" cards in a cabinet full of long drawers. She had learned the Dewey Decimal System in first grade at Fords Prairie Elementary School, just across town. Hours later, she stumbled on a title that captured her attention. Lauren read the description and her eyes widened as she realized what she was holding in her hand. It was the key to all knowledge about early religion, the Bible, and scriptures. A complete volume was at her grasp. Taking the 3"x5" card out of the catalog drawer, Lauren handed it across the counter to the librarian. She was an elderly woman who wore trifocals. Her grey hair was twisted into a bun on top of her head. The librarian peered through her thickest layer of glass as she strained to read the title: *The Codex Sinaiticus*. "Young lady, I'm not sure we have this book, look here," her raspy voice rattled, as she pointed at the bottom of the card.

"It is dated around the fourth century; that is a long time ago. They put this card in just for reference." She paused as she wheezed. "We wouldn't have a copy."

Lauren wasn't going to be put off, pressing her.

"Can you please look it up? Maybe there is a copy somewhere?"

The librarian sighed as she scrolled through the microfiche machine, scanning title after title. "Well, I'll be darned. A few copies do exist."

"Can you get it for me?" Lauren figured it was in Seattle or another major city close by.

"The closest library that has it, is in Chicago," she replied.

Lauren's face lengthened, dejection showing in her eyes.

"Oh. Don't be sad young lady, we might be able to get it on loan for you to read here."

Her face lit up. "Really? You can do that?" Lauren asked.

"Let me give them a call and see what we can do." The librarian scrolled through a rolodex, as she looked for phone number to the Chicago Public Library. "Here it is, let's see if they will help us."

She dialed the rotary phone like a pro, not missing a beat as her fingers scrolled through the numbers, the dial slowly returning to the home position between each number. Twenty minutes later and a promise to only let the book be viewed inside the confines of the library research office, Lauren had her book on the way, via US Postal Media Mail. Guaranteed delivery in four to six weeks.

"Six weeks!" Lauren yelled. "Can you get it here faster? They put a man on the moon quicker than that!" she spat.

"Quiet down Miss. There is no need to disturb the other patrons."

"I'm sorry," she whispered. "Is there any way to speed up the delivery?"

"I'm sorry dear, that is how long it takes; there is nothing we can do except wait for its arrival. I'll call you as soon as it gets in. Jot your name and number down for me." The librarian shoved a piece of paper across the counter at Lauren. Lauren wrote her name and number on it, shoving it back to the librarian as her head slumped against her chest.

20

ACROSS THE COUNTRY, ANOTHER LIBRARIAN prepped a book that had previously been incognito for decades. The event kindled his curiousity as he packed the book for shipping. He wrapped the book inside a cardboard box lined with felt, then placed the box inside a steel case, closing the top and locking it on one side. He had remembered a priest years before coming in and asking questions about the book. The man examined it then left his number and name with the instructions to call him if anyone checked out the book. Nosy intuition was jabbing the librarian as he scrolled through the file cabinet in the small office just off to the side of the desk. He had to locate the priest's number to find out why this book was so special. The cabinet was a jumbled mess as he thumbed through decades of correspondence, finding the handwritten note in the back. He dialed slowly, waiting as the phone clicked. It was ringing on the other end. Two minutes went by and he was about to hang up when a voice came on the line.

"Father Callahan here, who's calling?"

"Father, this is Samuel Sorenson. I am the head librarian at the Chicago Public Library."

"Yes Mr. Sorenson, how may I help you?" the priest asked.

"Your book, I mean, the book you came to look at years ago, has just been ordered for review by a patron in Washington."

The phone was silent for a few seconds. "Father, are you still there?" the librarian asked.

Static crackled through the phone as the priest cleared his throat. "Y—yes, I'm here, go on."

"The party in Centralia, Washington, will be receiving the book in a few weeks. I shipped it out this afternoon."

He waited to see what the priest was going to say, but the phone went dead.

"Father, are you still there?" The buzz of a dropped call filled his head. The priest had either hung up or the call was lost. The librarian hung up the phone and redialed the number, the phone buzzing a busy signal. His curiosity went unfulfilled.

Lauren finally had the book in her hands and was examining the pages one by one. Six weeks had gone by in a flash for everyone except her. She sat for hours in the confines of the private room just behind the librarian's station. The book was not allowed to leave the building. It was only viewable by one person at a time and for one week before it would be returned to Chicago. She digested the text page after page, writing notes as she went along. Within a week, Lauren had a view of religion she barely comprehended, but it did clear things up about her suspicions of Audrey. Chapter upon chapter had been reserved on the angels, and one in particular. She was beginning to believe it more and more, and now she had conclusive proof, although it was the author's rendition of the truth, even though it was written centuries before.

Saturday morning and just a few days before the book was scheduled to be sent to Chicago, Lauren arrived at the library to study the text one last time.

"Hello dear, are you here to view the book again?" the librarian asked.

"Yes, one more time, then I will be finished," Lauren answered.

"You weren't the only one interested in it..." the librarian whispered. "A young lady such as yourself viewed it yesterday while you were gone."

Lauren's face lit up. "Who?" Do you know her name?" she asked.

The librarian lifted her head, glanced left and right, then whispered, "She wrote her name on the register here," she said, pointing a bony finger down to the bottom of the journal entry. Lauren read it to herself.

Callie Elliot

"How long did she stay?"

"A couple hours."

21

"CARL NEWKIRK, AUDREY ANDERSON, COME HERE." They thought they were safe, sneaking through the back door of the lunch room, Carl's deal with the lunch lady to look the other way in trade for a fifth of whiskey only went so far; as long as the principal wasn't around. It was just bad luck; the principal had stopped by the kitchen to see what was on the menu.

"So you think you can ditch school and get away with it? That will earn you three days after school detention for both of you," the principal barked.

Audrey found it quite amusing: detention for showing up late. If she had done that at some of the other schools she had attended years past, she would have gotten a whack on the butt with a paddle, or at the least made to recite a lengthy poem in front of the class.

"Well, at least we will be together." Carl's sassy words angered the principal.

"Make it one week for both of you. Now get to class," he barked, pointing his finger toward the door, shooing them back to class.

Audrey could not have made a better decision coming in late with Carl that morning; it was the first time she would meet Mr. Gillingsworth. Most days the detention hall was an hour of sitting in a room, not allowed to do anything. Today was different. Audrey had noticed the history teacher in passing earlier, neither of them peaking each others interest. Detention was different now. She talked, he replied. She had his full attention.

Most of her answers were vague, but her questions were direct. She was delving into his knowledge of world history, specifically European history for the past six hundred years, Mr. Gillingsworth regaling her on the dark ages, the Mongols, Turks, and many more figures in history. A few gaps Audrey filled in, surprising him with her seemingly never-ending stories.

"Can we go now Audrey? Detention has been over for a half hour," Carl sighed, tapping his left foot.

“See you tomorrow Mr. Gillingsworth,” Audrey said as she waved, five fingers curling.

"Yes, good night Ms. Anderson—Carl." Mr. Gillingsworth smiled back at her.

Audrey and Carl walked down the hallway fifty feet, the other students running past them leaving them alone.

"I don't like the way he was looking at you."

"What way was he looking at me?"

"You know what I am talking about Audrey Anderson," Carl said as he grabbed her arm, stopping her. “He was flirty with you."

"Come on Carl, that is childish; he's the teacher."

"No, he was flirting with you, and I think you liked it."

Audrey didn't answer him as they walked down the hallway, and she could see now how deep Carl's jealousy had grown. She loved his childlike behavior at times but didn't appreciate that he was trying to control who she talked to.

“He’s smitten with you.”

“No he’s not; he’s too old,” she replied.

Audrey could tell that Mr. Gillingsworth, at twenty eight, was young enough to catch the attentions of many girls at the school, with his neatly trimmed brown hair and his disregard for the teachers dress code. She had watched him walk by in his blue jeans and a polo, which was his calling card, as a crowd of girls followed him to his class as he exited the teachers lounge.

“Audrey, I just don’t like how he talks to you.” Carl's voice was lower.

"How he talks to me? What are you getting at Carl? So, he is a bit flirty, big deal."

"Yes, how Mr. Gillingsworth talks to you, that's what I am saying." Carl shuffled his feet on the ground nervously as they walked out to his car, through the empty parking lot.

"Carl, I am not following what you are saying exactly, but if you are jealous of me talking to an older man, you will have to get over it." She picked it up in his eyes, his nervous twitches, and the shuffling of his feet.

"Well, I just don't like it. He never let anyone talk in detention before you came, and now he crossed the line and I don't like how he looks at you when he talks to you." He slammed the door of the car.

"I'm not talking about it anymore Carl. Don't bring it up again."

"Okay," he replied meekly.

"Start the car. I'm hungry."

He didn't revisit the topic that afternoon. They spent the rest of the evening at their favorite burger bar, a normal ritual for Audrey, one she enjoyed more each day. They were normally chatty. Today, the tension was as thick molasses and they sat in silence.

Carl dropped Audrey off at her house and watched her go inside before driving out of the valley to the strip where Frankie would race his car. Just west of Audrey's home, state highway 507 curved out of the north side of town. There was a long straight stretch where Frankie had marked a start and finish line in white spray paint. He had laid it out in the worst possible place to race: at the end of the strip, which was part of the two-lane state highway, a sharp ninety-degree left-hand corner jutted off to the north. It was a make or break decision for a racer caught in the left hand lane if oncoming traffic rounded the corner before you finished racing. Carl's testosterone and anger boiled over as he sat at the start line, revving his car up. He pushed the gas pedal to the floor; the car flew down the strip toward the corner, and the speedometer passed one hundred before he reached the halfway point. At one hundred five miles per hour, he had still not backed out of it when two cars rounded the corner. He's eyes grew large as he watched a large pickup truck passing a slower sedan, coming straight at him in his lane. Carl was sure they nearly hit each other as he slammed on the brakes, sliding back and forth, narrowly missing the pickup, the driver flipping Carl off as he swerved away from him. Mud splattered up on the windshield as his car slid off the road onto the flat ditch before it slammed into the middle of a large mud puddle. The engine sputtered then died. Carl placed his head on the steering wheel and breathed in and out. His head throbbed with adrenaline. Carl closed his eyes and counted backward from ten to one slowly. His emotions had gotten the best of him, nearly causing an accident. Carl turned the key and the engine sputtered a few times then died; the ignition points were wet. It was a spot outside town that you just did not want to spend time at alone and broke down. Carl cranked the engine again and it sputtered some more, then rumbled to life. His drive home was much slower, the entire front end of the car caked with mud. He drove ten miles per hour under the posted speed limit.

Audrey stood at the end of the concrete walkway in front of her house.

"Morning Audrey, I'm sorry about yesterday." He knew apologizing was the right thing to do, even before he had nearly killed himself, not having slept through the night with the thought of not seeing her again. It sobered him.

"Thank you." She slid across the seat, snuggling up to him. She gave him a light peck on his cheek, then they drove to school.

Carl only saw her during lunch, afterwards joining her in detention. Mr. Gillingsworth was seated behind his desk, not noticing the students file into the classroom.

"Hello Mr. Gillingsworth," Audrey said, peaking his interest as he raised his head. She was more intrigued now that they had engaged each other in stimulating conversation over history.

"Hello Audrey, how are you today?" He smiled at her, a smile that did not go unnoticed by the six other girls in detention that afternoon.

"Oh, I'm fine, just wondering if you would like to discuss the fourteenth century?" It was one of her favorite periods of time, the black death ravaging the people, the one hundred years' war and a time of extreme elegance where lords, ladies, and peasantry lived amongst each other in their bid to survive.

Audrey could tell he was interested as well as she watched Mr. Gillingsworth's face light up as a smile overtook him.

"I would, but let's see whether the rest of the class will mind us discussing it." He paused before addressing the other students.

"Normally, I do not allow you to talk during the detention period, but Ms. Anderson has piqued my interest with her vast knowledge of European history, so today, I propose a free day. Any student wishing to join in can talk freely with us or move to the back of the class and have an open discussion within your own group to your own liking." He was an intelligent man, with most of his conversation going straight over their heads and off into space.

"Does that mean we can talk with each other today?" The freckled faced girl behind Audrey had raised her hand as she asked.

"Yes it does Ms. Schmidt, just keep the conversation down to a low growl and enjoy the next fifty minutes courtesy of Ms. Anderson."

The students scrambled to the back of the room, leaving Audrey, Carl, and Mr. Gillingsworth up front. The teacher had taken a seat on top of his desk, his left leg hanging off one side, the other over the front. It gave him a position directly above Audrey. Carl knew exactly what he was doing, sending his teacher a direct signal of defiance by crossing his arms and frowning. Mr. Gillingsworth never noticed Carl's defiance during the fifty minutes of discussion with Audrey, his eyes glued on her. Audrey dominated the lecture, keeping the teacher's gaze on her as she laid out the events of the old world in detail, schooling her teacher on the events and specifics of life during the dark days.

"Ms. Anderson that was a fine discussion on life and times during the early centuries in Europe. I am very impressed with your knowledge." He paused. "I really am; in fact I am blown away by it."

She not only had his attention; she had turned on the flame. She watched his face glow after their discussion and could tell he was infatuated with her.

“Thank you Mr. Gillingsworth, it was quite pleasurable indeed,” she said.

“Nobody talks quite like you do Ms. Anderson, you are—unique,” he added. “Perhaps an old soul?”

“Thank you again Mr. Gillingsworth. I’ve been around the world a few times. History is my thing. You could say I invented it.”

“You are welcome, and please, call me Paul.” It burned Carl immediately; he could feel the acid rising out of the pit of his stomach and into his throat. *Call me Paul.* He milled it over in his head thirty times before he reached the door. *Call me Paul.*

“If you insist Mr. Gillingsworth—I mean—Paul," Audrey replied as the teacher's lips curled into a smile. Carl glared at him.

They walked down the hall and Audrey waited for Carl to explode.

“Audrey, it is not right.” She knew exactly what Carl was talking about and did not respond immediately.

“Did you hear me?”

Oh she had heard him and was ready to unload.

“Carl Newkirk, if you are saying I shouldn’t have a friendly discussion with one of my teachers without your permission then you are missing who I am to you.” He stood there stunned next to a row of lockers.

“And furthermore, if I have to ask your permission to do something or talk to someone, then we are through.”

He couldn’t believe she said it; Carl loved her, but he did not understand why she was so chummy with the teacher.

“I’m just confused Audrey, I thought you and I were together?” Carl said, stammering as they walked outside to his car.

“We are Carl, but that does not mean you control me or who I can talk to; that is the point of having a good relationship: equal trust.”

She knew he was milling it over in his mind and didn't know how to respond to her as they drove across town in silence.

“So you still love me?” he asked.

She slapped him on the cheek.

“Yes you big dummy. I do.” Carl grinned when she said it.

"So why do you like to talk to Mr. Gillingsworth so much?" Carl would not let it go until he was satisfied with her answer.

"It is hard for me here Carl; there aren't many people who know that much history, and it interests me, enough so that I am willing to have a teacher crush on me for my own pleasure."

It wasn't the answer he was looking for, but he understood it. Carl knew he was just an ordinary guy, and he was not college educated yet. He understood Audrey was exceptionally smart and smart people needed more input than a guy like him could give her. He had watched the gifted student program over the years as the genius students kept to themselves, spending all their time together studying at lunch breaks, before school and after school in study hall, when other kids had gone home. Carl never brought it back up; the last three days in detention were the same setup, with Audrey and Paul chatting away, the stir in the school growing like wildfire as the gossip got around about their discussions. The final day in detention, the class had filled to capacity with students standing along the walls; Mr. Gillingsworth was shocked to read the official roster from the principal. Every girl there had come to school late the previous day just to get sent to detention, to watch him sit on top of his desk, his manly physique on display, wooing their teenage hearts.

"Detention is canceled today."

He spoke lower than normal, his voice raspy. Nobody moved. It was as though a lamb had entered the slaughter house and thirty lions were standing ready to pounce on their victim. He rubbed his chin, scanning the young female faces, their dreamy expressions immediately apparent to him. He had never noticed many of them before, and it had all changed within the course of one week; Paul Gillingsworth was aware that he had commanded the attention of a large faction of the female student body.

The next semester, his dismally boring class that was usually only half filled because they had to take the class, was filled beyond capacity times three. Third period European history had to be rescheduled and the class moved into the larger auditorium to accommodate the seventy-five freshmen girls, fifteen senior girls that were retaking the class, and ten guys that had to take it for their graduation requirement. It was power he never had before. Thanks to Audrey.

22

ASSEMBLIES WERE SCHEDULED AT THE high school every Friday before the home football games. It was twenty minutes of screaming kids. The cheerleaders, and their boyfriends who were on the varsity football team, rallied together to fire up the team. Chloe was a natural-born cheerleader and captain; she was appointed to the squad as the top position because she had the most experience, having taken dance and gymnastic classes since she was three. She wowed the judges during her audition with a few backflips. Nobody could fly through the air as she could. Her roundhouse entry into a complete reversal and back flip left the high school gymnasium in awe during the pep-rallies, landing it perfectly right into the splits on the wooden floor. Chloe eyed Mona as she danced at the sidelines. She liked the way Mona's hair was shaved on one side, but shoulder length on the other. Chloe knew Mona was a loner and did not prefer to run in any clique or group in school.

Chloe ran up the bleachers, high-fiving her classmates, slapping Mona's hand, the two sharing a quick glance. Chloe could see that Mona was enamored with her. Her girl radar told her so. Chloe was falling for Carl's cousin.

The cheer squad stood shoulder to shoulder, with Chloe in the middle of them, waving her pom poms overhead as the senior class president introduced the varsity football squad. It was a short list of nobodies until they came to Pete, Chloe's older brother, the crowd of students going wild as Pete ran into the gymnasium wearing tiger-printed orange and black spandex tights. It was his trademark at every pep rally, and it drove the crowd crazy, the students stomping their feet as hard as they could, chanting his name over and over. Alan and Tommy were next, the crowd's cheers diminishing as they took their positions alongside Pete. Pete waited for the gymnasium to go silent as he raised his hands over his head. The class president handed him the microphone, Pete's gigantic hand smothering it.

"Ladies and gentle dudes—tonight, one night only, for your viewing pleasure, we, the varsity squad, will lay down the thunder on those swamp rats to the south." He had a way with words, the gymnasium erupting in cheers and clapping. The swamp rats he was referring to was the rival team from the small town four miles south of Centralia, Chehalis High School. Chehalis had an impressive high school football program, but as a rival, Pete used everything in his arsenal to get the students excited about the game.

"I expect each and every one of you to come to the game tonight." He pointed around the gymnasium, the teaching staff nodding their heads up and down in agreement. "...If you could come wearing your rain gear, I would be especially grateful." Pete knew it would be a psychological blow to the Chehalis team, mocking their town nickname: Swamp Town.

His speech worked. That evening, dozens of students attended wearing their father's yellow rain gear, and Pete capitalized on it before the game started. Walking off the sideline, he motioned for the students to come down on the track, the field microphone already in his hand. Pete had them line up on the track, the yellow hoard standing at the ready as he pumped up the crowd.

"Ladies and gentlemen and our esteemed booster club members," he said, holding his empty hand over his heart. "I present to you the first annual Swamp Town races." The crowd clapped and whistled, many stomped their feet. Pete raised his right arm as his classmates prepared themselves for the race.

Carl and Audrey stood together, arms locked, yellow rain gear drenched in sweat from the inside.

"On your mark, get set. Go!" Pete yelled, sending the students scrambling in opposite directions, as they ran awkwardly around the track, passing each other on the far side of the field, flipping off the Chehalis players and visitors as they slogged along in their heavy rubber boots. One two-some had lost a boot each but continued to run together, leaving their strays behind on the track, and that sent more fuel into the crowd, who roared with cheers for the hobbled racers. The crowd's roars subsided to hearty belly-aching laughter as many pointed at the stray boots. Carl and Audrey were scrambling along, the event one of their best days in high school, running as fast as they could, arm in arm, the yellow fisherman caps mashed down hard on their heads. They clambered around the outside of the track far ahead of the rest of the competition. The duo passed through the finish line first, breaking the paper ribbon, and Pete awarded them as the best team spirit, best couple, and winners, unofficially, before he joined his teammates on the sideline.

Mona had joined Carl and Audrey in the stands. Audrey did not have a clue how the game operated. The game was a blowout by halftime, the Centralia team in the lead, twenty-four to six, the Chehalis team struggling to even get close to the end zone. The second half, Chehalis did not fare well, Pete and his crew holding them to only one more touchdown, the crowd going wild as the final buzzer ended the game.

Audrey, Carl, Mona, and Chloe drove to the dance together, Pete and the players showing up a half hour later. More than two hundred students crowded around the dance floor as the disc jockey spun up the first song. Audrey jumped up and down, then pulled Carl into the middle of the dance floor as the slow song played on. She wrapped her arms around his neck as they danced. Audrey pushed her face into Carl's and kissed him passionately, blocking out everyone around them. He pulled his face away, toying with her. She pulled him into her and was oblivious to everyone around them, wanting nothing more than to melt into his arms. She didn't care about school policy or who might be watching. All that mattered was the feel of his lips on hers and the firm pressure of his groin against hers. She prolonged the duration of the kiss. Their eyes closed.

“Uh—hum,” Mr. Gillingsworth grumbled as he tapped her on the shoulder, Audrey faintly looking his way as they spun around.

“Audrey, you know better than that," Mr. Gillingsworth yelled over the music.”

“I’m sorry Paul, it won’t happen again,” Audrey giggled as she smiled at him.

“That’s okay, just keep it P.G,” he chuckled as he walked away.

Mr. Gillingsworth kept watch, breaking up a cat fight early on, separating a lovers’ spat, and keeping a close eye on Audrey throughout the night. The dance was nearly over when a fast song came on, Chloe dragging Audrey and Mona out with her to dance. Dancing with all girls was fashionable and a chance for them to talk about boys. Mona liked the crazy young gals’ antics and dance style, her energy infecting the entire student body that night, as the three of them orbited around, legs shooting out, arms flailing, half disco, half pop style. A slow dance filled the room, and Carl's cousin was taken off-guard when Chloe grabbed her, not letting her exit the dance floor as she threw her arms around Mona’s shoulders. Mona was nearly a full foot taller than Chloe, the matchup good proportionately for a slow dance.

“Chloe, we can’t dance together; people will talk,” Mona replied, shuffling her feet nervously.

“No they won’t. Nobody cares what I do; I’m the life of the party—watch.” Chloe hung onto Mona tight, spinning her around in a circle, then stopped abruptly as she flung her head back. Her friends cheered for her immediately, some of them clapping from the row of chairs from the side of the room. Mona's face turned deep red when Chloe kissed her on the neck—a kiss that she held for way too long. Mona’s face went flush.

“See, just two girls having fun,” Chloe laughed.

23

CARL'S FAMILY WAS DYSFUNCTIONAL; TO call it normal would have been a dishonor to all the good families in America. Mrs. Newkirk was a multifaceted person, shoved into the reality of raising a son at a time when she would rather be doing something else. Sure, she loved him, in her own way, but she was not the nurturing kind. Her enjoyment was reading fiction novels, not taking care of a family. Carl had prepared his mom for the dinner with Audrey Friday evening. Nothing would prepare Carl for the shock he got when he and Audrey entered the house, his mother drunk, stirring away at the pot of stew, still dressed in her housecoat.

"Mom, we're here," Carl yelled from the back door as Audrey followed him into the kitchen. His mom had her back turned away from them as she swirled the wooden spoon around the pot, the other hand holding the half-burned cigarette, the ash hanging out two inches, ready to drop on the floor. He looked his mother up and down, waiting to see if her words would be slurred, as his anger brewed.

"Mom," he yelled again, startling her, the fog of alcohol slowing her thoughts.

"Hello dear, Carl has told me so much about you."

Carl's anger subsided when he noticed that his mom was relatively sober. She was normal. Drunk, but normal. He was amazed at her capacity for presenting herself in a positive manner despite how she looked.

"Hello Mrs. Newkirk. I'm Audrey Anderson." Audrey moved in to shake hands, and Carl watched the interaction, wondering if his mom would put down the whiskey glass long enough to greet his girlfriend. She placed the glass on the table as she reached over and the two clasped hands.

"It is nice to meet you Audrey. Boy Carl, she is a looker," she added, as Audrey blushed.

"Thank you Mrs. Newkirk, it is my pleasure, really," Audrey replied, as his mom motioned for her to take a seat at the head of the table.

"Carl, can you set the table?" his mother asked.

"Sure," he croaked nervously, wondering if his mom would say something more to embarrass him or whether Audrey would ask her something that would make her think too hard and induce a brain fart.

"Is your dad here?" Audrey asked innocently.

"No, he does not come home for dinner now," Mrs Newkirk replied.

Carl knew what that meant. His father did work nights, but used to join them occasionally, parking the dump truck in the driveway, waiting for a call while he ate with them. He now elected to stay away, their marriage more a function of providing Carl a home for another couple years until he graduated, their marriage long but ended. The tension in the room was thick, the rest of the meal in silence. His mom left the teens at the table, retreating to her chair in the living room, opening the half read-horror novel of the week. She was thoroughly engrossed in it when Carl and Audrey walked into the room a few minutes later.

"I'm going to show Audrey the rest of the house." She hardly looked up from her novel, a fresh cigarette hanging out of her lips, the flame of the lighter consuming the first quarter inch as she lit it up.

"That's fine dear."

Carl took Audrey by the hand, dragging her up the narrow staircase into his room. It wasn't much to look at; the teenage boy's room was messy, the decorations an odd menagerie of street signs hanging on the walls, movie posters, and a framed photo of Albert Einstein nailed haphazardly to another wall. Carl watched Audrey as she studied a few of his pictures. One of them was a photo of a much younger Carl and Pete standing next to each other, holding onto an inner tube, their faces sunburned.

"That's Pete, Chloe's older brother?" She held the picture in her hands then looked over at Carl, who had laid back on his bed, arms folded behind his head.

"Yeah, we go way back, been friends since we were little. Not so much anymore. You know, Pete's a big-shot football star," he said as he shifted his body, pushing his head deeper into the mound of pillows.

A long couch lined the other wall, a throw-away he had found in the alley behind the theater, musty but in decent shape. Next to it stood a vintage fifties floor lamp, its glass body standing nearly three feet tall, the lamp protruding up another four feet above it. He had found it at one of the downtown antique malls and haggled with the proprietor of the shop until the man relented, selling it to him for five dollars. A small bookshelf stood at the other end of the couch; five years of National Geographic Magazines were lined up neatly. Audrey picked one up then sat on the couch.

"Do you like to travel Carl?" she asked as she flipped through the pages.

"Yes, I would, but I have never been out of Washington."

Audrey's brows raised, shocked. She had been virtually everywhere around the globe.

"I will take you sometime," she replied, acknowledging the fact in her mind that he didn't comprehend what she was saying. She knew he wouldn't believe her right now. She knew he wouldn't believe she had the means to travel. Audrey dropped the magazine as she crawled onto the bed, straddling Carl. She grabbed the back of his neck, pulling his face into hers as she kissed him.

"I would go anywhere with you Audrey," Carl replied, but was immediately quieted with more passionate kisses as her body melded into his. Their love was burgeoning. Audrey could sense that it was more than just a teen fling.

“Do you think your mom would let you go with me?” she asked between kisses.

“Maybe, depends on when you ask her—better to wait until late in the evening.” She kissed him again, pulling his shirt off as she ran her hands down his chest. Audrey had flipped her shoes off her feet and ran her toes up the inside of his leg.

“That tingles,” Carl giggled. She pressed her lips against his harder. Sweat ran down their brows.

“I want to take you with me to Europe.” More kissing followed as her hands rubbed his thighs.

“When are you going?” Carl choked out. Their breathing intensified.

“I go back in the summers when I can,” she answered.

“I don’t have the money to go.”

She did not care about money, nor the fact that Carl’s family had limited means.

“Don’t worry, I will pay for everything, just come with me when I ask.”

“Yes, I will,” he squeaked out through gasps for air.

They kissed for another two hours, their lips raw. Carl led Audrey downstairs, their hair matted from sweat. Mrs. Newkirk was passed out in her chair.

Carl pulled the afghan blanket over her, making sure the cigarettes in the ashtray were cold before they left. The lovers had run out of steam and were ready to get a burger across town before joining the cruisers. Audrey snuggled up next to him in the car, rubbing his chest as they drove over to the burger stand. The evening was cool but dry, a rare treat in the Pacific Northwest. Carl cruised with the window open, heater cranked up, his arm hanging out, waving to friends as they passed them by on the strip. The neon lights of the burger joint bathed the parking lot in bright reds and blues, cars stacked alongside each other, the occupants waiting for their orders to be called over the loudspeaker. Carl parked alongside a car he recognized, the inside of it empty.

“I’ll be right back. The usual?” he asked as he shut the door behind him.

“Uh huh,” she replied.

Carl stood in line to order and was interrupted by a sharp stab in the back.

Callie's high-pitched voice followed. "Hello Carl, how are you?"

Carl's nerves shot up, wondering if she would kiss him in front of Audrey or brush it off as two kids, that had a fling.

"I'm good. How have you been," he replied nervously as he looked across the parking lot at his car.

"I'm okay—still have nightmares. Are you back with Audrey?"

"Yeah, I guess so."

"Be careful Carl. She's not who you think she is—"

"What do you mean?" he asked.

"I-I got to go, Tommy's coming."

She had said the one name he did not want to hear. Tommy was the one guy he hated in high school. Tommy was part thug, star athlete, and popular with all the girls, most of them in the outlying schools around the county. Carl and Tommy had come to blows a few times over the years, mostly just shoving matches. Glancing over his shoulder nervously, he searched around the parking lot for Tommy. Carl was halfway through his order with the cashier when he felt a fist push him in the back.

"Hey Carl, what do you mean talking to my girl?" It was Tommy standing behind him and a full six inches taller, his broad chest stretching the t-shirt as his muscles fought to escape.

"No harm no foul Tommy, just said hello," Carl replied, wondering if it was convincing enough. He knew he was on Tommy's radar since he had been with Callie, even though it was obvious he was back with Audrey. If it had been Carl a year earlier, nobody would have paid attention, but now that Carl had the best looking girlfriend in the school, he was on Tommy's docket.

"Just stay away from my girl, geek." Tommy pushed Carl's shoulder hard, causing him to stumble backward. Carl stared at Audrey across the parking lot and wondered if she would think he was a wimp. He was sure that she saw the confrontation.

“Who was that Carl?” she asked him gently, knowing his pride was hurt, rubbing his shoulder.

“Tommy, from school,” he replied.

“What did he want?” she pressed.

If he told the truth, it could backfire on him, but that was one thing that Carl was not: a liar.

“He was mad because I talked to Callie,” he said, wondering if she would accept it.

“What did you say to her?”

Another pointed question—it wasn’t as though he had done anything wrong, just a thirty-second conversation with the other girl. His thoughts hit him immediately; her jealousy of Callie would never end, that was how girlfriends were. Carl thought about it; in Audrey’s mind, he could reason that she viewed they had never broken up.

“I said hello to her, was just being nice,” he glanced at her, one eye wider.

"Cool," she replied.

Carl’s window rattled as Tommy’s fist banged on it hard enough to break it.

“What do you want Tommy?” Carl was getting tired of him, and now he had crossed the line; touching his car was off limits.

“You stay away from my girl Newkirk; she’s mine now.” His finger was pointed straight into Carl’s face. Audrey leaned forward across Carl’s chest. The pair stared at each other intently. Carl could see the fire in her eyes. He watched Tommy choke up, momentarily unable to breathe, his throat tightening as his airway closed. Audrey leaned back as Tommy walked away coughing, massaging his throat with his hands.

Clint sped around the corner, the blue Nova bouncing into the parking lot as it navigated the rise in the pavement. The car screeched to a halt inches from Carl’s door. Clint jumped out, moving over to Carl’s window.

“Moose, Audrey, what’s going on.” Clint leaned on the door as he spoke.

“Not much Clint, just hanging with my girl.” Clint acknowledged Audrey, giving her a quick eyebrow raise.

“Hey catch ya later, Callie is waiting.” Callie was still standing inside the phone booth when Clint arrived. Clint pulled the Nova up alongside the booth and Callie jumped in, snuggling up next to him. Clint flipped his middle finger up at Tommy as he drove away.

24

INSIDE THE POOL HALL, SEAN flicked the cigarette, depositing an ash into the tray next to him. Tonight, the room was nearly empty, with only a handful of tables being used. Sean never approached them, staying back as they played, watching her move as he studied her shots. Audrey sauntered around the pool table with confidence. She glanced at the thug at the back of the room from time to time, taunting him. Her shots were effortless. Nobody noticed when Sean left the pool hall, but Audrey had gotten to him, and she knew he couldn't stand to be in the same room with the girl that had dethroned him, deflating his ego.

Audrey worked with Carl, showing him how to hold the stick better, lining up his shots and working on his drawback. He was learning, and maybe that is what Sean saw that pissed him off—the real pool shark teaching Carl her technique. Most pool table lamps in the front were turned off, leaving only Carl and Audrey's table illuminated in the rear of the hall, the attendant at the cashier booth in front of the room snoring, his feet propped up on the counter. Audrey slid around the table, getting ready for her next shot, leaning over the table as she brought the stick close to the cue ball. Audrey pulled the stick back as she watched through her peripheral vision. She saw Carl had moved one of the balls over to the corner pocket. She smirked.

"Carl Newkirk, are you trying to cheat me?" She slid up next to him, staring into his eyes, her stern look breaking into a smile, then a laugh as he grabbed her, setting her up on the table, standing between her legs. Carl moved in for a kiss, but Audrey moved her head away. He pulled her to him; she moved her head away. It went on that way for another thirty seconds before she let him kiss her. Their moist lips exploring each other as the pair meshed into one.

"Come home with me," she whispered.

“Are you trying to seduce me,” he replied, his voice trailing off into another kiss.

25

MONDAY MORNINGS IN HIGH SCHOOL start the same across America. Students arrive half-asleep, worn out from too much partying, too much drinking, and too little sleep on the weekend. Carl was no different, his morning routine of one fried egg, a glass of milk, and a piece of toast did nothing to revive him before noon. Audrey was a different story; he was surprised to see her waiting outside her house, especially on a brisk cold morning, her face still glowing. Her attitude was upbeat and chipper. The previous night's events still flush on her face.

"Good morning Carl." She kissed him on the cheek.

"Morning Audrey, how are you?"

"Wonderful, like I was just born last week."

"Where were you yesterday? I stopped by, and nobody was home."

"Church."

It was the one place he was not interested in visiting; Carl immediately dropped the conversation, enjoying the moment with Audrey at his side. She slid over next to him on the bench seat, snuggling up to him as they rode to school. The fifteen-minute drive was quality time where two teens could enjoy each other's company alone.

They were in full boyfriend–girlfriend mode now, a light kiss in the car, holding hands in the hallways before class, and Carl counting down the minutes until he could see her between classes.

Audrey, however, found that Lauren was less than cordial this morning. Lauren was still avoiding her, deliberately taking another hallway to go between classes. Audrey knew why but was determined to intervene, to let her know she did not appreciate the cold shoulder. Just before lunch, third period was in full swing. Audrey and Chloe were taking the same class: home economics.

"Chloe, do you know what's wrong with Lauren?"

"She does seem a bit off lately, but Lauren can be bitchy; just wait until you get to know her." Chloe was not exaggerating. Lauren's moods swung violently from crabby to pleasant then back to crabby five seconds later.

"She's probably on her period," Chloe chirped.

"She won't talk to me and keeps avoiding me in the hallway."

"I wouldn't worry about her—probably ticked off about who knows what. How are you and Carl doing? Becoming quite the item aren't you!"

"Carl is a nice boy, and he is good to me."

"Did you do it yet?" Chloe stabbed.

"Chloe, a girl doesn't kiss and tell."

"They do if they are screwing," she prodded.

"I'm not talking about this anymore. Your mind is in the gutter; it's not ladylike."

"I live vicariously through you Audrey. I don't know whether you've looked in the mirror lately, but you are the prettiest girl in the whole school, heck probably the prettiest in the entire state," Chloe said, a tinge of jealousy in her voice.

"You're just saying that."

Audrey never considered herself beautiful, although she had the drop-dead gorgeous looks of an angel. It had been a long time since she had seen her reflection, something she missed. Beauty to her was more about taking care of yourself, self respect, and acting like a lady. Audrey was truly refined, especially for a high schooler, which is what attracted people to her in numbers, whether teen or adult. She was—infectious.

Carl and Audrey practically sat on top of each other during lunch, Audrey feeding him off her plate. Lauren glared at them from the other side of the cafeteria, glares that didn't go unnoticed by Audrey. When lunch ended, Audrey parted ways with her friends, catching up with Lauren in the photo lab darkroom.

Unaware Audrey had joined among her classmates, Lauren jumped as she turned around, Audrey staring into her eyes a mere two feet away.

"What are you doing here?" Her voice shook.

"Just came by to talk to you."

"I don't want to talk to you."

"Lauren please."

"No—I saw—at the dance. I saw when you were braiding Chloe's hair in the bathroom—you, weren't there—"

"It's okay Lauren. I'm not a bad person. I'm here to be your friend. I can't explain it all right now, and you have to believe that I'm not here to hurt you."

"What are you?" Lauren asked as she pulled at the ends of her hair.

"I am before, and am now."

"A revenant?"

Audrey had heard people refer to her in that term before.

"It's not important. I am here now, here to be with you, Chloe, and Carl."

"Audrey. Or whoever you are—I—I need more time to sort this out."

"I understand. I won't bother you anymore, but please, do not be afraid."

Audrey watched the hair on Lauren's bare arms stand on end as goosebumps formed.

"I gotta go," Lauren croaked as she brushed past Audrey.

Students filled the hallways as the last bell rang, and Lauren pushed through them, catching a glimpse of Chloe in front of her.

"Chloe, wait up," Lauren yelled.

"Hey Lauren, 'bout time you came around."

Lauren stood a full four inches taller, as the two locked eyes.

"Come with me. I have something to show you in the library." Lauren nearly ripped Chloe's arm out of the socket as she pulled her into the library. The last two geeks in school were sitting reading in a far corner as Lauren searched for a dictionary on one of the shelves marked "reference."

"I just talked to Audrey in photo lab."

"You did?...Audrey?"

"Yes…."

Chloe paused, then added. "Yeah, she said she wanted to talk to you, said you were ignoring her or something like that."

"I wasn't ignoring her. I-I was just scared," Lauren said, breathing in deeply before continuing.

"The first dance when she was braiding your hair, I did not see her reflection in the mirror. Today when I talked to her, I asked her about it. She brushed it off, said she was, or is, or something like that?"

"What do you mean she didn't have a reflection?"

"She wasn't there. I don't know—I think she's a revenant."

"What's a revenant?" Chloe milled the word over in her mind, trying to catch on to what Lauren was trying to tell her. If there was one thing going for Chloe, it was her stunning looks and cheery personality. When it came time for academics, deductive reasoning, and general studies, she was lacking. Not that she couldn't learn, nor was she a complete idiot; Chloe was just like the other popular girls. Looks meant everything in high school, as well as how you were dressed. She put more effort into her looks and style.

"Read it, it's right here," Lauren said, pointing to the definition with her index finger as she held the book in the other hand.

rev·e·nant

ˈrevəˌnäN,-nənt/

Noun

A person who has returned, especially, supposedly from the dead.

"She's dead?" Chloe laughed.

"*Shh*, somebody will hear you." Lauren glanced around the library.

"So you think she is dead?" Chloe said just as loud.

"No, I don't think she is dead now—I think she is back from the dead."

"I don't believe it."

"Damn it Chloe, when was the last time I lied to you?" Lauren said, her tone forceful.

"Last year at prom, you said that—"

"That was last year, I'm telling you what I saw and what she told me."

"Let's just say you are right; what is she doing here and why is she here, and how can you prove she is a revenant?"

"I don't know yet; I'll think of something." Lauren's hands trembled.

"Well, when you do, then come get me, but if you are wrong, this will be social suicide for both of us. She has only been here a little while, and she is on top, and that is where I intend to stay. Dead girl or no dead girl, I'm not losing my social status."

Chloe knew the key to existing in high school was popularity; she knew she had to do anything possible to maintain that, even if it meant coexisting with the dead, the devil, or anything in-between.

"I think she is Apollyon as well," Lauren added, her voice trailing off.

"What is that?" Chloe asked. "Where do you come up with this stuff?"

"I was reading a book on the spirits. It's Greek for what they call the grim reaper, or angel of death."

"I thought the angel of death was a dude?" Chloe joked.

"Chloe, does it matter if it is a gal or guy?"

"No, I guess not, as long as she doesn't interfere with homecoming. I'm getting nominated, and there is a good chance I will be on the court."

"I'm done talking to you Chloe; you aren't even listening to me."

"Whatever Lauren, I think you are taking this all too seriously, lighten up; we are only freshmen. We've got three more years to screw up our lives."

Lauren would not let it go. Her plan of action already started in motion in her mind, if she could only get someone else to believe her, she could get her friends back on her side. She knew what she had to do: plan a party; her house was full of mirrors, they would see, just as soon as she could get Audrey in front of one of them.

The rest of the week passed slowly, Lauren studying every book in the library on anything pertaining to the undead, as well as spending equal amounts of time planning the party at her house. It was an easy subject to bring up to her parents. They were parents, having given birth to Lauren late in their forties, that didn't care what she did, as long as she did it at home. She took advantage of the fact that they were pushing seventy and retired to their bedroom by seven thirty each evening, TV blaring away as they dozed off, the blue glow shining out of their bedroom window.

By Thursday morning, rumors of the party circulated like wildfire. By Friday night, the entire street in front of her house was parked full of teenager's junkers. Music inside the home permeated the walls, drifting down the street to the neighbors, who had earlier ignored the loud wild get togethers. Hour after hour, Lauren waited for Carl and Audrey to show up. She chugged a beer, then another as she danced, getting more inebriated by the minute, her vision diminishing. By eleven thirty, they still had not made an appearance, and Lauren was on the verge of passing out when they strolled through the front door. Audrey stood directly behind her boyfriend, holding his hand, following him through the crowd of partiers into the living room. A red-eyed Lauren followed close behind as she worked hard to see if Audrey cast a reflection in the mirrors.

In the middle of the crowd, Lance Macintosh, king of the dance world, spun into a frenzy on his back, feet up, hands behind his head, the crowd moving away from him, clapping as they cheered him on.

"What is that called?" Audrey asked.

"Breakdancing," Carl replied.

"Break—dancing?" she asked. "What is he breaking?"

Carl chuckled. "It is just a form of dancing that involves spinning on your back, head, jumping up and down—breakdancing. You don't break anything."

"Oh."

Throughout the night, Lauren worked her way around the other teens, looking for a chance to expose Audrey. Carl and Audrey pulsated up and down to the music, mingling into the middle of the crowd of drunken kids, the mirrors around the house hardly noticing the absence of an image dancing next to her boyfriend. She brushed up against another guy and they had a brief moment of eye contact, sending a cold shiver up her spine. She had run smack into a demon, and he knew she was there for him at that moment. Opposing forces always attracted each other, no matter the circumstance. Their tensions climaxed as they kept an eye on each other throughout the dance.

"Carl, who is that guy over there?" She pointed as they spun facing her prey.

"Michael something or other—can't remember his last name—he's new, started this year—I think he transferred from Seattle?" Carl replied.

Audrey kept tabs on him as they danced, then lost sight of Michael as Carl spun her around. She let go of him and walked through the crowd to an open door that lead to the pool.

On the patio outside the back of the home, a small group of seniors and their girlfriends sat next to the pool, and a dare came up quick: jump into the pool naked. The testosterone of a football star got the best of him. He stripped his clothing off quickly and stepped up onto the diving board. Girls around him catcalled and whistled, egging him on. Audrey stared into his eyes from the other end of the pool. He gave her the finger. The board flexed up and down with each leap into the air as he catapulted himself into the water. Alcohol and teenage bravado should not go hand in hand. He smacked the water, and the girls screamed in horror, a few guys hollering as they cheered. His belly flop off the diving board sent him to the bottom of the pool, where his body lay motionless. Pete dove into the pool and swam downward to his friend. Audrey stared above the water line, her hand flexing, veins in her neck pulsating. Under her breath she chanted silently. Carl started to unbutton his shirt and she stopped him, holding her left arm across his chest.

"You shall return to your house from which you came," she whispered. "The redemption has come to take you home—fallen one."

"Did you say something?" Carl asked, grabbing her hand.

"No—"

Pete scooped up his friend and kicked for the surface, where a dozen students had waded in to help. They pulled the lifeless body out of the water and laid it on the concrete patio. Nobody moved for a few seconds.

"Do something!" a girl screamed from the crowd. *"C.P.R.—do C.P.R!"* she yelled again.

Pete knelt next to his friend and pressed his hands up and down, compressing the chest. Water shot out of his unresponsive friend.

"Come on buddy, you can do it," Pete yelled.

"Call 9 1 1," a girl yelled into the house from the patio.

Pete pumped away, compressing the chest, and more water gurgled from the lifeless mouth—then sputtering.

"That's it, come on man," Pete said as the ashen grey face below him came to life. Audrey stared at her prey in disbelief as his eyes opened, glaring straight at her. He drew in a deep breath, then exhaled. She squeezed Carl's hand tight as her eyes narrowed. A single breath exited the mouth of her rival and he was gone. One more opposing spirit she would not have to worry about.

Pete leaned back then placed his head in his hands.

"Carl, let's go."

"We can't go now. Michael died; we have to wait for the cops."

"I've done what I came here to do; I want to go home now." Her words were forceful. Her command was direct and effective.

"I'll drive you home, if that is what you want, but we should stay."

“Please take me home, I’m tired,” she replied as she pulled on his hand, leading him through the crowded patio through the home. They walked by Lauren, who was passed out on the couch, and out to his car.

Carl shut Audrey’s door, then moved around to the driver’s seat, cranking the engine over. The engine rumbled, then died as it coughed in protest.

“C’mon,” he mumbled as he turned the key again. The car chugged then caught as Carl pumped the throttle, throwing the transmission in drive just in time to pull the car into the street as the ambulance rounded the corner of the main road in front of them. He pulled over to let the ambulance pass.

“We should go back,” he choked out.

“*No*—we can’t, it is over,” she yelled, then added, “Will you stay with me tonight?” Her voice was timid, withdrawn.

“Sure Audrey, what’s wrong?”

“I’m really tired and I don’t want to be alone tonight—I don’t want to talk about it; just drive me home.”

“Okay.”

Inside the old house in the valley, Audrey led Carl up to her bedroom, her mood diminished. The glow of the single lamp on the table next to the bed beckoned him to her as they collapsed into the sheets together. Audrey fell asleep in an instant inside Carl’s arms; Carl drifted off minutes later.

26

LUNCH WAS AUDREY'S FAVORITE MOMENT at school—that twenty-minute interlude between classes, breaking up the monotony of the day. Centralia High's lunchroom was also the commons area, where they would hold the dances, house the lockers, and where the cheerleaders would practice after school. It was an odd arrangement: the concrete structure and open floor where the janitors would roll out the fold-up lunch tables just minutes before. Two-dozen tables jammed the floor space, directly in front of the lockers. The lockers were housed in a two-story structure made of solid concrete that held the senior class above the junior class's lockers. The senior deck, where their lockers stood, was a right of passage; only the seniors and a few lucky underclassmen, usually pretty girls, were allowed up there. Carl never went up there.

Carl met up with Audrey and the rest of the gang, their table reserved just for them, no sign needed. It was implied who sat with or near them everyday, the rest of the students giving them a wide berth. Audrey had their tray full of the usual: deep fried burritos, mashed potatoes, applesauce, and a piece of cake. She always called it food that was not fit for a rat, but ate it anyway, opting to have something to sit on their stomachs until they could get home for dinner. Today, their food would end up stuck in various places besides their stomachs. It was also the third time that the food fight would happen that quarter, and one of the last times before winter break. Nobody knew how it started; later it would be said that the same boy initiated it the same way he had gotten someone to start it last time and the time before. His name was Lance Macintosh, the same breakdancer she had watched at Lauren's house. He was a nobody really, but a somebody for everybody that had nobody. Lance was the king of the out crowd, if their ever was one.

Carl and Audrey were engaged in their own ritual of feeding each other one bite at a time while they talked among their group. Lance was a loud person, garnering everyone's attention as he jumped up on the top of his table and started gyrating his body around, waving his arms as if he were a lunatic. It was his way to get it started, the first chunk of food coming across the lunchroom, hurled at Lance by one of the football players. Lance ducked just in time as the piece of cake with chocolate frosting flew past him, hitting a boy in the back of the head. The recipient of the chocolate cake spun around fast, looking at the football player's table. Alan flipped him off. Chocolate cake boy, sprung into action. With chocolate frosting dripping off the back of his head, his target was the entire team as he launched his whole plastic tray of food at them. The contents of spaghetti, applesauce, and more chocolate cake splattered the football squad, and his tray bounced off the back of one of Alan's friends, nearly cold cocking him. The next few seconds seemed to last forever; Lance still danced in the middle of the table as hundreds of students joined the fight. Food and trays assaulted the unwary as the sky filled with debris. Although the food fight only lasted thirty to forty-five seconds, the ensuing damage of food on the ceiling, floors, and everyone's clothing would give the principal enough ammunition to send dozens of students into detention the following day. He had walked into the lunch room in time to catch the last few revelers as he flew into a tirade.

Lance came through the whole process completely unscathed, except for a small spot of chocolate cake that he licked off his sneaker. It was one of those high school events that would become legend. Lance was always landing on top, no matter what the circumstance. Audrey was appalled and amused at the entire spectacle.

27

ON THE OTHER SIDE OF the world, a meeting was held in secret as it had been for centuries, the location undisclosed. It was hidden from the outside by layers of brick, mortar, and the cobblestone streets above. Members of a secret religious order were making their way into the darkened alley, following one another down a steep set of narrow steps to a chamber below. One after the other, they worked their way into the cramped room, taking their assigned seats around a twenty foot long rectangular table. The wood was distressed and stained from centuries of spilled wine. A few names had been carved into the table top. Forty feet above them, people milled around the city of Rome unaware.

The twelve clerics attending the meeting had been recruited to do what their predecessors were reluctant to even speak about, much less comprehend: the full spectrum of the supernatural. Sure, they all believed in God and the afterlife, but none of them were fully prepared to be at odds with the church itself. Now they were being asked to put away everything they ever knew and believed to start a new era of darkness, going against the church in direct violation of persecuting an angel they believed had crossed the line.

A short gentleman wearing a business suit motioned for the others to be seated as he waved at his assistants to close and lock the door. He knew if they were discovered that they would be sent directly to the maximum security prison in rural Italy, never to be heard from again, or worse—killed.

"Please, take your seats. Welcome and thank you for coming on short notice. I know there is not much known about the actual appearance in modern times of an angel, but we are on the edge of a new millennium, a time when the world will be thrown upside down. Whose side are we going to be on?" he said, pausing. "I'm asking you, my brothers, to stand with me now. The time has come to leave the church and get back to the teachings that we know are found in the original scrolls." He continued speaking of the Dead Sea scrolls and his first-hand knowledge of their true content, having studied them in the temple on the mount in Jerusalem. Only a few religious leaders had been given access to the documents out of fear that the information would change the thoughts and minds of the religious followers. Immediately after he studied them, the Israelis revoked his visa and access, expelling him from the country. He had asked too many questions.

He stood, leaning with both fists on top of the table. He raised his right fist, then struck the table with it. "Now is the time; we must move swiftly with conviction and courage. What we do in the next few months will affect the world for thousands of years to come." Sweat poured off the top of his partially bald head, landing on the wood table next to his plate full of food. The other members sat quietly, drinking their wine and feasting on the roasted lamb.

"An angel of death has manifested and we must deal with it—" He was cutoff by another cleric.

"Am I to presume, you are asking us to go slay the dragon on our own?" he said between sips of wine.

"That is exactly what I am asking. We need to form a task force to take this apparition out. Nothing good can come from its continued existence."

Some of the clerics nodded their heads in agreement, but nobody spoke up except for the man who had posed the question about slaying the dragon. The dim lights flickered above, casting shadows of the clerics' bodies against the walls behind them. The plaster stuck to the walls was peeling off in chunks, exposing the bricks underneath, leaving powdery residue on the floor. Condensation dripped steadily from the ceiling.

"Who of us is ready to battle the supernatural?" the doubting cleric asked, looking around the table at his colleagues. Nobody spoke, some averting their gaze into their plate of food or across the table at the opposite wall. "We are old men, tired men; we don't have the stamina or strength to walk five miles let alone battle a superior force," he added.

The head cleric banged his right fist on the table again, startling the group. "Faith, you must have faith or it will be for naught." He studied the expressions of those in front of him, looking to see who would be on his side. "We will hire mercenaries to go out with each cleric." Half of the group nodded in agreement.

"Who will join me on this quest for justice?" His voice rose up, gaining strength. "Raise your glass if you are with me." One man after the other raised his wine glass, the others following suit all down to the last man at the opposite end of the table.

28

AUDREY HAD NOTICED THAT LAUREN was still keeping her distance as she fell out with the group of friends, growing more introverted by the week. Mona had joined the group as her replacement, like a pond filling in after a rock splashed through the surface. Audrey was still on top, the unofficial leader of her group. She was their pillar. It was obvious to everyone by now that her charm was guiding them into her realm. To Audrey, it was the exact opposite effect she'd intended. Although she loved the attention, her belief that some people were bad would haunt her thoughts from past experiences. The new trio plied the halls, arms interlocked, laughing, giggling and cutting up. They were having the time of their lives.

Carl had also blossomed over the last few months. His features were taking on a more rugged and mature look. His confidence was high for the first time in his life. Audrey and Carl were the talk of the school. They were the perfect couple, in an imperfect world—teenage romance.

Mona confided in Carl. He was her favorite cousin and they talked nearly every day. She was a year older, although they were in the same grade and she still held a position of respect for him. She had grown up with him, bike riding as kids throughout town nearly every year, until they drifted apart sometime around their thirteenth birthdays, the awkwardness of puberty alienating them for a few years. Now, their resurgence and friendship gave them a new lease together and a newfound respect. Carl was spending more and more time at Audrey's home, electing to stay overnight often.

A week before Audrey's sixteenth birthday; spring had arrived quickly, and she felt compelled to tell him her secret. She had formally invited him over for dinner. Carl had come and gone from the place as though he owned it, not paying much attention to the fact that the mother was still missing. He didn't want to know. Across from the small dinner table in the kitchen, Audrey guarded her thoughts; the nervousness in her voice spoke volumes.

"Carl, I need to tell you something."

He was all ears, not speaking.

"This place, the farmland, house—it is mine Carl. I own it all and I live here alone. It was my family's, now it is mine. I am the last of my kind."

She watched as her words bounced around in his head, knowing he was not fully comprehending what she was saying.

"You live here all alone?"

His statement cut into her and she could tell it was going to take time to get through to him.

"Yes, I have for a while now; it was very lonely for a long time. My life is meaningful now that you are here."

"You're only 16? How do you live alone? Where's your mom at? She's never been here?"

"That's what I'm trying to tell you; she isn't here. I'm alone—except now I have you." She moved up to him and wrapped her arms around his waist.

"I have a secret..." she added, her words trailing off in a whisper.

"What is it?" he whispered back, moving his face in close.

"I love you—" she whispered back, cutting the words off when her lips pressed against his.

She stopped the conversation, giving him just enough information to get him thinking—enough to keep him around, not quite enough to send him running away.

The following Saturday afternoon more of the pieces of mystery came together for him, a few days before her birthday. In the distance, Carl could see a moving van sitting in front of her house as he drove down the driveway. Two movers were exiting the house when he pulled alongside the moving van.

Carl walked past the burly movers as he entered the house. He was thick with trepidation, expecting it to be empty and Audrey missing. He was surprised when he found Audrey sitting on the piano bench, the baby grand top opened, the careful notes floating through the home as her fingers ran up and down the keys. Carl took a seat behind her on the couch and kept quiet. She played a dark and expressive tune he had never heard before. It was melancholy. For more than half an hour Audrey played on, unaware or uncaring he was there. Carl surprised her with his applause.

"Bravo Audrey, I didn't know you played the piano."

"It has been a while; I thought it might be time to have some of my things delivered."

Antique furniture plied every spot in the home. Persian rugs were laid out in the middle of the rooms, each rug more impressive than the last. Carl breathed in her sweet aroma as he buried his face in her hair. He kissed her neck. Carl could feel his chest aching with desire as he took Audrey into his arms, his gentle touch caressing her, her auburn hair and perfume intoxicating him. She pulled him over to the couch and laid down behind him. Carl's eyes drooped as he fought their closing, the glow of a small fire in the open fireplace dancing across the walls around them. She stroked his hair and he fell asleep.

Carl awoke hours later, foggy, Audrey not at his side. The fire had burned down to a small pile of red hot coals. Carl's vision sharpened as he walked around the downstairs, studying her things. Every corner, every table, had an object displayed. Things he had never seen before, odd things, old things. A pair of samurai swords were positioned on a table near the kitchen. A full suit of armor stood in the hallway next to the bathroom. Everything was there that should be in a home as regal as this—everything except a mirror.

He climbed the stairs and was not surprised to see her bedroom fully outfitted with fine antiques. The wardrobe looked as though it were centuries old, its door a fancy hand-carved scene of angels holding swords floating above a slain enemy. Her makeup table sat opposite the wardrobe, classy and ornate—the mirror missing. Carl sat down in the rocking chair and tried to put two and two together. Audrey's strange home, her things, living alone, it didn't add up for him. Carl shifted forward in the chair, his elbows on his knees, hands covering his face.

A floorboard creaked. Carl looked up.

"Carl, what are you doing in here?"

"I—I was looking for you," he replied.

The two locked eyes, startled by each other's presence. He had been there frequently before, wishing he could be more intimate with her. He had been waiting for a girl he thought was only fifteen to turn sixteen. She was waiting for the boy of only seventeen to turn eighteen.

"We're going to be late; Chloe expects us by seven." She pulled him out of the chair, kissing him lightly on the cheek as they ran down the stairs and out of the house.

"Sorry Aud, I fell aslee and when I woke up I couldn't find you."

The Nova rattled over the country road as the tires jumped in and out of potholes. Silence filled the car, Audrey sitting next to Carl; the rumble of the worn-out muffler filling in the void. Carl pointed out the window, as he watched Chloe leap off the porch and run up to the car.

"Hey there my lovelies, Chloe Bear missed you guys." She slid up next to Audrey, giving her a kiss on the cheek.

"Hey Chloe, how's Pete?" Carl asked.

"He's fine, still bummed about losing the game," Chloe chirped.

"Yeah, that one sucked, if I were bigger, I would play with them."

"It's okay, he will come around. So Aud, how you been? Haven't talked to you in like twelve hours."

"Good."

Carl and Audrey barely laid eyes on each other.

"Let's go to the burger bar tonight Carl." Chloe laughed nervously, her words cutting through the tension. Carl placed his hand on Audrey's thigh, eliciting a glance from her. He couldn't tell if she was mad, anxious or if she was hiding something from him.

"Sure Chloe Bear. As long as it is okay with Audrey."

"That's fine by me."

“Do I detect a lover’s quarrel?” Chloe chirped.

Nobody answered.

The burger bar parking lot was filled as the Nova rounded the corner, Carl easing it up between two hotrods. It was a cornucopia of 1960s and 70s muscle cars, and Carl felt at home there, although his car was far from being fast. Frankie was there as well, sitting in his usual spot, the hood of his car open, the chrome intake jutting skyward.

“Hey Frankie, got her dialed in yet?” Carl yelled as he walked up to him.

“You bet cousin; she’s running sweet. How 'bout following me out of town to see me run? Could sure use you at the finish line again.”

“Yeah, no problem, glad to do it.”

“Don’t you have to get permission from the ball and chain?” Frankie jabbed.

“Nah man, were good; she’s just moody tonight. I’m not sure what is going on.”

The girls were in a world of their own, Chloe chatting away with Audrey inside the car, oblivious to the conversation between the cousins. Carl rejoined them a half hour later, arms piled up with a box of burgers, fries, and drinks, the three of them gorging on the feast. An hour later, Carl brought up the subject about going out with Frankie to watch him run his car.

“I don’t like it Carl; I think it is dangerous, and I don’t want you to go.”

“Audrey, it’s no big deal, just like he did at the race track.”

“If it is no big deal, then you can take me home. I’m not going.” She folded her arms across her chest and a scowl crept across her face.

“Fine.”

The drive back across town was even more uncomfortable except for Chloe chattering away about making it on the wrestling cheerleading squad, her favorite clothing, and who she would ask to the spring dance. Her bad luck with not getting nominated for homecoming was a distant memory. The Nova rattled over the hill and down the long driveway up to Audrey's home, the breaks squealing as it slid to a stop a few inches from the concrete stairs leading up to the yard.

"See you in the am?" Carl wasn't sure if she wanted to talk to him or even hang out.

"Sure Carl, stop by after noon. See you Chloe," Audrey said, kissing Chloe on the cheek as the she stepped out of the car.

"Night Audrey, Love you," Chloe replied, sliding back inside, her hand immediately reaching for the heater dial. She twisted it to max heat.

Carl was still worried about Audrey's moodiness but brushed it off. He was happy to be in Chloe's infectious company. If ever someone in their group was depressed, it took only thirty seconds with Chloe to cheer them up.

"Can I go out to watch you guys race?"

"No, I think I better take you home; your brother would kick my ass if he knew you were out late with me."

"Please, please, please, pretty please Carl. I promise I won't tell anyone; besides, he's finishing off that case of beer he got from you."

"How do you know about that? Did he tell you?" Carl said, his eyebrows twisting skyward.

"I'm his little sister; I know everything he does. That way I can blackmail him later. So if you don't take me with you, I'll tell him I was out with you late tonight."

"That doesn't make any sense."

"Yes it does."

"No it doesn't?"

"Yes, yes it does." Chloe crossed her arms.

"I give up; you can come." He knew it was pointless arguing with a girl, especially one that had information that could get him in trouble.

"*Alright—*" Chloe cranked the stereo volume up, the loud thumping of the twelve-inch woofer in the trunk drowning out any chance for Carl to reason with her.

The drive out of town to the corner took less than ten minutes and Frankie, and a few other guys were waiting for him.

"Hey cousin, glad you could make it. What's up Chloe Bear?" Frankie said as he high-fived Chloe.

"Not much Frankie; let's see what that bad boy can do," Chloe said as she jumped up and down cheering.

"Were about to find out, soon as Carl drives to the other end of the strip. Signal me with your arm when you are ready for the first run Carl."

"Got it," Carl replied.

Carl slid behind the steering wheel as Chloe plopped into the passenger seat.

"Get out Chloe; it's too dangerous."

"Nope, not budging an inch, just remember, I know what you supply my brother with. I'm sure my parents would find it quite interesting."

"Fine, suit yourself, but stay in the car when we get down there."

She smiled.

Carl drove to the other end of the marked strip, a quarter mile away; the pitch-black night engulfed him, his headlights shining across the highway, marking the finish line. Chloe stared out the window as the wipers squeaked back and forth in the light rain. Carl stood in the middle of the road, waving a red handkerchief back and forth, dropping it to the ground to signal Frankie's first run. The Chevelle's race engine roared to life, the tires burning rubber on the asphalt, trying to grip the road in the slick conditions. The car catapulted forward gaining speed as it closed the distance to the finish line. Frankie slammed the shifter from second to third gear and the car lurched sideways.

Chloe counted in her head: *seven, eight, nine, ten, eleven, twelve*; her thoughts stalled in time as she watched Frankie lose it as the Chevelle slid then tumbled over and over toward Carl.

"Run Carl!" Chloe screamed.

The Chevelle continued tumbling sideways straight at him, going airborne. One of the front wheels had broken off and was thrown above the car as it shot skyward. Chloe blinked her eyes the second the impact was imminent, knowing Carl would be crushed.

"Carl!" Chloe screamed again.

She pressed her face up against the windshield, and for a split second, she was sure she saw Audrey standing next to Carl, holding his hand. She blinked. They were gone. A loud bang shook the Nova rocking her back in the seat. Chloe looked across the road where the Chevelle landed twenty feet down the bank, taillights glowing red. Steam poured out of the crushed radiator and around the mashed car. Chloe gasped as she sucked air into her lungs again, her heartbeat pounding in her chest. Adrenaline shot through her body—energy Chloe did not need.

Chloe stumbled out of the car, fell, stumbled again, then was up on her feet as she sprinted over to the edge of the road where Frankie's car lay smashed but upright. Chloe slid down the muddy bank to the driver's door. She yanked on the door handle but it wouldn't budge. It was smashed in and the roof was crumpled down around the roll cage. She could smell gasoline. Fear struck her with the thought of an explosion. She had to move Frankie if he was still alive.

"Frankie, Frankie, are you ok?" She touched his shoulder and his head rolled over to one side, the helmet cocked sideways.

"—ahh shit, I just killed my cousin," he mumbled.

"No you didn't, I'm right here man."

Frankie and Chloe stared through the car and broken passenger window at Carl. Chloe breathed in and out deeply. Her chest throbbed.

Carl helped Chloe drag Frankie up the muddy bank to the roadway.

"Man, I screwed it this time; it was too slick. Drive me home man, we need to get the truck and trailer so I can get my car out of here before the cops come."

"Yeah, sure thing Frankie. Can we drop Chloe off first?"

"Sure."

"Are you okay?" Chloe squeaked.

"Yeah Chloe Bear, I'm alright," Frankie said while Chloe squeezed him hard, hugging him, tears streaming down her cheeks.

"Damn it Frankie—I thought you were dead—and you too Carl," she cried. She broke down and continued sobbing. Frankie held her.

The three of them drove back to Chloe's house, nobody speaking a word the whole way. Chloe was near comatose, shaking at the premonition and thought of Audrey standing in the road. The tears continued, her mascara streaked.

"Night Chloe," Frankie yelled as she ran inside. No reply.

Carl and Frankie spent the next hour pulling the car onto the flatbed trailer, neither of them talking. Carl followed his cousin, breaking off on a side street as Frankie continued into town. Carl's short drive up to Davis hill seemed to take forever, the event swirling in his head. Did he really cheat death? A split second before the car was going to hit him, he must have knelt down or run out of the way; he could not remember. The only thing running through his mind was the cold chill of an icy hand on his.

Carl walked past his mother, placing the partially burned cigarette into the ashtray. She had passed out mid burn, uncaring. Carl collapsed in his bed and stared at the ceiling and tried to sleep, but his thoughts raced through his head. First the lack of reflection in the pool, her icy hands around his neck, and later a car crash that should have killed him. Pure exhaustion knocked him out; Carl would not wake up until 4:30 the next afternoon. Driving across town to Audrey's house, he mulled over the crash and the dance months earlier. With no logical explanation, he put it out of his mind, his thoughts going back to the beautiful auburn hair and Audrey's smell that was similar to a sweet morning dew. That is what it reminded him of. *Yes he thought, he had finally put a finger on it.*

Carl pounded on her door, but the house was empty. Audrey's absence was a mystery to him. She was probably spending time with the girls. *Sure that's where she is,* he reasoned. She was most likely at Chloe's house.

Carl knocked over and over on Chloe and Pete's front door, the maid opening it minutes later.

"Yes," the maid asked.

"Is Pete here?"

"Come in young man, take your shoes off."

Carl had never seen such a home. They hadn't hung out for years. Now, it was clear to him that they were extremely wealthy.

“He’s in his room; it’s down the hallway, last door on the left,” she pointed, resuming her duties.

Carl stared at the fine art plying the walls. He couldn’t make sense out of the finger-painting style. It looked as though children had made them, although he understood they must have cost a small fortune by the way they were framed in fancy oak and cherry.

“Pete, it’s me. Carl,” he said, while knocking on the door.

“Hey butthead, come in here. Close the door. What the hell did you do to my sister man? And be straight with me, no bullshit. I know she was out with you and Audrey last night, but she's not talking.”

“About that—she was with me. We took Audrey home, then I wanted to drop her off and she wouldn’t let me.”

“Come on man, she’s only fifteen, just kick her ass out of the car next time.”

“It’s not that easy; she knows about us. I mean, she knows how you get the booze.”

“Dammit, that little sneak, now she’s going to tell Mom. I’m screwed man. Talk to her, see what she wants—you’re the guy that can get anything,” he paused. “Chloe is sneaky, she will use this to blackmail me for the rest of my life.”

“True story, but I don’t think she will talk to me after what happened last night.” Carl didn’t want to tell him about the crash.

“Carl, I’m getting a picture in my head that does not look good for you.”

Carl watched as Pete’s nostrils flared and his face turned red.

“Nothing like that happened man; it’s your sister,” Carl replied, holding his hand up. “I promised she would be okay, and she is.”

“Then why isn’t she talking?”

Carl took in a deep breath before telling him the whole story.

“—After the crash, she thought I was dead, until I came up on the other side of Frankie’s car and scared the shit out of both of them—didn’t mean to—it was like she saw a ghost or something.”

“Alright man, you’re cool. I won’t have to beat the shit out of you. Go talk to her; she’s in her room and hasn’t come out all day.”

“Sure thing.”

Carl opened the door and stepped into Chloe's room. She stared back at him wide eyed, barely acknowledging him.

"Chloe, you all right? Your brother is pretty worried about you, me too. I'm sorry I scared you last night. I really don't know what happened for a few seconds, except that I was alive."

He had never been in her room before, and now was not the time to be staring at her walls full of her own hand-drawn artwork. His eyes were drawn to a sketch of a raven just above her pillow. He looked back at her.

Her eyes blinked a few times, but she remained silent.

"Those are really cool drawings Chloe; you're very talented."

She broke her thousand-yard gaze. "You really think so?"

"Yes, for sure Chloe; they're great," he replied, trying to soften her up.

"You—you should be dead Carl; I saw it. I saw it happen."

"I know, but I'm here. It's going to be okay." Carl sat down on the bed next to her and could feel her legs trembling.

"She was there, next to you on the road, holding your hand—a split second before the crash, then you were both gone—I can't get her out of my mind. I close my eyes and she is there, holding onto you." Her voice was still shaky.

Carl could see she had not slept last night, her eyes were sunken and dark bags had formed underneath them."

"It's on constant rewind Carl—over and over," she gurgled. "It's unnatural—there is no explanation for what happened."

"What are you talking about?"

"Audrey was there. I don't know how, but she was there holding your hand. Are you listening to me Carl?" her voice pitched up.

Carl searched his thoughts for an explanation, something tangible he could hold onto, his mind racing back to the center of the road hours earlier and the icy grip on his hand seconds before the accident. He closed his eyes and was staring at Frankie's car flying at him; he couldn't bring his head sideways to look at who was holding his hand, pulling him out of the way. He knew it was her hand, feeling every line in her palm. It was the right size and shape and cold. Everything told him it was her; he was not ready to believe it. He couldn't believe it.

“I went by her house today and she wasn’t home. I thought she might be here with you or maybe at Lauren’s house.”

“She never came by, and Lauren doesn’t talk to us anymore,” Chloe croaked, her body shaking.

“You need to get some sleep Chloe, you look terrible.”

“Thanks a lot Carl,” she replied.

Chloe slipped from underneath the covers and walked up to the mirror on her vanity, staring at her reflection. She ran a brush through her hair.

“—No, you are right. I do look like shit.”

“Call Lauren, see if she is there,” Carl asked.

Chloe picked up the pink phone next to her bed and dialed her former friend, the phone ringing a dozen times before it was answered.

“Hello?” the voice on the other end said.

“Is Lauren there? it’s Chloe, I need to talk to her, it’s urgent.”

“She doesn’t want to talk right now Chloe; you’ll have to call back later.”

“Alright Mrs. Reddick would you tell her I called?”

“Will do dear. Bye.”

Chloe hung up the phone.

“I’m not lying Carl. I know what I saw and I know she was there last night—drive me over to Audrey’s house, I want to talk to her.”

“I just came from there; she’s not home Chloe.”

“Maybe she didn’t want to answer the door, that’s all.”

Carl did as he was told, afraid Chloe would drop the bomb, letting her parents in on Pete’s arrangement with him. A cold North wind blew across town, scattering the leaves, the slight drizzle of rain returning from the evening before. The house was dark as they drove up the driveway.

“I'm pretty sure that she is not home,” he groaned.

Chloe stepped onto the porch.

“You know Carl, it’s weird. I’ve never been invited over,” she said as they approached the door. “You knock; she's your girlfriend.”

Carl knocked on the door lightly.

"Harder, she might be in the back."

Carl balled his fist up and rapped on the door. Chloe tried the handle. The door opened, creaking as it swung on the rusty hinges, the cool damp air hitting them both in the face.

"Audrey, are you home? It's Chloe," she yelled into the house.

Chloe pushed Carl in the back, shoving him through the front door into the parlor.

"Aud, it's Carl. Are you here?" Carl's knees trembled, the cool damp air chilling him to the bone.

"See, she's not home, can we go now?"

"Carl, you chicken shit; I'm going upstairs to see if she's in bed; maybe she's sick?"

"Chloe, I think we should leave. This place freaks me out now. I mean it is strange; how can she live in a place with no heat? Can't you feel how bone-chilling cold it is in here? It is like a coffin."

The second he said it, he realized how the home had felt before, but had put it out of his mind, now he wished he could take back his words. *Like a coffin.* Three short words that held a grisly meaning.

"Stay close to me," Chloe said as she grabbed Carl's hand, leading him up the stairs.

"Sure thing."

The stairs creaked underfoot as they climbed to the second floor, Chloe sticking her nose around the corner down the empty hallway to Audrey's bedroom.

"It's down there, last door on the left," Carl said, pointing over her shoulder.

He prodded her forward.

"Don't push me."

"Sorry."

Chloe's grip tightened, her heartbeat galloping as they approached the door hand in hand.

"I can't open it," she said as she let go of the door handle.

"Is it locked?" Carl asked.

"No—just—uhm…I'm not sure about doing this."

Carl grasped the nob and slowly turned it. The door swung open with a firm push, her bed empty.

"Nobody here—we can go now," Chloe said as she spun on her heels, dragging Carl behind her down the stairs and across the yard.

Chloe scrambled into the car, slamming the door. Carl paused as he walked around the front of the car, then looked back at the upstairs window to Audrey's room. It was just a fleeting glance, a simple motion that crossed his peripheral vision. He was sure he saw her pass in front of the window. Carl slid behind the wheel and cranked the engine over, the heater fan slowly ticking away as cool air hit them.

"Tell me what you know Carl. I know you know something; I've got to know."

Carl knew he had to tell her everything he had seen, felt, dreamed, but up until now, he wasn't prepared to fully believe it himself.

"I don't know, I mean, she…she is nice to me, the first girl ever to treat me like that."

"Carl, the house is weird; look at all those things in there. Where did she get all those things?"

"They were delivered the other day when I picked her up; she said she owned the whole place, by herself."

"Carl, there is something strange going on here!"

"Maybe she is just out of town for the weekend Chloe?"

"We'll see on Monday when we go back to school. If she shows up, I'll put her on the spot."

His head was full of resignation but Carl decided to hold back on his suspicions. He knew Chloe had had a rough enough time the last twelve hours, and he was not sure she could handle any more stress.

"I'm going to take you home."

"No, take me over to Lauren's, we need to talk to her."

"Okay but I'm pretty sure she won't talk to us."

Carl drove Chloe across town to see Lauren. The home was just two blocks to the east of the high school in an upscale neighborhood built in the late 1950s, when the single story rambler was king. Carl's stomach churned as they pulled up in front of the home. He hadn't been back there since the party.

"I don't know if I should go in," Carl said, his hands shaking.

"You don't have to go in Carl; I know you hate her guts. I can't blame you either; she never treated you very nice."

"It's all right, I should talk to her, or at least hear what she has to say."

Inside the home, Lauren's mother ushered them back to her daughter's bedroom.

"Lauren your friends are here to see you," she said through the closed door.

"You kids go in. She's in bed, not sure she want's to talk, but it will be good for her to have visitors," she added before disappearing down the hall.

"Thanks Mrs. R," Chloe chirped.

"You're welcome dear…" floated out of the kitchen.

Chloe pushed the door open and Carl looked over her shoulder at the lump in the bed, Lauren's face under the covers.

Chloe sat on the bed next to Lauren then shook her.

"Talk to me Lauren. I know you know something about Audrey," Chloe said as she looked at Carl, shrugging her shoulders.

"Tell her about last night. Tell her what you saw in front of my car."

Chloe took a deep breath.

"Lauren, last night I went out to the strip to watch Frankie run his car. Right before he hit the finish line, he crashed."

"Is he okay?" Lauren's voice came muffled from underneath the covers, her face poking out.

"Yeah, he's good, not even a scratch. That's not what I'm talking about though. Last night, in the road, Carl was waiting with his stopwatch at the finish line. When Frankie crashed, he rolled the car right on top of Carl. At least where he was standing."

Lauren stared at Carl, wrinkling an eyebrow.

"Audrey was right next to him, holding his hand, then they both disappeared. I watched it happen from Carl's car."

Lauren's body trembled as she sat up.

"Are you okay?" Carl asked.

"Last year at the dance, in the bathroom, when Audrey was braiding your hair, I was in the stall and watched her pass in front of the mirror. She wasn't there, in the mirror—she cast no reflection. I looked through the crack between the door and the edge of the stall, all I saw was you Chloe; remember when I told you what she was? Remember our talk in the library? You have to believe me, I'm not a freak; I'm just scared."

"I remember," Chloe replied.

Inside the small bedroom, it felt like all the air was sucked out at once. Goosebumps covered their bodies.

"What is she?" Carl asked.

"I don't know Carl; whatever she is, she is not from this world, at least not now. When was the last time you saw her?" Lauren snapped.

"We dropped her off at her house last night. Then Chloe and I went out to the strip. We just came from her house and she wasn't there."

"Take me out there Carl. I want to see for myself."

"Sure Lauren, but I'm getting Frankie...If he is feeling okay from the crash."

The group drove across town, picking Frankie up—backup for whatever they thought they were going to find. Crossing the low bridge just down the road from Audrey's ranch, the foursome held their breath as they viewed the house in the distance. Fading sunlight bathed the front porch in an orange glow.

The tinkling of the piano drifted onto the porch as the teens approached nervously. The latch yielding to his gentle turn as Carl's friends followed him inside the home. Audrey continued playing with indifference, her back to them.

"Audrey, you okay?" Chloe said as she walked up behind her.

She played on for another two minutes, Frankie grabbing a seat behind her on the couch. Chloe turned to look at her friends and shrugged her shoulders. The air in the room was palpable. The teens waiting to see what would happen.

“You were there last night Audrey. I saw you in the road standing next to Carl. You were holding his hand, then you were gone,” Chloe said softly.

Chloe's statement and Audrey spinning around on the piano bench startled Lauren; she grabbed Frankie’s hand.

“Things are not always what they seem. Do not be afraid,” she said, her face withdrawn, rugged but still beautiful. “Times have changed for me; people have not. It is always the same when they find out; you will react in the same way.”

“Audrey, what are you talking about? That doesn't make any sense,” Frankie said.

“You have come back…from where, I don’t know, but you've returned, haven't you?” Lauren spat.

“You are right Lauren; I have come back. It has been a long time since I was here before. Decades ago, long before any of you were alive, long before your parents. It was a simple time back then, but even then, people were afraid of what they did not understand.”

Her words sent chills up the girl’s spines. Carl had not moved from his spot near the doorway. He was comatose.

“What are you?” Lauren said, pressing her for more. “Are you a revenant?”

“I am the one that comes before the end; the one that guides those that need it. Many souls have wanted to stay behind; those are the ones I am here for. You have nothing to fear by being here or around me.”

“You really are—or were—dead,” Lauren replied to the chagrin of Chloe.

“Death is only the beginning…” Audrey said as she rose from the bench and moved toward Lauren.

Lauren stood up and walked backward one foot at a time, keeping her eyes on Audrey as she groped for the door behind her.

"I could kill you all right now," Audrey whispered.

Her words drifted around the teens’ ears, galvanizing them. Carl twisted the door knob but it would not turn. It was jammed.

"But that would not serve my purpose," she continued while moving around the back of the couch where Frankie and Chloe were seated together, placing her arms around Chloe's neck, hugging her.

"Besides which, I love you guys—especially you Chloe."

Chloe turned her head to the right to look at Audrey's face. Audrey moved around the end of the couch, taking a seat on the arm next to Frankie. Lauren tried the door knob, twisting it left then right, then gave up when she realized it was no use.

"The question is, what are you going to do now that you know what I am?" Audrey flipped her hair to one side with her hand.

"I want to go; let me out of here," Lauren pleaded.

"The door is open. All you have to do is walk out," Audrey replied, pointing at the door as it swung open a few inches. A cool breeze brushed across Lauren's face. Lauren reached for the door and was about to leave when Audrey spoke again.

"If you leave, you can't come back here—ever. Do you understand me? I can't associate with those that don't accept who I am."

Lauren turned to face her. "Why us? Why now?"

"I'm drawn to this place and this time, and one of you," Audrey replied.

Audrey walked around the room, lifting up a few objects at random: an antique pistol on a table, a hairbrush with an ivory handle. "I've been around for centuries; some would call me a ghost, others an apparition, and others would pursue me until the end."

"Are you an angel of death?" Chloe spat out before she could stop herself—silence from the others, their eyes pleading with her not to say it. She could see Carl mouthing the word *No* to her. She covered her mouth with her hand. It was the only way she could keep herself from talking.

"Some would call me that, usually those that don't understand. In the old world, we were called Abaddon or Apollyon; it is the same no matter the language you say it in."

"Audrey, I don't care what you are, just stay with us. Be my friend at school. I need you now more than ever."

"Chloe, it won't be that simple; you know what I am. They say for two people to be able to keep a secret, one of them has to be dead. There will be no way you all will be able to keep me a secret, then it will happen again: they will come for me, and the ending will be the same."

“But you can come back, right?”

“Yes, in time. It never happens the same way Frankie.”

“I won’t tell anyone Audrey. I love you and I know you love me,” Carl said.

“I know Carl. You are the reason I have stayed here this long. You are the kindest person I have ever met—the most innocent too.”

“How old are you?” It was a question they all wanted to ask, especially Carl, but only Lauren had the guts to pose it.

“I was born in the year 1241, in Poland, the same year that the Mongols invaded from the Volga in Russia.”

“That’s over 700 years ago,” Frankie spat out, his math off just a bit.

“Seven hundred and forty four, Frankie,” she replied, sending a chill up their spines.

“So you were not going to tell me that I have been dating an older woman all this time?” Carl said in anger.

“Dude you've been dating an older woman!" Frankie laughed.

"Very funny Frankie," Carl said, frowning, then turning his gaze back to Audrey.

“I tried to Carl, believe me, I tried, but there was never a good time.”

“Right on Carl; finally, something that is cooler than hell,” Frankie said, laughing out loud.

"Shut up Frankie," Chloe barked. "I'm still freaked out, but am okay with her being who she is."

Lauren ran outside and Carl chased after her.

"Lauren, wait up," he yelled, grabbing her shoulder as she yanked on the car door handle.

"Let go of me," she grumbled, spinning around to face him. Audrey was silhouetted in the open doorway behind them. "I can't do this, I can’t—”

Carl held up his hand. "Please Lauren—you have too. I love her too much to let her go. Besides, what's the worst that can happen?"

"She can kill us, that's what."

"No, I don't think so. If she was going to do that, we’d be dead already.”

Audrey walked down the steps and up to the two teens.

"Come back inside; it will be all right," she said, motioning for them to follow her. Audrey turned to walk back to the house, then looked back at Lauren.

"Come," she said, turning to walk away as they followed.

Audrey waited for Carl and Lauren before speaking.

“None of you can speak of what I have told you; none of you can talk about this outside this house.”

They all nodded their heads in unison.

“I’m not saying a word—ever.” Chloe broke the silence as she ran up to her friend, throwing her arms around her.

“I know Chloe—I’ve always known you would never betray me,” Audrey replied.

“Me neither—” Frankie added.

“I’m with you—babe,” Carl laughed, “—especially since I’m dating an older woman.”

“Lauren?” Audrey looked directly at the last to comply. “—are you with me? Or?”

“—I guess,” Lauren said, shifting nervously in the chair where she was seated. “Yeah, I’m fine.”

Summer came and went, and Audrey turned another year older, enjoying her time with the group of friends she trusted. She was happy they had accepted her. The events of that summer unfolded as she expected, her knowledge of things to come a premonition. That summer was one of the hottest on record, the temperatures soaring into the triple digits for weeks on end, nearly twenty degrees above average. It was the year when every teen in town abandoned the swimming pool for the cold water in the river just north of downtown.

Pete still had no knowledge of what was going on, nor what she was. The heat had pulled the kids to the bend in the river. Dozens of teens crowded the riverbank that gently sloped into the water, the rope swing a popular destination. As the teens would swing out above the water, they would arch their backs, trying to gain the most altitude before they let go, cannonballing into the sixty-two-degree water below.

Pete grabbed the rope as he waved to his friends on the bank, elevating their applause for him to do something a bit more risky than the last guy. Pete ran down the bank and swung out over the river, letting go of the rope early, plunging him into a shallow spot, head first straight to the bottom. The dull thud of his head striking a rock underwater was not heard above; a full minute passed by before Carl jumped in to drag Pete out. It was not the first time Pete had pulled the prank on his friends; even as Carl carried him up the river bank, laying him on the dirt, they still thought he was faking.

"He's not breathing," Carl shouted.

"Do something Audrey," Chloe cried.

Audrey leaned down next to him and touched his forehead. Pete gasped for air, spitting water out of his mouth, his eyes staring directly into Audrey's. Chloe hugged her brother and nearly squeezed the life back out of him.

"My head frigging hurts." The welt had already started to build on Pete's forehead.

"It should you big ass; you hit it on a rock," Chloe yelled.

"I'm sorry sis, I'm sorry."

Chloe looked over at Audrey, their eyes locked. She had not done anything, nor would it have been in her power—something she could not tell her friend now. Chloe believed Audrey had saved her brother. He had survived on his own, his will to live too great, robbing the grave again. They didn't return to that spot in the river all summer.

Carl spent more time with Audrey and less time at home, staying many nights at the ranch house in the valley.

Their love for each other grew enormously. Audrey was someone he thought unachievable, a beautiful smart precocious young lady, although she had a past like no one else. She was that one girl in school nobody had dared to approach except for Carl when he saw her again in the hallway.

Mona would visit on Sundays, still enamored with Audrey, excited for her cousin and his girlfriend, but still unaware of her true identity. Mona also was happy to spend extra time around Chloe.

Audrey and Carl spent their days alone, usually taking in the afternoon sun on top of the hill behind the house. The small meadow was the perfect spot for their picnics. She was caring to him, letting him mature at his own pace, a quality she enjoyed seeing as he developed into a man. He was completely and utterly head over heels in love with her, his concern for her true self never again coming up. Holding her in his arms that afternoon, Audrey talked for hours about her past experiences, good and bad: the relentless pursuit of her in the seventeen hundreds, the superstitious Europeans chasing her across the countryside, town after town, eventually capturing her and torturing her to death—another grisly ending. Carl could not imagine the horrors that had befell her, his sadness at her stories getting the best of him, his tears dropping off his face onto her forehead.

“It’s okay Carl. I’m not leaving you any time soon.”

"Good, because I'm not letting you go either," he replied.

29

SUMMER CRUISING WAS IN FULL swing, the gas gauge of Carl's car hitting empty twice a night. Audrey footed the bill when he would stop at the corner store. Jackpot gas and grocery was the one gathering place in town where ten guys could line up their muscle cars, pop open the hoods, and brag. It was also the first time Audrey had heard the story of Pickled Willie.

"Hey Audrey, are you going out to Pickled Willie's grave with us tomorrow?" Frankie asked.

"What's that?" Audrey replied, her eyebrows arched high above her eyes.

"Well, a long time ago, this family was traveling out to Washington by wagon train, you know, pioneer stuff and all. Anyway, this dude's son always wanted to see the Pacific Ocean. Not too long into the trip, the kid dies. But before he kicks the bucket, he has his dad promise to take him all the way to the ocean."

"It's more technical than that Frankie; tell it right. It's her first time to hear it," Carl said.

"In the mid eighteen hundreds," Frankie said, restarting, "a father and son were destined to make the trip from Missouri to Oregon by wagon train. Just days after their departure, the son, Willie, died of malaria. Keeping his promise to bring his son out to Washington no matter what, the father fixed a coffin, lined it with lead, and poured in gallons of whiskey to preserve the body for the long trip ahead. They buried him near Raymond. That's a town west of Chehalis. His grave is the Mecca for high schoolers during their senior year. Seniors have been doing that trip for decades."

"Reallly? Are you pulling my leg?" Audrey asked after he finished his long story.

"No, not at all Aud, that's the truth. Like I was saying, the kid dies somewhere out in the Midwest, maybe Kansas or some other cornfield state, and they haul him all the way out here, burying him west of Adna." Frankie smiled, adding in, "Pickled in whiskey. How cool is that?"

"Wouldn't the body get stinky after months of traveling?" Audrey asked. She smiled.

"Audrey, are you listening to me? He was soaking up all that whiskey—floating around for a couple of months—the body was preserved and probably smelled like Jack Daniels."

"It sounds interesting. What time are we going Carl?" Audrey hugged her boyfriend around the chest as she looked up into his eyes.

"Noon? Sound good Frankie?" Carl did not want to get up too early; the night was still young, and he had a few more rounds of cruising left in him.

"That sounds great, pick me up," Frankie said. "My car is still in pieces."

Chloe was inside the store picking up some red vines and had missed the whole story, although she had heard it many times before. Frankie yelled to her as soon as she exited.

"Hey Chloe Bear, you going with us to Pickled Willie's tomorrow?"

"Hell yeah, when we leaving?" she said jumping up and down a few times, the red vine flopping around in her mouth.

"Noon, we'll pick you up on the way to get Frankie," Audrey laughed as she said it, obviously amused by the prospect of going to visit a grave.

Audrey and Carl cruised around town for another two hours, closing down the strip, the last few cars driving past them as they left on their way out to Audrey's house.

The next morning, Chloe stood on the front porch, next to Pete. Pete could not stand that the group was going out to visit Pickled Willie's grave without him.

“Hey Carl. Chloe said we’re going out to Pickled Willie’s Grave, mind if I come with?” Pete said, frowning at Audrey as he leaned down to look through the window of the car.

“Sure, hop in.”

Pete was too big to get in the back seat with Chloe; his knees would have been shoved up into his face if he did, opting to sit next to Audrey in the front.

“Morning Audrey. Killed anyone lately?” he asked.

“Good morning Pete,” Audrey replied. “—and no, not today, just killing them with my good looks."

"Ha ha, funny Pete, funny,” Carl laughed unconvincingly.

“I just talked to Frankie on the phone, told him we would be there to pick him up in ten minutes,” Chloe chirped, her voice deafening Carl as she rambled.

Chloe chattered on as they drove through Logan district into town. Her voice dominated the confines of the car as she incessantly rattled on about the latest romance novel she had finished the evening before.

“What’s it about?” Audrey asked.

“This guy that has a vampire living next door to him,” she replied. “And he has gargels that protect him in the daytime. They live in the attic.”

“They’re called gargoyles Chloe,” Carl said, correcting her slang.

“That’s what I said gar-gels,” she replied, annunciating her word.

Carl laughed and Audrey elbowed him.

“I can’t help it. I had a lisp when I was younger. I still can’t say it right.”

“It’s cute the way you say it Chloe,” Audrey replied.

Carl laid on the horn as he pulled up in front of Frankie’s house. The blinds shifted sideways, Frankie’s nose poking through. Pete stepped out of the car to let Frankie into the backseat as he tilted the seat forward.

“Hey Chloe Bear,” Frankie said while hugging his friend.

“*Frankeee*,” she squeaked as he squeezed her.

Carl drove south on interstate five, searching the road sign for route six, spotting it a few minutes later south of Chehalis. Turning west onto route six, Carl pushed the car up to sixty-five miles per hour, ten faster than the posted speed. The two-lane country road meandered to the left miles ahead of them as the Nova passed multiple farms. The fields were muddy and the remnants of dried cornstalks jutted out of the ground like scarecrows.

"I need a can of chew, stop at the gas station in Adna," Frankie said as he groped his pockets.

"Damn it Frankie, we just got on the road." Carl was sure this trip would take all day if they kept stopping.

"I need to go to the bathroom," Chloe piped in. "Me too," Audrey said.

It always worked that way. One girl said she had to pee and the other immediately got the twinge to pee as well.

"All right, I'll stop, but then we are heading all the way to the grave—no more stopping. No cans of chew and—*NOOO PEEING.*"

"It's not my fault I have to pee—I have a tiny bladder," Chloe snickered.

Frankie cut up laughing, and the snorts shot out of him like a machine gun. That was all it took to get the whole group, including Carl, into a fit of madness as they let loose with uncontrollable giggles and belly-wrenching laughter.

Adna was a hole in the wall burg just west of Chehalis that had never grown up. The town was lucky to have an operating gas station, and to their credit, the high school football team was good for the small school and limited talent pool. At the gas station, Carl waited behind the wheel as the others attended to their needs. It was one of those pull offs next to the highway where everyone stopped. Today was no different, with two cars at the single pump and three rusty pickups parked in front of the convenience store: hunters likely stopping to refill their coolers with beer or the occasional farm kid taking dad's truck without permission.

Chloe brushed past a couple of high school boys next to the coolers, accidentally stumbling as she elbowed a young man in the side.

“Watch it shorty.” He was a rough-looking farm boy. Owner of said pickup in front. Hand-me-down from dad, three payments left. No interest for family.

“Who are you calling shorty?” Chloe barked, arms crossed, chest pushed out.

"How ‘bout you and I get together sometime?" the farm boy said while moving forward, grabbing Chloe's butt as he pulled her into his body."

"Pete. Pete!" Chloe screamed.

"What the hell is going on here," Pete said as he towered over the two farm boys.

"Nothing," the farm boys replied simultaneously.

"This guy grabbed my ass," Chloe replied, pointing at the young guy closest to her.

"Nobody touches my sister," Pete said as his fist rocketed toward its target. His knuckles made contact, melding to the boy’s face. The farm boy crumpled like a sack of potatoes.

"You broke my nose," he yelped, blood pouring out of his hands as he writhed on the floor.

The other boy grabbed Pete around the neck, putting him in a wrestling hold. Pete threw an elbow into his chest and a loud *pfft* exited the guy’s lips.

"You guys owe my sister an apology," Pete said, standing over top of them.

"Screw you man," the bloody-nosed kid spat.

Pete swung his right foot back and was ready to punt the guy across the store when Chloe pushed past him, raised her foot in the air, and brought it down on the bloody nosed boy’s groin.

"*Oouch!"* he yelled, grabbing his jewels.

The other farm boy had made it to his knees and lifted his head to look at Chloe. She stared down at him.

"Well?" she asked.

"Well what you bi—*oophh*,” he gasped as foot impacted his gut.

“You okay, sis?” Pete said as he placed his arm around Chloe, walking her outside to the car.

“Yeah.”

Frankie and Audrey ran out a few minutes later. "What happened to those guys in there? Somebody messed them up," Frankie asked, pointing at the store.

"Time to go Carl, kick this thing in the ass," Pete yelled. "Don't want to be here if and when the coppers get here."

"Next time you are going to roll someone, give me a call. I haven't had any action for months," Frankie replied, chuckling.

"It was nothing Frankie, just a quick tiff with some assholes," Pete replied.

Audrey had joined Chloe in the back seat, and the pair chatted away as the car pulled back on the two-lane highway.

Highway six was curvy, winding in and out of the hills past Adna, and through the smaller logging towns of PeEll, Doty, Dryad, and Menlo to name a few. Their trip took another forty-five minutes to the grave site. Pete had planned ahead as he produced the fifth of whiskey that was tucked inside his jacket. The teens stood in silent reverence as Pete raised the bottle.

"To Pickled Willie, may we never meet, a friend from beyond this world. I toast you my frothy pickled friend." He raised the bottle, took a swig, then passed it to Frankie.

Frankie coughed. "That's good," he said, then handed it down the line, the others taking their turn. Carl turned the bottle upside down on top of the grave, giving Willie the last drink, emptying the bottle.

"Well, now what the hell we going to do. It's only two o'clock."

"That is a good question Carl," Pete replied. Carl knew his friend was already planning something by the look on his face.

"Rainbow Falls." It was too cold to go swimming in the river at Rainbow Falls Park, but Pete did not have that in mind when he suggested it. Pete was still a risk taker, always trying something hair brained, his radar for danger broken.

"I'm not going swimming; it's too cold out," Chloe snapped. "You probably want us to jump off the bridge, don't you?" Pete grinned at his sister's reply.

"Rainbow Falls, here we come," Pete yelled. Carl shook his head back and forth.

Carl pulled the car off the road just past the sign to Rainbow Falls State Park. Pete scrambled out of the car and was standing on top of the bridge, stripped down to his underwear, daring the group to follow his lead before they knew it. “I jump, you jump. Come on you wimps,” he taunted.

"Are you crazy Pete, that water is forty-eight degrees," Frankie said.

"Nah man, closer to fifty-five. Besides, I will be in and out before I get cold."

"Whatever man, I'm not going in after you," Frankie said, crossing his arms.

Rainbow Falls had taken more than a dozen teens to an early grave, the pool under the bridge swirling with undercurrents, jagged rocks on the edges; the only point of entry was directly in the middle of the river. It was a sure way to kill yourself in the summer, let alone on a cool day with high water from the recent rains.

“Get down Pete. I’m going to tell Mom you if you don’t.”

“No you won’t,” he said mid leap, everyone leaning out over the bridge. Pete cannonballed. He hit the water hard and it swallowed him up as he disappeared into the depths.

“Where is he?” Carl said as he looked around the pool of water, searching frantically.

Frankie watched the second hand go around his watch, counting one minute out loud. Then two minutes twenty seconds.

"Where is he?" Chloe said as she ran up and down the bridge, searching for her brother.

Frankie was still timing him, knowing Pete could stay underwater for a full three minutes. It was four minutes now and still no sign.

“Go in Frankie, please,” Chloe cried.

Frankie stripped down to his underwear, then slid down the bank into the water just downstream from where Pete disappeared. Frankie dove down, groping around in the murky water, feeling his way around the bottom. Breaking the surface, he sucked in another breath and disappeared down to the bottom again. The rocks were slimy from algae growth. He surfaced, then dove down again, swinging his arms around in wide arcs.

30

MORE THAN SIX HUNDRED STUDENTS and their parents, aunts, uncles, and grandparents attended Pete's memorial service that next Friday. The high school was shut down. The crowd packed out the football stands. It was a solemn event, a first for many, having never known anyone that young who had died, nor ever attending a service. There was not a dry eye in the house as Chloe spoke about her brother through her sobs, choking up halfway through her speech. She described a side of her brother that most people had never seen before, and his compassion for his little sister, finishing off her speech with his crazy streak, playing as hard as he could at life as he did during the many football games over the past four years in school. She couldn't believe he was gone, even standing in front of a huge crowd; the realization she would never see him again was more than she was willing to accept. It was a time in her life that she needed him the most. He was taken from her too early. Their parents would never be the same afterward, hardly paying much attention to their surviving daughter.

A few teachers spoke of Pete's good humor and how they would forever miss his antics during the school pep rallies, showing up in the tiger-printed spandex, whooping the students up into a frenzy before the games.

Mr. Hollings had the most elegant speech prepared, handwritten on college-ruled single sheets of paper. “A few short years ago I met Pete Chambers during his freshman year. I could immediately tell this young man had high potential and would be crucial to the fabric of our student life in our school. Pete was a gentle, kind soul, wrapped up in a Paul Bunyon bigger-than-life package. He truly was one of a kind, treating others around him as equals or better than himself. I could see that early on as I watched his interaction with his peers and fellow teammates. On or off the field, he excelled and always strived for excellence. He was a good egg.” Mr. Hollings struggled to keep it together, choking up, as he stumbled through the final sentence. “And I will miss his smiling face and morning greetings—most of all his simple; Hey Mr. H. How’s it hanging?” Mr. Hollings dried his eyes off with his white handkerchief, snuffing his nose as he left the podium.

Weather in Washington can either be crappy or somewhat crappy, there is no in between; fortunately for the crowd sitting in the half-open stands that day, the sun came out briefly, the rain stopped, and the usually dismal grey overcast sky shined bright as the sun pushed through the clouds. It was a perfect moment the priest capitalized on during his speech. He explained how there was always a bit of sunshine and God’s plan was not always immediately realized or known.

Forty-five minutes had elapsed since the start, and most of the crowd had run out of tears in the first thirty minutes, Carl included. He had lost a childhood friend and did not know how he would be able to face Chloe from now on. Pete had always been stronger than him, a fact that Carl understood and did not seem to mind, though they had not been close for the past few years. Audrey held Carl’s hand tight, her way of telling him it would be all right. Not a single tear would roll down her face that day, and Carl wondered if there were something more that she knew or if it were just a cruel twist of fate, despite who she was. At the end of the prayer, the priest invited the close friends, football team, and family over to the Chambers’ home for a potluck immediately following the service.

Carl could tell that it was tough on Pete’s parents, coming to grips with the loss, without being able to lay his body to rest. Mr. Chambers had the monument company fashion a triangular shaped black marble headstone, placing it in Mt. View Cemetery. Musical notes and a football were carved into the stone, two of Pete's favorite activities. Frankie beat himself up over the whole event, questioning himself whether Pete would still be alive if he had stopped him from jumping. Frankie would run the day over and over in his head, rewinding the scene of Pete standing on the bridge ready to jump. His nights would be sleepless for many weeks.

Chloe milled around her relatives, nearly comatose as they worked their way through the line, paper plates in hand spooning up the regular funeral bean concoction and fried chicken delivered from the local grocery store chain where Pete had worked part time as a bagger. It was the first time that Carl and Audrey had seen Chloe's parents together; their blank faces and bloodshot eyes spoke volumes. Carl knew he had to say something to Mr. Chambers, but had never had any experience talking to a living relative of a dead friend. Summoning his courage, he left Audrey in a side room as he approached Mr. Chambers, who was seated on a couch in the middle of his family.

"Mr. Chambers, it's Carl." The words were hard to push up through his throat and out of his mouth. "I just w-wanted to tell you that—" Mr. Chambers interrupted him as he flew off the couch and into his face.

"Don't you even start Carl Newkirk. You should have stopped him. Don't ever tell me you are sorry. That will never bring my son back you son of a bitch."

He had let it fly, and Carl took it in silence, stunned. Mr. Chambers had always treated him like he was family, never questioning if he should stay for dinner or if he had money to go to the movies with them. Mr. Chambers always provided for him, knowing his family had limited means. The house had fallen into a hush; it was so quiet that you could have heard a mouse fart three blocks away.

"Daddy, it wasn't his fault; nobody could have stopped him. Pete would not listen to anyone that day." Chloe's words fell on deaf ears. Mr. Chambers stood his ground glaring at Carl, his face beet red.

"Carl, get the hell out of my house," Mr. Chamber's yelled.

Nobody dared say a word.

"Don't yell at him; it's not Carl's fault, we all miss Pete," Chloe sobbed.

"Come on Carl." Audrey's words were soft but firm and said loud enough to show disdain for how Mr. Chambers had treated one of Pete's best friends. Audrey pushed her way through the crowd as she led Carl outside and right into the midst of the football team.

"So Carl, thought you could stop by and smooth things over with the family huh," Tommy said as he stepped in front of them, blocking their exit.

"Get out of the way Tommy," she growled, tightening her grip on Carl's hand.

"Were not finished with this Newkirk, or with your bitch either." Tommy's words were laced with fire but had no effect on Audrey. Carl was still stunned by Mr. Chambers' tirade, and he had no reply ready for Tommy.

"Move out of the way Tommy, or so help me," Audrey said, her voice lower, menacing. It was enough to wise up a few of the other football players as they pulled Tommy back, letting Carl and Audrey go.

"Audrey, Carl, wait up." Chloe ran after them, catching them before they drove off.

"I'm sorry Carl."

He stepped out of the car, and hugged her as the young girl bawled openly.

"Can I go with you guys?" she sobbed.

"Chloe, you will always be our friend. Of course you can come with us," Carl said as he let her slide through his door across the seat next to Audrey. Audrey had finally let a few tears loose. None of the day's events really bothered her until Mr. Chambers blamed Pete's death on Carl. Chloe buried her head into Audrey's chest as Carl drove off, leaving the family to mourn among themselves.

The rains had returned, graying the sky, and the sunset was missing as darkness fell. Carl could not remember the last time he felt this bad, nor did he know where they were going. The normal routine of cruisers had already lined up at the Jackpot corner grocery store as they rolled past on their way into town. He didn't notice the cars. Nothing seemed to matter now, nor did he care about the things he thought were so important before. Time had stopped for the teens; their train had derailed.

"Let's go home Carl; I'm tired and Chloe needs her rest."

Carl steered the car out of town and through the valley to the ranch house, the large trees stretching over the two-lane country road, reaching their limbs out at the car as they drove underneath, the leaves blowing up behind the car.

Chloe stayed the night, sleeping on the couch downstairs in front of the fire, Audrey covering her up with a large hand-sewn quilt. She would come back to stay with them week after week, her routine of fighting with her parents, crying, then being consoled by Audrey repeated day after day. She knew she had a place with Audrey if she needed it but was trying to keep it together for her parents, who had all but gave up on life. The Chambers' walked around inside their house as though they were zombies, their demeanor less than cordial to the only living child they had left. Frankie visited a few times and came to grips with Pete's death. He was relieved when Chloe hugged him for the first time since the funeral.

31

MONA, CARL, LAUREN, AND AUDREY all gathered at Frankie's house for the end of summer party. It was the first time the group had all come together since Pete's death. Frankie's mom was a hit with the teenagers; everyone loved her wit. Frankie and Lauren had started dating shortly after Pete had passed away. She never called him Greasy Frank again, he calling her by her nickname every chance he got. It was catchy, the rest of the group following suit. Slim stuck with her for the rest of her life. Mona, however, was still an outsider, not privy to Audrey's secret. It was something the group never talked about again that summer. She belonged with them; they loved her more than ever now.

"Hey Audrey, are you getting your driver's license?"

"No Chloe, I don't think so. Carl can drive me around. I've seen most everything."

"That's true, you can ride with me when I pass drivers education next month too."

"I'll take you up on that Chloe. Carl may not always be around to take me places, and I can regale you about years past, sleigh rides in the snow, the dark days in Europe. You know, important milestones in history," Audrey replied, smiling at her protégé.

"I would love to hear about the sleigh ride and horses—you can keep the history tour," Chloe said. Audrey chuckled.

Mona seemed lost at the conversation, not really understanding the underlying meaning in their words, but she was good at figuring riddles out. She was a whiz at crosswords and a library of knowledge when it came to history. She unknowingly was sitting next to a huge resource of history that was gained firsthand. It was something she would have to wait to tap into. They had also put the Tuesday night party at the theater on hold after Pete's death, nobody wanting to come around with the thought of him not being there to liven the place up. It was too much to accept.

Across the patio, Frankie could not keep his hands off Lauren, their relationship a tumultuous affair. One minute they were kissing passionately, the next minute a slapstick comedy, she slugging him in the shoulder just to hear him scream out loud.

"I would love to hear about the history of Europe Audrey, I had no idea you knew so much about it," Mona quipped.

"In due time Mona, I would love to tell you," Audrey replied.

Chloe stood up and reached for the screen door leading into the kitchen.

"Does anyone want anything—I need to pee—will get it for you after?"

"No, I'm fine," Carl responded, Frankie and Audrey shook their heads.

Chloe slipped inside and was only gone a minute when Mona excused herself from the porch, the screen door rattling as it slammed shut. She moved through the kitchen, turned down an adjacent hallway, and ran smack into Chloe. Their bodies intermingled, meshed together in their short shorts and tank tops. Mona slipped her hand around the back of Chloe's neck, pulling their faces together in a warm embrace as the two mouths interlocked in a passionate kiss. Chloe didn't resist for almost a minute, then pulled her face backward, Mona's hand still holding the back of her neck.

"Wait a minute—we can't—" Chloe said, shocked, cutoff when Mona pulled their faces together again, the second kiss lingering for a few more minutes.

"Somebody will see us," Chloe whispered.

“Let them,” Mona replied, pressing her face into Chloe’s again. They held the embrace for another minute.

“Hey, where are you gals, the party is outside,” Frankie yelled as the screen door slammed shut behind him.

“Were right here,” Mona yelled back, stealing another kiss from Chloe as Frankie rounded the corner into the hallway.

“Hey what are you up to?” Frankie asked, catching Mona still holding Chloe.

“Uhh, Chloe’s got something in her eye. I’m trying to see what it is,” Mona replied, while Chloe played along, tilting her head back.

“Let me see,” Frankie said.

Frankie pulled out his penlight he used for inspecting carburetors and the dark confines under the dash of his car. He shined it into Chloe’s right eye.

“Can’t see anything,” he replied.

Chloe blinked a few times. “Must have been nothing, maybe a hair—feels okay now.”

The party ended late that evening, Chloe and Mona exchanging curious glances across the fire pit at each other throughout the night. They didn’t speak about it—not to each other, nor anyone else. A few weeks passed by, Chloe sneaking into the theater often to visit her new friend, the two of them disappearing into the dark of the projection booth where nobody could see their actions. They had met up nearly every day since the party and were at the theater one Tuesday night as their group of friends assembled for an after-hour party of hide and go seek.

“So,” Audrey started, “Who will be It first?”

The group looked around each other as they stood just outside the girl’s bathroom.

“I’ll be it,” Mona replied, “as long as Chloe is it with me.”

“That’s settled then,” Audrey said. “Into the bathroom, so we can hide.”

Chloe and Mona ducked into the bathroom and started counting out loud.

“One, two, three, four—” then silence. Audrey pushed the bathroom door open catching them mid kiss, hands groping each other.

“Uh hum,” Audrey cleared her throat.

Mona and Chloe were shocked, staring at their friend. They were caught red handed.

“So, this is what you have been up to Chloe,” Audrey laughed. “I was wondering why you were having Carl drop you off at the theater all the time.”

“Please don’t tell anyone Audrey,” Mona pleaded.

“Yeah Aud, they won’t understand,” Chloe added.

Their faces were flush and sweaty with passion.

“Okay, for now—but, it would be easier for both of you if you would quit hiding,” Audrey promised.

“Thanks,” Mona replied.

The game played on throughout the night, each person taking a turn or two as It. Hours later, the game was nearly played out when it rotated around to Mona, who immediately asked Chloe to be It with her again.

“You gals don’t have to do it together, just one of you,” Frankie piped up, fueled by a few beers.

“No, no it’s okay,” Chloe replied, dragging Mona into the bathroom with her.

They started counting again. “One, two, three, four—” silence. Inside the bathroom, the duo continued their interlude of passionate romance for another few minutes.

“Okay, Mona, we have to go look for them,” Chloe gasped as she came up for air.

“One more kiss,” Mona replied as she pushed Chloe up against the door. The door gave way on its double hinge, swinging outward, Mona’s weight against Chloe pushing them into the mezzanine lobby and right in front of the group of friends.

“I knew it!” Frankie exclaimed, pointing at Chloe and Mona. They were still hanging onto each other.

“*Chloe*,” Carl said, but was immediately elbowed in the chest by Audrey, shutting him down.

Lauren was sitting on top of Frankie’s lap on the couch where they had been kissing just seconds before.

"Well, that explains a few things," Lauren said.

"You guys can't say anything to anyone," Mona pleaded with the rest of the group.

"Uh yeah, no kidding, you could get kicked out of school—or worse, somebody might thrash you," Carl said.

"Carl's right—we should keep this to us; the world is still homophobic. There is no need to air the dirty laundry in public, so to speak. But I find it endearing," Audrey added.

"Thanks Aud," Chloe said, her voice trailing off.

The group stared at the pair for thirty seconds, then Audrey lowered the boom.

"Hey, let's get back to the game—I want to play another round,"

"Yeah, me too," Frankie yelled, "Might as well let Mona and Chloe be It—they are a bit chummy now."

"Ha ha Frankie," Chloe said, squinting her eyes at her friend.

"Ahh Chloe Bear, you know I love you," Frankie replied.

"I know you do."

Later that night, Audrey let Mona in on her secret. Mona had speculated about the supernatural since she had seen something in the mirror downstairs last year. Audrey spelled it all out to her, word for word. Mona was still skeptical.

"I need proof."

Audrey knew it would come to that at some point. The rest of them had seen something before, taking it in individually, each one of them coming to grips in their own time, even though they had found out together at her house. This time was different; she knew she had to satisfy Mona's curiosity and make her swear to never tell anyone. She knew she could count on her tight circle to enforce it, and Chloe's love for Mona was also a benefit now that their secret was out to the group.

"Alright Mona, but you may not like what you see tonight—none of you may—but some of you have already seen me. I gain no pleasure in showing you; do not be afraid."

Her words drifted in and out of their ears, syllable by syllable. Audrey walked out of the room, immediately reappearing at the top of the opposite staircase, a split second later. Mona's eyes widened. It wasn't the only thing she would show them that evening. Halfway across the mezzanine in front of them, she vanished, a light wisp of fog left where she was standing.

"Okay. Now I'm officially freaked out here—is anyone else?" Mona said, her hands shaking.

"Not really," Chloe chirped.

"Yeah we've known for a couple months," Frankie replied.

Audrey rejoined them, nonchalantly walking back up the stairs as natural as anyone would, taking a seat right next to Mona on the couch.

"Go ahead, touch me. I assure you I am flesh and blood just like you."

Mona raised her hand up to Audrey's face, touching her with her index finger. "Are you always this cold?"

"No, just when I move between dimensions."

"What is it like over there Aud?" Chloe said. "I can't take it anymore—I've wanted to ask you for months."

"It is dark and light simultaneously. Some places over there are for suffering; others are much happier. I tend to prefer traveling to the happier places."

"The hell you say!"

Frankie had a way with words—probably the only statement he could think of at the time. Lauren seemed unconcerned as she pulled Frankie's face into hers.

The rest of summer came to pass, the school year started up in full swing, the group making their presence known to the school on day one. Nobody questioned them; most stayed away, afraid of confrontation. There was an air of maturity among them keeping the other students at bay. On paper, Audrey was a sophomore, her boredom getting the best of her late one afternoon. She approached the counselor and talked her into letting her challenge every class the first week of her sophomore year. The testing took her nearly three straight days, the grading a week longer. The principal called Audrey into the office two weeks later to give her the news.

"It's okay Mr. Hollings; I already know I passed everything. Now it is official."

“Congratulations Ms. Anderson; in more than forty years of education, you are the first I’ve seen that has done what you did in that short amount of time. I’m still amazed. All I can say is congratulations—enjoy your junior year.”

“Thanks, I appreciate it,” she replied.

The news of her academic accomplishment flew around the school like wildfire, her presence garnering unwanted attention by numerous young men and women; it was a consequence of being too smart and having too much worldly knowledge. It occured at the same time when Chloe and Mona would move into the house in the valley; both of them gaining independence via court order of emancipation.

Chloe’s parent’s never contested her request, still shocked and grieving the loss of their son. Mona had been on her own for more than a year, her single mother in and out of drug rehab multiple times, unaware her daughter had moved out. Audrey welcomed them into the home, giving them the large suite down the hall from hers. They both were astonished when they opened the door to their room as they took in the huge canopy bed. It was one of the finest ones Audrey could find through an antique dealer in Seattle. The room was fit for a king—or two queens—a refuge for two lovers forbidden to show their love outside the residence.

Chloe was exuberant that first evening, jumping up and down on the bed as she did when she was a little girl.

“Come on you two, dinner is served; you can come back and enjoy the bed later.”

Audrey was the matriarch of the group; whatever she said was done immediately, the three friends never questioning her motives or direction. They relied on her maturity, growing more and more mature themselves by the day.

They sat around the table in bliss. Carl was all grins, his heart happy. Mona was there with her friend, allowed to be herself, even if only within the confines of the house.

“We should all go to the point tonight!” Carl said, smiling, holding Audrey’s hand in his on top of the table.

“Sure Carl, that sounds like fun to me. What do you think Chloe?”

Mona was sweet to her. There was no confusion in her mind; sure she had milled over the term lesbian, but to her they were a couple, plain and simple.

"Heck yes, as long as Audrey comes with us," Chloe chirped.

"I'm delighted to go with you guys."

"It's settled then. After dinner, we will go up to the point and watch the city lights," Carl finished.

Dinner with Audrey was a culmination of fancy cuisine the likes of which none of the three teens had ever seen. This evening was no different: the fancy roast beef entree was something she called bœuf à la Bourguignonne and a history lesson in of itself. Audrey explained where and when she learned the recipe long ago in the Burgundy region of France. They were enamored with her, soaking it all in, including the fancy china plates, real silver utensils, and crystal glasses for their wine. She was carefully refining and molding them into upper-class citizens.

As Carl drove up to the point, Chloe and Mona were all over each other in the back seat, their kissing a passionate prelude to the evening that would follow. He parked at the edge of the hill and cradled Audrey in his arms. The mood in the back seat had moved from a slow train departure to a full rocket launch, including the steam that fogged up the windows.

"You gals want to slow it down back there; you're spoiling the quiet solitude of the city lights and missing it all."

"Sorry Carl, I can't keep my hands off my Chloe Bear." It was the first time he had heard her say it, and the first time Chloe had been called that by her lover. Chloe cried.

"Why are you crying Chloe?"

"I'm sorry Mona; it's been tough without my brother."

Mona's embrace for her friend was comforting to Chloe, when she needed someone the most in her life. Mona had that special something that no one else could offer her, sincere compassion and love. She pulled her young friend's head onto her chest, Chloe's tears staining Mona's shirt.

"It's okay Chloe; I'm here for you. I love you," she whispered into her ear, kissing it gently as she pulled Chloe's hair away from her eyes.

Chloe needed those words. She knew she would find love, she just didn't realize it would be this soon and with a friend. They watched the city lights for another hour, then drove home.

The couples went their separate ways, Chloe and Mona sharing their own bed together officially for the first time without suspicion and the first time without being afraid of getting caught.

At breakfast, Chloe pushed a bit harder, asking Audrey the questions that haunted her. Audrey held back. She didn't want to trouble Chloe with her demise.

During school, Audrey had become quite popular after getting nominated for homecoming queen and Carl as king, easily outpacing their opponents twenty to one in the vote. Standing in front of the crowd at the football stadium during the historic homecoming game, they took their positions on the podium as they were crowned. Tommy and Lauren stood on the sidelines as their hatred blossomed. The fact that Lauren was pushed aside, garnering only a few votes, burned within her. She hid her true feelings from Audrey and the others. Tommy was more confrontational, going directly to Carl and challenging him to fight. Carl brushed it off this time, Audrey pleading with him to not fight Tommy. Chloe was on the sidelines with five other gals, all dressed in their skimpy cheerleading uniforms, her pompoms working overtime as she waved them around, unaware of Lauren and Tommy's hatred for Carl and Audrey. She did a backflip, then screamed at her friends.

"Right on Carl! Rock it Audrey!"

Winter dance came right before Christmas break, Audrey ordering three of the finest dresses ever seen at a high school formal dance. It was shear elegance. Chloe and Mona went as a couple, joining Audrey and Carl. Nobody in the school was wise to their affair; many high school girls were doing the same thing that year, electing to ditch the guys who would not commit to the dance. Lauren and Frankie met up at the dance, the group together again, a force to be reckoned with, the tensions among another popular group coming to a head with them.

"So Carl, looks like you have yourself a small harem," Tommy growled.

Carl never liked the cocky senior. Tommy had been Pete's friend and was now the captain of the football team. It was bound to happen one way or another, an event to throw the group into action.

"Tom, tonight is not the night; we don't appreciate your mouth, nor do we want to talk to you."

Carl was sticking up for the group, his cousin backing him up, Frankie's hands ready.

"Why don't we step outside and settle this once and for all Carl."

Tommy's words sliced into Carl, his blood coming to a low boil. "There is nothing I would like better, as long as it is you and me, nobody else."

"Sure, after I kick your ass Carl, I'm going to make your girl mine."

"Carl, don't go out there; he means nothing." Audrey's words had no effect on him this time; it was going to happen. Carl followed Tommy outside as he prepared himself for battle; Frankie came as well just to keep things fair. The fight lasted less than a minute, with Tommy only getting in one lucky punch to the face before Carl laid him out.

"Don't do that again Carl; it is not gentlemanly."

"I know Audrey, but sometimes you have to do things in this world that just don't make sense."

His hormones had taken over. For Carl, defending her honor was acceptable.

"Men have been doing the same thing for centuries; it has never solved a thing."

"I'm sorry Audrey, you are right. Can we go inside and enjoy the dance?"

"Yes. Please come inside."

It was an evening of slow dances, the girls unable to move around in their fancy dresses. Audrey looked like something straight out of a Dickens novel. Her vintage dress was imported from Eastern Europe, the black lace and silk giving her a dark look, a dress popular during the Victorian era. Audrey was on cloud nine. She had missed this faction of life, unable to attend formal dances. She taught Carl ballroom dancing. It was an awkward moment for him. Audrey had to show him his hand placement and footwork; he picked it up by the end of the night as he moved around the floor with a modicum of elegance. She had danced like a princess, her thoughts going back to a more elegant though simple time period as she spun around. Once again, the princess was regaled by all. Time seemed to stop for them as the dance floor opened up, the two spinning around in circles, oblivious to the onlookers. At the end of the dance, they were treated to applause and whistles.

"You've made me happier than you will ever know Carl; I have not danced like that for a very long time."

It was their last event before winter break, with only one week remaining in class. Audrey had a surprise that would blow them away, something she would wait to give them during dinner Friday evening.

Their dinner parties were a routine now, Lauren and Frankie attending without an invite, their presence always welcome.

She sprang the surprise on them at the dinner table.

"I have something for you guys," Audrey said, beaming.

"What is it Aud? Chloe Bear wants to know."

"Hold on, I'll be right back."

Audrey returned a few minutes later after retrieving a letter for each one of them. She passed them around the table and the friends stared at the fancy brown envelope. Their names were written in the Cyrillic alphabet, the writing style for Eastern European countries and Russia.

"Well, open them."

Frankie tore into his envelope shredding it. He pulled out a plane ticket, holding it up in front of him.

"You're taking us to Europe? Get the hell out of here."

"Yes Frankie, and I still don't like that language; it is not becoming of a gentleman."

"Yes Mom, sorry. How effn cool is this!"

Lauren was always the doubter in the group, coming up with the obvious. "How can we do this? My parents will never agree to let me go."

"Au contraire mademoiselle. I've already talked to them and they said you could go."

"I—I don't know what to say," Lauren replied.

"That's okay, you don't have to say anything."

Chloe was the first to show true appreciation as she squeezed Audrey heartily.

"I love you Audrey," she said as she kissed her on the lips. It was a chummy sisterly kiss.

"I know you do Chloe. Pack a small bag you guys, and be ready to go at six tomorrow morning."

32

SIXTEEN HOURS CLICKED OFF SLOWLY as the plane cruised across the Atlantic from Seattle. First-class seats comforted the group as Audrey taught Carl how to play cribbage. It was a game she loved and rarely one she would let him win. The plane touched down in Berlin and the group disembarked on the second leg of their journey. They traveled by train throughout the night to an unknown destination. Audrey would not give them the destination, holding off until they saw it in person. The train lurched from side to side as it rumbled down the track, the thumping of the road wheels hitting the joints in the track was rhythmic and annoying at first but quickly faded away as they endured the trip.

Chloe sat next to Audrey, snuggling in for the journey. She was elated but could not fathom traveling to Europe before she was an old woman. She didn't let go of Audrey's hand as she stared out the window into the German countryside as they crossed the Polish border town of Zasieski. Audrey interpreted the announcements as the towns and crossings were broadcast in German first, then Polish.

"How much longer?" Chloe asked, shaking Audrey's hand. Chloe shifted back and forth in the seat next to her.

"Not much farther. Take a short nap; we will be there in just a few hours."

She snuggled up against Audrey in an embrace of her friendship and loyalty to her. Audrey stroked Chloe's hair softly and it was all she needed to be able to sleep, the gentle touch soothing her. Audrey had the feeling that Chloe was extremely special to her. There was a deeper kinship. She knew they were more than just friends. She could not put a finger on it, even having out of the world knowledge, but her vibe was good. Chloe would have a pivotal relationship with her. Audrey stared out the window, watching the lights of small towns pass by, the faint moonlight glowing across the countryside. Its beams casting shadowy hands through the spindly leaf-barren trees.

Mona wouldn't sleep. She did not want to miss anything. She was in awe, never looking inside the train once since they started moving, and had never-ending questions for Audrey: history, timelines, how, when, where. Audrey was patient, holding off on their true destination as the train moved toward her hometown of Moszna, located in Southwestern Poland near the German border. They talked for hours, Mona learning a lot about Audrey's past life and her vast knowledge of the Slavic region. Chloe slept peacefully, laid across Audrey's lap. Mona smiled at the pair, knowing Audrey would always look out for both of them.

The train screeched to a stop as the road wheels slipped on the rusty rails. The group shuffled out of their cars half asleep, pulling their fatigued bodies off the train to the van waiting just outside the terminal. Audrey spoke with the driver. The conversation was short, but you could tell by her demeanor that she was in charge; he complied immediately with her orders, loading up the baggage as the group loaded into the van. The drive was only twenty-one miles further, about forty-five minutes on the narrow rural country roads. The driver pushed the van past posted speeds, its wheels slipping on the broken pavement, throwing the passengers back and forth. Each turn felt similar to a fairground ride through the haunted house. The van pitched around another bend in the road and through a small grove of trees as it slowed to navigate through the narrow entryway into the estate.

Chloe spoke first as the van moved up the long driveway. "We're staying here? In a castle! How cool is that!"

"Get out of town!" Frankie exclaimed.

Carl and Lauren were speechless, soaking in the castle as they unloaded. The teens craned their necks upward to view the spires reaching out of the top of the castle high above them.

They were met by the caretaker, who was expecting their arrival.

"Welcome home madam. I have prepared everything as requested. Please, come inside."

"This is like a fairytale," Chloe squealed. "It's the castle in my dreams."

"For sure it is Chloe," Audrey replied.

"I'm not kidding, I dreamt about this castle the other night!"

The castle had withstood the test of time, completed early in 1679, it had gone through renovation and additions for the next two hundred years. All in all, it had ninety-nine turrets in the style of spires, three hundred sixty-five rooms, for a total of seven thousand square meters. It was huge.

"How long are we staying here?" Frankie asked.

The main foyer was a palace in its own right, leading right up to the curved marble staircase. It also served as the main ballroom, where she had hosted many fine events.

"As long as we want to stay, or at least until school starts next year."

"It must cost a fortune to stay here," Mona blurted out before she could stop herself as she stood there, her body wavering, euphoria taking over.

"Audrey, is that a painting of one of your relatives?" Carl asked as he pointed to the monolith above the fireplace, his eyebrows raised. He glanced back and forth from the painting to Audrey—painting—Audrey—painting.

His question was pointed.

"It's me; it was painted here, during the winter sometime around seventeen twenty, I think."

"Get the hell out of here," Frankie said.

"Don't cuss Frankie, and Mona, you are only partially right. This place did cost a fortune, but that was nearly three hundred years ago."

"You own this place?"

“Yes Chloe, it is mine, as well as the grounds around it as far as you can see.”

“Audrey, you were cool before, but this, this shit is epic; I mean epic!” Chloe flailed her arms around as she talked.

“I can’t believe you held off telling us you owned a castle—not that it would matter. I would still love you even if you didn’t,” Carl said.

“You will find your rooms ready. Take any one of the rooms that aren’t marked *A.A.* on the door. That one is mine.”

“You really own this place! I’m in heaven!” Chloe chirped, leaping up the stairs as she skipped every other step, vanishing into the second floor. Mona chased after her.

Frankie was more reserved; his thoughts were not only on the room but what he planned on doing with Lauren. You could see it in his eyes. They would disappear for the evening, not showing up until lunch the next day.

Carl and Audrey would retreat to the other side of the castle, the castle within the castle. It was her master bedroom, a four thousand square-foot mansion, complete with its own fireplace, where six-foot logs would sit burning all day. The king sleigh bed was waiting for them, where they slept like babies until the next morning. Audrey was sure sometime that night she heard Chloe running around the castle, Chloe’s laughs waking her a few times.

They awoke to a heavy snowfall the next morning that had silently coated the grounds as they slept. Breakfast was followed by a tour through the home, a light lunch, then an afternoon spent in the game room. Around four p.m., Audrey ordered the team hitched up to the large sleigh. She had planned a ride through the countryside that evening for a perfect introduction to her homeland. The neighing of the horse brought Chloe outside. If there was one thing she really had a heart for, it was horses. The pair hitched to the sleigh were the finest you would find for nearly a thousand miles. Chloe was enamored by the horses, talking to them as she climbed into the sleigh, bundled up in one of Audrey’s fur coats she found in her room’s wardrobe. The others joined her and were whisked away through the countryside by her driver, sliding across the snow-covered roads, the scrape of the sleigh runners and clop of the hooves filling them with sounds of the past. Audrey had a specific destination in mind, the driver pulling the sleigh up in front of a small restaurant just outside town. The waitress brought out course after course of traditional old world style food. They spent the evening eating, drinking, and enjoying each other's company, their lives in Washington forgotten.

"I could stay here for the rest of my life." It was something Audrey was hoping Carl would want.

"Chloe Bear would too Carl, as long as Mona stays with me." Mona couldn't speak, her love for Chloe still blossoming, her face flush with embarrassment. They were holding hands and it was the first time that the two of them had shown affection for each other in public. In Europe, people were less homophobic. Same sex couples had walked around freely without discrimination for nearly a decade. Mona was still warming up to the idea but enjoying it more and more—cautiously. Chloe did not care, nor did she take her hands off Mona when they were out, no matter who the company was. Nobody would tell her that she couldn't love or touch someone anytime she wanted.

"I will visit you guys, but my baby is waiting for me back home," Frankie said. "I'm not leaving my car for that long—it would miss me."

"I'm coming back here at the end of the school year; you are all invited. Please consider spending the summer with me. I have so much to tell you, and so many things to show you."

"I'll come back to visit, as long as they have this dessert—" Frankie replied through a mouthful of mush. "What is it again?"

"Baklava, Frankie," Audrey replied.

Frankie finished off the pastry, ordered another, and finished off what Chloe left on her plate as well, his belly aching as he climbed the stairs up to the bedroom. Audrey and Carl sat on the sofa inside their room, cuddling in front of the fireplace, drifting off to sleep in each other's arms.

Mona was excited for her day Audrey had planned for them. She was waiting for Audrey for an hour, sitting in the foyer. Audrey had promised to take her on a historical tour of the grounds and surrounding countryside. It would be the day she posed the ultimate question. Mona rode alone with her in the sleigh as she listened intently. Audrey laid out her life in vivid detail. How she came upon rebuilding the castle, her love affair with a wealthy Polish gentleman in the late sixteen hundreds, and their luck at stumbling on the empty castle. It was abandoned by its previous owner during an outbreak of cholera, she explained. Mona soaked up everything she heard, not interrupting Audrey for hours as they rode farther away from the grounds of the estate, finally stopping at the foot of a small hill.

"This is it, the place where they chased me down. We were pursued by the townspeople, after they accused me of sorcery. I was stabbed and left for dead, my husband drawn and quartered, his body pulled apart by horses, scattered to the wind."

"But you came back didn't you!"

"It was the second time. A friend found me two days later and carried me to the chapel, where he laid me at the foot of the cross. He prayed for a miracle. Sometimes it feels as though I am cursed."

"But you get to live forever?" Mona asked. "You are totally unencumbered by death aren't you?"

"Mona, there are worse things than death. A life lived happily, is worth more than anything in the world—worth more than immortality."

"I have so many questions. I can't even think straight right now," Mona replied.

"Mona, I will tell you everything in time. Let's enjoy the rest of our day; there is so much to see here, a lifetime of beauty."

They rode on, throughout the countryside, stopping on top of a bridge. Mona stared at the stream below, the frozen branches of an elm tree above them glistening in the waning sunlight. Their afternoon together was what Mona needed. She had come to an understanding that she could live happily here in this country. She was certain she knew how it felt to be an outcast as Audrey had centuries before.

"Driver, take us back; it's getting late. Dinner will be ready soon."

"Yes madam," the driver replied, cracking the whip to prod the horses.

Inside the castle, Frankie was up to old tricks again, his version of hide and go seek going awry. Lauren searched and searched for him in the three hundred plus rooms. She was not amused as she looked through a dozen wardrobes. She found him in the last room she checked. Frankie jumped out at her as she opened the wardrobe.

"Damn it Frankie," she growled.

"What?" he replied as he struggled with her. Lauren gave him a light slap on the cheek before kissing him.

"Dinner is ready, we have to go," Lauren replied.

"One more kiss."

"No, Audrey will be waiting for us, we can't be late."

"I'm not going until you kiss me," Frankie said, laughing.

Lauren gave Frankie a quick peck on the cheek then slugged him. He stood there as she ran out of the room.

"Wait up," Frankie yelled.

Downstairs, in the dining hall, the meal was being set by a half dozen maids, all hired locally, clueless to Audrey's past. As far as they knew, it was a wealthy group of American kids, sent over on their Christmas break. The table was filled from one end to the other with game hens, roast beef, stroganoff, and dessert spread out on the finest china. Audrey and the rest of the group were waiting as Lauren ran down the stairs and took her seat across from Chloe'. Frankie was a few seconds behind.

"Sorry we're late," Frankie said.

"That's okay," Audrey replied.

"I propose a toast to Audrey, and this magnificent place."

"Here here, Frankie, well said," Carl replied jubilantly, raising his wine glass above his head.

"To Audrey," Frankie cheered, the group following in.

"Thank you, thank you all," Audrey replied, adding, "Tomorrow is our last Friday night here; it would be nice to invite some local teens over for a dance."

"Audrey, that sounds like a bitchin idea. I like it, but what do we say to them when they get here? We don't speak Polish," Frankie asked.

“You might be surprised to find out that all students in Poland are taught English as a second language. I am sure you will find something to talk about.”

“I’m game!” Chloe chirped.

“It is settled then. I will send word and have one of the maids deliver a flyer into town.”

Friday evening rolled around quickly and a local disc jockey was brought in from the nearest populated location. Surprisingly enough, most the music was from American artists. Audrey's flyer stated that the dance party in the castle would start promptly at eight. At seven thirty, more than two dozen teens were waiting outside, ready to party.

“Welcome, friends. Come in out of the cold, enjoy yourselves,” Audrey said as she stretched her arms out, welcoming the locals.

She was the most gracious host. It was the event of the decade in this small community, the local teens co-mingled with the American teens, their use of English enough to bridge the gap between them. They danced for hours, both sides of the world enjoying themselves. The Polish girls were as beautiful as Audrey, with natural features that did not go unnoticed by Frankie and Carl. It was their last evening in the old world, their return the following day ending an experience they would never forget.

Booking passage back to the states through Paris, the group traveled across Europe into France. They stayed the night in a hotel with a view of the Eiffel Tower.

"How long has it been since you were here last?" Mona asked. Chloe was sandwiched in the middle of them, arm in arm. Audrey had not been back to Paris for a long time, a trip she had wanted to do for decades. She marveled at the size of the city that evening as she chatted with Mona.

"Quite some time,” Audrey replied, adding, “It was not always like this—not nearly as busy.” She sighed; the old Paris had changed. Crowds filled the streets and the modernization of the 21st century startled Audrey. Even though the city had changed, Paris was still a magical place for her. It was also a place where Mona and Chloe could sit on a park bench with each other, holding hands unmolested.

“It must have been grand, centuries ago?” Mona asked, always seeking knowledge.

“It was magic. The people were so elegant back then.” Audrey breathed in the sweet smell of pastries that lined the shop windows nearby.

“I wish I could have lived with you in those times,” Mona replied. "I would trade anything to have lived here then."

"Anything Mona?" Chloe quipped. "Even me?" she joked.

"Well, nearly anything. Just not you,” Mona replied, as she gave Chloe a peck on the cheek.

33

LIFE WAS BACK TO NORMAL as the teens transitioned from world travelers back into local yokels at the burger stand in Centralia. Frankie and Lauren were on again, off again, and then a nasty breakup split them apart—their love affair too hot and tumultuous to handle even for them. Lauren was spending her time with Tommy and Alan, split off from the group that had taken her in. The group had provided her with unending love and compassion, and she threw it away for the next hot guy. Mona was back at the theater, and Chloe was spending every moment she could with her, seated on the floor under the counter of the ticket booth. She was there nightly, hiding just out of sight from the patrons outside, their chatter going unnoticed.

A month after they returned from Europe, Mona had her first run in with Lauren, Tommy, and Alan.

"Hey bitch," Lauren spat as she approached the ticket booth.

Mona glared at her.

"We want three tickets." Lauren didn't even specify a movie, and Mona didn't care, printing out three tickets to the downstairs show.

"Four fifty," Mona replied as Lauren shoved a five under the slot in the window.

"Keep the change, skank," Lauren growled.

"What is wrong with her?" Chloe had heard everything. "I'm going to take her out; nobody calls my girl a bitch or a skank." She tried to stand up, but Mona held her down with her foot, standing on her legs that were crossed Indian style. “Leave it alone Chloe, she means nothing to us now.”

“I’m not leaving it alone; let me up.” Chloe threw Mona’s leg off her, slamming the door of the booth behind her. Mona couldn’t follow her because of the line of people going out the door and around the block waiting to buy a ticket; tonight’s movie would be sold out.

Chloe stepped into the theater, letting the door close behind her slowly. Her eyes adjusted to the dark. She scanned the seats, then spotted Lauren and the boys halfway down in the middle, unaware she was watching them. She rung her hands at her sides of her thighs. Her fists pulsed as she opened then closed them, then opened them again. Her pulse sped up.

"Call my girl a skank,” Chloe muttered under her breath.

Chloe shoved the theater door back open and stood at the corner of the concession stand, motioning for one of the attendants to get her a large soda, no ice. It was common practice by now to give Chloe whatever she wanted, Mona taking care of the inventory at the end of the night to make the numbers right on what they had sold. With the large soda in hand, Chloe returned to the theater. Concealing herself from Lauren, she pulled the hood up over her head, taking a seat behind them. Minute by minute, Chloe waited for the perfect time when the crowded theater was cheering loudly. Twenty minutes passed as she sat quietly. The crowd roared with laughter and claps. Chloe slipped the lid off the cup of soda and pushed it between the seats in front of her, dumping the contents into Lauren’s lap. Lauren had no clue what was happening until it was too late. Her crotch was soaked. Chloe's timing was perfect. Lauren screamed at the exact time when the crowds reaction to the movie was the loudest and nobody noticed what had happened. Chloe slipped away, Lauren only seeing the back of a short person’s head covered by a hooded sweatshirt. She ran after Chloe.

“Gotta go, see you later,” Chloe yelled as she ran past the ticket booth. Mona jumped up, watching her bolt out the door and down the street. Lauren came out a few seconds later, her white pants stained brown.

“Where is that little bitch?” she yelled. Mona shrugged, then smiled as Lauren flew out the door. Chloe circled the block as Lauren chased after her, just catching sight of Lauren rounding the corner. Tommy and Alan had not realized Lauren had had a run in with the soda and were still watching the movie. Chloe's aim and slow pour kept all the liquid confined to Lauren's crotch.

Chloe had made it around the block unscathed and ran back inside the theater. She hid in the ticket booth with Mona. Lauren burst through the door a minute later.

"Where is that little bitch?" she yelled. Mona shrugged her shoulders again as Chloe snickered, covering her mouth with her hands. It was a struggle for Chloe to hold in her laughter. Lauren couldn't see Chloe who was just underneath the counter. A few inches of plywood separated her from danger.

"I know she is here; you tell her that she is dead, you hear me!" Lauren's eye shadow ran down her cheeks from sweat.

"I think you better leave Lauren, you are disturbing my customers; don't make me call the police." Mona stifled a giggle with the back of her hand, then burst out laughing, unable to hold back any longer. She wasn't sure why Lauren hated her so much; maybe it was her half-shaved head or the other half of her hair that was shoulder length. Mona knew she was an outsider to most people, but it did not concern her. Lauren glared at her through the glass, and Mona could see the hatred in her eyes. It was disturbing. With the next rush of patrons lining up outside the theater door, Lauren had no recourse but to leave. Mona was busy printing out tickets, taking money, and trying to hold in her laughter, as Chloe giggled underneath the counter.

"What did you do?" Mona asked her between customers.

"She never saw it coming. I waited until everyone was laughing at the movie, then dumped my soda on her crotch from the seat behind her."

Mona roared with laughter again as tears rolled down her face until her stomach ached.

"Then, she let out this scream, but nobody noticed because they were laughing at the movie at the same time," Chloe laughed, snorting a few times as she talked.

"You should have seen her face Chloe, she looked evil; her eyes burned with hatred."

“Good, that’s what she gets for being an ass.”

“Be careful, I don’t want you getting close to her anymore; she is dangerous Chloe.”

"She got what she deserved,” Chloe replied.

“Chloe, look at me.” Mona looked down into Chloe’s eyes. Chloe opened them real wide, goofy eyed.

“Yes Mom!” She couldn’t contain her laughter, snorting again as she went into a fit of spasms, grabbing her belly.

“Be careful, okay?” Mona pointed at her as she attempted to stifle her giggles.

“Okay, I will, but I will not be nice to her.”

“That’s fine. I didn’t ask you to be nice, just be careful.”

Mona was worried that Lauren would assault Chloe, who was much smaller. As the pair drove home that evening, Mona was still harping at Chloe, chastising her as she told her to keep her distance from Lauren. The small confines of her 1978 Ford Mustang made the conversation more intimate. Chloe didn't say a word for nearly five miles as they drove out of town to Audrey’s mansion. It was a dark night with no moonlight. The tall fir trees blocked out the rest of the light.

“Are you done yet?” Chloe spat.

“No, I’m not done Chloe; listen to me. She is dangerous! I’m telling you to stay away. I forbid you to get closer than one hundred feet from her. Promise me you will stay away from her.”

Chloe crossed her arms and clamped her mouth shut. The rest of their trip onto the dirt driveway was silently uncomfortable, the headlights of the car throwing shadows into the field next to the road from the cedar fence posts that lined the drive. Chloe slammed the car door, then ran up the short hill and into the house, right past Carl and Audrey, who were lying on the couch together.

“Hey Chloe.” Carl barely got it out as she ran upstairs. Mona walked in a few seconds later, sighing.

“What’s up with her?” Audrey asked.

“She’s just mad because I told her I didn’t want to see her around Lauren.”

Mona told them what had happened at the theater and how evil Lauren looked when she came back after chasing Chloe, as well as her conversation they had while driving home.

"Let me talk to her; she just needs time to cool off," Audrey said calmly.

"Chloe, you in here?" Audrey stepped into the dark bedroom, her eyes adjusting to the light, Chloe's small body was humped up in the middle of the bed underneath the covers. Audrey waited for her to respond as she sat on the edge of the bed.

"Chloe, if you don't want to talk to me, I understand," Audrey prodded.

Chloe poked her head out of the covers and Audrey could see that she had been crying. Audrey dried Chloe's tears, brushing her hair back away from her face, the mascara staining her hands.

"She yelled at me; I've never heard her be so mean," she sobbed, her face hot to Audrey's touch.

"I'm sure she did not mean for it to come out that harsh; sometimes when we love someone so much, we forget and our words come out abrasive."

Chloe sat up next to her.

"You want to come down for cocoa?" Audrey asked,

"Yeah, I guess so," she sobbed. "It is my favorite…"

Chloe and Audrey slipped down the stairs and into the kitchen, returning to the living room a few minutes later. Chloe had two cups of cocoa in her hands, marshmallows humped up to the rim.

"I'm sorry Mona, you were right; I will stay away from her," she said, handing the other cup to her lover.

34

LAUREN LET AUDREY'S SECRET SLIP out one day, Tommy feeding off every word she said. She did not tell him about Audrey's exact physical presence, but did tell him more than enough to send him into an incessant desire to destroy everything about that house, and its occupants. It took them a few weeks to convince the rest of his friends to help them, but once they summoned enough courage, fueled by alcohol, which was all it took to set things in motion, Audrey's fate was be sealed.

Lauren had been researching more and more in the library, looking for answers. She had a curiosity that was more than a morbid fascination. She had been planning her vengeance for over a year. Their hatred was fueled more each week as Tommy would stare up into the bleachers at Audrey. Lauren had turned him into a heinous ally.

Weeks before they would put their plans into motion, Tommy and Lauren secretly conspired together in her bedroom, filling him in on everything she knew about the afterlife. Tommy fed on it as though he was a grizzly eating salmon in late summer. He was fueled with rage and hatred too, his loathing of Carl the top thing on his mind. Now, he had a way to hurt him. He had found a way to wound him to the core. If they could get the rest of his close teammates to follow his lead, they could put the plan in action. Tommy was on top for sure, but to convince your friends into doing a dirty deed was another matter. He knew it would be best fueled by alcohol at their next weekend bonfire. It was Lauren's idea right from the start, pulling Tommy into her web, the one guy she needed to put it together. Tommy put the word out that week, calling his friends up one by one. *"I have free beer,"* he said. It was another ritual partaken by teens in Lewis County, traveling out past the town of Cinnabar to the tall hill above called Rooster Rock.

Rooster Rock was legendary for bonfires and inner tubing in the snow during the winter. It was a muddy remote location when it rained, a four-wheel-drive show most of the time. The trek to the top was arduous. Tommy had scavenged two truckloads of pallets from Harden's lumber company in Centralia. When Lauren and Tommy arrived, there were half a dozen four wheel drives parked in a half circle around the pallets, waiting for Tommy to light it off. He grabbed a can of gasoline out of the back of his pickup and dowsed the pile with two gallons, the flammable liquid throwing a vapor cloud out around the pile. The next part was tricky; even Tommy knew the vapor would ignite way before he could get the flame near the pallets. Standing back by his truck, he lit a flare, tossing it thirty feet into the top of the pile of pallets. Time was in slow motion at that moment, the gasoline vapor igniting, then setting off a concussion that knocked two of his friends to the ground, singeing their eyebrows.

"Damn it Tom, that was too freaking close for comfort. Next time don't use so much gas." His teammate brushed the dirt off his pants. Tommy laughed as he pulled a case of beer out of the cab of his pickup, tossing a can to each of his friends. Lauren did not drink, keeping herself sober for events later that night. She was a permanent fixture by Tommy's side, hanging onto his arm as the boys did what boys do on a weekend bender. Tommy had specifically requested no girlfriends, and they all complied. *"Boys night out,"* he said, except Lauren.

"Tommy man, watch this." Alan bent over at the waist as another boy stuck a lighter near his butt, lighting his fart, the flame blowing upward.

"That's freaking gross Alan," Lauren cringed.

Lauren didn't laugh, but the rest of the group roared. Another hour passed by, Lauren judging their sobriety as she elbowed Tommy.

"Bring out another case," she whispered into his ear.

Tommy complied explicitly, his vision blurry from the three beers he had pounded when he got there. The fire raged as flames licked the sky.

"Another round for my friends." Tommy passed the cans around, chucking them football style to the group. They were already slowing down; the pile of aluminum cans scattered all around them. The party was losing momentum.

"Hey man, let's shotgun this one."

Tommy pulled his keys out of his pocket.

"How do you do it?"

Tommy frowned at his center.

"Take a key, turn the beer upside down, and poke a small hole into the bottom near the side, then put it up to your mouth like this and open the pull tab, sucking the beer in." He guzzled the beer down in seconds.

"Look guys." It always began that way when Tommy wanted his teammates to do something against the grain.

"I—me and Lauren I mean, need your help," he slurred.

"What is it man?"

"We have a problem that needs your special attention. You all know what Chloe Chambers did to Lauren at the theater. Now, we are going to get some payback against her and that bitch she calls a friend, Audrey Anderson—throw some real fear into them."

"How we going to do that?"

Tommy looked around the group, eyeing each one of them.

"Fire. That's how!" He threw it out there to see whether it would stick, just as you would when cooking spaghetti: take one piece, throw it against a wall. If it sticks, great. If not, let the spaghetti simmer in the boiling water a few more minutes.

"You want to invite them out to the next bonfire?"

"No you idiot, that is not what we have in mind. We were thinking of taking the fire to them, out in the valley at Audrey's house." He studied their faces to see if they would accept what he had said.

"I'm not burning her house down," Alan replied. "That's illegal, and someone could get hurt."

"We aren't going to burn her house down man, just light a fire real close and scare them, that's all." Tommy lied, his web intertwined with

Lauren’s, her lips curling up like the Grinch's. People were like that in a small town, as they plotted revenge.

“So just light a fire next to it?” a player quipped.

“Yes, we will sneak out there early one evening and dump cans of gas in a circle around the house, then let the fire flare up; nothing will happen, except the flames will jump up above the windows, scaring them.”

“I’m in man.”

“Me too.”

“Count me in.”

They all ponied up just as Lauren had hoped.

“When we going to do it?”

“Maybe a week or so; just wait for my call, then come as fast as you can.” Tommy didn’t have the exact date but knew his teammates would rush to the location at his disposal as soon as he requested. Their evening in the woods, on top of Rooster Rock, ended a few hours later. Most of the team passed out in the cabs or pickup beds. Lauren drove Tommy back to her house, where she intended to sleep with him but he passed out minutes after he climbed into her bed.

35

TOMMY WAS THE BIG SHOT on campus now, a point that did not go unnoticed by Carl. He had his eye on Carl, and the revenge he would exact on him. Audrey's group had rejoined their classmates, who were unaware of their holiday in the old world an ocean away.

Friday night football games had ended, replaced by basketball; Audrey and Carl were regulars, never missing a game. It was bittersweet for Chloe; her brother would have been the team captain, replaced by Tommy. The extra burden of not being able to have a relationship out in the open put a strain on her and Mona. It was an on-again, off-again affair, although they stayed out at the old house in the valley, never straying too far from each other. Frankie was back in full swing, rebuilding his car, making it better than before, and Lauren had turned her attentions full time to Tommy. That is how it all started: too much knowledge from a girl who had an ulterior motive, more than likely from the start, and how they had initiated the plan weeks earlier at the bonfire.

Tommy had followed them around often, waiting to strike as the cruising scene was going full force that winter, Frankie and Carl constant participants. They drove their cars back and forth for hours through town, Audrey grew weary the first couple of months, electing to stay home. Tommy knew it was their time to strike, a moment when she was alone, or at least that is what they thought as they surrounded the house, cans of gasoline in their hands.

Lauren had spearheaded the assault on the house, reciting the spell that would hold Audrey inside, binding her from leaving. Tommy had brought nearly the entire senior squad of the football team, and as captain, they would follow his lead, doing whatever he asked. Surrounding the house with cans of gasoline, they poured the liquid out, Tommy splashing it high up on the siding in the back of the house where the teammates couldn't see, each one of them pushed to act recklessly by Lauren's hatred for her former friend and her fear of the supernatural. Lauren lit the match, throwing it at the house. It flew through the air, igniting the fumes before hitting the ground. The flames raced around the ground and up the back side of the house.

"Audrey Anderson, demon. I banish you back to where you came. By fire I send you into the afterlife, and fire will consume you for the rest of your days."

The fire crept around the outside of the house and filtered through the cracks in the windows as it engulfed the upstairs.

"Audrey—Audrey," Chloe screamed as she stumbled out of her bedroom and down the hallway. Smoke was billowing through the top of the home, choking Chloe, her face pushed into her arm to block out the retched pollutant.

"Audrey, are you in there?" she yelled, slamming her body into the bedroom door. She pushed on it hard and it gave way and Chloe ducked into the room. Fire had erupted up the rear of the house and had burned through the wall, leaping onto the ceiling above, bathing the room in an orange glow. Chloe dropped to the floor and groped around the room, finding the bed a few feet in front of her. She reached up into the middle and could feel her friend lying there.

"Are you okay? Let's go, we have to get out of here," Chloe screamed.

Audrey's voice was just a whisper. "It is over, save yourself—"

"No, you have to come with me," Chloe coughed, pulling on Audrey.

"I can't, I'm bound here now."

“I’m not leaving you,” Chloe gasped as she climbed onto the bed next to Audrey. She held her friend as the fire raced down the wall behind them, igniting the bed. Chloe breathed in one last breath.

Carl drove around the corner, missing the perpetrators by minutes. They had taken a side road before he arrived, concealing their exit. The fire raged in the distance. Carl could not believe his eyes as he watched the house being consumed in front of him. His anguish flooded over him as huge embers launched high above, drifting into the heavens. He slid into the driveway and stepped out of the car. Carl ran up the sidewalk as he held his arm in front of his face. It was too hot to get any closer. Carl stood there weeping.

At daybreak, the fire investigator confirmed Chloe’s death, her body nearly consumed by the fire. Carl could not believe it; he was grief-stricken. The only place he thought of going to was his cousin’s house. He drove over to Frankie’s and collapsed on the couch in the garage. He didn’t speak for hours. Frankie was distraught as well when Carl told him the girls were gone.

It was a steel grey overcast day at the cemetery, dozens of students surrounding the open hole, the ornate silver coffin suspended above. Mona took it the hardest as she wept uncontrollably. Chloe was one of the kindest people she had ever known. Her eyes burned from rubbing them.

“I’m sorry Mona,” Carl choked out.

“I’ll never love anyone again,” Mona sobbed. Carl put his arm around his cousin.

The preacher spoke for nearly a half hour about life, death, and the resurrection, finally signaling to the groundskeepers to lower the coffin into the ground. At that moment it hit Mona the hardest, her love slipping away from her as the casket descended into the grave a few inches at a time. The priest grabbed a shovel and spoke the words that he had said at every funeral.

“Ashes to ashes, dust to dust, we commend this soul to the heavens, this body to the earth,” he said, shoveling dirt onto the casket below. A low thud vibrated out of the grave as the earth slipped around the sides of the casket.

Mona wept harder as the priest handed her the shovel. Mona scooped up a pile of dirt, casting it into the grave. It hit the top of the casket with a hollow thud. She handed the shovel to Carl, and he did the same, passing it along the line. Each student pitched a shovel full in as well, a few declining due to the solemn morbidity of the day.

Carl cruised the streets more than ever in the weeks afterwards, spending time alone. His heart was broken. Nearly two months to the day after the accident, she reappeared. He was driving to Chehalis on the freeway. Just after crossing the Skookumchuck River, Carl saw her walking along the frontage road. He turned to look at her in the rearview mirror. There was no way to turn around before the next exit. Carl pushed the throttle down as he searched for the exit two miles away. He swung off the exit, crossed over the freeway and onto the entrance ramp. He knew it was her. The engine roared as he pulled out the stops. Soon, the speedometer passed through 120 mph, settling on 125 where it topped out. Cars stood still as the Nova slid past them in a blur. He was back to the spot where he saw her and she was gone. Had she come back already? Or was his mind playing tricks on him? Later that afternoon, Mona left an urgent message at his parent's house to come by and see her.

They had not talked since the funeral, and Carl was afraid to tell her what he saw.

"She is gone Carl."

"I know, they are both gone."

"No, not Audrey. Chloe's grave is empty. I went there this morning to lay flowers on her tombstone; it was empty.

"What the hell?"

"The coffin was dug up and left open, her body was not inside. What does this mean?"

"I was not going to tell you this, but you should know if anyone should. I saw Audrey today, walking next to the freeway."

"Are you sure it was Audrey?"

"Pretty sure."

“What do we do Carl?”

“We wait.”

“Do you think Chloe is coming back too?”

“I don’t know,” he replied.

Waiting was the only thing they could do; school was wrapping up in just under a month, and they would have to figure out what to do with the rest of their lives. Carl’s mind was on who started the fire. He was sure that Lauren had something to do with it. Graduation came a few weeks later, the confrontation between Tommy and Carl a major event at the party directly afterward.

“Tommy, I already kicked your ass once; don’t make me do it again.”

“I won’t fight you again Carl, but I will race you pink slip for pink slip.”

It was the one challenge Tommy thought would break Carl’s soul and his resolve. Carl wanted it as well. Tommy was unaware Frankie had swapped out the 327 for his race engine while he fixed up the body of his wrecked car. The challenge was accepted, the race location just outside town alongside the highway. It was a long straight road, one guy’s hot rod against the other. The crowd that gathered on that stretch of road grew to nearly thirty kids, Lauren included. Frankie waited at the end of the road, then waved the flag. The car’s tires squealed as both cars shot down the road at the crowd of people. The crowd of teens pushed in closer to the edge of the roadway, right up to the fog lines. It was neck and neck most of the way, with Carl pulling away from Tommy hundreds of yards before the finish line. At nearly one hundred twenty miles per hour, Tommy started to lose it. Then horror flashed in his eyes; Audrey was standing right in front of the car, just fifty feet away. He pushed his foot down harder on the throttle to run her into the ground as his anger boiled. Seconds later he crashed into Lauren. Dread crept through him as the car slid off the road and into the ditch, bursting into flames. Carl slammed on the brakes, the Chevy sliding back and forth down the road. He had a fleeting glance of Audrey in his peripheral vision as he flew past her, then she was gone.

The next day, Carl listened intently as the newscaster broke into the regular program on TV. "Eleven teens dead in a mysterious bus crash," the news anchor said. "We don't have all the information yet, but it looks like the bus rolled over as it went off the road, landing upside down in the Chehalis River."

Carl stared at the TV, motionless, contemplating the deaths, wondering if it was anyone he knew, wondering if Audrey had anything to do with it. The other deaths were masked by the bus crash.

36

TOMMY AND LAUREN HAD BEEN gone nearly a week, their deaths rocking the small community. School was canceled for three days preceding their funerals and the town buzzed with the mysterious bus crash, its cause unknown. Across town, Sean was plying the local pool hall as usual, his latest victim closing the door, leaving him alone at a table in the back. The deaths were barely a blip on his radar, although he had participated in burning down Audrey's house. Sean was not at all bothered by the events of the past week; his concern was at the pool table and the game itself. The bell above the door jingled when the young girl walked through.

"We're closed, get the hell out." His yell went right past the young girl, who continued walking between the rows of pool tables to him, the darkened interior of the pool hall masking her face. Sean strained his eyes to get a look at the intruder through the shadows.

"I said we are closed," Sean yelled again.

"Hello Sean. I thought we could play a round," she said.

He didn't recognize her voice or face. Her clothing was neither stylish nor well fitting. She was dressed in black.

"I don't usually play after hours. How much do you want to play for?" A musty smell hit his nose, similar to a summer rain on a dusty road.

The girl racked the balls. They clicked sharply as she shoved them together. Her fingernails were un-manicured and protruded an inch past the tips of her fingers. Her hair was deep auburn and matted.

"These," she said, pulling out a few gold coins.

"That is a lot of money you have there. Two ounces? I'll play you for that. Let's flip to see who breaks."

"Sure, flip it," she replied.

"Heads I break; tails you break," Sean said as he flipped the two headed coin. It bounced on the table, flipped over then stopped on the headed side.

"Go ahead Sean, give it your best shot." She never spoke another word as he broke, sinking the first ball. Sean ran the table, winning the game without her playing. His smile was growing wider by the minute as he gloated at her. His zealous ego emanated from his pores. Sean reached across the table to grab the coins. He rolled them over in his hands and was elated.

"Good game. Do you want to play another?" she asked.

"How much are you willing to lose?" he said as he upped the ante.

"More than you can handle. More if you are willing to make the ultimate bet, a bet you have never had nor will ever have a chance of getting again."

"What do you have in mind?" he spat.

Audrey walked over to his side of the table and placed her hand on his. Visions of luxury and opulence flashed across Sean's consciousness. Another vision of a large mansion with a half dozen fine automobiles inside the garage made Sean's pulse race, and the vault inside the home was stacked full of cash and gold. It added to his frenzy and was enough to suck him in.

"Your soul. I bet your soul against what I just showed you. You win, I will make sure you become the top player in the world. Money, fame—the cars, all yours. You lose, you surrender your soul immediately."

"Sure, I'll play for that. As long as you throw in two more gold coins. I know you have more."

She did have more, throwing them on the table in front of him. He was not sure what had just happened, the fog of gold clouding his judgment.

"So is it a bet, Sean? Are you ready to bet your soul and two gold coins that you can beat me again?"

"Yeah sure, my soul and two gold coins I can beat you. I'll even let you break."

"It's your life." Her words echoed through him, unaware of what he had done. Audrey's boney fingers shuddered as they slid down the pool stick. Her fingernails scraped the finish off as she drew it through her hand. A gust of wind shuddered across the front of the building rattling the windows. The front door blew open, ringing the bell above it.

Audrey pulled the cue stick back, leaning over it as she rested it on her left hand. She thrust the stick forward and the tip of it propelled the cue ball directly to the center of the rack. The cue ball crashed into the other balls, sending a spark upward. Sean watched as three balls shot into opposing pockets. His demeanor never changed; he figured he would get a shot after she missed. Audrey lined up another shot from the far end of the table, sending the cue-ball back down, banking it off the right side around the eight ball. It rolled past the two ball, then hit the five, throwing it into the corner pocket directly in front of him. Shot after shot she sent each ball into a pocket until only the eight ball remained.

"This is for the game, Sean, and your soul," she laughed as Sean saw her for who she was. Dread crept over him in a sobering moment.

"You're dead? I watched the house burn. We killed you!" he said.

You could see the confusion and madness in his eyes. Sean watched the eight ball go into the far pocket she had just called; his fate was sealed. Audrey's green eyes glowed in the night, her face turning from the pale skin to a gray skeleton.

"You lose. Payment due! Now!"

She reached her hand up to his throat, lifting him off his feet, his gasps for air a raspy wisp in the silent pool hall. Sean could feel his soul leaving him, his labored breathing and realization death had come scaring him as he stared into her face. He kicked his feet violently to try to release her grip as her bony hand tightened on his throat. Sean struggled again as he grabbed her hand with his. She had him immobilized as the hands tightened, clamping his airway off. His vision faded as blackness overtook his mind. He could still hear her just seconds before his brain ceased to function.

"Mercy for those that honor the father. Damnation for those that seek ill reward," she said through the rotting stench that emanated from her breath as her grip loosened and Sean's body crumpled to the floor.

Sean lay there on the floor, his body discovered the following morning, the horror in his eyes still apparent to the responding officer. The coroner wrote it up as a drug overdose, although he knew by the ligature marks on the body's neck that he was strangled. Sean was well known as a thug and drug dealer in the area, and even the coroner was unwilling to spend time on a frivolous investigation.

A FEW DAYS LATER:

"Hey man, did you hear about Sean?" Alan's high school buddy had heard the scuttlebutt from his uncle who was a custodian at the police station.

"No, what happened?" Alan was not much for conversation, his brains had been bashed a few times too many during football.

"Sean died last night." The words punched Alan in the stomach.

"Really?" Alan asked.

"Yeah, my uncle said he overheard the coroner telling the chief of police that his eyes were wide open and he was scared when he died."

"Man you watch too many movies. Sean was an asshole anyway. The best thing he ever did was to help us burn that psycho's house down."

"Damn it Alan, we were never going to talk about that. What if somebody tells the police?"

"Don't worry, just keep your mouth shut and we'll be all right," Alan said.

The tall football jock had left Alan in his room, running home as the night approached fast. He did not want to be caught out after dark. Outside Alan's room, the window above his bed rattled. Alan jumped up and backed away from it.

"Who's there?" he squeaked.

He turned and grabbed the door handle to get out of the room. The knob was stuck. Alan pushed on the door with his shoulder as he tried to break through. A cold chill wrapped around him, and he was afraid to turn around. He could feel the presence in the room.

"Who's there?" he whispered.

"You know who it is," the voice replied.

"It can't be," he replied, turning to face her. "You're dead—how—" she cut his words off as her hand slid around his throat.

"Redemption and mercy for those that have faith," Audrey whispered.

Alan stared into her eyes as they glowed deep green. "I—I don't believe—"

"Maybe you should," she replied squeezing tighter as his veins bulged in his neck.

"WHHYY—" he gasped as a vessel ruptured in his brain.

"Death. The end for you," she replied.

Audrey stood over the lifeless body, then uttered under her breath. "Evil knows no bounds; the wicked shall perish. Righteousness is honorable even in death."

Across town that evening, she visited two more players, their fate just as grisly. They did not seek redemption.

37

CARL SPENT THE SUMMER WORKING at the local lumber mill, his mind on Audrey and Chloe twenty-four hours a day. Mona kept the theater going. She was still distraught by the loss of her friend but anxious to put the pieces together about the events that happened the weekend Audrey was spotted and Chloe's grave found empty. Carl was formulating a plan, rat-holing every dime he could as weeks turned into months, his bank account growing slowly. He was saving his money to go to her in the old world. Mona had never thought of it; she always imagined Audrey would return to them in Washington. Carl met up with his cousin at the theater.

"Hey Mona, how are you?"

"I'm good; you know you don't have to buy a ticket."

"I didn't come to see a movie, just to talk to you."

"Come around, I'll unlock the booth."

Carl joined her inside the ticket booth while the evening shows filled. He broke the silence a few minutes later.

"I'm going over there, as soon as I can earn enough money to travel."

"How do you know she will be there? Besides, you don't know any foreign languages." Mona was torn. She did not know what to do now. Should she go with her cousin or stay in America and risk not finding the truth.

"Please come with me. I need you," Carl pleaded.

"I don't know. What if she is not there? She never told us how soon she returns; she already came back once, maybe that is all she will get?"

"No, I don't believe it; we're connected, I can feel it. She comes to me in my dreams."

"Recently?"

"Yes."

"Did she say anything?"

"No, not yet. I know she wants to say something; I'm not sure why she doesn't or if she's not able."

"I will think about it Carl. I don't know if I can do this. I'll think it over."

"Good."

Nights were the hardest on Carl; he couldn't sleep. His hours were spent staring at the ceiling above. The hours meshed together as he strolled down memory lane with Audrey holding his hand. Her smile stuck with him and that is what drove him to find her. He knew she would be in her homeland if he could get over there.

That summer in Washington was another cooker. Carl was melting in a pool of sweat as he lay in bed. The moonlight shimmered through the open windows and onto the floor. Audrey came to him a few hours later. Carl was unsure whether he was awake or dreaming, but she was there, standing at the foot of the bed. She was a shadow of her former self. Her lips moved as the words drifted across the bed to him.

COME TO ME. The phrase echoed in his head when he woke up the next morning.

At the end of the summer, Carl found himself driving out to the house in the valley. The burned-out remains were no higher than a few feet off the ground, the large chimney standing above, the last pillar towering over the rubble.

Carl climbed through the knee-high grass to the short hill above the house and breathed in the late summer flowers. He wanted to visit the meadow where they had spent time together. The meadow was a place of solitude for him and a place of healing. His heart was no longer in pain. It was in that moment that she came to him again as a vision on the hill; the same ghostly apparition he had seen before. She stretched her arm out to the east, pointing. He knew for sure that she was calling him back to the castle in Moszna. Carl could not get down the hill fast enough, tumbling down a few feet, then standing back up, sliding his way to the car. He drove as fast as he could back to the theater, where he knew he would find Mona.

"I saw her." He was nearly out of breath, screaming it through the small holes drilled into the plexiglass window of the ticket booth.

"Carl, quiet down. Come around the side, I'll let you in."

She had barely unlatched the door when Carl pushed it in, knocking her backward, his hand grabbing her arm before she hit the floor. Carl slammed the door behind them, making sure nobody was around to eavesdrop on their conversation as he stared through the glass front of the booth into the lobby.

"She came to me. She came to me Mona."

"Where?" she asked.

"In the meadow on the hill above the house." He still had her image in his head in sharp detail.

"What did she say?"

"Nothing, she just pointed to the east. She stuck a single finger as she stretched her arm out. We have to go to her; I know she is waiting for us."

"I don't know Carl. I can't leave now; I start college in a few weeks. What if she isn't there, then what?"

"You have to believe me."

"I believe you Carl, and I believe she came to you, but I don't know if I can handle not finding anything when we get there. I'm sorry. I can't go. Please understand," she said.

"I'll send for you, you'll see, as soon as I get there and find her, I'll send for you."

"Okay. Give me a hug," she said as they embraced. "Call me as soon as you get there," she replied.

Carl spent the rest of the summer working every day, his thoughts stuck in the past. He focused on her hand in his those many times they drove around town and her elegance while playing the piano, while the group of friends sat around the fireplace. Those were days he knew he would never get back, but he was still willing to go searching for her, just as soon as he could earn the rest of the money. Carl visited Frankie a week before he was scheduled to leave.

"Hey Carl, she still sounds sweet under the hood."

"Yeah thanks Frankie, I have not had much time to run her since the last race."

"I was meaning to talk to you for a long time, just couldn't get myself to come around."

"That's okay Frankie, it has been hard on all of us." Carl paused, catching his breath. "I'm leaving on Monday to fly over to see if I can find her. Do you mind if I store my car in the shop while I am gone?"

"You don't even have to ask; I will take care of it until you get back."

Carl was refreshed knowing he could count on his cousin. Frankie never brought up the accident with Lauren, preferring to remember the good times he had with her. They pushed the car up to the back of the long garage, next to the wrecked Chevelle. Frankie helped him jack it up to take pressure off the tires. Carl gave it a last look over his shoulder as he stepped out of the garage. Frankie closed the door and they shook hands. Carl waved from the street, then headed to the railroad tracks and shortcut home. He could not remember a more lonely time as he walked on the tracks that evening. The Skookumchuck River was just a trickle below him as he crossed the bridge, his ears straining to listen for an oncoming train. Assured he could make the six hundred yards across the river, he slowly stepped from tie to tie, watching the river below him. It was a wicked twist of fate as he heard the horn blaring at the railroad crossing a quarter mile away. Carl knew it wasn't the time to make quick movements. If he made one false move, he would get stuck between the railroad ties. His pulse raced. He was only halfway across the trestle and the train was picking up speed as it filled the track in front of him. His only option was to jump off the trestle into the murky water below him. He jumped, holding his breath a second before he hit the water. His feet slapped the water and he slipped under the surface. Carl emerged a few yards downstream and on the opposite bank. At least he was on the right side. The train rumbled overhead on the trestle as he stood in the muddy water shivering. He trudged up the bank and walked home.

PART II
THE SEARCH

38

THE WHINE OF THE TURBINE engines escalated as the airliner climbed skyward. Carl watched Seattle disappear beneath him from his coach seat near the back of the plane, the next sixteen hours a quiet time of reflection and planning. Traveling with Audrey was easy; she had done everything, down to the last detail. The fact that they made it through three countries without passports was a mystery to him. He sat there with his passport in hand and would be entering Europe legally. His arrival put him there in late fall as he stepped out of the airport in Berlin. Oktoberfest was in full swing, with drunks filling the streets.

Carl boarded the train to Poland and joined a group of young tourists sharing their six-passenger cabin. It was not as luxurious as when he traveled last winter, but it was getting him there.

"Hello, I'm Carl."

"Ah you're American. I'm Stephan, my friends don't speak very good English, so you are stuck with me I guess. Where are you going?"

"Moszna, it is in the southwest region of Poland."

"Ah very good Carl, we know that area. You are traveling alone, no?"

"Yes, I'm alone. I'm looking for someone."

"I hope you find her my friend. It is a girl right?"

"Yes."

Carl could not sleep in the cramped compartment. His companions had stretched out in the cabin, taking up all the leg room. And they snored incessantly.

Opole train station was deserted when they arrived at the end of the train line and jumping off point to the estate. It would be hours until daylight, and Carl had no clue how he would make the twenty-one mile trip.

"Where you going Carl?" Stephan asked as they stepped onto the platform in front of the terminal.

The tourists had hit the end of the road as well and were studying their guidebook, looking for a place to stay.

"My friend lives down the road from here. I just need to get a ride," Carl said, pointing.

"You probably won't find anybody to take you out there until tomorrow. Why don't you hang out with us; we're going to camp out in the park tonight."

He had not planned any farther than getting to Opole, and now it was evident he would have to wait.

"Okay," Carl replied.

Morning came early for them, the group sleeping under a large tarp to keep the dew off. Carl stretched his aching muscles as he stood. He stared at the courtyard. It dawned on him that he did not remember much about the town, other than its small size. Most of the two dozen houses were run down and appeared vacant.

"Carl, come with us to breakfast, my girlfriend found a restaurant just across the street; it is cheap. Then we can talk about how we will get you out to your friend."

Stephan seemed genuine enough to him, and it was unlikely Carl would find anyone in town that spoke English, nor would they be willing to help him. The small town had minimal services. A single-story two-tone mint-green restaurant building sat in stark contrast to the brick-and-mortar homes around it. He followed the tourists to the restaurant on the other side of the town square.

The group sat around a long table, waiting for service. It was the kind of place staffed by family. A young waitress was behind the counter, chatting to the patrons. They paid no attention to the group of teens. In the kitchen you could hear two elderly ladies chatting away, the conversation lost in translation to Carl.

"What do you want?" the waitress barked.

"Yes, we will take breakfast for us, pastries, whatever you have. And coffee, Carl wants coffee," Stephan growled.

The waitress wrote on her notepad then hurried off to the kitchen. Carl asked Stephan about his life and where they were going. It was the usual conversation you would have when you meet someone for the first time.

"Ask the waitress if someone has a car to give me a ride up to my friend's house."

"Sure Carl, no problem."

When the waitress returned, her arms were loaded down with plates full of pirogues, the traditional style of wrapped dough pastry in Poland. She had one hand holding the pot of coffee, which she nearly dropped on the floor when Stephan asked her about a ride for Carl. Their conversation was heated, or so it seemed to Carl. A guttural banter took place back and forth for a minute. Stephan's friends were less on the convention of showing good manners, shoving the food down as fast as they could.

"She said there is a man sitting at the bar that might take us; she is asking him now."

Carl watched the young woman as her arms flailed around. She smiled, then her face grimaced, as the old man turned to look at the group of teens. She pointed in their direction. The old man nodded. What it meant, Carl had no clue.

"Ask her if she has seen my friend Audrey; you would remember her if you saw her."

"You ask her, here she comes."

"Excuse me, I was wondering if you have seen my friend. She may have traveled through here a few months ago?"

"What does she look like?"

Carl did not even have a photograph of her, nor did he know if she could have one taken, but her image was burnt into his mind in vivid detail.

"She is five feet six, maybe one hundred twenty pounds, beautiful face, auburn hair, but her presence would tell you she were here, just by looking at her."

The waitress shrugged her shoulders. “No, I have not seen someone like that. That older man will take you wherever you want to go. But it will cost you, he said.”

“How much?” Carl was not one to beat around the bush, hitting her right between the eyes.

“Two hundred dollars American, is the minimum he said he would take to drive you,” the waitress replied.

“Okay.” Carl glanced at the driver, nodding his head up and down, signaling him that he would accept his price.

“Carl, you did not even negotiate with him. Let me talk to him. I’m sure I can get a cheaper price.”

“No Stephan. I'll pay it.”

Stephan stared at Carl as his eyes darted around the table at his friends. “Okay Carl it is your money. If you don’t mind, we would like to come with you.”

“Sure, I could use the company and an interpreter.”

They finished their breakfast, then stepped outside where the old man was waiting for them. Blue smoke tumbled out of the exhaust and rolled across the cool pavement.

“You sit up front Carl; I’ll tell him where you want to go.”

The van had seen its better years. It lurched back and forth as it rumbled down the road, the shocks completely wore out, each bump felt for another thirty seconds as it oscillated up and down. Farther out of the village, the driver slowly steered the van around the narrow roads leading up to the castle. Carl remembered the route exactly, down to the stone walls outside the village. Further down the road, a group of old men were raking leaves into piles at the sides of the road. The driver stopped the van as he approached the castle's entrance; his argument with Stephan in back told Carl something was wrong.

“What is it Stephan?”

“He says he won’t drive inside. Something about the castle being haunted and nobody lives here. Are you sure this is the place?”

“Yes, I’ll walk.”

“We’re coming with you.”

Stephan said something to the driver before he left. The driver pulled onto the road and the engine coughed as it sped off, spewing more noxious smoke. An early morning fog had blanketed the countryside, concealing the castle in the mist.

Carl walked through the entrance gate, noticing that the huge gargoyle statues on the twin pillars of the entrance had changed their facial features. Their eyes looked straight at him. Goosebumps crawled up his skin. His new friends whispered amongst themselves.

"The old man said that spirits of the dead live here. He said it has been that way for a long time. Are you sure you want to go in there Carl?"

"Look Stephan, if you don't want to come with me, fine. But, if you are going to come, stop acting like a weeny."

"Weeny? Stephan is not a hot dog?"

"No, like a spineless man that is afraid of his own shadow."

"I'm not scared Carl," Stephan replied, pushing his chest out.

The castle materialized out of the fog as they walked closer, the young gals in the group marveling at the tall spires.

"Wait here. I'm going to find the caretaker. I'll be right back."

"Sure Carl, whatever. We will just hang out here and wait for—for whatever comes for us."

Carl ran across the estate grounds to the caretaker's small cottage; he could see smoke rising from the chimney as he approached the front door. Carl knocked on the door, shaking it. The caretaker opened the door, with a deepening smile coming across his lips.

"Karl!" he exclaimed, as he threw his arms around Carl.

The caretaker loosened his embrace, then motioned for Carl to step inside as he disappeared into a bedroom, returning a few seconds later.

"Here," the caretaker said, handing Carl the large skeleton key to the front door.

"Thank you," Carl replied.

Carl's mind raced. Would she be there waiting for him? He had no answers; his new friends were still standing in the same spot when he approached them. They followed like a herd of cows going to slaughter, single file. They watched him turn the large key in the lock, the door taking nearly all his effort to swing open. The castle had been shut up since last year, and they could smell the dank conditions inside, its cool interior unnerving his new friends.

"Do you think she is here? Maybe we should come back when she is home?"

"She's not here Stephan. Not yet."

They wandered around inside, looking at all the fine furnishings while Carl built a fire, the main room glowing in warmth a few hours later.

"Your friend, she is very wealthy Carl."

"She does have some money," Carl replied.

"I think she needs a maid," Stephan said, running his hand along the dusty fireplace mantle.

"There are more than three hundred rooms here. Take whatever ones you want, just leave the one with the initials A.A. on the door alone; that room is off limits. Tell them for me Stephan, tell them that one is haunted."

"Okay Carl, no problem," he replied, relaying the message to his friends.

Inside Audrey's chambers, Carl collapsed on the bed he had shared with her last winter, the huge covers engulfing his body as exhaustion overtook him.

39

THE DEATH OF THE TEENS in Centralia had garnered much attention. In Seattle, the top newspaper had sent down their best investigative journalist to dig into the story. Tracking down the students who were at the scene of Lauren and Tommy's deaths, he interviewed them one by one, each one telling a slightly different account of the events. After months of research, he broke the story. The headlines stated a grisly tale.

13 Teens Die

His article chronicled the timeline of events starting with the car crash, and Lauren getting run down. It ended with the last teen dying in his sleep. Paragraph after paragraph, he quoted the surviving teens, their comments about seeing an apparition floating in the middle of the road right before Lauren was struck, each detail of the night, each recollection of Audrey jotted down in his notes, coming to life on the page. The article would have died having made only the third page, if it had not caught the attention of an archbishop of the local diocese. His faith had prepared him for the possibility of the spirit world clashing with the physical world, sending him into offense mode. His superiors across the Atlantic Ocean were alerted within hours.

Near Rome City: Undisclosed underground location.

"Finally, we have decisive evidence and eyewitness accounts to the actuality that a Smeric is loose. The time has come, we must prepare ourselves."

The words of the priest enlivened the group of soldiers sitting at the large table around him. The other priests stood in unison behind them.

"Where do we start, Padre?"

"It was spotted in a small town south of Seattle, Washington."

"America. Good."

"You will leave in the morning, get some sleep, then we will meet again in the chapel for your blessing and sendoff."

"Yes Father."

The group of hunters had been formed centuries before, during the dark ages. Their mission was the enforcement of the holy sacrament of the church. They had not failed, ever, their military tactics unmatched. They were hand picked from elite forces around the world. There were six regular soldiers; the seventh was a high priest, knowledgeable of all things living, dead, or in-between.

Waiting for nearly two centuries for an event like this, the church had kept detailed records and procedures for dealing with the undead; the priest had his work cut out for him. He burned the midnight oil as he poured over secret church documents in the hidden library. It was outside the reach of the ordinary citizen, its review reserved only for the high clergy. Thumbing through an age-old script, the priest adjusted his bifocal glasses, as he strained to read the small text. His Latin was rusty from a lack of use, his interpretation of the text incomplete. The priest prayed for forgiveness as he spent the last few hours before daylight on his knees in humility.

The team landed in Seattle two days later, then traveled to Centralia, looking for the students who were interviewed in the paper. They tracked down one of the teens that was interviewed, and she pointed them straight to Frankie. Their arrival in his driveway was similar to the FBI appearing, down to the black SUV.

"Young man, we'd like to have a word with you."

"Whatever it is I didn't do it; I'm on the straight and narrow now. Got a full-time job turning wrench at Toads Auto Shop down the road."

"It is only partly about you. Did you know the girl who was killed earlier this year? Her name was Lauren."

"Yeah, I knew her."

The priest pushed through the soldiers to present himself to Frankie.

"Son, I am from an organization that is centuries old; we need to know what happened. Do you know what I am talking about?"

"No, I'm not following you." Frankie was playing dumb with the priest; he knew what a priest wore and could tell immediately that this man with his starched white collar and black shirt was not from the burger joint in town.

"We're here because some kids saw something. They say they saw—an apparition."

"A ghost? Is that what you mean?" Frankie said, his statement a jab at the authority figure standing in front of him.

"It is the modern term people use, yes."

"Sorry, can't help you, don't believe in them. All I believe is in a good race car and a six pack of beer. If you don't mind I've got to get ready for work."

"So you don't care that your friend was killed by this thing."

"Nobody said Lauren was killed by a ghost; I didn't. She ran out in front of a car; it was her fault. I've got to go."

Frankie knew these guys meant business. He also knew he had to get away from them as fast as he could. He was sure the thugs would come back, and their second visit would probably not be as formal as the first. He watched his mirror as he drove across town, the black sport utility vehicle following him block after block. He lost them as he sped up, leaving them at a red light, swinging the car around into an alley as they passed by. He ditched the car, then ran the two blocks down the alley to the back of the theater, banging on the door frantically hoping someone would open it. Mona appeared at the door minutes later, the first show still an hour away.

"What is it Frankie?"

"Somebody is here looking for information about Audrey; they came to my house a half hour ago."

"Who was it?" she asked.

"A priest and six thugs. I don't know who the hell they are—bad people. I think they will come to talk to you soon. We need to get out of town."

"Where would we go? Are you sure they weren't just another news crew?"

"No dammit, they wanted to know if I had seen an apparition—how clear could they be? I'm scared Mona."

"Okay, okay Frankie, calm down. Take my car to get some clothes and I'll wait for you here."

He did not want to go back home, but she was right. If he were going to leave town for a while, he needed clothes and money that he had stashed at his house. Frankie stepped back into the alley and closed the door behind him, then turned, running face to face into one of the soldiers.

"We are not here to play games, young man."

The hand around his throat told him that these guys meant business. The solid punch to his stomach left him bent over in the alley, spitting up blood.

"Kiss my ass, I'll never tell you anything. Beat the crap out of me if you must."

"Oh, you will talk," the priest replied. "Everybody talks—one way or another."

With his hands bound, the back of the truck was his immediate home, Frankie unaware where they were going. The truck pulled alongside the large ornate church located across town, the team carrying Frankie downstairs into the cellar.

"We have ways to make you talk."

Frankie was coming to from the first knockout when a fist to his face knocked him unconscious again. He regained consciousness as they stuck a needle in his arm. "There, a few minutes and we will get the truth."

"What did you give me? I'll freaking cut your heart out; let me out of here." Frankie struggled, pulling hard at the ropes bound around his wrists holding him to the chair as he screamed at the top of his lungs. His cries would go unanswered, the basement walls too thick to let even the loudest noises outside.

"Now who was the apparition that was here the night Lauren was killed?" The priest pushed his face inches away from Frankie's.

"She won't like it if I tell you. She'll come for you."

“Ah it is good you are talking. Tell us more.”

“She lived here with us.”

“Who?”

“Audrey.”

He told them more than he wanted to. It was something he could not stop as the psychoactive drug loosened his lips. Frankie spilled it all. The priest pushed more drugs into his arm as a soldier worked Frankie over, slapping him around as he slurred his words. He died early the next morning after another fatal dose.

“Get rid of the body. Let’s find his cousin.”

40

CARL HAD SETTLED INTO THE castle as though it was home, his new friends unsure of their surroundings, all of them visibly shaken by what the driver had told them. Stephan seemed less concerned, and Carl decided to use him to research Audrey's background. His insatiable appetite to see her again never waning as Carl searched the castle room by room before stumbling on the closed-up wing and archives of the library. Thousands of books lay in front of him, most of them in Latin, some in German. The most recent were in English, although those were from the late eighteen hundreds. With Stephan's help, he searched the volumes for anything around the years of the late sixteen hundreds to seventeen twenties, the only dates he could remember Audrey telling him.

"Here Carl, I found a book that is from seventeen twenty." The volume was large, the leather cover closed with a strap with pages inlaid with gold.

"What does it say?" Carl asked.

"It says Aniela Andrysiak. Maybe she changed her name? You said she called herself Audrey Anderson. Well, A.A., same, but an English name does sound better in America, right?"

Carl nodded his head but did not tell about the first time he met Audrey at the river, when she said her real name to him as he held her. He had remembered it—in his subconscious.

Stephan flipped the pages as he read the titles. The book was a chronological family history of who and where, Aniela's name coming up page after page.

"Look here, it says she was married to a wealthy land baron and they rebuilt this estate some time in the seventeen hundreds, adding onto it for several years. No children, but it says they lived here a while. I'm not sure how long. Maybe there are more books?" Stephan said, looking around the library for another volume.

Carl rummaged through the shelves as he searched for a book with the initials A.A. on the front cover. They worked throughout the night as Stephan translated innocuous facts, most of them unrelated to Audrey.

Mona waited for Frankie to come back to the theater, unaware she was being watched from across the street until she noticed the dark smokey exhaust spewing from a black SUV. She stared at the truck from the ticket booth. She was thinking that it was odd they would leave their vehicle running all night, the shadowy figures inside never moving. It unnerved her, as it finally hit her that these could be the guys who questioned Frankie. The fact that he did not come back scared her. She dialed the phone. A police dispatcher answered, listened to her concern, then relayed the information to the field. Officer Spence showed up a few minutes later, parking opposite the SUV. He stood outside the theater a few minutes watching the SUV, then went in to talk with Mona.

"Hey Mona."

"Officer Spence, thanks for coming, I don't know if it is anything, but that black SUV has been sitting there idling for the last two hours and it's freaking me out. Can you go talk to them?"

"Sure thing."

Officer Spence stepped off the sidewalk and into the street; the guy in the driver's seat stared back at him as he moved across the road, then he threw the truck into drive, burning rubber on the asphalt as he shot out of the parking spot, narrowly missing the cop. Officer Spence sped after them, siren blaring, lights flashing, the SUV weaving in and out of the city streets as they tried to shake him. The driver of the SUV put caution to the wind as they flew across the river bridge, speeding out of town to the north. Officer Spence was close behind when they slammed on the brakes, the entire team of soldiers exiting their rig with automatic weapons drawn. The hail of gunfire shattered Officer Spence's windshield, sending him careening off the side of the road and into the ditch. The patrolman's face burned as he pulled himself off the steering wheel; a trickle of blood oozed out of his nose. The black SUV disappeared into the night.

Mona closed the theater ticket booth and clocked out. Her walk through town was lonely and full of anticipation of being abducted. She stumbled upon Frankie's car a few blocks away from the theater. She reached around the steering column and located the key in the ignition. Mona drove it back to his house. She searched the garage then his house and her fright escalated further when she was not able to find him. Two days later, his body was found floating alongside the river bank a mile from his house. Mona knew what she had to do; her only choice was to flee the country and join Carl. She was able to slip out of town a few days later.

The black SUV rolled through town a week later, this time meeting up with the local travel agent, their information easily obtained for a few dollars. The agent figured the priest was just interested in helping Mona, and what harm could come from that? Mona was already on her way across the ocean, landing in Paris, on the only flight she could get to Europe on short notice. Mona bought a rail pass and worked her way across France, then Germany, before entering Poland a few days later. Her journey was not as pleasant as Carl's, but she had the female card on her side, getting a ride from the same gentleman at the restaurant for only thirty dollars, her smile filling in for her lack of money. She stepped out of his van at the front gate and he bid her farewell in Polish. Mona was still unsure if Carl had made it.

She crept through the entrance as the gargoyle's eyes followed her. The castle rose up in the distance: dark and menacing. Mona approached the door, raised her hand to knock, then paused. Her hand reverberated as she struck the door multiple times. Her knocks on the large wooden door went unanswered for a few minutes. She was preparing to turn around when the door swung open. The bleach-blond companion of Stephan stood in front of her.

"I'm sorry, is Carl here?"

The young girl had no idea what she said except for Carl's name.

She pulled Mona inside without speaking and led her back to the library, where the two researchers had spent the last few weeks studying.

"Carl?" she called out.

Carl stepped out from behind a long bookcase. "I'm glad you came. What took you so long?"

"Carl, they killed Frankie," she said, running up to him and throwing her arms around him as she teared up.

"What happened? Who killed Frankie?" Carl choked as he spit the words out, trying to clear his throat.

"These guys came into town with a priest. They wanted information about Audrey. Frankie said they came to see him at his house, then he came by the theater; he was so scared. He was supposed to meet me at the theater that night, but after he left, he never came back and then they found his body a few days later in the river."

The air left Carl's chest as he sat there stunned. His cousin was everything to him. Frankie was that one guy he really looked up to, and now he was gone.

"Who were they?"

"Frankie said one of them was a priest, the others must have been guards or something. I don't know; I was so scared."

"That's crazy—"

"That's not all. A black SUV pulled up in front of the theater that night. I called the cops, and when Officer Spence went to talk to them, the sped off, nearly running him down."

"What the hell—" Carl mumbled. "Were they waiting for you?"

"I think so. Who else would they be looking for?"

"I don't know. Do you think they followed you here?"

"I'm not sure," she finished.

Carl filled her in on all their research and the volumes of information they had scoured out of the books. He filled her in on Audrey's real name, and the fortune she had amassed. She filled him in on the sleigh ride Audrey took her on the year before, traveling out into the countryside, right to the spot where she was killed. Carl's mind tabulated the information quickly, coming up with a new direction, but waited until he could talk to Mona alone.

"Who are these people here?"

She had meant to ask, but in all her excitement to see her cousin, she bypassed Stephan, not acknowledging his existence.

"Stephan, Mona. Mona, Stephan. He's helping me translate these documents, and I am already learning Polish and some Latin."

Stephan smiled at the new acquaintance; his other friends lounged in the great hall.

"It is a pleasure to meet you Mona. Carl has told me all about you."

She shook his hand, but the apprehension in her eyes told Carl she was nervous to have an outsider among them.

The afternoon sun cast rays of orange light across the side of the castle. The sunlight pushed a kaleidoscope of colors through the stained-glass windows before the orb slipped below the horizon. Carl lit a few lamps so they could make their way back to the kitchen. The flames bathed the library in a yellowy cast as the shadows of their bodies danced behind them on the bookshelves. They searched for another hour, then gave up when Stephan complained for the third time that his stomach was painful.

The group had taken turns fixing different meals, and tonight was Carl's attempt at cooking. It was something he did not put much effort into, his longing for a fine meal with his love prodding him to work harder and longer. The other teens sat around the table discussing something in German. They dropped their plans halfway through the meal as they spoke with Stephan about their desire to leave in the morning.

"They are leaving tomorrow Carl, but I will stay, I can catch up to them in Switzerland after the new year; they want to go to the mountains."

"Thank you for staying Stephan. Tomorrow, Mona is going to show me something up the road. If you want to come, we would be glad you did."

"Sure, I am here to help you."

Mona shook her head back and forth.

Mona's distrust of her new friend was growing by the minute; she did not understand why a foreigner would help them so willingly with nothing to gain in return, other than a free place to stay. Stephan was a drifter, not settling into one area more than a couple of weeks, and had tagged along with his gypsy friends for more than a year.

"We found a book in the library a few days ago, and Stephan has translated it. I think it is the key to finding Audrey. You gotta see it Mona, it is very old, and written entirely in Latin."

Carl did not want to tell Mona exactly what the book was in front of Stephan and his friends, although he had translated the entire text; Carl had written it down word for word as Stephan spoke. It was a book older than anything he had ever seen, dating from the twelfth century. The transcript was a bundle of loose-leaf pages, hand scribed and placed in a traditional wooden box.

Mona came to Audrey's chambers where Carl was waiting for her. The yellow glow of her lamp barely illuminated the expanse.

"I could not tell you about the rest of the book Stephan had translated, and he never asked why I wanted it translated. It was a prayer, or a spell. I think it is a spell to raise the dead."

"Really?" Mona smiled.

"There is more. Audrey's name was scrolled in the book on the side of one page, right next to the spell. I mean her real name was there, Aniela Andrysiak, and here is the best part. Her name means '*Angel* and *The Messenger'*."

"I don't know Carl, what happens if we bring her back and she is pissed off at us? Then what?"

"I'm willing to risk it. I'd rather die now than live without her. Don't you want to see her again?"

"Of course I do, but I'm scared. Can't you tell? I'm on the run, and who knows when those guys will show up here; it is only a matter time before they put it all together."

Carl had not put much thought into the hunters, his goal of researching Audrey filling his head twenty-four hours a day. Now things had changed. They were on a mission, and time could be running out for them.

"You're right, we need to prepare for their arrival, and you're probably right about them killing Frankie too. First thing in the morning, I'm going to see if Stephan will help us get some guns. Somebody in this country must have access to weapons."

"I'll stay with you Carl. I owe Chloe and Audrey that much, although I don't like the idea of getting weapons."

"I know you don't, but we may need them."

41

OUTSIDE THE CASTLE, THE CARETAKER had hitched up the team to the covered coach at Carl's request. The rest of the staff was gone, so he acted as the driver as well. Leaving the estate grounds, he took them outside into the country, where Audrey had shown Mona where she had been slain. The smell of the leaf piles burning alongside the road filled the air. The old men were doing the age-old job of cleaning up before the long freeze of winter. It was full daylight, but the smokey air and fog had nearly choked off the sun, the sky steel grey. The driver stopped the carriage outside a locked gate to the graveyard. A small chapel sat on top a short rise in the middle of the tombstones. Mona recounted the story she had heard from Audrey; Carl listened intently.

"Is her grave around here somewhere?"

"She never said anything about that, Carl. What are you thinking?"

"The book said if the body were brought out of the grave on the eve of the winter solstice, then there would be a chance for resurrection, or an awakening. The words don't really translate that well."

If Stephan did not think Carl was crazy before, he surely did now, especially with the addition of his cousin, who was as eager to dig up a grave that was centuries old. His morbid curiosity was the only thing that was keeping him there, and his plot of stealing money from them. Mona, Carl, and Stephan searched the graveyard near the chapel, then separated, each taking a different section. They walked among the hundreds of tombstones that were worn away from the weather, making them nearly illegible. Headstone after headstone, Carl searched the rows before meeting up with Mona. They stood between two large stones. The cool air radiated off them into Carl. Mona scanned the graveyard but couldn't come up with an answer. It struck her a minute later.

“She would have a large tombstone; they were wealthy right?” she blurted out. She said it louder than she wanted it to come out, her words echoing across the empty graveyard.

"I guess so," Carl replied.

“Or a crypt!” Mona added. Carl had walked past a half dozen crypts. He had not looked at them; his mind was stuck on finding her name on a tombstone. They ran back, scanning the front of the crypts. The cousins eliminated four of them right off the bat, the last names nothing close to Audrey’s.

"There. It's right there!" Carl yelled.

Aniela Andrysiak.
1722

Carl ran up to the crypt. It was the most ornate in the graveyard, and the largest, measuring twenty feet across by fourteen feet deep. Aniela’s name was carved into the door in fancy script. Pieces of the slate roof lay on the ground in front of the door. Carl stepped onto one of the tiles and cracked it.

“We’re going to need a pry bar.” The words had barely come out of his mouth when an axe flew past his head, shattering the rusted lock.

“Are you trying to kill me?” Carl yelled.

“You want inside. Stephan is here to help, as long as I get money.”

Carl saw a new side to Stephan. Stephan was a grifter. If money was the only thing that motivated his new friend, Carl would oblige him.

Carl pushed the door open and descended the wet stairway into the cavern below. He moved forward slowly as he inched into the dark confines of the burial room. He could barely make out the solitary coffin that was perched on a marble bench, unseen for nearly 250 years.

“Now what?” Mona asked. "Think she is still inside?"

Carl wasted no time wondering, as he pushed up on the coffin lid. It creaked as the rusty hinges broke free. Audrey was lying inside peacefully, her skeleton still wrapped in her opulent clothing. Her burgundy dress that was made centuries before was worn away by time.

"We take her back home; she will be safer there," Carl replied. "This will be the first place they look, as soon as they find out who she is."

VATICAN CITY

"Let's hurry gentlemen; we don't have much time left." The priest pushed the team of soldiers as they worked against the clock and Audrey's return.

Armed with their new found knowledge about Audrey, the team of seven loaded onto the train in Rome. They traveled throughout the night, crossing the Alps into Austria. Behind them, a team of researchers in Italy were working on Audrey's background with the information they were able to pull out of Frankie before they killed him.

Carl and Stephan loaded the skeleton into the carriage.

"Driver, take us back to the castle," Carl ordered. "As fast as you can go."

"Yes sir," the driver replied as he shook the reins, spurring the team of horses into action, the carriage lurching forward, jolting the occupants inside. The carriage slid around a corner in the road, as the right rear wheel scraped against a stone wall. The passenger's held on tight as they were thrown around. The horses pulled harder with the crack of the driver's whip. Steam billowed out of their nostrils as their hooves gained purchase on the pavement. Miles away, the castle loomed ahead of them. Carl could see it in the distance, silhouetted by the moon rising behind it.

"Stephan, can you get some rifles? Or guns?" Carl asked.

"Yes Carl, but it will cost you a lot of money. This is not America; not everyone is allowed to own them here."

"Fine, get as many as you can buy with this," Carl replied, pulling a wad of hundreds out of his pocket.

"Carl, where did you get all that money?" Mona asked.

"It's Audrey's. I don't think she would mind now," he replied.

Stephan grabbed the wad out of Carl's hand. "I will get guns, knives, whatever you want Carl."

Stephan was the unlikely henchman they needed, bribed with more money than he had ever seen. He did not disappoint, buying four assault rifles left over from the last world war. They were antiques, but functional enough to make a stand if it came to that.

Winter solstice was a few days away, and the train crossing the Alps was delayed because of an avalanche, holding the team back, prolonging the inevitable confrontation.

"Carl, you ever shoot a rifle before?" Stephan's words had a ring of condescension in them. The more time Carl spent with Stephan, the less he liked him.

"Yes, a few times."

"I never have; it is illegal to own a gun in most countries in Europe. Only the wealthy own them, but now that I have one, I will keep it."

"You keep it Stephan, as long as it makes you happy. But remember, the man that lives by the gun, is the man who dies by the gun."

Stephan sat on the couch, cradling the weapon.

Audrey lay on her bed in the master suite, Carl's love for her growing stronger every day. He left her alone, afraid to disturb her for the next seventy-two hours, until the solstice.

Mona had practiced the ceremony, going over every detail dozens of times. She recited the passage until she memorized it word for word.

Carl had ordered the caretaker to shut the front gate, locking it with a thick chain, the first line of defense against the team.

"Carl, CARL—" Mona screamed down the hall to her cousin.

Carl poked his head out of the library. "What is it?"

"Come here, I found her!" she yelled back.

Carl ran down the hall, following Mona into a vacant room. A small casket sat in the corner against the stone wall.

"Is it her?" he asked.

“Yes, look at the end,” she replied.

Carl knelt down next to the casket and rubbed his hand across the nameplate.

*“**CHLOE**,” he whispered.*

"It's Chloe’s,” Mona said, breathless, collapsing on her knees.

"How did it get here?" he asked. Mona had kept her distance, covering her mouth with one hand.

"There is a shipping label on the side," he said, pushing his face closer to read the label. "It's tagged for transport here in Moszna.”

"What else does it say?" she asked.

"Uhm, just some numbers for tracking…” he paused, “and…Audrey's signature."

"Really?" she asked, whispering. "How can you tell?"

"It's hers. I'd recognize it anywhere,” Carl replied. "Come look at the other end. It's Chloe's name in cursive.”

“I’m fine over here,” she replied.

Tears ran down Mona’s face; her emotions were flooding back full force.

Two more days went by with the Stephan brandishing the automatic rifle, laughing and acting the fool. Carl and Mona wondered if Stephan would step up when the time came. They had no other choice but to ask him to stay; an extra gun was better than nothing.

The train carrying the team pulled into the local station late the next evening.

"Grab the bags, I'll secure transportation," the priest ordered, stepping off the train, leaving his crew behind to gather their things. He returned a few minutes later.

"Follow me," he said, grabbing a heavy tote as the others followed him out of the terminal to a waiting van. Their heavy baggage was a precursor to the events that would transpire that evening. The long plastic cases were full of an arsenal of weaponry and gadgets for dispatching the living as well as the dead.

Inside the castle, Carl was prepping his friends for the fight.

"We have three hundred rooms here; we can use that to our advantage, holding them off for as long as possible. Stephan, you take the downstairs. Mona and I will position ourselves upstairs. Try to get them to spread out. If we can separate them we may have a chance."

Stephan moved around the main level of the castle, looking for a place to hide.

Carl climbed six stories into one of the high towers where he could see the front gate. Minutes clicked by, his breath materializing through the open window as the evening grew colder. A flash of light bounced across the sky. Carl followed the source back to the gate where the team was using a torch to cut open the lock. He ran down the stairs, stumbling at a landing. He scrambled to his feet as he picked himself back up, then down the remaining flight.

"They're here!" Carl yelled to Mona at the other end of a long hallway.

"Okay—I'm ready," she yelled back.

Mona moved up to the bannister overlooking the living room.

"Stephan, they're here," she whispered, eliciting no response.

Stephan stepped out of a side door from the kitchen, moving quietly around to the front of the castle, stooping down behind a row of hedges. He watched the soldiers approach and waited for them to come into range.

"Aiyeee!" he screamed. The assault rifle roared as he squeezed the trigger, the muzzle spraying bullets haphazardly into the opposing force. The team ducked for cover.

Stephan poked his head above the hedge to an empty driveway. He searched the hedgerows that lined both sides of the road, spotting a lifeless body partially obscured by the shrubs.

"Come on—what are you waiting for?" he yelled.

The silence of the night was shattered with return gunfire directed at Stephan's last position.

Stephan crept around the end of the circular hedge separating him from the force. The soldiers continued firing. They reloaded then fired again as they moved forward, spraying the whole area with lead as they pushed toward the castle. Stephan crawled to the corner of the hedge, poking his nose out to take a look at the opening between the driveway and circular hedgerow. A soldier moved across the road, then crouched down.

"Hey—" Stephan yelled as he jumped up, his AK47 rifle lighting up the sky as fire flew from the barrel. The soldier stood there stunned for a few seconds and it was too late, the bullets tore into his chest, ripping through muscle, bone, and a single bullet piercing his heart before exiting his back. He fell forward, dead. His teammates returned fire again as Stephan ran wildly back and forth, the bullets whizzing past his body. He zigged, then zagged again. Round's bounced off the dirt and one ricocheted off the corner of the building as he disappeared around the castle and inside the kitchen unscathed.

Stephan reloaded as he hid in the kitchen just down the hallway from the living room. Mona was hiding in the same spot, her nose jutting up above the bannister every few seconds to see if anyone had made it inside.

"Do you see anything?" Carl whispered.

"No, it's too quiet," Mona replied.

Carl watched the front door from the balcony. The door latch clicked as it was pushed in. He had left it unlocked on purpose.

Carl aimed his rifle at the open door, waiting. A few seconds later, a shadowy figure moved inside quickly, then took a knee as he turned to motion for the others to follow.

"Get out!" Carl yelled.

"We can't do that," the priest yelled back from just outside the front door.

"We don't have to do this. Just leave us alone," Carl yelled back at him, ducking behind the large bannister at the top of the stairs. The soldier just inside the door moved to the right, ducking behind the large couch in front of the fireplace, aiming his rifle over it at the stairs where Carl was hiding.

"There is no way out; we're not leaving," the priest yelled back.

"I know, it was just a thought," Carl replied, his ears straining as he listened for any movement below him. He poked his head up above the railing, and wood splinters sprayed up around him as the sound of the rifle hit his ears. Blood trickled down the side of his face where a splinter of the bannister had grazed him.

Shattering glass broke the silence of the lower residence. Stephan crept to the source, his breathing fast and labored. A rush of adrenaline pumped through his body. He moved around the large prep island in the kitchen, straining his eyes in the darkness. His feet moved a step at a time as he crept toward the other end of the kitchen and open door. Gunfire erupted again from the living room where Carl was keeping the soldier behind the couch at bay. Stephan turned to step through the doorway and a shadowy figure stepped up behind him.

"Ooohph," Stephan gasped. "What—" he whispered as a sharp pain pierced the middle of his back, taking the wind out of him. The knife plunged deeper as the soldier pushed it in, pulling it upward. Stephan dropped his rifle as his body tingled before he slumped to his knees. He could feel the cool blade against his neck, then his world went black.

Carl crept around through the back of the castle, slowly working his way to the front, waiting for the right time to strike. His hands ached as he gripped the rifle tight. He did not have to wait long, hiding in an alcove behind a large statue. A soldier stepped out in front of him and he hit him in the back of the head with his rifle butt. Carl stepped over the lifeless body as he moved through the main level, keeping to the shadows next to the walls. His breathing slowed as he peeked around the corner and into the living room. The soldier that had fired on them was still crouched behind the sofa, bathed in the yellow glow of the fire behind him. Carl raised his rifle, pointing it directly at the soldiers head. *Click—*

"Misfire," he said. The silence of the room was immediately shattered by gunfire from the soldier as bullets tore into the wall above Carl's head. He ducked back down the hallway, running as fast as his legs would carry him. The soldier leapt into action and gave chase, catching a glimpse of Carl as he rounded the far corner. The soldier crept down the hallway, gun pointed ahead. Carl glanced around the corner.

"Almost," he mouthed to Mona.

She stood motionless behind a large statue with a sword in her right hand. The soldier stepped closer, close enough that Mona could smell him. She lifted the sword above her head in the shadows, bringing it down swiftly, catching the soldier mid forearm. The soldier moved slightly to deflect the blow, most of it absorbed by the rifle. He grunted from the pain, then swung his good arm across his body, catching Mona in the face, sending her tumbling backward. Carl ran down the hallway brandishing a short dagger and plunged it into the soldiers chest.

"Take that," Carl whispered as he pushed it in deeper. The soldier stumbled backward, the knife protruding from his chest as he fell over.

"Mona, you okay?" Carl asked as he picked her up off the floor.

"No, my face is killing me," she replied. "I think I have a loose tooth," she said, sticking her finger in her mouth."

"Come on, we don't have time for teeth, there's more of them. We have to move."

Mona slid her arm around Carl's neck as he carried her down the hallway and out a side door. He leaned her up against the building.

"Stay here, I'm going around back. If anyone comes—shoot first."

"No problem Carl."

Carl left her, making his way around the back of the castle to the broken window of the kitchen. He climbed inside, stepping on broken glass. Carl shifted his feet onto solid ground. He found Stephan's body a few feet further inside the kitchen. Carl looked at the living room through the oval window in the kitchen door. Something wasn't right. He moved forward to look through the window again and the living room was empty. Hair stood up on the back of Carl's neck as he noticed the reflection of a soldier in the glass. He wasn't sure how far away the man was, but he was sure that the guy was right behind him. Carl stood there motionless. If he spun around, he was sure he was dead. If he moved he was dead. Carl lowered the weapon.

"I know you are behind me," Carl said.

"Time for you to die," the soldier replied.

Carl turned to face him.

The soldier raised his weapon.

“Aiyee!” Stephan yelled as he plunged his switchblade into the soldier’s leg just below the knee.

“OOWWW,” the soldier yelled.

Carl raised his rifle, pulling the trigger, and a mass of bullets riddled their intended target ten feet away, killing the soldier.

“Stephan, are you okay?” Carl asked, kneeling down next to him.

“I’m out of here Carl—goodbye,” Stephan replied with his dying breath.

Outside near the front of the castle, the priest was preparing his ceremony.

"Holy father, maker of peace," he said while reading from an open book.

Mona walked up behind him, scanning the front of the home.

“If you are going to pray, you should pray for your soul, because you will be joining your maker soon enough.”

"You don't know what you are doing," the priest replied without turning to face her.

"Maybe. That's not for me to decide," she replied. "It's time."

"Prepare yourself, we will never stop looking for you," he whispered as gunfire erupted, knocking him to the ground.

“Mona, are you all right?” Carl yelled.

“Yeah, I'm over here."

Carl stepped through front door, where he could see Mona. His peripheral vision caught the movement of the last soldier. Carl swung the rifle to his right just as the soldier was taking aim at Mona. Gunfire erupted from both rifles. The soldier stepped back. A bullet whizzed past Mona's face. The soldier stumbled, then fell backward and clutched his chest, blood oozing around his fingers.

42

DAYBREAK CAME A FEW HOURS later as Mona and Carl hid the bodies inside the dungeon. Carl repaired the front gate, welding it shut with the torch to seal them off from the outside. Their preparation for tonight's ceremony had to go undisturbed; they were not even sure it would work, but had to try.

"I'm nervous Carl."

"Me too," he replied.

"What if it doesn't work?" She shuffled her feet, wringing her hands. "What do we do then?"

"Try again? I don't know," he replied, his voice wavering.

Mona prepared the ritual in Audrey's chambers just as the text described. She lit seven candles and placed them around the room in accordance to the diagram in the book. Mona read the Latin text a dozen times, memorizing it.

"I guess I'm ready?"

"Yeah, me too," Carl replied.

Mona stood at the head of the bed, cleared her throat, then started reading.

"Oh father, we prepare this sacrament for your honor, we pray for those that have gone before and those that will be guided by this soul. The angel of death we summon with your honor. Amen."

She had remembered the text exactly as it was written, but held it open as she uttered the words in Latin.

O pater paremus tibi, hoc sacramentum, et qui nos praecesserunt et orate pro ea sequi anima tua honor. angelum vocat mortem.

Carl stood just inside the doorway, waiting as he held his breath. Minutes passed.

"What time is it?" he asked.

"A quarter to twelve. Do you think we started too soon? Are you sure Stephan translated it correctly, or was there more to it?"

"I don't know Mona."

They were at a loss for words; it was beyond their comprehension, having never done anything like this before. The sound of the large grandfather clock struck midnight downstairs as it echoed throughout the castle. Carl stared intently at the remains of his beloved.

"Maybe we will have to have this text translated by someone else? Someone smarter than Stephan," she replied.

"Who can we ask around here? We don't know anyone?"

"I don't know Carl, but someone must know Latin in this country or at least across the border in Germany. Lets figure it out in the morning, I'm tired. I'm sorry Carl." Her chin slumped to her chest.

"That's okay, we tried."

Mona left him lying next to Audrey's corpse, his hand gripping hers. He ran his finger over the large wedding ring. Carl slipped into a deep sleep. A dream state ensued, and he was with her again, holding her soft hand. He twitched back and forth on the bed as he dreamed. The air in the room grew colder. Carl pulled the covers over his body as he shivered, slipping back into the dream. Her face glowed porcelain as the flesh was renewed. The bed next to him slowly sunk in. Carl rolled over and up against her body. It felt different to him. He opened an eye.

"Audrey?" he whispered. "Are you there?" Carl shook his head, rubbing his eyes. He was still half in dream state, half awake. His vision cleared and he focused on Audrey's face, the complexion creamy, complete. Hot breath bathed his face and he could smell her. She was…*alive*.

"You came for me Carl. You're here," she whispered.

"I love you so much Audrey; I love you," he said, kissing her.

"Carl, stay with me—forever."

"I will. I promise."

Mona slept soundly until late the next morning, the sound of footsteps outside her room waking her up. "Carl, is that you?"

There was no answer. She tried to stand up but her feet were asleep. Pins and needles jabbed at her toes as the feeling came back. Mona walked across the hallway to Audrey's chamber and placed her ear up to the door, trying to hear if Carl was awake. She was surprised to hear laughter.

"Carl, are you okay?"

"Come in Mona, we have been waiting for you to wake up." The voice was female, high pitched. Mona pushed the door open and could see her friend, Audrey's face young and as beautiful as she had remembered.

Carl held Audrey in his arms.

"You came back!" she said.

"I knew you would release me; that is why I trusted you. It's why I brought you here last year. I knew you of all people would figure it out if it came to that."

"We can't stay here Audrey; they will find you again." Mona wanted to ask her about Chloe's remains, but held off, not wanting to hear the answer that would mean she would never see her again.

"We have time. I can feel when they get close; that is what has kept me safe from them for centuries, the priests always give off a seed of doubt."

"But Tommy's friends were able to kill you?"

"It is harder with the nonbelievers, they give off no energy. We will be more careful from now on. Come in, let me see you, we have plenty of time before we have to leave."

Mona had a hard time believing what she was seeing and hearing; she was not a religious person, and now she had brought back the dead—or at least released the Angel of Death. Either way, she was in shock. Mona hugged her friend tight and their energies exchanged as their hearts met.

"Don't worry Mona, I have more than one place in Europe. This was just my favorite, and we will leave soon enough. They will not find us again as long as we stick together."

Mona cried and Audrey brushed her tears off her face.

"Don't cry, it is a joyous time, a time for celebration."

Audrey cupped Mona's face in her hands as they lay next to each other, staring into each other's eyes, hugging.

The next day, Audrey prepared them a meal to celebrate her rebirth, the trio laughing, dancing, and partying the day away, late into the evening and next day. Carl was fulfilled again, his passions reserved for their night together alone in her chamber. He had waited months, not knowing whether he would see her again, and now he was holding her in his arms again, the gentle kiss sending his heart into overdrive. She had come back to him, something she had never done before, returning to a living friend. It was the one thing she had vowed never to do the first time she was released. She had made a covenant to keep the faith, guiding those that had passed and taking on those that were evil. Audrey had brought things in motion that she could not stop, their love for each other too much for even the afterlife to contain. Audrey needed Carl just as much as he needed her, they were bound together: two souls connected across the dimensions.

The moving vans came and went for a whole week, hauling all the furnishings out of the house and into a large storage building in the town of Ogola a few miles down the road. Audrey had ordered a van to take them to the train station with a driver from outside the country—somebody who would not ask questions, someone that would keep their mouth shut for money.

"I don't think we should trust the driver."

"Don't worry Carl. After he drives us to the train station. I will kill him."

"What? No more killing, Audrey."

"I'm just kidding, you have to lighten up my love."

"That is easy for you to say. We just raised you from the dead; our nerves are on edge."

"I'm sorry. I won't joke about it again."

"Please don't," he replied. Their were some things Carl did not want to know.

They left the castle on a Sunday morning, its interior deserted and the contents stored away for safekeeping. The trio traveled by private rail car, staying out of sight, leery of anyone that looked at them twice, leaving their past behind them. Audrey held off telling them where they were headed; Carl never asked, but Mona was curious, prodding her for answers.

The train rumbled on through the day and into the night, stopping at the border crossing between Poland and Belarus, their journey partially completed. There would be two more days traveling into interior Russia, where Audrey had purchased a mansion in the Ural Mountains a century earlier. Carl and Mona were tired, sleeping most of the trip, while Audrey stayed awake, watching over them. The countryside rolled past the window, blanketed in a deep layer of snow, the tight grip of winter in full glory. Audrey sighed as she stared out the window, her breath exiting onto the glass, fogging it, the realization of another start in a foreign land on her mind, her love laying next to her, sleeping peacefully.

Chloe's remains lay protected in the cargo car at the end of the train. The small coffin Audrey had placed her in was nondescript, except for Chloe's name on one end.

Months earlier, the ground crew had unloaded the coffin out of a plane from the states, placing it into the back of a utility van, the company liaison giving the driver explicit instructions where to deliver it. The shipping was paid in full with bonus, Audrey's name scrolled across the label as Carl had found it.

"Where are we?"

"Belarus my love. Go back to sleep, we will be there in another day and a half."

Carl placed his head back in her lap, his fatigue overtaking him seconds later. She stroked his hair away form his face, caressing it as he slipped away. She could not remember a time since her birth centuries before when she was this content, despite the events that sent her back a few months earlier.

In the town near the castle, the restaurant patrons could tell the older man who had just walked through the door was not from around there. His solid black suit and black shoes gave him away as an official in some capacity. He took a seat at the far end of the restaurant and waited for the young waitress to come over. His use of Polish language was enough to get by, accurate enough to speak with her candidly.

"What will you have sir?" she asked.

"I would like a cup of coffee, and the stew."

The waitress scurried off to the cook with his order, then turned her attention to the patrons seated at the counter. She chatted with the three locals, glancing over her shoulder at the stranger. The waitress turned her attention back to the patrons sitting at the counter. The stranger stared at her, making her uncomfortable. He waved and she ignored him. He waved again, then cleared his throat as she was serving the old men at the counter. She hesitated as she looked at the stranger in the corner booth. Her radar for creepy old men was pinging loudly. He nodded and she couldn't ignore him any longer.

"More coffee sir?"

"Yes, thank you. You wouldn't happen to know of a young American lady that lived around here recently, would you?"

"Maybe, what would you give me if I knew something," she said, rubbing two fingers together.

He produced his wallet out of a coat pocket and she could see the wad of money stacked neatly together.

"Twenty dollars," he replied.

"Thirty," she challenged.

He threw it down on the table in front of her. She snatched it up.

"She came here with friends last year; they left a few weeks later."

"Where did she go after they left?"

"Back to America, I guess?"

"Is that all?" he asked.

“No, her friend came back here a couple months ago; he was traveling with a group from Germany.”

"He was the only American?" he asked, eyebrows lifting.

“Another American came just last week,” the waitress added.

“Who?” he asked. “A girl that was here with them last winter?”

“Yes, she was here last year.”

“Thank you,” he replied, handing her a few more small bills.

The castle walls were barren inside as the man in black stepped through the front door. The movers had left little evidence to their existence just a few days prior, the entire library packed up, waiting for shipment later on.

“You can’t be here; Ms. Anderson would not like it that you are in here.”

The caretaker did not know who this man was, but it was still his job to protect the place from vandals.

“I was just looking for some information; do you know where they went?”

“No, they just left yesterday; I didn’t ask where they were going.”

He thought that odd, a caretaker not asking if his employer would be returning or where to find her. It was a dead end, with little to no leads to go by. But this man was not your ordinary tourist traveling to find a friend; he was on an official mission, one that he had done before, right after World War Two, tracking down Nazi war criminals. There was no way that he would not find who he was looking for. With his work cut out for him, he returned to Opole, the town just outside the village of Moszna. His first plan was to study the train schedules and destinations, a tall feat for anyone. Staying at a small inn a few blocks away from the train station, he toiled day and night making notes of all the routes out of Poland. There was a dozen directions, years worth of research and traveling on foot. He would leave a week later, train route number one, his first search of many.

43

THE TRAIN RUMBLED NOISILY DOWN THE TRACKS, flying past multiple unmapped towns, through the dark of night. Their trip would take them another two days, traveling halfway across Russia, their location a secret. The town was not even on the map, resulting from the Russian government's attempt at hiding the large manufacturing area from the world during the cold war. The city of Perm was the perfect place to hide out. Amongst its nearly one million residents, nobody in Perm would notice three more people getting off a train, least of all in winter, when thousands of citizen's flocked to the city for work. Audrey had found a townhouse in the central district, the rent paid in full for a year until her home in the mountains to the north could be renovated.

Carl was still shaking off the three long days of travel when the train pulled into the station. The structure was bigger than anything he had ever seen. They waited in a beat up ugly van. The driver sat motionless as the train crew loaded the coffin into the back, closing the double doors with a loud bang, shaking the vehicle. Russia was still a closed country; nobody would inquire into their travels. Audrey had been able to get them into the country without a question asked, and they virtually dropped off the end of the earth. Her intention was to keep them safe while they reestablished themselves.

"It's colder than crap here," Carl said.

"You will get used to it my love. I will keep you warm," Audrey replied.

"Is there a library in town?" Mona asked.

"Yes, a nice one—but I'm sure most everything is printed in Russian," Audrey replied.

"Crap," Mona grumbled. "Can't we settle somewhere warm?"

"Yeah like the Caribbean!" Carl added.

"It will warm up next summer," Audrey laughed. "Besides, you will be busy learning Russian all winter; it doesn't have to be warm for that."

"Ahh that sounds wonderful," Carl replied, shaking his head.

The driver weaved in and out of the heavy traffic as he maneuvered the van across town. They drove alongside the Kama River. The Kama was one of the longest rivers in Russia and a vital transportation hub in the Soviet countryside. The van's tires thumped on the metal grating as it crossed a long bridge before pulling up in front of the townhouse. Their residence towered three stories above them. Carl strained his neck as he looked up. It was located in the middle of the block, sandwiched between two townhouses. It did not look like much on the outside, built at the height of communist rule, but the inside was outfitted luxuriously: everything she requested, and every detail attended to.

Carl and Mona were happy to finally settle into the three-story residence. Mona had staked out her claim for the entire second floor. Carl and Audrey would retreat to the top floor penthouse every evening, time spent alone, her kind spirit molding him into a gentleman. Days turned into weeks, and the trio finally decided to venture outside. It was late February and still bitter cold. Dressing up in locally made clothing, they blended in, Audrey speaking in Russian as the mood hit her. Most people were still extremely introverted and left them alone. They took in the winter ballet weekly so Carl and Mona could experience real culture in the foreign land while their daily schedule of Russian language lessons drug on. Carl complained the most, while Mona picked it up fast.

Work on her mansion in the Ural Mountains just northeast of the city continued all winter. The home was a large stone palace fashioned after a French chateau and had sat in ruin for nearly sixty years. Life crept into the building week by week. The large stone pillars were rebuilt, windows reinstalled, and the roof replaced. None of the crew had questioned the rebuild. It was something you did not do in Russia, especially since they were being paid in cash, many of them remembering the dark times where people would disappear just out of suspicion of being a dissident.

"My love, I don't think your cousin is very happy."

Audrey was very perceptive, not missing anything, in tune to their needs and feelings.

"She is still very sad that Chloe is gone. Do you think we could have a crypt built for Chloe?"

"That is a fine idea, I'll order it done. The workers can start on it next week," she replied.

Carl was more than a boyfriend now, at nearly twenty years old, he had grown physically and matured emotionally as well. Audrey would come to rely on him, giving him access to her finances; it was then that he realized she had amassed a sizable fortune, investing in railroads and lumber mills, and trading rare jewels. He had never seen a bank account that large before; it was a number that was unfathomable to him. He would repeat the sum in his head: four hundred fifty million. How could a person gain that much wealth? The most he ever had in his pocket at one time was when he traveled to Europe alone, and that was only a couple thousand. Although he was impressed with the large sum, it did not matter; he would have given it all away just to be with her for another day.

Their love affair continued to grow that spring as the winter slowly faded away. Flowers bloomed around town and the heavy coats stored in the closet. Carl would prepare breakfast daily, bringing her a tray to their room. It was her favorite time with him, as the two of them would sit in silence, staring into each other's eyes. She'd had lovers in the past, but none as caring as Carl and none as dedicated. Audrey's heart melted every morning when she awoke, her first look at his boyish smile bringing her happiness.

"It would be nice to visit our new home tomorrow. What do you guys think?" Audrey asked.

"I can't wait to get out of the city, can you Mona?" Carl said as he tried to engage his cousin.

"I guess," she replied meekly.

"Carl, can you leave us alone for a while. I want to speak with Mona in private."

"Of course."

He never questioned her, nor worried about her motives. It was the one thing that made their relationship solid. Audrey stared into her friend's eyes, the anguish on Mona's face apparent to her.

"Come with me into the parlor." It was not a request, but an order.

Audrey had framed Chloe's picture and placed it on the fireplace mantle as a show of respect for her friend.

"It has been over a year since she has been gone, and I know it is hard on you."

Mona sobbed as Audrey wrapped her arms around her.

"Will I ever see her again?"

"Mona, there are still things I am not sure of. If I had all the answers, she would still be alive today. I promised you I would tell you everything. You have to trust me; that time is coming soon."

"But we brought you back, can you bring her back?"

"I only take life. I cannot give it; that is how it works. I'm sorry, it is not up to me."

They stood there hugging for a long time, Mona still upset, but at least she was healing, one day at a time.

"Get a good night's sleep. I have a surprise for you tomorrow." Her hand caressed Mona's face, wiping a tear off her cheek.

Audrey had given Mona a small piece of hope, and she slept more soundly that night than ever before, her thoughts and dreams of her days with Chloe, her first and only love. She missed her giddy smile, her childish laughter, and her antics. Those were the best days of her life—something she wondered if she could ever get back.

Spring was in full glory and a flock of ravens crossed the sky in front of their van as Carl drove them out of town and up into the mountains, their destination hours away from the hustle of the city. The trip was theraputic for Mona, and she was gaining some peace from her loss. The hurt would never go away entirely, but she was beginning to feel whole again. Nearly three hours later, Carl pulled the van off the main highway and onto the dirt side road leading to the mansion. It was almost as big as the castle in Poland as it came into view.

"This is ours?"

"Yes Mona, it is all ours, a place where we can stay forever. We can move in soon; they are almost finished renovating it."

"Awesome," Mona replied.

Audrey walked them around the home as she showed them everything that had been rebuilt, finally coming into the main garden where she had the crypt built for Chloe.

"I know this may be hard for you Mona, but it is proper to have a resting place for her; it was Carl's idea, but we both want you to know how much she meant to all of us."

"It's beautiful. I don't know what to say."

It was magnificent. Audrey had spared no expense on the structure. It was built in a gothic style reminiscent of the castles in eastern Europe. The outside had two large gargoyle statues standing guard on both sides of the large door. Behind them were two large columns carved out of marble. Above the front door, a multi-colored stained-glass window was installed. Two angels floated above a shepherd that was holding a lamb. It shimmered in the sunlight.

Carl had hoped she would appreciate the gesture, although she had already been to one funeral for her friend.

"You don't have to say anything, Audrey and I are here for you as long as you need us and as long as you want to stay."

Her tears were tears of joy, seeing the large crypt with Chloe's name etched on the door. It was a fitting tribute to her friend. The inside was equally impressive. A bench sat against one wall opposite the stone perch where the casket would be placed. Mona sat down on the bench for a few minutes, the cool stone soothing to her, the colored sunlight pushing through the window bathing the interior in a rainbow.

“Thank you Carl, and especially you Audrey. I know I have been down in the dumps lately, but I’m a lot better now.”

They stayed in the gardens all afternoon, chatting about their times in high school. Audrey told them more about her life in the early centuries; she had nothing to hide now, her friends the closest confidants she had ever had, fully trusting them.

Move in day was cheerully warm as spring was in full bloom. A steady stream of delivery trucks ferried her furniture from Perm. The precious cargo, Carl had the movers load into the van under his direction. They laid her to rest in the large crypt early that evening. Chloe was safe. Mona would visit her nearly every day, picking fresh flowers to place on top of the coffin, her tears less each time she left. She thought about asking Audrey about her reflection she saw in the river by the castle a year earlier but never felt the right timing to bring it up. Audrey held off telling Mona about her vision.

44

SPRING HAD BROUGHT THE EMERGENCE of fresh flowers pushing through the fertile earth of the estate. Yellow daffodils lined the sidewalks. Mona was spending more and more time outside with Audrey, their daily walks past the crypt into the gardens invigorating them. It had occurred to Audrey that they should travel away from the home for the summer and spend time at her cottage on a lake in the east. She brought the idea up with Mona one afternoon. Audrey convinced her that it would be good for her body and soul to seek relaxation on the lake property. Mona agreed with her, even though she did not want to leave Chloe behind.

A month later, the trio headed to the train station. Carl got the same feeling he had on the trip out of Poland as he boarded the train. His nerves were telling him that this may be a dangerous trip, exposing them to the searchers. On board the train, they quickly settled into their private car, Carl finally noticing Mona's hair had grown longer since the previous year. Her brunette locks fell just above her shoulders, the short haircut no longer evident. Mona still seemed to be extremely withdrawn to him and distant.

"What is the house like?" Carl asked.

"Hmm, it is older, but has a nice view of the lake, but it has been a very long time since I have been there." This was true; Audrey had not returned to her lake home for nearly a century, and the fact was that it may not be standing.

"Is the lake warm enough to swim in?" His questions would go on and on for hours.

"Could be, depends on the time of the year," Audrey replied.

"Good, I can't wait to go swimming." His smile was infectious, uplifting the gals. Mona smiled back at her cousin for the first time since before Chloe had passed away.

They rode in a luxurious cabin in the first-class train, their needs and wants attended to by the concierge. The train twisted through the Ural Mountains eastward. Carl and Audrey took the time to enjoy the scenery in the main viewing train, commingling with the common citizens of Russia. Traveling throughout the night, the train stopped at town after town, never staying more than ten minutes at each stop. It was just enough time for Carl to step off the train onto the station platform and stretch his legs.

"Where you going?" The conductor was chummy with everyone, but Carl had peaked his interest early on.

"To the lake." Carl was not giving him much information and considered it a nicety to say something, even though Audrey had warned him not to say anything more than how the weather was that day.

"It is getting warmer, should be very nice at the lake this time of year."

"Yes, I can't wait to go for a swim when I get there."

"You must re-board, sir, the train will be pulling out in two minutes." The conductor seemed to be studying Carl's features, staring at his face longer than would normally be acceptable for a Russian. Citizens were on edge with the impending crash of the economy and collapse of communism.

Carl rejoined Audrey and Mona in their private cabin. The pull-down bunks were setup for the night, and Audrey was already snuggled into the back wall. He snuggled in and stared at Mona, who had taken the opposite bunk and was fast asleep.

"What did you see?"

"Nothing much here; I'm pretty sure this town only has a few residents. I only counted three people getting off."

"Go to sleep, we will be there in the morning."

Carl drifted off to sleep as Audrey kept watch. The train lurched forward as it left the station on the way east once again, quickly gaining speed as the darkened countryside passed them by. Carl slept undisturbed. Mona woke up a few hours later. Continual sleep had evaded her these last few months, awakened by a noise or maybe a premonition, she was not sure. Something, or someone, called to her. Her pain and loss of her friend was still current. Mona closed the door to their cabin softly, then made her way to the dining car and took a seat at the end of the bar.

"Vodka on the rocks," she said. The bartender did not speak, pouring the native spirit into a glass while adding in a few square ice cubes. Mona grasped the glass in her hand, then tipped it back, the potent drink sliding down her throat, a quick burn replaced by the numbing tingle of the start of a nice buzz.

"Another one." She did not have to ask; the bartender was already pouring her a second one as the glass touched down on the oak bar. At the opposite end of the train car, she had sparked the attention of a young man. He moved over and took a seat next to her as he waved at the bartender to bring him another drink.

"Make that two, one for my new friend here," the young man said.

"Thank you," she replied casually.

"My name is Alex."

"Very nice to meet you Alex, I'm Mona." They shook hands and his grip was soft.

"You traveling alone?" he asked pointedly.

"No, my friends are asleep. You?" The warmth of her third drink was filling her body and clouding her mind.

"Yes, I am on my way to the University in Vladivostok."

"What do you study there?"

"I am an engineering student."

It was a lie, and one that he had told many times before. The truth was, this gentleman belonged to the new KGB, renamed the FSB (the secret police), and it had been formed as the Soviet Union was collapsing. He was a new protégé, sent out to the east undercover as a university student. The Soviet Union was still paranoid of all people, continually watching for the wayward nonconformist. Fortunately for Mona, even though he was lying about who he was, Alex was only interested in her in a physical way.

"I must tell you that I am flattered and appreciate the drinks and conversation, but I am not interested in men," she replied.

"Oh, you have a lover?" It was a question she had not been asked before and was unprepared to answer immediately. She relented. "I do."

"Bartender. Two more drinks." Mona had ordered this time, and Alex eased up on his questions about her past relationship.

"You are American?"

"Yes, but I live here now," she said, unable to stop herself.

"Mona, you should come back to the cabin." Audrey's voice was firm, startling Mona into instant sobriety.

"Sir if you would excuse us. Good evening." Audrey nodded her head at Alex as she helped Mona back to the cabin.

"I'm sorry Audrey, it was just a friendly conversation and drink," she slurred as she collapsed into the bed.

"All right Mona, just sleep. We will be there soon." Audrey placed a finger on Mona's lips as she was about to speak, quieting her.

Four hours later, the train slowed down as it entered a curve a few miles outside of the lake town, and their intended destination. Brake squeal and the jolt of the cars slamming together woke Carl and Audrey, his cousin still fast asleep. After they unloaded their luggage, they had to carry Mona off the train, placing her into the back seat of the transport van waiting for them at the station. Minutes later they were on their way out of town, traveling up the western shore of the long lake towards her summer home. Sunlight and orange hues filled the sky, the glow of daybreak presenting itself. It was Carl's first glimpse of the lake, its deep blue color filling his vision. It overwhelmed him. He had never experienced something that grand before. He hugged Audrey hard, giving her a light kiss on the cheek.

"What was that for?" she asked.

"Nothing, I'm just happy," Carl replied, smiling.

Their two-hour trip clicked off without a hitch, with Mona passed out and snoring in the back seat behind them. She seemed heavier as Carl carried her out of the van and into the large two-story lake house, placing her in an upstairs bedroom. On the back deck, Audrey had already setup the lounge chairs and was quickly soaking up the sunshine when Carl joined her.

"It is beautiful," he said.

The lake was fifty feet away from the house as the ground sloped from the deck to the waterline. Carl stared across the open expanse and judged the lake to be more than a couple miles across to the distant shore. He lay next to Audrey on her lounge chair, the two of them entwined in embrace, a perfect ending to the trip.

Upstairs, Mona slept for another eight hours before waking, her head pounding from the hangover. She could hear her cousin and friend laughing downstairs through the screaming headache. Audrey had ordered groceries from town with the driver, and he had already delivered. The meal was sitting out on the table as Mona joined them.

"My head freaking hurts," Mona said as she massaged her temples.

"It should. When I found you last night, you were quite inebriated." Audrey was not happy with her friend getting smashed and talking with a stranger.

"Yeah, about that. I'm sorry, it was just innocent drowning of my sorrows. But other than this hangover, I'm feeling much better."

"Good, I am glad you are feeling better. We will talk about your conversation with that young man last night later on."

Mona sat with her friends at the table, a nice evening in their summer house together, her hangover subsiding two hours and four aspirin later. "I'm going down to the lake for a walk. To clear my head," Mona said as she left Carl and Audrey alone.

She walked along the water, squinting her eyes at the distant shore. The water shimmered in the afternoon sun. Mona looked to her left, closed her eyes, then opened them up again. She closed her eyes again and rubbed them before opening them.

Chloe startled her. She thought she was hallucinating from the hangover. It was Chloe—a wispy apparition of fog—but sure enough Chloe reaching out to her. Mona turned back to look at the house, scanning the balcony to see if Audrey and Carl were seeing Chloe as well. The balcony was empty. They had already retreated upstairs to their bedroom. She turned back around and Chloe was gone, her image vanishing before Mona could get a second look. Mona ran back to the house, skipping stairs as she leapt up the three flights to the top floor, bursting into Audrey's room. She caught them mid stride through a love-making session and their naked bodies were entwined on top of the covers. The shocked look on their faces said it all.

"I saw her, down at the lake," she yelled, pointing out the window.

"Mona, can you knock next time?" Carl had scrambled to put on his robe, leaving Audrey sitting on the bed naked, her modesty still intact but uncaring that Mona was staring at her.

"Where?" Audrey asked.

"Down on the lake shore. She came to me, just for a few seconds, but she was there. What does this mean?" Mona could not contain her excitement, the realization her friend had come to her hitting her like a punch in the stomach.

"She is still present." Audrey's words echoed through the room, bouncing around inside Mona's head, taking effect a few minutes later.

"Is she coming back to me?" Mona asked. "I have to know."

"Maybe, there is no way to tell about these things; if it is supposed to be, then it will happen."

The words were enough for Mona. She had been waiting to hear them for over a year and now she had hope.

They stayed at the lake house for the rest of the summer, swimming, partying, and waiting to see if Chloe would make another appearance. She never came to them again. One visit from her was enough for Mona. It had spurred her into action as soon as she could get back to the library at the mansion. Soon she would start researching. She was determined more than ever to bring her lover back. Her winter would be spent leaning over a pile of books, reading, studying, and waiting. Her dreams of Chloe were vivid in every detail. She missed her blond-haired friend more than ever. She longed to be with her. Nothing would keep her from finding her...nothing.

END

Tiffany “I think we’re alone now.” *Tiffany.* MCA Records, 1987, Single/cd

Def Leppard “Armageddon it.” *Hysteria.* Mercury, 1988 CD,CDV 7”,12”

Billy Idol 1981 “Mony Mony.” Originally released by Tommy James and the Shondells, 1968. Roulette

Sam & Dave “Soul Man.” Soul Men. Stax/Atlantic 1967

Fox Theater, 20th Century Fox “The last word in motion picture entertainment,” as seen on the top of the theater in Centralia.

Harold’s Burger Bar- Centralia Wa. Best Burger joint west of the Mississippi R. 727 S.Gold st.

www.ingramcontent.com/pod-product-compliance
Lightning Source LLC
Chambersburg PA
CBHW030818310726
48980CB00006B/543/J

* 9 7 8 0 6 9 2 8 4 2 9 1 1 *